SHUGGIE BAIN

Douglas Stuart was born and raised in Glasgow. After graduating from the Royal College of Art in London, he moved to New York City, where he began a career in fashion design. *Shuggie Bain* is his first novel.

SHUGGIE BAIN

DOUGLAS STUART

PICADOR

First published in the UK 2020 by Picador
an imprint of Pan Macmillan
The Smithson, 6 Briset Street, London EC1M 5NR
Associated companies throughout the world
www.panmacmillan.com

ISBN 978-1-5290-1928-5

7 9 8 6

A CIP catalogue record for this book is available from the British Library.

Printed and bound by CPI Group (UK) Ltd, Croydon, CR0 4YY

For My Mother, A.E.D.

SHUGGIE
BAIN

1992
THE SOUTH SIDE

One

The day was flat. That morning his mind had abandoned him and left his body wandering down below. The empty body went listlessly through its routine, pale and vacant-eyed under the fluorescent strip lights, as his soul floated above the aisles and thought only of tomorrow. Tomorrow was something to look forward to.

Shuggie was methodical in setting up for his shift. All the pots of oily dips and spreads were decanted into clean trays. The edges were wiped free of any splashes that would go brown quickly and ruin the illusion of freshness. The sliced hams were artfully arranged with fake parsley sprigs, and the olives were turned so that the viscous juice slid like mucus over their green skins.

Ann McGee had the brass neck to call in sick again that morning, leaving him with the thankless task of running his deli counter and her rotisserie stand all alone. No day ever started well with six dozen raw chickens, and today of all days, it was stealing the sweetness out of his daydreams.

He pushed industrial skewers through each cold, dead bird and lined them up neatly in a row. They sat there, with their stubby wings crossed over their fat little chests like so many headless babies. There was a time he would have taken pride in this orderliness. In reality, pushing the metal through the bumpy pink flesh was the easy part; the difficult part was resisting the urge to do the same to the customers. They would pore over the hot glass and study each of the carcasses in detail. They would choose only the best bird, ignorant to the fact that battery farming meant they were all identical. Shuggie would stand there, his back teeth pinching the inside of his cheek, and indulge their indecisiveness with a forced smile. Then the pantomime would really begin. "*Gies three breasts, five thighs, and just wan wing the day, son.*"

He prayed for strength. Why did no one want a whole chicken any more? He would lift the carcass using long prongs, careful not to touch the birds with his gloved hands, and then he would dissect the parts neatly (skin intact) using catering scissors. He felt like a fool standing there against the broiler lights. His scalp was sweating under the hairnet and his hands were not quite strong enough to artfully snap the back of the chicken with the dull blades. He hunched slightly, the better to throw his back muscles behind the pressure in his wrists, and all the time he kept smiling.

If he was very unlucky, the tongs would slip and the chicken would thud and slide its way across the gritty floor. He'd have to make an apologetic pretence of starting again, but he never wasted that dirty bird. When the women turned away he would put it back with its sisters under the hot yellow lights. He believed in hygiene well enough, but these little private victories stopped him from starting a riot. Most of the judgy, man-faced housewives who shopped here deserved it. The way they looked down on him flushed the back of his neck scarlet. On particularly low days he folded all types of his bodily discharge into the taramasalata. He sold an uncanny amount of that bourgeois shite.

He had worked for Kilfeathers for over a year. It was never meant to be that long. It was just that he had to feed himself and pay his own dig money each week, and the supermarket was the only business that would take him. Mr Kilfeather was a parsimonious bastard; he liked to staff the shop with anyone he didn't have to pay a full adult wage, and Shuggie found himself able to take short shifts that fit around his patchy schooling. In his dreams he always intended to move on. He had always loved to brush and play with hair; it was the only thing that made time truly fly. When he had turned sixteen he had promised himself he would go to the hairdressing college that sat south of the River Clyde. He had gathered up all of his inspiration, the sketches he had copied from the Littlewoods catalogue and pages ripped from the Sunday magazines. Then he had gone to Cardonald to see about the evening classes. At the bus stop outside the college he alighted with half a dozen eighteen-year-olds. They wore the newest, most-fashionable gear and talked with a buzzing confidence that masked their own nerves. Shuggie walked half as fast as they did. He watched them go in the front door, then he recrossed the street to catch the bus going the other way. He started at Kilfeathers the following week.

Shuggie killed most of his morning break poring over the damaged tins in the discount bins. He found three small cans of Scottish salmon that were barely damaged, the labels were scuffed and marked, but the tins themselves were intact. With the last of his wages he paid for his small basket and placed the tins of fish inside his old school bag, which he locked again inside his locker. He sloped up the stairs to the staff canteen and tried to look nonchalant as he passed the table of university students who worked the easy summer shifts and spent their breaks looking self-important, surrounded with thick folders of revision notes. He fixed his gaze to the middle distance and sat down in the corner, not with, but near enough to the girls from the tills.

In truth, the girls were three middle-aged Glasgow women. Ena, the ringleader, was a rake-thin, poker-faced woman with greasy hair. She had no eyebrows to speak of, but she did have a faint moustache, which seemed unfair to Shuggie. Ena was rough even for this end of Glasgow, but she was also kind and generous in the way hard-done-to people often are. Nora, the youngest of the three, wore her hair scraped tightly back and held in place with an elastic band. Her eyes, like Ena's, were small and sharp, and at thirty-three she was a mother of five already. The last of the group was Jackie. She was different to these other two in that she very much resembled a woman. Jackie was a riotous gossip, a big, bosomy sofa of a woman. It was her that Shuggie liked best.

He sat down near them and caught the ending to the saga of Jackie's latest man. It was guaranteed that the women were always full of good-hearted patter. Twice now they had taken him along on their bingo nights, and as the women drank and howled with laughter, he sat amongst them like a teenager who couldn't be trusted to stay home alone. He had liked the way they sat easily together. How their bulk surrounded him and the softness of their flesh pressed into his side. He liked how they fussed with him, and although he protested, how they pushed his hair from his eyes and licked their thumbs to wipe the corners of his mouth. For the women, Shuggie offered some form of male attention, and it did not matter that he was only sixteen and three months. Under the La Scala bingo tables they had each tried at least once to brush against his cock. The strokes were too long, too searching, to be truly accidental. For Ena-with-no-eyebrows it could become almost a crusade. The deeper she went into drink, the more brazen she became. With every passing graze of her ringed knuckles, she clamped her fat tongue between her teeth, and kept her eyes burning into the side of his face. When Shuggie had finally flared with embarrassment, she had tutted, and Jackie had pushed two pound notes across the table to a beaming, victorious Nora. It was a disappointment, sure, but as they drank deeper they decided it had not been a rejection exactly. Something about the boy was no right, and this was at least something they could pity.

Shuggie sat in the dark listening to the unsteady snores through the tenement walls. He was trying, and failing, to ignore the lonely men who had no people of their own. The morning chill had turned his naked thighs a tartan blue, so he wrapped a thin towel around himself for warmth and chewed nervously at the corner, soothed by the way it squeaked between his teeth. He arranged the last of his supermarket wages along the table's edge. He ordered the coins, first by worth, then by their mint and shine.

The pink-faced man in the room next door creaked to life. In his narrow bed he scratched noisily at himself and sighed a prayer for the will to stand. His feet hit the floor with a thud, like bags of heavy butcher's meat, and it sounded like an effort for him to shuffle across the small room to the doorway. He fumbled with the familiar locks and came out into the always-dark hall, blindly feeling his way, his hand sliding across the wall and falling against the outside of Shuggie's door. The boy held his breath as the fingers ran across the beadwork. Only when he heard the *plink-plink* of the bathroom light cord did Shuggie move again. The old man began to cough and hauch his lungs to life. Shuggie tried not to listen as he pissed and spat gobs of phlegm into the toilet at the same time.

The morning light was the colour of too-milky tea. It snuck into the bedsit like a sly ghost, crossing the carpet and inching slowly up his bare legs. Shuggie closed his eyes and tried to feel it creeping there, but there was no heat in its touch. He waited until he thought it might have covered him entirely, and then he opened his eyes again.

They were staring back at him, a hundred pairs of painted eyes, all broken-hearted or lonely, just as they always were. The porcelain ballerinas with the little puppies, the Spanish girl with the dancing sailors, and the rosy-faced farm boy pulling his lazy shire horse. Shuggie had arranged the ornaments neatly along the bay window's ledge. He had spent hours with their made-up stories. The thick-armed blacksmith amongst the angel-faced choirboys, or his favourite, the seven or so giant baby kittens smiling and menacing the lazy shepherd.

At least they cheered the place up a little. The bedsit was taller than it was long, and his single bed stuck out into the middle like a divider. An old-fashioned two-seater settee, the wooden kind, whose thin cushions meant you always felt the slats in your back, was on one side. A small fridge and a double-ringed Baby Belling cooker was on the other. Except for the rumpled bedding, nothing was out of place: no stour, no yesterday's clothes, no signs of life. Shuggie tried to calm himself as he smoothed his hand over the mismatched sheets. He thought how his mother would have hated these bedclothes, the odd colours and patterns, layered one upon the other as if he didn't care what people would think. This mess would have hurt her pride. Someday he would save some money and buy new sheets of his own, soft and warm and all the same colour.

He had been fortunate to get this room in Mrs Bakhsh's boarding house. He was lucky the old man before him had liked his drink too much and had been jailed for it. The large bay window jutted out proudly on to Albert Drive, and Shuggie supposed at one time the room must have been the living room of a fairly grand three-bedroom flat. He had seen into some of the other rooms in the house. The kitchenette Mrs Bakhsh had turned into a bedroom still had its original checkered linoleum floor, and the three other boxier rooms still kept their original threadbare carpets. The pink-faced man lived in what must have been at one time a nursery, still with its yellow-flowered wallpaper and a happy border of laughing rabbits around the cornicing. The man's bed, his settee, and his kitchen stove were all lined up on one wall and all touching. Shuggie had seen it once, through the crack of a half-opened door, and he was glad of his grand bay window.

He had been lucky to find the Pakistanis. None of the other land-lords had wanted to rent to a fifteen-year-old boy who was pretending to be one day past his sixteenth birthday. The others didn't say it outright, but they had too many questions. They had looked up and down at his best school shirt and polished shoes suspiciously. *It's no right*, their eyes had said. In the corners of their mouths he could see they thought it was a disgrace for a boy of his age to have no mammy, no people of his own.

Mrs Bakhsh hadn't cared. She looked at his school backpack and at the month's rent he had in advance and went back to worrying about feeding her own weans. With a blue biro he had decorated that first rent envelope specially for her. Shuggie had wanted to show her he cared about being good, that he was reliable enough to put in this extra effort. So he took a piece of paper from his geography notebook and drew swirling paisley patterns on it, intertwined it around her name, and coloured in between the lines so that the peacock shapes stood out in cobalt glory.

The landlady lived across the close, in an identical tenement flat, richly furnished and flushed hot with central heating. In the other, cold flat she kept five men in five bedsits for eighteen pounds and fifty pence each a week, week to week, cash only. The two men who were not being paid for by the social services had to slip the first of their wages under her door on a Friday night before they took to drinking the rest. On their knees, on her doormat, they would linger a moment over the content-ment radiating from inside: bubbling pots of perfumed chicken meat, happy noises of children fighting over television channels, and the laugh-ing sounds of fat women talking foreign words around kitchen tables.

The landlady never bothered Shuggie. She never set foot in his bedsit unless the rent was late. Then she came with other thick-armed Pakistani women and knocked heavily on the doors of the men. Mostly, she visited only to hoover the windowless hallway or to wipe around the bath. Once a month she poured bleach around the toilet bowl, and from time to time, she laid a new scrap of carpet remnant around its base to soak up the piss.

Shuggie leaned his face against his door and listened for the pink-faced man to finish his ablutions. In the quiet he heard him undo the snib on the bathroom door and step out into the hallway again. The boy slipped his feet into his old school shoes. Over his underpants he pulled on his parka, a noisy nylon-skinned thing that was trimmed with a matted fur hood. He zipped it closed all the way to the top, and into the large army pockets he stuffed a Kilfeathers shopping bag and two thin tea towels.

There was a school jumper stuffed into the gap at the bottom of his door. As he removed it, he could smell the other men carried in on the cold draught. One of them had been smoking through the night again; another had taken fish for his supper. Shuggie opened his door and slid out into the darkness.

Mrs Bakhsh had taken the single light bulb from the overhead fix-ture, saying the men had wasted good money by leaving it burning at all hours. Now the smell of the men lingered across the hallway like a trail of ghosts, with no breeze or light to disturb it. Years spent smoking where they slept, eating fried suppers in front of Calor gas fires, and passing summer days with windows closed. The stale smells of sweat and cum mixed with the static heat of black-and-white televisions and the sting of amber aftershave.

Shuggie had begun to be able to tell the men apart. In the darkness he could follow the pink-faced man as he rose to shave his face and comb Brylcreem through his hair, and he could smell the musty overcoat of the yellow-toothed man who ate only what smelled like buttered popcorn or creamed fish. Later, when the pubs had reached closing time, Shuggie could tell as each man returned safely home again.

The shared bathroom had a mottled-glass door. He snibbed the lock and stood a moment pulling on the handle, checking it had caught. Unzipping the heavy anorak, he placed it in the corner. He turned on the hot tap to feel the water, it ran a leftover lukewarm and then sputtered twice and ran colder than the River Clyde. The icy shock of it made him put his fingers in his mouth. He took up a fifty-pence piece, turning it mournfully, and pushed it into the immersion heater and watched as the little gas flame burst to life.

When he turned the tap on again the water ran ice cold, and then, with a cough, jets of boiling water streamed out. He soaked the wet dishcloth, running it over his cold chest and white neck, glad for the steaming heat of it. He sank his face and head into the rare warmth, held himself there and dreamt about filling a bath to the very top. He thought about lying under the hot water far away from the smells of the other lodgers. It had been a long time since he felt thawed all the way through, all of him warm at the exact same time.

Lifting his arm he ran the rag from his wrist up and over his shoulder. He tensed his arm muscle and circled his fingers around the bicep. If he really tried, he could almost wrap his whole hand around it, and if he squeezed hard, he could feel the contours of his bone. His armpit was dusted in a fine lint, like baby duck feathers. He brought his nose to it; it smelled sweet and clean and of nothing at all. He pinched the skin and squeezed, milking the soft flesh till it flushed red with frustration; he sniffed his fingers again, nothing. Scrubbing at himself harder now, he repeated under his breath, "*The Scottish Premier League Results. Gers won 22, drew 14, lost 8, 58 points total. Aberdeen won 17, drew 21, lost 6, 55 points total. Motherwell won 14, drew 12, lost 10.*"

In the mirror his wet hair was black as coal. As he brushed it down over his face he was surprised to find it nearly to his chin. He stared and tried to find something masculine to admire in himself: the black curls, the milky skin, the high bones in his cheeks. He caught the reflection of his own eyes in the mirror. It wasn't right. It wasn't how real boys were built to be. He scrubbed at himself again. "*Gers won 22, drew 14, lost 8, 58 points total. Aberdeen won 17, drew . . .*"

There were footsteps in the hallway then, the familiar squeak of heavy leather shoes, and then nothing. The thin door moved insistently against the hasp. Shuggie reached for the army parka and slipped his damp body inside.

When he had first moved into Mrs Bakhsh's bedsit, only one of the other tenants had paid any real notice. The pink-faced man and the yellow-toothed man had been too blind or too ruined with drink to care. But that first night, as Shuggie sat on the bed eating the buttered end of a white loaf, there had been a knock at his door. The boy stayed silent a long time before he decided to open it. The man on the other side was tall and thickly built and smelled of pine soap. In his hand he held a plastic bag with twelve tins of lager that clanged together like dulled chapel bells. With a hard paw the man introduced himself as Joseph Darling and held the bag out to the boy with a smile. Shuggie had tried to say, *No, thank you*, in the polite way he had been taught, but something in the man had intimidated him, and so instead Shuggie let him in.

They had sat quietly together, Shuggie and his visitor, perched on the edge of the neat single bed and looking out on to the tenemented street. Protestant families were eating their dinners in front of televisions, and the charwoman who lived opposite was eating alone at her drop-leaf table. The pair drank in silence and watched the others go about their normal routines. Mr Darling kept his thick tweed coat on. The weight of him on the bed rolled Shuggie into his broad side. From the corner of his eye Shuggie watched the yellow tips of his thick fingers stab nervously at themselves. Shuggie had only taken a mouthful of the lager to be gracious, and as the man spoke to him, he could think only about the taste of the tinned ale, how sour and sad it tasted. It reminded him of things he would rather forget.

Mr Darling had a considered, half-closed way to himself. Shuggie tried his best to be polite and listen as the man told him how he had been a janitor at a Protestant school that they had shut and merged with the Catholic one to save the council money. To hear him tell it, Mr Darling sounded more astounded that the Proddy weans should be running with the Catholic ones in peace than he was to find himself out of a job.

"Ah jist cannae believe it!" he had said, mostly to himself. "In ma day a person's religion said something about them. Ye came up through the school having to fight yer way there through bus-fulls of cabbage-eating Catholic bastards. It was something to be proud of. Now any good lassie will sleep with any dirty Mick as soon as she'd lie with a dog."

Shuggie pretended to take a light tug on the beer, but mostly he let it swirl around his teeth and trickle back into the can. Mr Darling's eyes were searching the walls for a sign. Then he stole a sideways glance at the boy and asked, suddenly unsure of his audience, "So, what school did ye used to go to?"

Shuggie knew what he was after. "I'm not really one or the other, and I'm still at the school." It was true, he didn't belong to either the Catholics or the Protestants, and he still did go to school, when he could afford to not be at the supermarket.

"Aye? What's your best subject then?"

The boy shrugged. It wasn't modesty, he generally wasn't good at anything. His attendance had been patchy at best, and so the thread of learning was difficult to follow. Mostly he went and sat quietly at the back so that the education board wouldn't come after him for truancy. If the school knew how he lived, they would have been forced to do something about it.

The man finished his second can and quickly set about his third. Shuggie felt the burn of Mr Darling's finger against the side of his leg.

The man had set his hand on the mattress, and the little finger, with its gold sovereign ring, was barely touching him. It didn't move, or wriggle. It just sat there, and that had made it burn all the more.

Now Shuggie stood in the damp bathroom holding his parka closed. Mr Darling pulled at the edge of his tweed bunnet in an old-fashioned greeting. "Ah jist chapped to see if ye were around the day?"

"Today? I don't know. I have some messages to run."

A cloud of disappointment crossed Mr Darling's face. "Miserable day for it."

"I know. But I said I would meet a friend."

Mr Darling sucked at his large white teeth. The man was so tall he was still straightening to his full height. Shuggie could imagine generations of Protestant weans lined up in single file and terrified in his long shadow. He could see now that the man's face was flush, a line of drinkers sweat already on the edge of his brow. The man had been bent at the keyhole, Shuggie was sure of that now.

"That's a pity. Ah'm jist away to cash ma dole, might stop in at the Brewers Arms, then put a wee line on. But afterwards ah was hoping we could share a few cans. Mibbe watch the fitba results on the wee telly? Ah could teach ye about the English leagues?" The man looked down on the boy, he dug his tongue into his back molars.

If he played it right, the man was always good for a few pounds. But it would take too long to wait on Mr Darling to cash his unemployment; to stoat from the post office to the betting shop to the off-licence and then home, that was if he found his way home at all. Shuggie couldn't wait that long.

The boy let go of the parka then, and Mr Darling pretended not to stare as the coat gaped slightly. But the man seemed unable to help himself, and Shuggie watched as the grey light in his green eyes dipped. Shuggie could feel it burn into his pale chest as the man's gaze slid down over his loose underwear to his bare legs, the unremarkable, white hairless things, that hung like uncut thread from the bottom of his black coat.

Only then did Mr Darling smile.

1981
SIGHTHILL

Two

Agnes Bain pushed her toes into the carpet and leaned out as far as she could into the night air. The damp wind kissed her flushed neck and pushed down inside her dress. It felt like a stranger's hand, a sign of living, a reminder of life. With a flick she watched her cigarette doubt fall, the glowing embers dancing sixteen floors down on to the dark fore-court. She wanted to show the city this claret velvet dress. She wanted to feel a little envy from strangers, to dance with men who held her proud and close. Mostly she wanted to take a good drink, to live a little.

With a stretch of her calves, she leaned her hipbone on the window frame and let go of the ballast of her toes. Her body tipped down towards the amber city lights, and her cheeks flushed with blood. She reached her arms out to the lights, and for a brief moment she was flying.

No one noticed the flying woman.

She thought about tilting further then, dared herself to do it. How easy it would be to kid herself that she was flying, until it became only falling and she broke herself on the concrete below. The high-rise flat she still shared with her mother and father pressed in against her. Every-thing in the room behind her felt so small, so low-ceilinged and stifling, payday to Mass day, a life bought on tick, with nothing that ever felt owned outright.

To be thirty-nine and have her husband and her three children, two of them nearly grown, all crammed together in her mammy's flat, gave her a feeling of failure. Him, her man, who when he shared her bed now seemed to lie on the very edge, made her feel angry with the littered promises of better things. Agnes wanted to put her foot through it all, or to scrape it back like it was spoilt wallpaper. To get her nail under it and rip it all away.

With a bored slouch, Agnes fell back into the stuffy room and felt the safety of her mammy's carpet below her feet again. The other women hadn't looked up. Peevishly, she scraped the needle across the record player. She clawed at her hairline and turned the volume up too loud. "Come on, please, just the one wee dance?"

"*T'chut*, no yet," spat Nan Flannigan. She was feverish and arranging silver and copper coins into neat piles. "I'm just about to pimp out the lot of ye."

Reeny Sweeny rolled her eyes and held her cards close. "Ye have one filthy mind!"

"*Well*, don't say I didnae warn ye." Nan bit the end off a slab of fried fish and sucked the grease from her lips. "When I am done taking all your menage money at these cards ye're gonnae hiv to go home and fuck that bag o' soup bones you call a husband for more."

"No chance!" Reeny made a lazy sign of a cross. "I've been sitting on it since Lent, and I've got no intention of letting him get at it until next Christmas." She pushed a fat golden chip into her mouth. "I once held aff so long I got a new colour telly in the bedroom."

The women cackled without breaking their concentration on the cards. It was sweaty and close in the front room. Agnes watched her mammy, little Lizzie, carefully studying her hand, flanked by the bulk of Nan Flannigan on one side and Reeny Sweeny on the other. The women sat thigh to thigh and tore at the last scraps of a fish supper. They were moving coins and folding cards with greasy fingers. Ann Marie Easton, the youngest amongst them, was concentrating on rolling mean-looking cigarettes of loose tobacco on her skirt. The women spilt their housekeeping money on to the low tea table and were pushing five- and ten-pence bets back and forward.

It bored Agnes. There was a time before baggy cardigans and skinny husbands that she had led them all up to the dancing. As girls, they had clung to one another like a string of pearls and sang at the top of their voices all the way down Sauchiehall Street. They had been underage, but Agnes, sure of herself even at fifteen, knew she would get them in. The doormen always saw her gleaming at the back of the line and beckoned her forward, and she pulled the other girls behind her like a chain gang. They held on to the belt of her coat and muttered protest, but Agnes just smiled her best smile for the doormen, the smile she kept for men, the same one she hid from her mother. She had loved to show off her smile back then. She got her teeth from her daddy's side and the Campbell teeth had always been weak, they were a reason for humility in an otherwise handsome face. Her own adult teeth had come in small and crooked, and even when they were new they had never been white because of the smoking and her mammy's strong tea. At fifteen she had begged Lizzie to let her have them all taken out. The discomfort of the false teeth was nothing when compared to the movie star smile she thought they must give her. Each tooth was broad and even and as straight as Elizabeth Taylor's.

Agnes sucked at her porcelain. Now here they were, every Friday night, these same women playing cards in her mammy's front room. There was not a single drop of make-up between them. Nobody had much of a heart to sing any more.

She watched the women fight over a few pounds in copper coins and let out a bored huff. Friday card school was the one thing they looked forward to all week. It was meant to be their respite from ironing in front of the telly and heating tins of beans for ungrateful weans. Big Nan usually went home with the winnings from the kitty, except for the times when Lizzie would have a lucky-handed winning streak and got a slap for it. Big Nan couldn't help herself. She got jumpy around money and didn't like to lose it. Agnes had seen her mother get a black eye over ten bob.

"Haw you!" Nan was shouting at Agnes, who was engrossed with her own reflection in the window. "Ye're bloody cheatin'!"

Agnes rolled her eyes and took a long mouthful of flat stout. It was too slow a bus for where she wanted to go. So she filled her gullet with stout and wished it was vodka.

"Leave her be," said Lizzie. She knew that faraway look.

Nan returned her gaze to her cards. "Might have known you two were in cahoots. Thieving bastards the pair o' ye!"

"I've never stolen a thing in my life!" said Lizzie.

"Liar! I've seen ye at the end of a shift. Lumpy as porridge and heavy as oats! Stuffing your work pinny full of rolls of hospital toilet paper and bottles of dish soap."

"Do you know the price of that nonsense?" asked Lizzie indignantly.

"Aye, of course I do," sniffed Nan. "Because I actually pay for mine."

Agnes had been floating around the room, unable to settle. Now she nearly upended the card table with an armful of plastic shopping bags. "I bought youse a wee present," she said.

Nan usually wouldn't have allowed the interruption, but a gift was free and she knew better than to pass that by. She tucked her cards securely into her cleavage, and as they passed the plastic bags around, each woman drew out a small box. For a while they sat in silence contemplating the picture on the front. Lizzie spoke first, a little affronted. "A bra? What am I wanting with a bra?"

"It's no just any bra. It's one of those Cross Your Heart bras. It does wonders for your shape."

"Try it, Lizzie!" said Reeny. "Auld Wullie will be at you like it's the Fair Fortnight!"

Ann Marie took her bra from the box; it was clearly too small. "This bra isnae my size!"

"Well, I tried my best to guess. I got a couple of spare, so mind and check all of them." Agnes was already unzipping the back of her dress. The alabaster of her shoulders was shocking against the claret of the velvet. She unhooked her old bra and her porcelain breasts slid out; she slipped herself quickly into a new bra, and her breasts lifted several centimetres. Agnes dipped and spun for the women. "A fella was selling them off the back of a lorry down Paddy's Market. Five for twenty pound. Pure magic, eh?"

Ann Marie rummaged and found her size. She was more modest than Agnes, so turned her back to the room as she took off her cardigan and slipped off her old bra. The heaviness of her tits had left red strap welts on her shoulders. Soon all the women except for Lizzie had unfolded their dresses or unsnapped their work coveralls and were sitting in their new bras. Lizzie sat with her arms across her chest. The others, almost bare from the waist up, were running their hands along the satin straps and staring down at their own tits and cooing appreciatively.

"This might be the most comfy thing I've ever worn," admitted Nan. The bra was too loose across the back and was doing its best to hoist her enormous breasts off the shelf of her belly.

"Now *those* are the boobs I remember from when we were lassies," said Agnes approvingly.

"Dear God, if only we had known then what we ken now, eh?" said Reeny. "I would have let any bastard that wanted a feel play wi' them right then and there."

Nan rolled her tongue lasciviously. "Pure shite! You were never one to keep your hand on your ha'penny anyway." She was already keen to get back to business and was pushing coins around the table again. "Right, can we all stop looking at oorsels like a bunch of stupit lassies." She gathered the cards back up and started shuffling the deck. The women still hadn't drawn up their tops.

Lizzie tried to quietly burst the cellophane on a new cigarette packet. The other women were hawkish, growing sick of smoking harsh rollies and picking tobacco off the ends of their tongues. Lizzie sniffed, "I thought we were smoking our own?" But it was like eating ham hock in front of a pack of strays; they would give her no peace. She grudgingly passed around the fresh pack, and everyone lit up, enjoying the luxury of a manufactured cigarette. Nan sat back in her bra and held the smoke deep in her lungs as she closed her eyes. The air in the room grew hot and curdled again as the smoke swirled and danced with the paisley wallpaper.

Now and then fresh air pulled in and out of the sixteenth-floor window, and the women blinked at the sharpness of it. Lizzie drank her cold black tea and watched as the women all descended towards the darkness in their moods. Fresh air always did this to the drunk. The light, gossipy energy was leaving the room and being replaced by something stickier and thicker.

There was a new voice. "Mammy, he won't go to sleep!"

Catherine stood in the living room doorway with a look of exasperation on her face. She held her little brother on her hip. He was becoming too big to be held like that, but Shuggie clung to her tight, and it was clear how he loved the bony comfort of her.

Catherine, sour-faced for sympathy, pinched at his wrists and pried him from her. "Please. I can't handle him any more."

The little boy ran to his mother, and Agnes swept Shuggie up into her arms. There was the static crackle of nylon pyjamas as she spun him, content at last to have someone to dance with.

Catherine ignored the fact that the women were sitting, half-naked, in new bras. She searched the debris of fish suppers. She preferred the smallest brown chips, the curly skins that spent too long in the fryer and became crispy in the hot fat.

Lizzie smoothed her hand across Catherine's hip. Everything about her granddaughter seemed meagre, somehow unfeminine. At seventeen Catherine was long-limbed and boyish, with waist-length, poker-straight hair and no real curves. Fitted skirts seemed a disappointment on her. Lizzie had an absent-minded habit of rubbing her hand over her granddaughter's hip, as if this might cause some sudden femininity to raise up. From pure routine, Catherine pushed Lizzie's fussing hand away.

"Here!" said Lizzie. "Tell them about that smashin' job ye've tain in the city." She didn't pause to let her granddaughter speak but instead turned to the women. "I'm that proud. *Assistant* to the chairman. That's almost like being the gaffer yourself, eh?"

"Granny!"

Lizzie pointed to Agnes. "Well! That one thought she was going to get by on good looks. Thank fuck somebody's got brains." Lizzie crossed herself quickly. "I'll gladly go up the confession for boasting."

"And swearing," said Catherine.

Nan Flannigan did not look up from her cards. "Now that ye're working, doll. First thing to do is open two bank accounts. One for when ye take a man. The other one for yersel. And never fuckin' tell him about it, eh."

The women all murmured agreement at Nan's wisdom.

"So, no more school then, hen?" asked Reeny.

Catherine stole a sly glance at her mother. "No. No more school. We need the money."

"Aye. The state of the day's world ye'll be supporting any man ye do get." The women all had men at home. Men rotting into the settee for want of decent work.

Nan was growing impatient again. She rubbed her chapped hands together. "Listen, Catherine, I love ye, hen." She sounded insincere. "When ye are our first Scottish space cadet I'll be sure and pack ye some sandwiches for yer trip. Till then . . ." She motioned to the cards, then pointed to the door. "Fuck off."

Catherine slunk over to her mother and reluctantly took Shuggie from Agnes's hip. Her little brother was fascinated by the plastic slider on his mother's bra strap.

"Is our Alexander in for the night?" Agnes asked.

"Uh-huh. I think so."

"What do you mean, you *think* so? Is Alexander in the bedroom or not?" The bedroom was too small to misplace a lanky fifteen-year-old. It barely held the bunk beds for Catherine and Leek and the single bed for Shuggie. Still, Leek was a quiet soul, given to watching from the edges, capable of disappearing even when someone was talking to him.

"Mammy, you know what Leek's like. He *might* be." That's all she would say. Catherine spun on her heels, a whirling fan of chestnut hair, and as she carried Shuggie out of the room, she sank her fingernails into the soft of his thigh.

More hands of cards were dealt, more menage money was lost, and Agnes kept the records on rotation even though no one was paying any mind. Predictably, coins started piling in front of Nan as the piles of the others got smaller. Agnes, with her drink in hand, began to spin alone on the carpeted floor. "Oh, oh, oh. This is my song, ladies. Get up, get up!" Her twirling fingers implored them to their feet.

The women rose one by one, the unlucky ones happy to step away from Nan's conspicuous pile of silver. They danced happily in their new bras and old cardigans. The floor bounced under their weight. Nan spun around a shrieking Ann Marie until the two of them knocked into the edge of the low tea table. The women danced with abandon and took big mouthfuls of lager out of old tea mugs. All their movement became concentrated in the shoulders and hips, rhythmic and lusty, like the young girls they saw on television. It was a certainty that the poor skinny husbands they kept at home would be suffocated later that night. The women, smelling of vinegar and stout, would go home and climb on top of them. Giggling and sweating, yet feeling for a moment like fifteen-year-olds again in their new bras. They would strip to holey tights and unclasp their swinging tits. It would be drunk open mouths, hot red tongues, and heavy clumsy flesh. Pure Friday-night happiness.

Lizzie didn't dance. She had proclaimed herself off the drink. She and Wullie had tried to set a good example for the family. It had made her a bad Catholic to be tut-tutting at Agnes while enjoying a wee can or two herself. So she had stopped with the sweetheart stout and haufs of whisky, *almost*. Agnes looked over at her mammy sat with her cold mug of tea, and didn't believe it for a minute. Sitting with a proud back, Lizzie's eyes were still rheumy and damp-looking, her pink face clouded with a distant look.

Agnes knew Wullie and Lizzie had taken to slipping out of the room when they thought no one was watching. They would get up from the dinner table on a Sunday or make one too many trips to the bathroom. In secret they would sit on the edge of their big double bed with their bedroom door closed and pull plastic bags out from underneath. Into an old mug they would pour the bevvy and drink it quickly and quietly in the dark like teenagers. They would come back to the kitchen table and clear their throats, their eyes happier and glassier, and everyone would pretend not to smell the whisky. You only had to watch her father try to eat his Sunday soup to tell if he had a drink in him or not.

The record hissed to the end of the first side. Lizzie excused herself and wobbled off to the bathroom. Big Nan, thinking no one was looking, took the opportunity to peer slyly at Lizzie's cards. Her eye caught a glint of unopened stout tins behind Wullie's old comfy chair. "Jackpot!" she shouted. "That auld yin has a hidden carry-oot stuck down the back o' his chair!" She sat down, sweaty and out of breath, and helped herself. Nan was here on business, staying a little soberer than the others. All night she had been closely counting the money on the card table, thinking about the bit of ham she could buy for Sunday's soup and the money the weans would need for next week's school. Now the card business was over, Nan was thirsty for the hidden stout.

"Lizzie Campbell. That auld liar. She's not aff the drink," said Reeny.

"She's as aff that drink as I'm aff the pies," said Nan, buttoning her cardigan tight over her new bra. She shouted for Lizzie's benefit in the direction of the dark hallway. "I don't know why I'm pals wi' you robbing Catholic bastards anyhows!" Nan took the stout and filled the mugs and glasses on the table; the drunker she could get them the better. Suddenly she was all business again. "So. Are we gonnae finish these cards or get the catalogue out? I'm tired o' watching you auld wummin dance like youse are Pan's People." From a black leather handbag at her feet she pulled out a thick, dog-eared catalogue. Across the front cover it read *Freemans*, and there was a picture of a women in a lace dress and straw hat in a happy golden field somewhere far from here. She looked like her hair smelled of green apples.

Nan opened the catalogue on top of the playing cards and flicked through a couple of pages. The noise of the plasticky paper was like a siren's song. The women stopped throwing themselves around to the music and gathered around the open book, pressing greasy fingers on pictures of leather sandals and polyester nighties. They opened to a double spread of women riding bikes in pretty jersey dresses and cooed as one. At this Nan reached into her leather bag again and pulled out the handful of Bible-size payment books. There were groans all around. They were her pals, sure, but this was her job, and she had weans to feed.

"Och, Nan, I've just no got it this week," said young Ann Marie, almost recoiling from the catalogue.

Nan smiled and through closed teeth replied as politely as she was capable. "Aye, ye've fuckin' goat it. An' if ah have to dangle you out of the window by they fat ankles, you'll be paying me the night."

Agnes smiled to herself and knew Ann Marie should have quit while she was ahead. But the young woman ploughed on. "It's just that swimsuit doesnae actually fit."

"Yer arse! It fit when you goat it." Nan searched through the grey books. She pulled the one that read "Ann Marie Easton" in curly black biro and dropped it on the table.

"It's just my boyfriend said he's no able to take me away on holiday anymair." Ann Marie looked big-eyed from face to face for a trace of pity. The women couldn't care less. The last holiday most of them had seen was a stay on the Stobhill maternity ward.

"Too. Fuckin'. Bad. Pick. Better. Men. Pick. Better. Claes," Nan applied the pressure like she had a thousand times and went about collecting money from all the women and marking it in their books. It would be an eternity to pay off a pair of children's school trousers or a set of bathroom towels. Five pounds a month would take years to pay off when the interest was added on top. It felt like they were renting their lives. The catalogue opened to a new page, and the women started fighting over who wanted what.

Agnes was the first to lift her head at the change of pressure in the room. Shug was stood in the doorway, his thick money belt heavy in his hand. The damp wind was sucking through the room, telling Agnes that he had left the front door open, that he was not staying. Agnes stood and moved towards her husband, her dress still folded down at the waist. Too late she straightened her skirt, then she clasped her hands and tried to smile her soberest smile. He didn't return her it. Shug simply looked through her in disgust and abruptly said, "Right, who needs a lift?"

The unwelcome presence of a man was like a school bell. The women started gathering their things. Nan slipped a couple of Lizzie's hidden stouts into her bag. "Right, ladies! Next Tuesday up ma hoose," she barked, adding, for Shug's benefit, "and any man who thinks he can break up ma catalogue night will get battered."

"Looking lovely as ever, Mrs Flannigan," said Shug, picking his thumbnail with the hackney key. Of all of the women to fuck, it would never be her. He had standards.

"That's nice of ye to say," replied Nan with a thin smile. "Why don't ye shove yer arms up yer arse and gie yer insides a big hug from me."

Agnes pulled her velvet dress back over her shoulders. She stood still, her palms flat on her skirt. The women buttoned themselves into heavy coats and nodded politely to her as they squeezed uncomfortably past Shug, who still stood in the doorway. They all lowered their eyes, and Agnes watched as Shug smiled from under his moustache at each woman on her way out. He stepped aside only for the bulk of Nan.

Shug was slowly losing his looks, but he was still commanding, magnetic. There was a directness to his gaze that did something funny to Agnes. She had once told her mother that when she met Shug he had a gleam in his eye that would make you take your clothes off if only he asked. Then she had said that he asked this a lot. Confidence was the key, she explained, for he was no oil painting and his vanity would have been sickening in a less charming man. Shug had the talent to sell it to you like it was the thing you wanted the worst. He had the Glasgow patter.

He stood there, in his pressed suit and narrow tie, the leather taxi belt in his hand, and he coldly surveyed the departing women like a drover at a cattle auction. She had always known that Shug appreciated the very high and the very low of it; he saw an adventure in most women. There was something about how he could lower beautiful women, because he was never intimidated by them. He could make them laugh and feel flushed and grateful to be around him. He had a patience and a charm that could make plain women feel confident, like the loveliest thing that ever walked in flat shoes.

He was a selfish animal, she knew that now, in a dirty, sexual way that aroused her against her better nature. It showed in the way he ate, how he crammed food into his mouth and licked gravy from between his knuckles without caring what anyone thought. It showed in how he devoured the women leaving the card party. These days it was showing too often.

She had left her first husband to marry Shug. The first had been a Christmas Catholic, pious enough for the housing scheme but devout only to her. Agnes was better-looking than him in a way that made strange men feel hopeful for themselves and made women squint at his crotch and wonder what they had missed in Brendan McGowan. But there was nothing to miss; he was straightforward, a hard-working man with little imagination who knew how lucky he was to have Agnes and so he worshipped her. When other men went to the pub, he brought home his wages every week, the brown envelope still sealed, and handed it to her without argument. She had never respected that gesture. The contents of the envelope had never felt like enough.

Big Shug Bain had seemed so shiny in comparison to the Catholic. He had been vain in the way only Protestants were allowed to be, conspicuous with his shallow wealth, flushed pink with gluttony and waste.

Lizzie had always known. When Agnes had shown up on the doorstep with her two eldest and the Protestant taxi driver, she had had the instant compulsion to shut the door, but Wullie would not let her. Wullie had an optimism when it came to Agnes that Lizzie thought was a blindness. When Shug and Agnes finally got married, neither Wullie nor Lizzie went to the registry office. They said it was wrong, to marry between the faiths, to marry outside the Chapel. Really, it was Shug Bain she disliked. Lizzie had known it all along.

Ann Marie was one of the last to leave, taking too long a time in gathering her cardigan and cigarettes, even though it was all there, exactly as she had dropped it when she arrived. She made to say something to Shug, but he caught her eye, and she held her tongue. Agnes watched their silent conversation.

"Reeny, how you feeling, doll?" asked Shug with a cat's grin.

Agnes turned her eyes from Ann Marie's shadow and looked at her old friend, and her ribs broke anew.

"Aye, fine thanks, Shug," Reeny answered awkwardly, all the while looking at Agnes.

Agnes's chest caved into her heart as Shug said, "Get your coat, you'll catch your death. I'll drive you across the street."

"No. That's too much bother."

"Nonsense." He smiled again. "Any friend of our Agnes is a friend of mine."

"Shug, I'll put your tea on, don't be long," Agnes said, sounding more of a shrew than she wanted to.

"I'm no hungry." He quietly closed the door between them. The curtains became lifeless again.

Reeny Sweeny lived at 9 Pinkston Drive in the tower block that stood shoulder to shoulder with number 16. The black hackney just needed to turn its neat pirouette, and Reeny would be home in less than a minute. Agnes sat down, lit a cigarette, and knew she would wait long hours before Shug showed his face again.

She could feel the burn of Lizzie's eyes on the side of her face. Her mother said nothing, she just glowered. It was too much to be trapped in your mother's front room and judged by her, too much to have her be a front-row spectator to every ebb in your marriage. Agnes gathered her cigarettes and went along the short hallway to look in on her weans. The room was dark but for the focused beam of a camping torch. Leek was clutching it under his chin and drawing in a black sketchbook with a look of stillness on his face. He did not look up, and she could not see his grey eyes under the shade of his soft fringe. The room was warm and close with the breath of his sleeping siblings.

Agnes folded some of the clothes that were strewn across the floor. She took the pencil from his hand and folded the book closed. "You'll hurt your eyes, darling."

He was almost a man, far too old to kiss goodnight now, but she did so anyway and ignored it when he recoiled at the smell of heavy stout on her breath. Leek shone his torch on the single bed for her. Agnes checked on her youngest, drew the blanket tight under Shuggie's chin. She wanted to waken him, thought about taking him to her bed, overwhelmed by a sudden need to have someone wrapped tight around her again. Shuggie's mouth hung open in sleep, his eyelids flickering gently, too far away to be disturbed.

Agnes closed the door quietly and went to her own room. She felt between the layers of the mattress and took out the familiar vodka bottle. Shaking the dregs, she poured herself a pauper's mug, and then she sucked on the neck of the empty bottle and watched the city lights below.

The first time Shug went missing after his night shift Agnes spent the dawn hours worrying the hospitals and all the drivers she knew from the taxi rank. Working through her black book, she called all of her female friends, asking casually how they were but not admitting that Shug was roaming, unable to admit to herself that he had finally done it.

As the women gabbed about the routine of their lives she only listened to the noises beyond them and strained for any sounds of him in the room behind. Now she wanted to tell the women that she knew all about it. She knew about the sweaty taxi windows, his greedy hands, and how they must have panted at Shug to take them away from it all as he stuck his prick into them. It made her feel old and very alone. She wanted to tell them she understood. She knew all about its thrill, because once upon a time it had been her.

Once upon a time the wind whipping off the sea had turned the front of her thighs blue with the cold, but Agnes couldn't feel it because she had been happy.

The thousand blinking lights from the promenade rained down on her, and she moved towards them with a slack mouth. She was so struck she hardly drew a breath. The black paillettes on her new dress reflected the bright lights and sent them back twinkling into the Fair Fortnight crowd till she looked as radiant as the illuminations herself.

Shug lifted her and stood her on an empty bench. The lights were afire all along the waterfront for as far as her eye could travel. Every building was in competition with the next, blinking with a thousand gaudy bulbs of its own. Some were western saloon signs with galloping horses and winking cowboys, others were like the dancing girls of Las Vegas. She looked down on Shug, beaming up at her. He looked smart in his good, narrow black suit. He looked like he was somebody.

"I can't remember the last time you took me dancing," she said.

"I can still trip the light fantastic." He helped her gently back to the pavement and took a lingering squeeze of her soft middle. Shug could see the waterfront through her eyes, the tawdry glamour of the clubs and the adventure of the amusement halls. He wondered if this, too, would lose its shine for her. He took his suit jacket from his back and draped it over her shoulders. "Aye, the lights from Sighthill aren't going to seem the same after this."

Agnes shivered. "Let's not talk about home. Let's just pretend we've run away."

They walked along the shimmering waterfront trying not to think of all the small, everyday things that pushed them apart, that kept them living in a high-rise flat with her mother and father snoring through the bedroom wall. Agnes watched the lights flash on and off. Shug watched the men swivel their greedy eyes to look at her and felt a sick pride burst in his chest.

In the grey daylight of that morning she had seen the Blackpool seafront for the first time. Her heart had quietly broken in disappointment. Shabby buildings faced a dark, choppy ocean and a cold, stony beach where blue weans ran around in their underclothes. It was buckets and spades and pensioners in rain bonnets. It was day-tripping families from Liverpool and coachloads from Glasgow. He had meant it as a chance to be alone. She had bitten the inside of her cheek at the commonness of it all.

Now, at night, she saw its draw. The true magic was in the illuminations. There wasn't a surface that wasn't glowing. The old trams that ran down the middle of the street were covered in lights, and the shaky wooden piers that jutted out into the brackish sea were now festooned like runways. Even the Kiss Me Quick hats blinked on and off as though demented with lust. Shug took her wrist and led her through the crowd and along the blazing promenade. Children were screaming from the waltzer ride on the pier. There was the roar and flash of the dodgem cars, the *clink-clink* of the manic slots. Shug kept pulling her through the crowds towards the Blackpool Tower, twisting this way and that in the habit of a taxi driver.

"Darlin', please slow down," she pleaded. The lights were all flying past her too quickly to drink in. She wrenched her wrist from his grasp, there was a red ring where he had gripped her.

Shug was blinking and red-faced in the holiday crowd. He flushed with a mixture of anger and embarrassment. Strange men shook their heads as if they would have known how to handle this fine woman better. "You're no starting, are you?"

Agnes rubbed at her arm. She tried to soften the frown on her face. She hooked his pinkie with hers, the gold of his Masonic ring felt cold and dead against her hand. "You were rushing me, that's all. Just let me enjoy it. I feel like I never get out of the house." She turned from him, back to the lights, but the magic was gone. They *were* cheap.

Agnes sighed. "Let's have a wee drink. It'll take the chill off, maybe help us get back in the spirit of things."

Shug narrowed his eyes and ran his fist over his moustache like he was catching all the hard words he wanted to say to her. "Agnes. I'm begging you. Please can you take it slow the night?" But she was already gone, over the tramlines towards the winking cowboy.

"Howdy," said the barmaid in a thick Lancashire accent. "That's a right purdy dress."

Agnes lifted herself up on to the swivelling plastic bar stool and crossed her ankles daintily. "A Brandy Alexander, please."

Shug turned the bar stool next to her, spun it like a top, till it was taller than hers. With a hop he pulled himself up and twisted until they were eye to eye. "A cold milk, please." He drew two cigarettes out of a packet, and Agnes motioned for him to light one for her. The barmaid put the drinks down in front of them. The milk was in a child's tumbler, and Shug pushed it back towards her and demanded a different glass.

He slid the lit cigarette between Agnes's lips and stroked the nape of her neck where a soft curl was escaping. She reached into her handbag and then, pushing the hair back into her crown, with a *skoooosh* she blasted it with sweet-smelling hairspray. Agnes took a long mouthful of the sweet drink and smacked her lips. "Elizabeth Taylor has been to Blackpool. I wonder if she likes whelks?"

Shug picked the inside of his nose with the ringed pinkie. He rolled the mucus between his thumb and forefinger. "Who doesnae?"

She spun to face him. "Maybe we should move here. It could be like this all the time."

He laughed and shook his head at her, like she was a child. "Everyday it is something different with you. I'm exhausted trying to keep up." He traced a finger along the shiny hem of her skirt as she watched the summer crowds push by outside the bar. Ordinary folk, already in winter coats.

"You know what I want? I want to play some bingo." The warmth of the drink was in her now. She wrapped her arms around herself in a contented hug. "All these lights. I'm feeling lucky."

"Aye? I asked them to turn them on just for ye."

Fresh drinks came. Agnes fished around and pulled out the straw, the stirrer, and the two fat ice cubes. "This time I mean it. I'm going to win big. I'm going to start living. I'm going to give Sighthill a showing up. I can just feel it." She finished the brandy in one swallow.

Their rented room was at the top of a Victorian house that was set three streets back from the promenade. It was plain even for a Blackpool B & B, and it smelled like the kind of place that rented rooms to temporary lodgers, not families on holiday. Each carpeted landing had a different, settled-in musk. The place smelled of burnt toast and TV static, as if the landlady never liked to open a window.

It was quiet at that hour in the morning. Agnes lay in a pile at the bottom of the carpeted stairs singing tunelessly to herself. "*Ahh'm onny hew-man. Ahh'm just a wooh-man.*"

There were feet moving behind closed doors and old floorboards creaked overhead. Shug put his hand lightly over her mouth. "Shh. Be quiet, will ye. You'll wake up every soul in the place."

Agnes pushed his arm away from her face, threw her arm wide, and sang louder. "*Show me the stairwaa-ay ah have to cli-imb.*"

Lights came on in one of the rooms. Shug could see it from under the thin door. He put his hands under her arms and tried to pick her up, drag her up the carpeted stairs. The more he pulled the more easily she slid through his hands, like a boneless bag of flesh. Each time he got leverage, she would become formless and slip free. Agnes spilt back on to the stairs with a giggle and went on singing to herself.

An Englishman in one of the rented rooms hissed through his closed door, "Keep it down. Before I call the poh-lice! People are trying to sleep." To Shug he sounded like a small effeminate man, the way he dribbled out his sibilant esses. Shug would have liked him to open the door. Shug would have liked to leave a sovereign print on his face.

Agnes feigned affront. "Aye, phone the police you spoilsport. I'm on my holid—"

Shug clamped his hand tight over her wet mouth. She only giggled. With mischief in her eyes, she licked the inside of his palm with a fat tongue. It felt like a warm wet slab of flank mutton. It turned his stomach. Tightening his grip, he dug his ringed fingers into her cheeks till he forced her dentures apart. The smile left her eyes. Leaning his face close to hers, he hissed: "I'm only going to tell you this the once. Pick yersel up. Get yersel up they stairs."

Slowly he took his hand away from her face. There was a pink mark where he had squeezed her jaw. There was fear in her eyes, and she looked almost sober again. As he drew his hand away, the fear melted from her eyes and the demon drink came back into her face. She spat at him through the ceramic teeth. "Who the fuck do you think y—"

Shug was on her before she could finish. Stepping over her, he reached backwards into her hair. The hardened hairspray cracked like chicken bones as he wound his fingers into the strands. With a tug hard enough to rip handfuls out by the roots, he started up the stairs, dragging her behind him. Agnes's legs splayed awkwardly, she flailed like a clumsy spider as she tried to find her footing. The ripping pain stung her skull, and she wrapped her hands around his arm for purchase. Shug barely felt the sharpness of her nails as she pierced his skin. He pulled her up a stair, then he pulled her up another, and then another. The dirty carpet burnt her back, rubbed the skin from her neck, ripped the paillettes from her shiny dress. Hooking his thick arm under her chin he dragged her across the next carpeted landing. In one motion he dropped her at the door, fished out the key, turned on the bare light, and dragged her inside.

Agnes lay abandoned behind the door like a ragged draught excluder. The beaded dress had worked itself up her white legs. Her hand reached to her head, feeling for where her hair had started to tear. Shug crossed the room and pulled her hand away, suddenly embarrassed at what he had done. "Stop touching at yourself. I've no hurt you."

She could feel the blood of her scalp on her fingers. Her ears were ringing from the *bump, thump, bump* of each stair. The numbness of the drink was leaving her. "Why did you do that?"

"You were making a show of me."

Shug took off his black suit jacket and laid it over the single wooden chair. He took off the black tie and wound it neatly upon itself. His face was flushed red, and it made his eyes look somehow smaller and darker. While he'd dragged her upstairs his hair had come undone from the bald patch he tried hard to conceal. The loosened strands hung by his left ear, thin and ratty-looking. There was a *cluck* in the back of his throat, like a switch firing, and then his hands were on her again. She felt the claw on her neck, felt it on her thigh. He used his fingers and dug into her softness, wanting to be sure he had a firm grip. As flesh separated from bone she cried out from the pain, and he hammered his sovereign ring twice into her cheek.

When she was quiet again, Shug bent over and dug his nails into her shoulder and thigh and threw her on to the rented bed like a burst bin bag. He climbed on top of her. His face was a blazing shade of scarlet, his limp hair swinging free from his swollen head. It was as though he was filling with boiling blood. Using his elbows he pushed all his weight on to her arms, shoved them into the mattress until they felt like they might snap. He took the bulk of himself, all the driving weight he had gained from being so sedentary, and pushed it into her and pinned her there below him.

With his right hand he reached below her dress and found the soft white parts of her. She crossed her legs below him; he felt the ankles lock one over the other. With his free hand he gripped her thighs and tried to pull the dead weight of them apart. There was no giving. The lock was tight. He dug his fingers into the soft tops of her legs, digging the nails in until he felt the skin burst, until he felt her ankles open.

He pushed into her as she wept. There was no drink in her now. There was no fight in her any more. When he was done he put his face against her neck. He told her he would take her dancing in the lights again tomorrow.

Three

That summer, when it finally came, was close and damp. For a nocturnal man, the days had felt too long. The long daylight was like an inconsiderate guest, the northern gloam reluctant to leave. Big Shug always found the summer days hardest to sleep through. The sun brightened the thick curtains till they were a vibrating violet, and the children were always noisiest when they were happiest, the door going constantly with mouthy teenagers from other flats and women in strappy sandals traipsing the hall carpet, clacking pink feet and pink gums at all hours.

As night finally fell, Big Shug pulled his black hackney round in a small tight circle. It spun like a fat dog chasing its tail and headed out of the Sighthill estate. Seeing the lights of Glasgow, he relaxed back into the seat, and for the first time that day his shoulders fell from around his ears. For the next eight hours the city was his, and he had plans for it.

He wiped the window and got a good look in the wing mirror. Smiling to himself, he thought how smashing he looked: white shirt, black suit, black tie. It was a bit much for work, Agnes had said, but then she said altogether too much these days. As the smile travelled through his body he wondered whether taxi driving was in his blood. Between him and his brother Rascal it was practically a family business. His father would have enjoyed it too, had the shipbuilding not killed him.

Shug pulled up at the lights under the shadow of the Royal Infirmary and watched a gaggle of nurses smoke a crafty fag. He watched them rub their pink arms in the cold night air and shelf their tits over tight-folded arms. They smoked without using their hands, afeart of losing any body heat. He smiled slowly and watched himself react in the mirror. Night shift definitely suited him best.

He liked to roam alone in the darkness, getting a good look at the underbelly. Out came the characters shellacked by the grey city, years of drink and rain and hope holding them in place. His living was made by moving people, but his favourite pastime was watching them.

The thin driver's window made a sharp slicing sound as he slid it down and lit a cigarette. The wind came rushing in, and his long strands of thin hair danced like beach grass in the breeze. He hated going bald, hated getting old; it made everything hard work. He adjusted the mirror lower so that he couldn't see the reflection of his bare head. He found his long, thick moustache and sat absent-mindedly stroking it, like a favourite pet. Under it his spare chin wobbled. He tilted the mirror back up.

The Glasgow streets were shiny with rain and street lights. The infirmary nurses didn't linger, flicking half-smoked fags into the puddles and tottering back inside. Shug sighed and turned the taxi past Townhead and pointed down towards the city centre. He liked the drive from Sighthill, it was like a descent into the heart of the Victorian darkness. The closer you got to the river, the lowest part of the city, the more the real Glasgow opened up to you. There were hidden nightclubs tucked under shadowy railway arches, and blacked-out windowless pubs where old men and women sat on sunny days in a sweaty, pungent purgatory. It was down near the river that the skinny, nervous-faced women sold themselves to men in polished estate cars, and sometimes it was here that the polis would later find chopped up bits of them in black bin bags. The north bank of the Clyde housed the city mortuary, and it seemed fitting that all the lost souls were floating in that direction, so as to be no trouble when their time blessedly came.

Pulling past the station, Shug was glad the rank there was full of taxis and empty of punters. Tourists were dull, talkative, and fucking cheap. They'd be an eternity lugging massive cases into the back and then would sit there steaming up the taxi in squeaky Pac-a-Macs. Those ugly tight-arsed bastards could shove their ten-pence tips. He gave a snide toot to the boys and drove on lower towards the river.

Rain was the natural state of Glasgow. It kept the grass green and the people pale and bronchial. Its effect on the taxi business was negligible. It was a problem because it was mostly inescapable and the constant dampness was pervasive, so fares might as well sit damp on a bus as damp in the back of an expensive taxi. On the other hand, rain meant that the young lassies from the dancing all wanted to take a taxi home so as not to ruin their stiff hair or their sharp shoes. For that Shug was in favour of the endless rain.

He pulled up Hope Street and sat at the rank. It shouldn't be long. Only two or three of the old boys were sat there, waiting for a hire. From here it was a short stoat from the dancing on Sauchiehall Street or a frozen trot for the working girls pitched out on Blythswood Square. Either way, it was a good spot for an interesting night.

Shug sat smoking in the dreich and listened to the crackle of the CB radio. The lady dispatcher announced fares up in Possil and runs to be had down in the Trongate. Joanie Micklewhite was the only voice on the radio, and every night he listened to her hold this repetitive circular monologue asking for help, waiting for answers, giving orders, and bluffing any backchat. Always only half a conversation, like she was talking to herself or talking, it seemed, only to him. He liked the peaceful sound of her voice. He took a comfort from it.

He finished his cigarette and watched young couples huddle together as they left the late picture. The drivers in front slowly started to pull fares and rattle off into the night. Alone at the head of the rank, he watched a group of young lassies dribble chips on to the street as they had a fight over how they should get home. It looked like they'd get in the taxi, but no, the fat practical one wanted to wait for the night bus. *Leave her*, he thought, *let her get wet*. The prettiest, most guttered one was still stumbling towards him. Shug practiced his smile in the half-light.

He was dragged from his dirty thoughts as a set of bony knuckles rapped on the window. "Ye fur hire, pal?" said a man's voice.

"No!" shouted Shug, pointing in the direction of the wrecked girls.

"Right, then," said the old man, not paying any heed. He opened the door before Shug could hit the automatic lock and pulled his small frame and voluminous coats inside. "Dae ye ken the Rangers bar on Duke Street?"

Shug sighed, "Aye, pal," as the pretty girl slid along the queue to the taxi behind his. He gave her a half-smile, but she paid him no mind.

Ignoring the black leather seat that ran the width of the taxi, the old man pulled down a folding seat and sat directly behind Shug. This was the sign of a talker. *Here we fuckin' go*, thought Shug.

It was wet outside but humid inside the cab. The hackney filled with the smell of old milk. The old man sat in a yellowed shirt and a crumpled grey suit, over which he had piled a thin wool coat and on top of this had added an oversize topcoat. It gave him the look of a refugee, his tiny frame drowning in yards of Shetland wool and gabardine. On his head he wore a Harris bunnet, from the shadows of which only his red round nose protruded. The patter started almost immediately. "Did ye see the game the day, son?" asked the milky passenger.

"No," answered Shug, already knowing where this was headed.

"Aw, ye missed a great game, a bloody great game." The man was tutting to himself. "Who *do* ye support then?"

"Celtic," he lied. He was no Catholic, but it was the shortcut to ending the conversation.

The auld man's face crumpled like a dropped towel. "Oh, fur fuck's sake, might've known ah'd get in a Pape's taxi." Shug watched him in the mirror and snorted under his moustache. He didn't support Celtic; he didn't support the Rangers either, but he was proud to be a Protestant. He would have turned his Masonic ring around, but the old man was paying no heed and moving like he was underwater.

Bemused, Shug watched as the man worked himself up into a state of distracted despair, swinging from lachrymose to belligerent. He held his hands in front of him like he was pleading with God. Then he laid his arm across the back of the partition and brought his face inches from the glass separating him from Shug's ear. Wet-lipped with the drink, he was spitting out random streams of patter, making faces like a toddler learning to talk. Big globs of wet spit misted the partition. Shug deliberately tapped the brakes, and the man's forehead made a *thunk* sound as it skelped off the glass. Bunnetless but undeterred, he kept on with his rambling. Shug frowned. He'd have to give that a good wipe later.

The auld Glasgow jakey was a dying breed—a traditionally benign soul that was devolving into something younger and far more sinister with the spread of drugs across the city. Shug looked in the mirror and watched the man continue his drunken solo, the conversation so low and incoherent that he could pick out only certain words like *Thatcher* and *union* and *bastard*. With no feelings of sympathy, he watched as the man laughed and then sobbed at intervals.

The Louden Tavern sat dark and windowless, the door well recessed into the brick face of the low building. It was by design rock-proof, bottle-proof, and bomb-proof. The facade, painted with the red, white, and blue of the Glasgow Rangers, was gloriously defiant in the shadow of Parkhead, the home of Glasgow Celtic, the sporting Mecca of all Catholics.

Shug told the man the fare was a pound seventy and watched him ferret in one pocket after another. All the Glasgow jakeys did this. Their Friday wages were splintered by every bar they passed till they rolled around in pockets as five and ten pence in change, the cumulative weight of the heavy small coins giving them a waddling walk and a hump. They would live on the coins for the rest of the week, taking their chances with their random findings. Even in sleep they were never to be separated from their trousers and large coats for fear their wives or children would tip them out first and buy bread and milk with the shrapnel.

The man was an age looking in every pocket. Shug listened to the soft voice on the CB and tried to stay calm. By the time the jakey had paid and sailed into the dark mouth of the pub Shug was thundering back along Duke Street, trying not to miss the dancing letting out. Outside the Scala an auld dear stuck her hand out, waving it like a small bird. Shug had to stop short or run her over.

He watched her climb into the back of the taxi and felt relieved when she sat square in the centre of the wide black seat. "The Parade, please." She sniffed, wrinkled her nose, and looked scornfully at Shug. It must have smelled like someone pissed in a pot of old porridge back there.

The taxi started climbing the tenemented hills of Dennistoun. Shug looked in the mirror and watched the woman, who was watching him. The Glasgow housewives always sat square in the middle, never to the side looking out of the window or on one of the fold-down seats like the lonely old men who were hungry for company. She sat as they all did, upright and rigid, like a Presbyterian queen, knees together, back straight, with her hands clasped on her lap. Her coat was pulled close around herself, her hair was set and brushed, even in the back, and her face was set tight like a mask.

"It's a wild terrible night, right enough," she said finally.

"Aye, the radio said it would piss all week." There was something about the woman that reminded him of his own mother, dead and gone. The raw hands and tiny frame belied the strength and power that surely ran through her. He thought of the nights his father would raise his fist on his mother. The more she took it the more he rained down on her, turning her red then blue then black. Shug thought about her at the mirror, pulling her hair over her face, pushing her make-up wider around her eyes to cover the bruises.

"Ah wis just saying I don't usually get a taxi." She was searching for his eyes in the mirror.

"Oh, aye?" said Shug, glad to have his thoughts interrupted.

"Aye, but I've had a wee win the night, you see. Just a wee one, mind, but it's nice all the same." She was rubbing her thumbnail raw. "It'll come in right handy, you see, now that my George is out of work," she sighed. "Twenty. Five. Years. Out at the Dalmarnock Iron Works, and all he got was three weeks' wages. Three weeks! I went up there maself, chapped on the big red gaffer's door, and I telt him what he could dae with three weeks' wages." She opened the clasp on her small hard bag and looked inside. "Do you know what that big bastard telt me? 'Mrs Brodie, your husband was lucky to get three weeks. I have some young boys wi' their whole lives ahead o' them and they only got paid till the end of their shift.' Made my blood absolutely boil so'in, it did. I said to him, 'Well, I've got two grown boys at home to feed, and they cannae find any work either, so just what do you suppose I do about that?' He looked at me and he didnae even blink when he said, *'Try South Africa!'*"

She closed the bag. "They've never even been to South Lanark-shire, never mind South Africa!" She kept rubbing her red thumb. "It's no right. The government should dae something. Shutting down the ironworks and shipbuilding. It'll be the miners next. Just you watch! South Africa! *I never!* Go all the way to South Africa so they can build cheap boats there and send them home to put more of our boys out of work? The shower of swine."

"It's diamonds," Shug offered. "They go to South Africa to mine diamonds."

The woman looked as if he had contradicted her. "Well I don't care what they mine, they could be pulling licorice out a black man's arse for all I care. But they should be working here at home in Glasgow and eating their mammy's cooking."

Shug put his foot on the accelerator. The city was changing; he could see it in people's faces. Glasgow was losing its purpose, and he could see it all clearly from behind the glass. He could feel it in his takings. He had heard them say that Thatcher didn't want honest workers any more; her future was technology and nuclear power and private health. Industrial days were over, and the bones of the Clyde Shipworks and the Springburn Railworks lay about the city like rotted dinosaurs. Whole housing estates of young men who were promised the working trades of their fathers had no future now. Men were losing their very masculinity.

Shug had watched the thinning out of the working classes from their poor neighbourhoods. Middle-class civil servants and city planners had seen it a stroke of genius to ring the city with new towns and cheaply built estates. Given a patch of grass and a view of the sky, the city's ills were supposed to disappear.

The woman sat stiff and still on the back seat. The skin was wearing off around her thumbs, and worry sat around the corners of her mouth. Only when she patted the back of her hair did Shug know she was still alive. The taxi dropped her at the mouth of her close, and she pushed a pound tip into Shug's hand.

"Here, what's this?" He tried to pass it back. "I'm no needin' that."

"Gies peace!" she shushed. "It's just a wee bit of my winnings. I'm spreading my luck around. Luck's the only thing that's gonnae get us out of this mess."

Shug took the tip reluctantly. Fuck the English tourists and their bastarding Kodaks. Shug had seen it before, those with least to give always gave the most.

By the time Shug got back to the city centre the last picture had let out and the city was settling in for a few hours of cold sleep. Some of the late-night clubs were banging out music, but it was suicide to sit outside them waiting for a fare because the first drunks wouldn't be spilling out till well after midnight. Shug sighed and thought about waiting around. Maybe he'd pick up a bird who'd been left holding all the Babycham while her pals danced with some fellas. The ugliest bird usually left first. He'd driven them home before, even waited with the meter off while they got some consoling bags of crisps and chocolate biscuits from the corner Paki. If you talked nice to them they were dead nice back.

He had loosened his tie and settled in for the long wait when the soft voice came over the radio. "Car thirty-one. Car thirty-one. Come in." His heart sank. It was Agnes, it had to be.

He picked up the black reciever and pressed the button on the side. "Car thirty-one here." There was a long pause, and he waited for the news.

"You've been requested up at Stobhill, car for Easton," said Joanie Micklewhite.

"I've got a fare, and I'm taking them out to the airport. Do you no have a car closer?" he asked.

"Sorry, sunshine! You've been specially requested." He could almost hear the smile. "Punter said to take your time, there was no rush."

He hadn't thought it'd be this. Agnes surely, or even his first wife after money for their four weans, but he hadn't thought it would be this. They weren't there yet, surely?

The drive up to the old hospital was quick this time of night. The Royal Infirmary was where the football stabbings and giro-day domestics went. Stobhill was where Glasgow was born and where Glasgow died. Now a mousy girl was stood there in the glow from the foyer, wearing a blue cleaner's apron. She clawed at her saggy tights and wriggled them straight and flat. Her make-up had spread from the cold and the tears, and he could see the ring of burnt doubts at her feet, like she must've been waiting in the cold for him her whole break. Shug smiled. She was only twenty-four and already his doormat.

"I didnae think you were coming," she said, climbing into the back of the taxi.

"What did you call me out here fur?"

"I missed ye, that's all," she said. "I haven't seen ye in weeks." She rolled her thick legs open and shut coquettishly. "You've no gone off o' me, have ye?" She grinned.

Shug turned in his seat. "Who the fuck do ye think ye are, Ann Marie? I'm tryin' to make a livin', and ye call me across the city like I wis a dog that pissed on yer carpet." He slammed the heel of his fist on the glass partition. "We have to be discreet. Cool like. What the fuck do you think would happen if Agnes found out, eh? I'll tell you what would happen. She'd get a haud of you by the scruff of yer neck and drag the length of the Clyde wi' ye for starters. When she was done dragging yer body she would drag yer good name. She'd phone yer parents every night just after they'd gone to their beds. She'd wake them up and tell them that their good wee Catholic girl was carrying on with a married man." He paused, watching his words take effect. "Is that really what you want?"

The tears were running down her face and pooling on her apron. "But ah love ye."

Shug pulled the taxi in a sharp arc and parked in a dark corner of the empty car park. He glanced at his watch and then met her gaze again in the mirror. "Aye, well, take yer fucking knickers off then. I've only got five minutes."

Shug felt hungry as he headed back into the city. He was certain Ann Marie wouldn't call the rank for him for a while. She was a nice lassie, heavy tits and eager too, but she was cramping his style. That was the problem with the young ones; they saw no reason to not expect better for themselves. She'd definitely have to go.

He was just thinking of the voice on the radio when it spoke to him again. "Car thirty-one, car thirty-one, come in."

He picked up the receiver and held his breath; he was running out of luck. "Joanie?"

"Phone. Home. Now," came the terse reply.

He pulled the hackney over at the mouth of Gordon Street, and clipping coins out of his dispenser he made a quick dash through the rain to an old red phone box. It was wet on the inside and smelled like piss. He had tried ignoring Agnes's orders before, but that just made things more difficult. She would be insistent and get more abusive as the night wore on. The best thing to do was *Phone. Home. Now.*

It barely rang once before it was answered. She would have been sat at the pleather phone table in the hall, just drinking and waiting and drinking.

"Hell-o," said the voice.

"Agnes, what is it?"

"Well, if it isn't the chief hoor-master himself."

"Agnes," Shug sighed. "What is it this time?"

"I know," spat the drunken voice.

"Know what?"

"Know. *Everything*."

"You're no making any sense." He shifted uncomfortably in the tight phone box.

"I knoo-ow." The voice boomed, her wet lips too close to the mouthpiece.

"If you're gonnae keep this up, I'm gonnae have to get back to work."

There was a deep sob on the end of the phone.

"Agnes, you cannae phone the rank any more, I'll get the sack. I'll be home in a few hours, and we can talk then. OK?" But there was no answer. "Well, do you want to know what I know? I know I love you," he lied. The sobbing got louder. Shug hung up.

The rain and piss had soaked through his tasselled brogues. Picking up the black receiver again, he hammered it against the side of the red booth. He knocked out three panes of glass before the receiver broke, before he felt better. Back in the taxi he had to sit still for ten minutes until his knuckles would let go of the choke they had on the steering wheel.

Maybe he would feel better if he ate something. He fished around under his seat for his plastic piece box. It smelled like margarine and white bread, like marriage and cramped flats. The corned beef pieces Agnes had packed turned his stomach. He dumped them into the gutter and cut up several side streets till he pulled up in front of DiRollo's chippy, open twenty-four hours, bog-standard. DiRollo's was popular with both cabbies and prostitutes because of the unsociable hours and the discretion of its owner. There was a big red lobster painted on the sign, but nothing as exotic on offer inside.

Joe DiRollo stood behind the counter, as he seemed to do every hour of the day. At night the fluorescent light made him look deceased. A small man, hair thin and slicked back off his face, with chip grease or Brylcreem or both. Like an oily iceberg only his swollen head and shoulders were visible above the counter. The rest of his sallow bulk was squished up against the machete he kept under the counter. He greeted everyone with a phlegmy clearing of the throat and tilting of his fat head.

"How ye doin', Joe?" asked Shug, with no genuine interest.

"Aye, no so bad."

"Been busy with our fair ladies the night?" Shug shoved his thumb in the direction of a gaunt-looking customer who, eyes closed, was swaying on her feet.

"Ehhhh, they been a-cumming and a-going, you know?" He laughed at his own joke. "No' so good for business any more. They eat half a bag of chips, drink a ginger, that's it! They ask to use the toilet, my own toilet, and auld Joe says, *OK*. He's a nice guy, but they don't come out for an hour, you know. They eat a half a bag of chips, and then they wash their cunts in my toilet."

Shug was eyeing the fried fish in the hot counter. "It's the drugs. I widnae dare stick it in them any more."

"Aye, they're dropping like flies. If the drugs are no doing them in, then some bad bastard's choking the life out of them."

"You'll put me aff ma whelks." Shug pulled a tight face. "Gies a fish supper, extra salt and vinegar, would ye?"

Joe took the white paper and dropped a heaped scoop of fat chips and a big bit of golden battered fish on it. He drizzled the hot food with salt and vinegar, and Shug circled with his fingers. "Mair, Joe. *Mair.*" The man piled it on till it was sodden.

He handed Shug his parcel. "So, you never give me an answer to my offer. You want the wee house or no?"

As well as running the chippy, Joe DiRollo was famous for grifting the Glasgow City Council. He signed up for subsidized flats under the guise of one of his many daughters. Then he rented them along, skimming an extra tenner a week over what the council originally charged him.

"I'll let you know," Shug said, backing out the door. "Mrs Bain, well, she's difficult."

"I'm surprised you want to move at all. Thought you would be living like a king up there in that Sighthill sky."

"The King is fine; it's the Queen that wants a beheading. Just hold on to that empty house of yours a while longer. There's a lot that has to be lined up first. I want it all to go perfect." He smiled and bit into a fat chip.

By the time Shug finished the last of the whelks there was only an hour or so left on the clock. He rolled down the windows as the sun broke the top of George Square, bathing the city in a warm orange light and setting the statue of Rabbie Burns on fire. It was the best time of day, the city at peace, before it got ruined by the diurnal masses. He watched the clock in anticipation and set off early for the North Side.

Driving slowly all the way to Joanie Micklewhite, he left the windows down and flicked the green air freshener with his forefinger. She would finish her shift soon, and then they could say all the things they could not over the CB radio. He pulled the taxi in tight amongst four or five others and waited for her, slumped forward in his seat, grinning like a daft boy, watching the front door like it was Christmas.

Four

They were both still damp and sitting on the edge of the bed when the evening street lights came on. Agnes had run Shuggie a deep bath, and then, feeling lonely, she'd climbed in beside her youngest. Lizzie would've had a fit if she had seen. It would have to stop soon, he was too canny for five. It was the first time he'd looked at her privates and then considered his own, like a spot-the-difference puzzle.

The water had grown cold as they made a great game of filling the shampoo bottles and then soaking each other with the soapy jet. She let him scrape at the old nail polish on her toes, his care and attention feeling like a penny dropped in an empty meter.

At the edge of her bed, she combed the boy's glossy black hair, as his head lowered in concentration. He made the Matchbox car squeal through the paisley maze of bedspread, it climbed over her bare leg as easily as the Campsie hills. Without knowing what he was looking at, he traced the white scars, the memories of Shug's fingernails, that lined the inside of her thigh. Then the car careened back to the bedspread. The tyres would scream loudly, and the boy would look up at her and smile with the self-satisfied face of his father.

Agnes drew a fresh can of lager from a hidden place and gently pulled at the ring top. With a careful finger she gathered the bubbly drips and popped them into her mouth. She gave the boy the empty Tennent's can. He had always liked the half-naked beauties photographed on the side. Shuggie was intent on this one, he hadn't seen her before, and he liked the way her name sounded when he spelt it out slowly, just like his Granda Wullie had taught him. *Shh-hee-nah*.

Shuggie would collect the empty cans from around the house and line up the women on the edge of the bath. He would stroke their tinny hair and make them talk to each other in imagined conversations, rambling monologues, mostly about ordering new shoes from catalogues and whoring husbands. Big Shug had caught him once. He had watched proudly as Shuggie lined up the women and spelt out each of their names phonetically. He bragged about it later down the rank. "*Five years old, eh!*" he would say. "*What a chip aff the auld block.*" Agnes had looked on sadly, knowing what was really going on.

Later that week she took Shuggie into the BHS and bought him a baby doll. Daphne was a chubby little toddler, with the tufted coif of a fifties housewife. Shuggie loved the doll. He put all his lager ladies in the bin after that.

Shuggie had been watching his mother quietly. He was always watching. She had raised three of them in the same mould, every single one of her children was as observant and wary as a prison warden.

"Howse aboots some light entertainment?" he asked, mimicking some nonsense from the telly.

Agnes flinched. With her painted nails she cupped his face and squeezed his dimples gently. She pushed until the boy's bottom lip protruded. "Ab-oww-t," she corrected. "Ab-OU-t."

He liked the feeling of her hands on his face, and he cocked his head slightly and baited her. "Ab-ooo-t."

Agnes frowned. She took her index finger and pushed it into his mouth, hooking his lower teeth. She gently pulled his jaw open, and held it down. "There's no need to sink to their level, Hugh. Try it again."

With her finger in his mouth, Shuggie pronounced it correctly if not clearly. It had the round, proper *oww* sound that she liked. Agnes nodded her approval and let go of his lip.

"Dus that mean the wee mooose wisnae loose aboot the hooose?" He was giggling before he could even finish the cheeky nonsense. Agnes hunkered down to chase him, and he squealed with happiness and terror as he raced around the bed.

A pile of cassettes sat next to the alarm clock. He raked through them, scattering them to the floor until he landed on the one he was after. Shug had bought the alarm clock for her. He had saved bricks of petrol coupons, rubber-banded together, and handed them to her like they were gold bullion. The plastic button released the cassette drawer. Shuggie punched the tape in and rewound it, screaming, to the beginning. It sounded tinny and hollow on the alarm clock, but she didn't care. The music made the room feel less empty. Shuggie stood on the bed and put his arms on her shoulders. They swayed that way for a while. She kissed his nose. He kissed her nose.

As the song changed, Shuggie watched his mother clutch the can to her chest and spin around the room. Agnes screwed her eyes shut and went back to a place where she felt young and hopeful and wanted. Back to the Barrowland, where strange men would follow her hungrily across the ballroom and women would drop their eyes in jealousy. With fingers unfurling like a beautiful fan, she ran her hand over her body. Just above her hips, she touched the stubborn roll of fat she had earned from birthing her three weans. Suddenly her eyes opened, and she returned from the past, feeling rotten and stupid and lumpy.

"I hate this wallpaper. I hate those curtains and that bed and that fucking lamp."

Shuggie rose to his stockinged feet on the soft bedspread. He wrapped his arms around her shoulders and tried to cling to her again, but this time she pushed him away.

The small flat was never quiet, the walls were too thin. There was always the drone of the big telly turned up too loud for her father. The low complaints of Catherine, with the telephone pulled into her bedroom, the cord saw-sawing the good veneer off the bottom of the door as she paced and moaned about the slights of being seventeen. There were neighbours on every side and on the sixteenth floor, the wind, always the pulsing wind, rattling against the ill-fitted windows.

Agnes put her head in her hands. She listened to her parents roar with laughter at some effeminate English comedian. Her eldest two were out, who knows where. They always seemed to be gone now, ducking her kisses, rolling their eyes at everything she said. She ignored Shuggie's light breathing, and for a moment it was like she was not nearly forty, not a married woman with three children. She was Agnes Campbell again, stuck in her bedroom, listening to her parents through the wall.

"Dance for me," she said suddenly. "Let's have a wee party." She stabbed at the alarm clock, and the cassette squealed forward, the slow sad music speeding up to something happier.

Shuggie lifted her lager can. He put it to his lips like it was a magical power juice. The bitter oaty flavour made him flinch, the way it tasted like fizzy ginger, milk, and porridge all at the same time. He danced for her, stepping side to side and clicking his fingers and missing every beat. When she laughed, he danced harder. He did whatever had caused her to laugh another dozen times till her smile stretched thin and false, and then he searched for the next move that would make her happy. He bounced and flung his arms out as she laughed and clapped. The happier she looked, the harder he wanted to spin and flail. The vibrating patterned wallpaper threatened to make him sick, but he kept going, punching the air and rattling his hips. Agnes threw her head back in peals of laughter, and the sadness was gone from her eyes. Shuggie snapped his fingers like a hardman and jutted his head, still missing the beat. It didn't matter.

They were both breathless from laughing when they heard it.

In the hallway the front door opened and closed. It was more a sucking of wind and a contracting of space than a noise. Heavy footsteps came slowly up the carpet to the bedroom door. Agnes gathered the spent lager cans and hid them on the far side of the bed. She twisted the rings upright on her fingers and, turning expectantly to the door, she practiced her most lighthearted smile. The heavy footsteps stopped outside. Agnes and Shuggie listened to the soft *chink-clink* of small change in a trouser pocket. Then there was a low sigh, and the footsteps passed on down the hallway to the living room. He was home for his first tea break. It should have been a time to spend together. Now she listened to Shug say hello to her parents, his voice flat and without warmth. Agnes knew her father would have looked up, the television reflected on his glasses, and smiled. There would be a moment when Wullie would have stood and offered Shug the comfy armchair. Both men would have circled it, in an awkward game of musical chairs, until Shug put his hand on Wullie's shoulder and lowered him back into the seat. Lizzie, stony-faced, would have stood to boil the ketttle and shivered likely, as though it was not Shug but the cold Campsie wind itself that had arrived.

Agnes listened to it all through the wall. In a single sweep, she caught the creams and perfume bottles on her dresser and sent them across the room. The lamp lay broken on its side. The bare bulb glaring up at her changed her features so completely that it scared Shuggie. Everything had turned upside down so quickly.

Agnes sank to the edge of the bed. Shuggie could feel her can of lager spill on to the mattress and start to soak through his socks. Burying her face in his hair, she sobbed her dry, frustrated tears; her breath was clammy against his neck. Falling back on the bed, she pulled him down beside her. As she gripped him, he could see her face was lopsided, the paint on her eyes was blurred and running away. It looked like the lager beauties sometimes did, a careless printer and a misaligned screen, and suddenly the woman was no longer whole, just a mess of different layers.

Agnes reached across the mattress for her cigarettes, she lit one and sucking loudly, she coaxed the end into a blazing copper tip. She looked at the light for a moment, and her voice cracked with the poor me's as she sang along with the cassette. Her right arm extended gracefully, and she held the glowing cigarette against the curtains. Shuggie watched as the ash started to smoulder and then gave off a grey smoke. He started to squirm as the smoke burst with a gasp into orange flame.

Agnes used her free arm and pulled him tighter towards her. "*Shhh.* Now be a big boy for your mammy." There was a dead calmness in her eyes.

The room turned golden. The flames climbed the synthetic curtains and started rushing towards the ceiling. Dark smoke raced up as though fleeing from the greedy fire. He would have been scared, but his mother seemed completely calm, and the room was never more beautiful, as the light cast dancing shadows on the walls and the paisley wallpaper came alive, like a thousand smoky fishes. Agnes clung to him, and together they watched all this new beauty in silence.

The curtains were almost gone, they dripped like ice cream on to the carpet. Some of the wallpaper that had come loose around the damp window was alight, and the plastic curtain track melted in two and swung down like a broken bridge. A large bead of bubbling curtain landed on the corner of the bed, and the smoke grew around them. Shuggie started to squirm again. He couldn't stop coughing. A dark cough, sticky and bitter, like the time one of Lizzie's bingo pens had burst ink into his mouth. Agnes never moved, she just closed her eyes and sang her sad song.

Big Shug stood framed in the darkness of the doorway. As fresh oxygen entered the room the flames ran across the ceiling to greet him. He was on and over the bed and had the window open in an instant. With his bare hands he pushed the burning polyester out the window. He picked the largest pieces of melted magma off the floor and threw them after the flaming fabric. Suddenly he was gone again, and Shuggie cried out for his father, certain he had left them alone.

When Shug returned he was swinging wet bath towels. They sprayed sour water each time they found their mark and the flames died under them. Shug turned to the bed and slapped the damp wet towels across the tangled bodies. Shuggie tried not to cry out as the whipping stung his skin. Agnes lay stiff, her eyes closed.

When the last of the flames had died Shug stood with his back to his wife and son. Through stinging eyes Shuggie watched his father's shoulders shake with anger, and when he turned around Shuggie could see that his face was flushed with the heat and his fingers were curled, scarlet and sore where he had burnt them.

Lizzie and Wullie stood in the darkness of the hallway. Shug ripped his son from under Agnes's arm and shunted him into Lizzie's embrace. Agnes lay still and lifeless on the bed, and when Shug pinched her face in his hand, her lips parted in an odd fishlike expression. Bending down he shook her sharply and repeated her name over and over, till the corners of his mouth were filled with spit.

It was no use.

He looked to Lizzie, who held the boy close. Wullie ran his thick, calloused hand under his glasses, tears already running down his face. Shug looked down at his wife and her lifeless body. The room was silent. No one knew what to say.

Agnes did not trust the quiet.

She opened one of her eyes; its pupil was dark and wide but focused and clear. She put the mangled cigarette back between her lips. "Where the fuck have you been?"

Five

The city centre was full of Orangemen. With their flutes, fife, and drums they had paraded from the cenotaph in George Square through the city to Glasgow Green. From the office window Catherine had watched the banners and sashes of the different lodges go by. At first the Protestants sang their support of King Billy, and later, after the pubs had opened, they screamed, "*Get it up ye, ya Fenian basturts*," to some tune Catherine did not know and doubted they did either.

All day policemen in reflective jackets sat on nervous horses. Now that the march was finished, young men gathered and sang sectarian songs like hateful carollers. They shouted at young girls that passed by and chased any man who wasn't wearing the correct colours.

Catherine left the office as late as she possibly could, hoping to avoid the worst of it. She stood outside the sandstone building, deeply regretting her new emerald-green coat and high-heeled suede boots. As rain clouds covered the July sun she cursed having to work the Orange Saturday. It wasn't like she was that great with numbers, but Mr Cameron insisted she be there when he was, to answer the phones that never rang, to make the tea he never drank.

It wasn't a bad first job, her stepfather, Shug, had argued, especially for a daft lassie just out of school with her brain rotten on boys and clothes. Credit lending was boring, but she did like the way everything had to be neatly organized and squared away. She loved looking at the neat red pen at the bottom of each ledger page, tallied, undisputed, and true. In a way it was her inheritance from Agnes, this neat fastidiousness, this keen eye on what you had and what you could spend.

It wasn't a bad job, and besides, Mr Cameron had a son who was a big handsome sort, and as Catherine skulked home she let herself think about the boy. Up at the cinema Campbell Cameron had been all slithering hands, like a dirty octopus. Even his tenderest winching had felt entitled and demanding.

Her granny had taken her aside once and told her that she was daft, that she should marry Seamus Kelly. Lizzie explained how she had married her good Catholic boy, and he had stood by her for over forty years, through all sorts of problems. It was easy to ignore her granny's advice. After all, Lizzie had only had two new settees in as long as Catherine could remember, and there had to be more to marriage than chapped hands and scullery knees. Lizzie needn't have worried about the young Cameron anyway. Catherine's stepfather was busy pushing his own nephew, Donald Jnr, on her.

When she had first seen her step-cousin, she had been secretly thrilled at the way he carried himself, how he made himself feel right at home in their small front room. Donald Jnr sat with his legs confidently open, taking more space than was his to take and talking about himself with no modesty. She liked the subtle ways he let her know that he was more important than her. It was the way that Proddy dogs always looked, like they were so loved, so well fed, the centre of their own lives. They were their mother's pride, even in their shame or shortcomings, and Donald Jnr seemed entirely free from conscience or burden. He was golden, though in reality, he was more of a dewy translucent pink.

Catherine liked to watch him eat. She was scandalized by the way he preferred lamb meat dripping to cabbage soup and the way he always expected three whole sausages in his plate of stovies. She had watched him hand his plate back to Lizzie and ask for more. So how could she tell her wee granny she felt lucky to have him? It was common knowledge that he'd winched dozens of girls while she had been sharing a bedroom with her two brothers. Donald Jnr didn't have to pay digs in to his mother. He didn't have to feel grateful or guilty for anything.

Almost as soon as they had met, he had been trying to separate her from her virginity. Catherine had lectured him in the first Communion, and he had guffawed when she earnestly said she was waiting for marriage. He was Shug's nephew right enough. She dug her nails deep into the palm of her hand and chastely turned him down. Secretly, she liked this rare imbalance of power, though part of her had assumed he would dump her for it. Yet somehow Donald Jnr never turned back. Instead, he spoke to his Uncle Shug, and on her seventeenth he proposed to her, his step-cousin, on the top deck of a Trongate bus in a showy scene that was more about him than it ever was about her.

As the rain fell harder, Catherine started into a small trot on the high boots. There had been all kinds of lurid stories splashed in black and red across the front of the evening papers, with photo-booth pictures of young women who had been raped and murdered in the shadows of the city. The papers said they were prostitutes and published biased stories about the drug problems they had to feed. One of the young girls had been strangled and dumped in a shallow burn by the edge of the motorway. The killer had folded her abused body neatly and slipped her inside a black bin bag. She had lain there for months until some fly-tippers had burst the bag, and her purple hand slid out. In all that time no one had reported her missing. It made Wullie suck at his dentures in pity and Lizzie ask where the Chapel was in all this.

Catherine had studied the newspaper photos of the dead girls with horror. Their hollow cheeks and sunken eyes were stark against the photo-booth portraits with their blanching orange background. A murdered young girl, and the best photo her family could provide was the extra copies she had done for her monthly transit pass.

It wasn't yet dark when she reached the concrete forecourt of the tower block. In the gloaming there were several young weans standing in a circle and poking something with a stick. The weans were too young to be out this late, and some had no coats or shoes on in the July rain. Something in the damp pile caught her attention, something familiar but out of place. Catherine crossed the forecourt and hoped it wasn't a dead dog again. Someone had been rat poisoning all the Sighthill strays; they had thought that kinder than watching them writhe in heat.

On the ground lay a wet heap of smouldering curtains, purple paisley that she recognized to be the same as her mother's, burnt and still smoking. Counting in twos she found the sixteenth floor and saw that all the lights were on and the windows were flung open at this late hour. It was not a good sign. Chances were that her brother Leek wouldn't be home. If the night had gone as she expected, he would have seen it coming at dinner and sloped off and hid. He was good at that. Being quiet nobody missed him much.

But she had to find him. She couldn't face their mother alone.

There was a dark alley with the iron railings of Saint Stephen's on the right and the chain-link fence of Springburn Pallet Works on the left. It was known as a dangerous walk; once you had started down the path there was no turning back till you reached the far end. Gangs loved it. About halfway down the alley an old drunk couple was staggering through the windblown rubbish. Catherine could hear the woman whispering dirty promises to the old man. She hurried along and then dipped down and crawled under a gap in the chain-link fence. The fence caught the back of her hair, and for a panicked moment she thought they had a hold of her. Catherine pulled, the hair ripped, and as she freed herself she fell backwards into the mud. Wet and scalped, she watched her hair hanging there like animal fur and thought about the ways she could take it out on Leek.

Inside the pallet factory there were thousands of stacked cubes made up of blue shipping crates. Each cube stood around thirty feet tall and was as wide as the foundation of any tower block. The foreman had arranged them like tenemented streets, ten blocks wide by ten blocks deep, set with just enough space in between to move a little pallet truck up the aisles. She counted the way as Leek had grudgingly taught her. It would have been easy to get lost amongst the pallets in the daytime and was much easier in the dark. Spotlights mounted on the side of the warehouse cast a weak glow down the north-south lines of pallet cubes, but turn a corner and it was instantly as black as night.

By the time she noticed the orange embers dancing in the dark it was too late. She tried to turn, but the wet heels of her suede boots slipped, and she slid further into the darkness. Hard hands grabbed her arms and pulled her towards the swarm of fireflies. She made to scream, but a hand closed over her mouth. She could taste the nicotine and glue that lingered on the fingers. Many hands moved on to her body, roaming and searching. There was a swishing sound of corduroy as a pair of legs moved closer behind her. The legs pressed into her, and she could feel the man through the thinness of his tight trousers. He was bloating with blood and excitement.

One of the burning embers came closer and glowed ominously in front of her face. "Whit the fuck do ye want?" it asked.

"It's goat nice tits," said the embers to her left. All the burning fireflies laughed and danced.

"Gies a feel." She felt a small hand, almost like a woman's, pull at her work blouse.

A silver light cut through the darkness, and Catherine felt cold metal press against the side of her face. The dirty hand over her face moved down to her throat. The silver fishing knife touched the side of her mouth and pushed inside a little. It tasted metallic, like a dirty spoon. "Celtic or Rangers?"

Catherine let out a sad whine. It was an impossible question: if she answered wrong the blade would leave her with a Glasgow smile, a scar from ear to ear, a marking for life. If she answered right she might just get raped.

Many nights Catherine had sat up in bed, brushing her long hair, and watched Leek ask the same nonsense of Shuggie. Leek would straddle his baby brother with his lanky limbs and pin him to the floor. He would make two fists, holding them inches from Shuggie's face, and would ask,

"Cemetery? Or hospital?" It was pointless. All answers gave the same result. You were going to get whatever the bad bastard on top of you wanted to give.

"I'm no gonnae ask you again."

The gutting knife rattled against her teeth as it tested the inside of her cheek. A single tear escaped her left eye. Catherine thought of the gluey fingers and forced a guess. "Celtic?"

The man huffed in disappointment. "Lucky answer." He drew the knife out slowly from between her lips; he was enjoying the terror on her face. Catherine put a finger inside her cheek, tasting the warm salty tang of blood, but the skin was still blessedly together.

A bright light shone directly into her face, and she shrank back against the man behind her. "Fuck me!" said the voice. "It's wee Leek's sister." It took a moment for her eyes to adjust to the torchlight; she put her hand on the tip and angled it down to the ground. The men standing around her were only boys, younger than her and probably younger than Leek. They had been smoking and waiting in the dark. With no peace at home they were waiting for someone to molest or for a chance to knife the night watchman.

Her hand shot out and connected with the owner of the silver knife. She felt no better, so she made another fist and rained it down on his neck, head, and shoulders. The boy covered his head and danced away, laughing.

Catherine pushed through the boys in disgust and ran the last block of pallets. She could hear feet, fast and flat, behind her. She grasped the wall of rough blue wood, and as quick as she could, she hauled herself up the stack of pallets. Behind her she felt a hand wrap around one of her new boots; it gave a quick tug, and her foot came free from its ledge. It took all of her strength to hold on to the splintery wood. She swung her boot back and heard it crack off a thick skull bone, and lifting her knee she found some purchase and scrambled up the rest of the tower.

The torchlight shone up her skirt, trying to illuminate her gusset. They were taunting her, their voices pitched, ready to break, the dangerous sound of little boys coming into the intoxicating power of manhood. She pulled herself the last ten feet to the top. She wanted to lie down for a moment and catch her breath, but she forced herself to stand up and look defiantly over the side. There were five of them, pockmarked and fuzzy-faced. They were grinning up at her, as the eldest was pushing his forefinger into a donut hole he had made with his other hand. Catherine spat over the side on to them. It was a wide shower of white foam, and the boys shrieked like the children they still were and scattered like laughing rats.

Standing on top of the flat pallet stack, she looked over the uniform fields of bright blue wood. The boys had made her lose count, and she hoped she had climbed the right tower. Leek could leap the eight feet or so between the stacks, but she never could. In wet boots she would slip and fall to the ground. She shuddered to think what the neds would do to her body as she lay there with a broken neck.

Catherine counted four from the fence and counted five from the turning. It was right; she hadn't lost count. Searching the top of the stack, she decided on a pallet that was about four by four in from the southeast corner. Checking over her shoulder, as she had been taught, she bent over and lifted a blue pallet free from the rest. A flickering light shone from somewhere within.

Catherine put her head into the opening and hissed her brother's name in the direction of the faint light. "*Leek, Leek!*" There was no answer. She hissed again, and suddenly the flickering light was snuffed and it went dark in the hole. Rain dripped from the end of her nose as she peered closer into the void. Suddenly a white face with small pink ears shot up at her from the darkness. "Boo!"

Catherine fell backwards. If she had been closer to the edge she would have fallen over the side. She hauched a wad of spittle into Leek's white face.

"Aw, fuck's sake!"

"Well, what the fuck did you try to scare me like that for?" Catherine pulled her knees together and searched her red hands for blue splinters. The fear and shame flooded her then, and her face was awash in frustrated tears.

Leek wiped his mouth with his jumper sleeve. He misunderstood her weeping. "Don't start greetin' about it. You coming in or what? You're letting the rain in."

Catherine sulked over to the opening and climbed down into her brother's den. Leek pulled the loose pallet closed over their heads. Inside it was as musty as an open grave and dark as a closed coffin. Catherine no sooner began the low exhale that preceded her moaning than Leek warned her, "Haud yer wheest," as he shuffled about in the pitch-blackness. In the farthest corner there was a clinking of metal, and the space lit up with a faint smoky light.

The camping lamp threw long shadows around the cave-like space. The centre of the hollowed-out pallets was easily twice the size of their bedroom at home, but the ceiling was only about six feet high. Leek had covered the floor and the walls in old bits of discarded carpet and flattened cardboard boxes. Through the narrow hole in the top he had dragged old bits of furniture and broken kitchen chairs. The pallets had been arranged to make supporting columns, and some had been angled and covered with old rugs to make a type of hard-looking set-tee. On the carpeted walls were naked pictures of Page Three girls. Someone had put up a picture of Maggie Thatcher and another joker had drawn a veined cock going into her haranguing mouth.

Catherine watched her brother go about making his home comfort-able for her. She had known some of the older Sighthill boys who had hollowed it out a few years before. After the wildest of them had stabbed a nosy night watchman they had been left pretty much alone. It was a great place to get drunk and sniff bags of glue. Most of the younger boys just liked that it was a space free from their heavy-handed fathers. Some of the boys brought girls here and would make beds out of bor-rowed coats and jumpers. Slowly, as good reputations became ruined, the Sighthill girls stopped coming to the pallet den. The boy's voices kept breaking and their hormones kept raging, so most of them skulked away in randy pursuit. The pallet house became emptier and quieter. Now Leek could often spend the entire weekend there alone.

If Agnes would take a drink on a Thursday, then Leek would take some tins of beans and powdered custard from his granny's kitchen and come here to hide. When he'd come back on a Sunday night, they would all be watching the television. Agnes would be soft and repentant, the demon drink having left her. She would make a cuddling space on the settee next to her, and he would sit close, enjoying the warm, perfumed smell of her bath. Lizzie would look at him with a distant smile and ask him if he'd been in his bed all weekend. It was good to be a quiet soul.

Not that he was small. By the time he turned fifteen he was already over six feet tall. He had always been skinny, and as he grew he became even more thrifty and efficient in build. His hair, like his build, he had inherited from his long-forgotten real father. It was fine and wispy, mouse brown in colour, and hung softly over his ears and eyes. His eyes were grey and clear but always slow to show emotion. He had long perfected the art of staring through people, leaving conversations to follow his daydreams through the back of their heads and out any open window.

Leek was as economical with his emotions as he was spare in build. From his real father he had inherited a gentle personality, quiet and pensive, lonesome and faraway. His only real physical concession to his mother was his nose, large and bony, too severe to be Roman. It broke the line of his soft, shy fringe and sat upon his thin face like a proud monument to his Irish Catholic ancestors. Agnes had gotten it from Wullie, and Wullie had gotten it from his own father, who had brought it from County Donegal. It left no one unscarred and overlooked no man or woman in the Campbell lineage.

The den was a carpeted fort, a boy thing. It smelled like beer, glue, and semen, and Catherine did not personally see the appeal. Walking around the room, she shrank from the mess and the tins of half-eaten food. She wiped the tears from her face and sniffed. "How long have you been here today?"

"Dunno," he said, pulling a discarded coat from a mouldy heap in the corner. "She blootered the dregs of the christening whisky by lunchtime."

He held the dry overcoat out to her. Catherine stepped out of her good green coat and slid into the man's Harris tweed. It smelled of lanolin and sweat, but the crispy dryness of the rough wool felt good. Leek took an old biscuit tin from the shelf above the girlie pictures and handed it to her. They sat together on the home-made sofa. He put his arm gently around her and climbed inside the coat till they had an armhole each.

Catherine lifted fingerfuls of the sweet cake from the tin. She could taste the amber sugar of the syrup her granny was fond of. It made her feel better. "I haven't eaten anything the day. There was no one to cover the phones, and Mr Cameron said he would bring me in a sandwich when he got his own lunch. But he didn't. And, well, I didn't like to say, or else he would know he had hurt my feelings."

"*Feelings are for weaklings.*" He was using the Dalek voice she hated.

Catherine drew her head out of the collar and looked at him coldly. "Well, hiding is for cowards." The long shy eyelashes fell low on his pink cheeks. Ever since he was a boy, he had been easy to hurt. She drew her arm back inside the mothy coat and wrapped it around his back; she could feel his thin ribs through his school jumper. "I'm sorry Leek. It's terrifying coming out here to find you. I'm wet, and I was afeart, and now my new boots are ruined."

"You can't keep anything good around here."

She pulled him to her, two years younger and already a foot taller. She buried her damp crown in the crease of his broad chin. She let herself cry quietly and tried to let the anger she felt for the neds and their fishing knife bleed out of her. "Have you been hiding here all day?"

"Aye." His sigh ran through her. "I told you. She woke up and I could tell over the cartoons that there was a belter coming. She was shaking something terrible, so she asked me to watch the wean while she went out to the shops . . ." He trailed off.

She knew he was staring into the distance. "Did she take a drink in a pub?"

His eyes had glazed over again. "No. I . . . I don't think so. She had the whisky, then I think she got a carry-out and battered some in the lift back up."

"Well, it is *very* dry up at that altitude." Catherine licked the last of the sticky mess from her fingers and put the tin down.

"Aye, she seemed fair parched," he said sadly. There was a long silence between them. Leek took out his top set of porcelain dentures and rubbed at his cheek as if they had been pinching. Agnes, annoyed with the constant trips to the dentist, had convinced him to have his teeth, weak and riddled with aluminum fillings, pulled for his fifteenth birthday.

"Do they *still* hurt?" Catherine asked, grateful that her teeth were still her own.

"Aye." He flicked the slabber from the plate and put it back in his mouth.

"I'm sorry, Leek, and I'm sorry I left you the day." She gently kissed his cheek.

It was a tenderness too far. He put his hand over her face and held her away from him. "Get off me, ya minger. Besides, don't ever feel sorry for me. I'm done feeling bad about this shite." Leek unbuttoned the oversize coat and stepped back out into the cold. He pulled the sleeve of his black school jumper over his knuckles and wiped his sister's kiss from his face.

Watching him, Catherine thought how Leek would have looked twelve had it not been for the large Campbell nose. She watched how his long fingers, as delicate and fine as a clockmaker's, worried it, ran the length of it constantly, fidgeted with it, measured it, and then regretted it. He lowered his hand from his nose. "Stop gawking." He stepped out of the lamplight into the dark side of the den.

Catherine picked up a black sketchbook. Leek had been drawing again. She flicked through the pages holding intricate sketches of bikini-clad beauties sitting on top of a muscular Ferrari or astride winged wyverns. Leek's was as good as any rock-album artwork, a beautifully rendered world of shy fantasy. The muscles and sinew and naked beauties eventually gave way to precise, ruler-drawn plans for architecture and woodwork, technical drawings for futuristic buildings and smaller, more thorough ones for record player units and one for a home-made easel. There wasn't a minute she could remember that he didn't have his pencil in hand.

She was smiling proudly to herself when Leek emerged from the darkness and snatched the sketchbook from her. "I don't see your fucking name on it." He lifted his jumper and tucked the book into the waistband of his denims.

"Leek, I think you are very talented."

He made a raspberry noise and disappeared back into the darkness.

"I mean it. You are going to be an amazing artist, and I'm going to get married, and between us we're both going to get the fuck out of here and away from this dump."

The hissing came from the dark. "Fuck you. I know you are going to leave me. I've seen you making eyes at that Orange prick. I know that you are going to leave me to deal with her on my own."

"Leek. Can you not stay in the light, where I can see you?"

"No. I like it over here."

Catherine dried her hair on the coat sleeve and thought for a moment. She pushed back against the fear the neds had left inside her. "Shame, I'm here to take all my clothes off and wrestle a giant winged snake for you."

He stepped from the darkness, shaking his head. "Dinnae bother. I prefer to draw bigger tits."

Catherine flinched, but she said, "Use that imagination of yours."

"I don't have a pencil fine enough to render their intricate, *miniatur-ey-alley-osity.*"

They glowered at each other with serious expressions. Catherine made the dry boak face first and pretended to throw up all over the old man's coat. Leek copied her, until they were swimming in imagined vomit. Catherine watched her brother's shy smile return, and she thought how it was a shame he didn't do that often enough any more. Leek caught her searching his face. "Take a picture, why don't ye?"

Catherine tried to soften her gaze, afraid she might send him back into the shadows. "So did Mammy look in a fighting mood or more of a maudlin mood when you left her?"

He shrugged. "She was on the phone most of the day looking for Shug. I could just tell it was gonnae end badly."

"How comes?"

"She was drinking like she wanted to get somewhere else."

"Was she loud?"

He shook his head. "More sad than loud today."

Catherine sighed. "Fuck. We'd better get back. I think there's been some trouble."

"No way. I stole enough food to stay here the night." He was halfway back to the dark already.

"You'll catch your death of cold."

"Guid."

"Come on, Leek. You're a bit bloody old for a Wendy house." It was a mean thing to say, and she knew she wouldn't win if she continued in this way. Her brother had been gifted with legendary stubbornness; he just stared through you and floated away, leaving behind his frame to be pecked to pieces. Catherine didn't want to face their mother alone. She did not want to walk back through the darkness without him. "Please. I came to get you. I didnae give your glue-sniffing pals a look up my skirt for nothing." She bit her lip pitifully. "They have a fishing knife, Leek. They grabbed my tits."

Leek looked very angry then. She was always scared and secretly delighted by the sudden force of his temper. It always came quietly and brutally, and the smallest slight could turn horseplay into horsepower. "*Please.*" Her arms went limp by her side in a gross pantomime of helplessness. Being pathetic was not in her true nature.

Leek went back into the dark corner of the cave and returned with his hooded anorak and the broken handle of a garden shovel. He turned it menacingly in his hands. He put out the smoky camping lamp, and together they climbed quietly back up the hole and out on top of the pallets. Leek slid the trapdoor shut, and they stood looking out over the glistening city below. It was beautiful. Catherine lifted her right hand and pointed into the darkness far beyond the orange city lights. "Leek. Do you see that o'er there?" she asked.

It was a line of emptiness on the horizon, black like the edge of nothing. He followed the line of her finger. "Nope."

"There!" she said and pointed harder, as if this might help. "Look past Springburn and Dennistoun. Look past the very last scheme."

"Caff! Just because you make your arm go stiff it doesn't help me see any better. It's pitch-black. There's nothing there."

"Exactly!" She considered this before lowering her finger and turning back towards the high-rise. "That's where I overheard Shug say we were flitting to."

Six

Agnes had lain with fits of coughing and hacking most of the night. Now the morning light that was pushing in through the curtainless window would give her no peace. She could no longer ignore the wet draught that was pushing into the room and down on to her clammy body. Opening her eyes, she searched the room feebly for a solution to this nuisance. Her eyes hadn't expected to find the black fingers of soot. She had bolted upright in a panic before she recognized the burnt bedroom as her own. Like a terrible postcard from the night before, her reflection stared back, fully dressed, with a face full of spoilt make-up. She looked at the pillow behind her and at the wet blue mess she had left there. Her gaze shifted across to Shug's side of the bed. It hadn't been slept in.

Agnes lowered her chin back to her chest and tried to clear her blackout. The correct images wouldn't come. Running her fingers through her black curls she felt the crispy brittleness of too much hairspray. From habit she placed her head in her hands and dug her nails sharply into the hairline, feeling the poisoned blood flush to her scalp. It felt good. The memories of the previous night started to ring like large chapel bells in her skull.

Clang, here is the wean dancing on the bed.

Clang, here is the flame on the curtains.

Clang, here is Shug, twisting his wedding band with a face full of disappointment again.

Agnes lay back in bed. She sobbed, but it was the self-pitying kind that brought no tears. She thought about holding the wean down as the flames raced up the curtain. She pushed the memory away and willed herself not to look at it again, yet the more she looked away the more it blossomed like a terrible flower. The guilt sank like dampness into her bones, and she felt rotten with the shame. She searched for a cigarette to coat her sore throat; it felt as black and sticky as tarmacadam in July. There were no cigarettes left in the room and no matches either. She had been placed under surveillance. This at least cheered her a little.

Out in the hallway the house was quiet. It must have been late enough, because the door to her parents' bedroom was open and she could see their bed was neatly made. She went into the windowless bathroom and closed the door, sitting on the toilet. She thought about taking a bath and sinking to the bottom to wait for the Lord. In the tub were two sodden bath towels, badly blackened by fire. She couldn't bring herself to move them.

Agnes wrapped her lips around the cold metal tap and gulped the fluoride-heavy water, panting and gasping like a thirsty dog. She began to wipe the ruined make-up off her face; the cotton wool came away blackened with soot stains. Opening the medicine cabinet, she searched the plastic shelves for Wullie's medicine, something to take the edge off, but the painkillers were gone. She lifted a bottle of congealed cough syrup and took a mouthful, and then she took another.

When she finally emerged into the dark hallway, she stood for a long time arranging herself. In the dark she tried on different smiles, small apologetic ones where she lowered her eyes and looked up through heavy brows with tight trembling lips. She tried some light casual smiles, like she was just back from the shops. She tried a large, toothy, beaming smile, a gallus head nod that said, *So what? Fuck you*. If Shug was in there, this would be the one she'd wear.

Wullie and Shuggie were sitting at the round dining table eating soft eggs and soldiers. Sixty years apart, they were huddled together in the far corner like old drinking pals. Leek was upended on the settee, his bare legs up and over the back, a sketchbook in hand. When he saw his mother, he got up very quietly and passed her with a polite nod, like a stranger in the street.

All the windows were thrown open, the house already scrubbed with bleach. The air was bitter and sharp. Wullie turned his head back towards his eggs when he saw her. He must have been at early Mass, his good suit was folded neatly over the kitchen chair. He sat in his undervest, his thick arms a tapestry of faded blue ink from his wrist to his shoulder meat, names and places never to be forgotten from the War, a laughing black-haired girl from Donegal, and Agnes's own name and birthdate in proud elegant letters.

"You've missed Mass."

Agnes tried several faces and finally decided on contrite. She heard sniffling in the kitchenette. "Is Shug here?" she asked nervously, a grin breaking over her false face.

Wullie shook his head. It had all been too ugly for him: the fight, the fire, the wean crying. He pushed his glasses up his nose and stared deeper into his eggs. "Please don't grin, Agnes. Please don't smirk at me like that."

Her son, God bless him, had lit up like the Blackpool illuminations when she came into the room. Shuggie's eggy hands were outstretched towards her, a bath towel tied around his head like a turban. "Mammy, Catherine wasn't very nice to me this morning. She said I was a sook." Agnes picked the boy up. He wrapped himself around her sore bones, squeezed the life back into her. "Granda said I can have three empire cakes the day."

"Hugh, come back over here and finish your breakfast or there will be *no* cakes." Wullie waved a thick hand at the boy, and with a sullen *tut* Shuggie slid down from his mother's trunk. She felt the shaking in her bones start again. Her father shovelled a mouthful into Shuggie's pursed lips before he spoke again. His voice was measured, but his eyes would not meet hers. "I know it's my fault, Agnes. I know I'm the reason you are the way you are."

Agnes shifted in irritation. *Not this again.* Her throat was desperate for a smoke.

"Hear me out. I know I spoilt you when I should have given you that belt. I know I'm sentimental, and I know I'm soft. But you have no idea. *No* idea what it was like." Wullie rubbed the meat of his fist across his lips. He looked to the door of the kitchenette like there was someone offstage feeding him lines. "Fourteen of us there was. My auld ma saw none of them get what couldn't be earned by their own hands. Not even our baby Francis, with his twisted leg. Poor wee bastard had to fight and shove like the rest of us. So when your mammy tells me I'm to be blessed with you, I prayed to let it be different. I promised that you'd never know want the way I knew want."

"Daddy, please, you don't have to . . ." *Where were the fucking cigarettes?*

He cracked his rough hands together; the sound was like booming thunder. "Am I always to be a milksop in my own house?" He was not a man who raised his voice. Agnes buttoned her lip; even Lizzie stopped her sniffling in the kitchenette. Wullie Campbell was a man built for loading granary barges down on the Clyde. She had seen him single-handedly clear a pub of a half dozen disrespectful Liverpudlians.

"Every day at a quarter past five you'd come running down that road to meet me as neat as a new pin. I asked your mammy to make sure you were clean. She used to say to me, 'Wullie is all this palaver really necessary?' But sure it was the only thing I ever asked her to do. A man needs to take pride in his family. But people don't care about things like that any more, do they?" Wullie's tattooed knuckles were knitted together in anger. "It gave me that much pleasure just to be proud of you. I could tell they were jealous, hanging out of their windows with tight faces. Grown men and women, jealous of a wee shiny bit of life like you. I used to laugh when they said you'd be ruined."

"You did good, Daddy. I was happy."

"Aye? Then what have you got to be so unhappy about now?" He sucked at his teeth and placed his hand on top of the boy's head, the weight of it looked like it might buckle Shuggie's neck. There were sentimental tears in Wullie's eyes, but he was watching her coldly, like it was the first time he had seen her properly. "So tell me, Agnes. Am I to belt you?"

Agnes's hand went to her throat, she felt like she might laugh. "Daddy! I'm thirty-nine!"

"Am I to beat this selfish devil out of you?" He rose slowly from the table. His arms were loose at his sides, his hands massive silt buckets at the end of iron cranes. "I am tired of you coming first, Agnes. I'm tired of watching you destroy yourself and knowing it's my fault."

Agnes took a step backwards. She wasn't smiling any more. "It's not your fault."

Wullie closed the living room door quietly. He drew his heavy granary belt from his wool trousers, the Meadowside Union logo was debossed into the leather, and the sheer weight of it dragged on the carpet. "Aye, mibbe it's for the best."

Agnes held her hands out and backed slowly to the door. The gallus grin was gone from her face. As her father advanced she kept walking backwards, until she felt the living room cabinet at her back and heard the glass-eyed ornaments tinkle in warning. The boy was at her legs now, his head hidden halfway behind her denims. Wullie twisted the belt around his hands, once, twice, for a better grip. "Put that wean away from you."

She held the boy closer. Wullie folded his hand around her soft upper arm. With his other hand he separated the boy gently but surely from her leg. He led Agnes over to his chair, where he sat down and pulled her over his knee.

She didn't struggle, and no more begging words would come.

"Lord Jesus Christ, I ask You to give me the strength to forgive." The union belt came down with a loud crack on the back of her soft buttocks. Agnes did not cry out. Wullie raised his hand again. "I thank

You that my burden is never more than I can bear." *Crack*. "Show Agnes the many blessings of her life." *Crack*. "Quiet her needs." *Crack*. "Show her some peace."

There was a soft shuffle at her side, and Agnes felt her left hand be taken up. She felt the cooling of bloodless hands on the back of her clammy neck; she felt the gentle stroke of her mother. Lizzie knelt on the floor by her side. Her voice joined Wullie's in prayer. "Lord, it is only through your forgiveness that we can forgive ourselves." *Crack*.

After the fire Shug had gone out on the night shift, and for the second time that week he hadn't come back in the morning. Besides his brother, Rascal Bain, and a few boys at the taxi rank, he didn't have many male friends. Still, Agnes knew, there was a million other places he could happily be.

She sat gingerly on the edge of their bed. The backs of her legs were scalded red from Wullie's belt, and she couldn't concentrate as she folded Shug's clean socks, one inside the other, matching the faded hues together exactly as he liked. Whose arms would he be in now? She felt the fight inside her begin to grow again. Could he be as close as the next tower block, with big Reeny?

She had to get out, she had to show face.

From the linen cupboard she picked up one of the folding deckchairs they would take to the fair-week caravan. She took out and rinsed her dentures under the warm tap. In tight denims and wearing her new black bra as a bikini top, she went out into the landing and waited for the piss-stained elevator. When she made it down the sixteen floors, she was relieved to see there were no burnt curtains lying around.

Except for petrified dog shit and some faint scorch marks, the fore-court was empty. Agnes checked out back of the tower block to see if Shug's taxi was parked there. She had caught him out like that once before. When he was supposed to be working a day shift he had been upstairs fucking some unknown wifey. His sweaty shenanigans had been separated from his family by a few feet of council-grade concrete. Agnes had ridden the Sighthill elevator all that afternoon with a mop bucket full of cold tea dregs and piss. She waited at each landing for the doors to open on him and called off the hunt only when they opened on a group of bonnie young girls who were going outside to play. The children took one look at her and fearfully refused to get in the lift with the mad-looking woman from the sixteenth floor.

At first she had thought how stupid Shug was to get caught out so easily. Only later, when she confronted him, did she learn that she was the stupid one. He hadn't been caught out. He wanted to make sure she knew all about it. Some things were not to be missed.

The sun was white in the sky. The concrete was already vibrating with the morning heat. On the waste ground, Lizzie was sunbathing on an old blanket with her back against the foundation. Her floral dress was opened to the breastbone and pulled apart to make the most of that rarest of occurrences, sunshine. Her hair sat in tight baby-blue curlers and was carefully wrapped in a gingham tea towel. She was reading the day's paper and gossiping with a clutch of old dears on the patchy grass. The other women sat in a cluster of kitchen chairs and were peeling the skin off big brown potatoes and dropping them into an old plastic bag.

Agnes set her deckchair a respectful distance from her mother and her gang. Lizzie barely looked up from her paper, and Agnes knew she was being punished. She tried to settle herself casually into the warmth of the sun, but her eyes kept flitting to Lizzie, wanting only a sliver of friendship to ease the loneliness in her chest.

There was new graffiti on the wall above Lizzie. It sprang like a dirty thought bubble from her curls: *Don't be Shy . . . Shows Yer Pie.* To Lizzie, the graffiti could have been a helpful plea to a bashful baker. Agnes knew better and couldn't help but laugh.

Lizzie scowled at her. "What do you find so funny?"

It was the first time she had spoken since the front-room chapel that morning, and Agnes took a moment to consider whether she felt like encouraging it or ruining it. "Nothing. Where's my wee man?"

Lizzie answered as spartanly as she could. "At the bakers, getting his cake." She went back to her paper.

Agnes knew the routine. Saturday and Sunday afternoons, Wullie walked with his grandson the half mile or so to the shops. It was a scant row of half-shuttered storefronts set into a shadowed recess that never seemed to catch the daylight. They had dragged families out of the old Glasgow tenements for this scheme, and it was meant to be different, futuristic, a grand improvement. But in reality the whole scheme was too brutal, too spartan, too poorly built to be any better.

Shuggie would stand well behaved inside the Paki shop while his granda bought a noose of sweetheart stouts and a half-bottle of whisky, enough to carry them through Saturday night and discreetly through the Sabbath. The growing boy gave Wullie and Imran something to talk about as the bags were loaded with the alcohol. It was a routine in which neither man was allowed to acknowledge the drink moving between them, as though it would have broken the charade. Across the shadows, inside the bakery, Wullie would make small talk with the pretty girls while Shuggie greedily eyed the cakes. Shuggie always chose the same bright pink sponge pyramid, covered in red and white desiccated coconut and trimmed with a sugary sweetie on top. He would walk home very slowly in Wullie's shadow, enjoying his spoils.

Agnes looked in the direction of the shops but couldn't see them. She rose and stood on the edge of the waste ground. In her black bra she threw her head back and stretched her arms wide to enjoy the sun's tingle on her pale skin. She caught a sideways glance from Lizzie. There was the start of a puce bruise on her lower back. It was this that held her mother's attention. Agnes's ringed fingers traced the belt welt, and she winced dramatically.

Lizzie stiffened proudly and hissed, "For the love of God. Cover yourself."

The women peeling potatoes exchanged a sympathetic glance that said they knew how bruises could be more plentiful than hugs in a marriage, and not just for the women. Agnes was not to be told. Irritated now, she collapsed into the deckchair again and bounced it gracelessly like it was a child's space hopper, bouncing, bouncing, till she was sat closer to her mother.

Agnes sprawled out luxuriously, her skin already poaching to a light rose colour. She reached out her foot and played with the hem of Lizzie's yellow floral dress like a child. Lizzie lowered her newspaper and pushed Agnes's foot away. "Stop fussing with me," she said. "You've got a cheek to show your face around me this morning." Lizzie undid the tea towel wrapped around her curlers. She opened a plastic bag at her side and started unravelling her hair.

Agnes took her mother's pick comb and slouched in the sticky deck-chair again. "My head is throbbing."

Lizzie drew out a curler and held the kirby grip between her lips. "Oh, poor you. I hope you don't expect any sympathy."

"*You should have stopped him.*"

Lizzie was watching Agnes out of the side of her eyes now. "M'lady, let me tell you, in forty years of marriage I have never once seen your father raise his hand in anger." She turned to the women with the potatoes. "You know, Maigret, he's that soft I thought he'd come back dead a week into that bloody War."

"Aye, he's a fine man, right enough." The potato women nodded in unison.

Lizzie turned back to her daughter. "I don't want you dragging his good name down with your own."

Agnes ran the pick through a painted tangle. "Am I that low?"

"Low?" Lizzie scoffed. "Do you know I've just been sat here on my lonesome getting a wee bit of colour, and I've no been able to get any peace from anybody. A woman cannae even run her messages, but she's got to cross this grass and ask me, *how I'm holding up?*"

"People should mind their own."

"I'm just after having Janice McCluskie drag her Mongoloid son across those weeds to me. She goes, '*I've heard your Agnes has no been keeping that well. How's her wee problem?*'" Lizzie's knuckles were white with indignation as she twisted a kirby grip. "I'm sat here with my dress unbuttoned down to my God's glory and that pair of mouth-breathers gawping down at me."

"Ignore them, Mammy."

"Bastards! No keeping well? *No fucking keeping well!*" Her hands clawed at the imagined offenders in front of her. Lizzie exhaled loudly, and her anger shifted to a look of tired defeat. "I don't deserve their hand-wringing, Agnes. I've worked hard my whole life without a day's rest, and for what?"

Agnes knew the next line well enough. Agnes still shook her head.

"So you could have everything you ever wanted."

Lizzie seemed so far away then. Agnes had the urge to wrap her mother in her arms, beg for her forgiveness, even though she felt not a shred of remorse. "Can't we be pals again?"

"No. It's not as simple as that any more." The corners of Lizzie's mouth turned down in a mocking way. "*Let's just kiss and make up?* No, I think not." She uncurled another clump of hair. "How many women will it take, Agnes?"

Agnes bristled. "I need a cigarette."

"You need a lot of things." Then she added, "You should have stayed married to that Catholic."

Agnes rooted around in her mother's curler bag. She took out the Embassy packet and put two cigarettes in her mouth. She took a long draw and held the smoke inside for a long while. "Jesus can't pay my catalogue."

Lizzie gave a fake laugh. "No. But hell will mend you."

Agnes got up then and sat on the blanket by her mother's side. The lit cigarette was a measly peace offering, but Lizzie took it and said, "Help me take out these curls. I must look half-mental." Agnes took her mother's head in her hands and ran her fingers through the thinning hair. Lizzie softened slightly. "You know, your faither always used to come in on a Friday night, half past six. Every other working fella on the street would go missing. There wouldn't be a man's voice till Sunday afternoon, not in all of Germiston. I remember that you could hang out that window and watch them all stoat home on a Sunday teatime. All of them addled wi' the drink."

The potato peelers were nodding in unison again. Lizzie said, "I'm no judging the men. That was just what they did in those days. If you wanted your housekeeping money you had to go dig your man out of the pub on a Friday teatime. But your faither would come singing

Friday night, his wage packed in his hand and a fresh parcel under his arm. Silly fool would have been down that market on his way back from Meadowside and picked up a wee dress or a new coat for you. I never knew a man know the size of his weans, let alone go shopping for them. I used to tell him to stop it, he was spoiling you. But he would say, '*What's the harm?*'"

"Mammy, I can't talk about this again."

"Honestly, I was that happy for you when you married that Brendan McGowan. He seemed like he could give you what your faither had given me. But look at you, you had to want better."

"Why shouldn't I?"

"*Better?*" Lizzie used her clenched teeth to itch the tip of her tongue. "Look where *better* has gotten you. Selfish article."

Agnes brushed out the last of her mother's curls. She had to restrain herself not to give them a sly tug. "Well, seeing as you think I'm selfish then, I need to ask you for a favour."

Lizzie sniffed. "It's a bit early in our friendship to be calling in favours."

She rubbed the lobe of Lizzie's ear gently, manipulatively. "I need you to tell him for me. Tell him that we're moving. Will you do that?"

"It'll kill your faither."

"It won't." She shook her head. "But if I stay here I know I am going to lose him."

Lizzie turned and studied her daughter closely. She stared coldly at the flicker of hope in Agnes's eyes. "You will believe anything, won't you." It wasn't a question.

"We just need a fresh start. Shug says it might make everything better. It's only a wee place, but it's got its own garden and its own front door and everything."

Lizzie waved her cigarette airily. "Oh, la-di-dah! Your very own front door. Tell me: How many locks do you suppose this front door is going to need to keep that wandering bastard at home?"

Agnes scratched the skin around her wedding band. "I've never had my own front door."

The women were silent a long while after that. Lizzie spoke first. "So, where is it then? This front door of your own."

"I'm not sure. It's way out on the Eastern Road. It used to be rented by an Italian chippy or somebody Shug knows. He said it was very green. He said it was quiet. Good for my nerves."

"Will you have your own washing line?"

"I would think so." Agnes rolled on to her knees. She knew how to beg for what she wanted. "Listen, we're pals again, right? I need you to tell my daddy for me."

"Your timing is beautiful. After this morning's nonsense?" Lizzie pulled her chin into her chest and made a long, low clown mouth. "If you leave he'll blame himself to his dying day."

"*He won't.*"

Lizzie began rebuttoning her summer dress. The buttons were lining up wrong, and it was testing her patience. "Mark my words. Shug Bain is only interested in Shug Bain. He's going to take you out there to the middle of nowhere and finish you for good."

"*He won't.*"

Wullie and Shuggie came lumbering across the forecourt then. Lizzie saw them first. "Look at the state of that. A walking advert for soap powder."

By the time Agnes looked up, the last of the Eiffel Tower was being licked from between the boy's chubby fingers. She couldn't help but smile at her father, the giant with his shirt tails untucked, like a schoolboy shirking his uniform. They walked slowly, swinging between them the Daphne dolly that Shuggie treasured so much.

"If you cannae make Shug do right by you, at least make him do right by the boy." Lizzie narrowed her eyes at her grandson, at his blond dolly. "You'll be needing that nipped in the bud. It's no right."

Seven

Agnes followed Shug's red leather cases as they migrated around the flat. They had shown up out of nowhere, earlier in the week, with no price tags and the faint look of having been gently used. Shug had neatly folded all of his clothes, setting socks within shoes and rolling underwear into tidy jam rolls, before packing everything thoughtfully inside. Often, during the week, he would open one of the red cases and study the contents closely, as though memorizing the inventory, then close and lock it securely again. Agnes could see the cases were half-empty, that there was still valuable space inside. Several times she left small piles of the children's clothes near them and then watched with bubbling jealousy as the cases up and moved to the other side of the room, still with nothing belonging to her or the children placed inside.

On the day of the flit he had set the red cases by the bedroom door. Agnes worried the suitcase lock with her nail. She wondered why she hadn't seen the new house herself. Shug had come home with the idea after one of his night shifts spent talking to a Masonic pal who owned a chippy in the city centre. A council flat in a two-up two-down that he said had its own front door. Shug signed for it there and then with all the casualness of buying a raffle ticket.

Agnes wrapped the last of her glass ornaments in newsprint and lined up her old green brocade cases next to Shug's. She intermixed them, rearranged them, but no matter what she did there was a sense that they didn't belong together any more. In the luggage tag that hung from her case was a handwriting she barely recognized now. It was the happy, confident loops of a much younger her, running away from her first husband for a promise of a life that was worth living. Her fingers traced the forgotten name: *Agnes McGowan, Bellfield Street, Glasgow.*

When Leek was still in nappies, Agnes had run away.

On the night she finally left she had packed the green cases full of new clothes, showy, impractical things she had bought on the last of Brendan McGowan's tick and had kept hidden for the past long year. Before she ran away she had scrubbed their tenement flat one last time. She knew the news would bring in the neighbours. With beady eyes they would pour in to offer condolences to her man, hoping to gnash their gums at her uppity ways. She wouldn't dare give them the pleasure of thinking her slatternly too.

On the plush hall carpet she had tamped a loose corner with her toe, pushing it back in place, and she was sad to hear the crunch of carpet tacks grip the wood once again. Earlier in the day she had tried to lift it. She had broken two good wedding spoons and bloodied her fingers before sitting back in frustrated tears. As the mascara ran down her face she had wondered if maybe she should stay on, just a little longer, just till she had gotten good use out of that new Axminster. She hadn't tried to take *everything*, but that carpet was new, and she had enjoyed how the old wife across the close blanched every time she saw it. It was the kind of hall carpet that you left your front door open for, the beautiful thick kind that you wanted all the neighbours to see. She had nagged and nagged until she got it installed, wall-to-wall, Templeton's Double Axminster, but the tingly feeling hadn't lasted this time, not even half as long as she had expected it to.

Living with the Catholic, in the ground-floor flat, all she could see was a wall of grey soot-covered tenements across the street. The night she ran away, Agnes had watched the lights go out, one by one, good, hard-working folk getting an early night for an early start. Outside in the rain was the purring hum of the hackney engine. She could not help but feel some excitement, and inside her, underneath the doubt, was a rising thrill.

Over the back of the sofa lay two miniature effigies; studies in neat melton and soft velvet and uncomfortable shoes of patent leather with gaudy silver buckles. She woke her sleeping toddlers. Catherine looked like a drunken old man, her sleepy eyelids opening and closing in big distressed gulps. As Agnes kissed them awake, there was a low scratch on the tenement door. She crept out to the hallway. The door opened with a low whine, and a man's round, tanned face twitched anxiously in the bright tenement light. Shug moved impatiently from one foot to the other, ready it seemed to run at any moment.

"You're late!" Agnes hissed.

The smell of sour stout on her breath made him swallow his half-smile. "I don't fucking believe it."

"What do you expect?" she hissed. "My nerves are shot waiting for you." Agnes pulled the door open and passed the heavy cases to Shug. They bulged at the zippers and tinkled happily, as if they were full of Christmas ornaments.

"Is that it?"

Agnes stared at the deep, swirling carpet and sighed. "Aye. That's it."

With the cases in hand the man shuffled into the street. Agnes had turned then and looked back into the flat. She went to the mirror in the hall and ran her fingers through her hair; the black curls bounced and folded back on themselves tightly. She ran a line of fresh red lipstick across her mouth. *Not bad for twenty-six*, she thought. Twenty-six years of sleep.

In the children's bedroom she finished making the beds and put the dirty pyjamas into the pocket of her mink coat. Without negotiation she gave them each a single toy to bring and led them out into the hallway. Stopping in front of the big bedroom door, she turned to them. She looked at the lovely carpet and in a low voice urged, "Right, no matter what, no crying, all right?" The shiny heads nodded. "When we go in there, do you think you can give me a big, *big* happy smile?"

She found the bedroom switch through habit. It flicked on with a click, and the dark burst with bright, unflattering light. The room was small and tight, dominated by a rococo-style bed that was much too large. The boy happily called out, "*Daddy!*" and the messy hump in the royal bed stirred. Brendan McGowan sat up in shock, blinking at the Victorian carollers stood at the foot of his bed. His mouth went slack.

Agnes pulled the collar up on her mink coat in a grand gesture. It was a coat he had bought for her on tick, an unneccesary extravagance that he had hoped would make her happy and hold her at peace from want, if just for a while. "Right. Thanks for everything, then." It was coming out wrong. "I'm away," she said, in a clumsy understatement, like a maid who had finished her chores and was leaving for the day.

The sleeping man could only blink as his waving family filed out of the room. He heard the front door close gently and the heavy hum of a diesel engine. Then they were gone.

As they roared away that night, the black hackney taxi sounded solid and heavy as a tank. Agnes sat on the long leather banquette flanked by her warm babies. The four drove in silence through the wet and shiny Glasgow streets. Shug's eyes kept glancing in the mirror, flitting over the faces of the sleeping children and tightening slightly. "Where are we going, then?" he asked after a while.

There was a long pause. "Why were you late?" asked Agnes from behind the collar of her coat.

Shug didn't answer.

"Did you have second thoughts?"

He stopped looking in the mirror. "Of course I did."

Agnes brought her leather-gloved hands up to her face. "*Jesus Christ.*"

"Well, didn't you?"

"Did it look as if I did?" she replied, her voice higher than she would have liked.

The streets of the East End were empty. The last pubs were closed, and decent families were tucked in together from the cold. The hackney pulled along the Gallowgate and drove on through the market. Agnes had never seen it empty before; it was usually full of people buying their messages or new curtains, nice bits of meat or fish for a Friday. Now it was a graveyard of empty tables and fruit boxes. "Where are we going to go?"

"I left mine at home, you know." He was glowering at her in the mirror. "We agreed. We said a fresh start."

Agnes felt the hot heads of her children burrowing into her side. "Yes, well, it's not that easy."

"Aye, but you said."

"Yes, well." Agnes fixed her eyes out the window. She could feel him still staring in the mirror. She wished he would watch the road. "I couldn't do it."

The man looked at the children in their Sunday finest, old-fashioned clothes worn for the first time, expensive clothes bought for a midnight escape. He thought about all their clothes neatly folded in the cases. "Aye, but you didnae even try, did ye?"

She fixed her eyes on the back of his head. "We can't all be as heart-less as you, Shug."

He had tapped the brakes as his body spasmed in anger. All four of them lurched forward, and the children started to gripe. "An' you fuckin' ask me why I wis late?" Bits of spit landed, gleaming, on the rear-view mirror. "Why I wis fuckin' late wis because I had to say goodbye to *fo-wer greetin' fuckin' weans*." He drew the back of his hand across his wet lips. "Never mind a wife that threatened to gas the lot of them. Telt me if I left her that she would put the oven on and not light the ignition."

The taxi screamed off again. They drove in silence, watching empty night buses grumble by and dark windows on cold houses. When he spoke again he was quieter. "Have you ever tried to walk to the front door with your bastarding family stuck into you like fish hooks, eh? Do you know how long it takes to peel four screaming weans off your leg? To kick them back down the hall and shut the door on their wee fingers?" His eyes were cold in the mirror. "No, you don't know what it's like. You just tell muggins here to come get ye. You sally out with suitcases like we were off to Millport for the day."

She was sobering up. She stared silently out the window, trying not to think of the trail of fatherless children and the childrenless father they were leaving in their wake. In her mind it looked like a trail of viscous, salty tears being dragged along behind the black hack. The excitement had left her by then.

When they had passed under the iron railway bridge at Trongate for the third time, the sun was starting to rise and the fresh fish vans were being unloaded at the market. Agnes stared at the women crowded at the bus stop, the early-shift charwomen getting ready to clean the big city-centre offices. "We could go to my mammy's new flat," she had mumbled finally. "Just till we find a place of our own."

All these years later, Agnes didn't want to think about that night because it made her feel like a fool. Now she had packed the Catholic's suitcases again. These brocade cases that were now carrying her away were the same ones that had brought her here to her mother's. She looked down on the green cases and ripped the old McGowan label in two.

After Agnes had left the Catholic, Brendan McGowan had tried to do the right thing by her. Even after she had stolen away in the night, he had hounded her to her mother's and made promises of what he would change to have her back. Agnes had stood there, in the shadow of the tower block, with her arms folded, as her husband offered to rearrange himself so completely into whatever she wanted that he would not have been recognized by his own mother. When it was clear she wouldn't take him back, he had asked the parish father to talk with Wullie and Lizzie and guilt her into returning. Agnes would not be told. She would not go back to a life she knew the edges of.

For the next three years Brendan McGowan had sent his money every Thursday and taken the children every second Saturday. The last thing Catherine remembered about her real father was sitting in Castellani's café as Brendan wiped vanilla ice cream from Leek's face. Agnes had dressed them both deliberately in the best clothes they owned, and an older lady, with pearls about her neck and ears, had complimented Brendan on their neatness and good manners. The woman leaned down to Catherine's height and asked the pretty girl what her name was. Clear as a Cathedral bell, the little girl had replied, "Catherine Bain."

Brendan McGowan had excused himself from the table then. He had wound between the clusters of happy families towards the bathroom, and then he had turned and gone out into the street. Catherine didn't know how long they had been sitting there alone, but Leek had eaten his ice cream and then hers and was dipping his finger into the melted dregs at the bottom of the shell-shaped glass.

The good Catholic had done all he could to hold his restless wife. She had run from him, and he had lowered his pride and asked for her back. She had divorced him, and he had lowered his pride again and had taken any time he could with his children as sacred. Then she had given them the Protestant's name, and like lambs who had wandered from their field, they were sprayed with the indelible keel marks of another. Agnes had found his limit. Now, thirteen years on, Leek and Catherine could not have picked him out if they met him in a crowd.

Agnes had to restrain herself from picking at the brocade handle. She had packed her questions and doubts into the Catholic's cases again and cheerlessly carried them to the taxi. To look at it now, the black hackney felt like a hearse. Wullie wouldn't speak to her as he helped carry the children's clothes down in the rusted lift. Lizzie stood over the big soup pot in the kitchen and wrung her chapped hands on her apron. As Agnes watched her mammy stir, she could see the gas wasn't on.

Leek and Catherine had sat up in their beds at night talking about the ominous pull of this new life. Agnes could hear the low mumble of their worries through the wall. Lizzie had come to her earlier in the week and said the children had asked to stay on with her. She pleaded with Agnes to let Leek finish school and let Catherine be close to the factoring office. The day of the flit, Agnes had noticed how Leek had been gone the whole morning, slunk off with his pencils and secret books to some hidey-hole or other. Catherine had quieted her trembling lip and dutifully helped her mother pack. All morning Lizzie hugged Shuggie close and whispered prayers for safe return into his pale neck. Agnes watched Leek, when he thought no one was looking, plead to his granny again; she heard him say that he would be good, that he would behave. Agnes was glad when Lizzie rebuffed him gently. "No, Alexander, your home is with your mammy."

As the rain started to come down, the last things to be loaded were Shug's two red leather suitcases. Only when they were stowed in place did Agnes admit to herself that it was time to go. Lizzie and Wullie stood in the rain looking as grey and stiff as the tower block behind them. Their goodbyes had been casual and distant. Lizzie wouldn't have them make a scene in public. A crack in the facade might open a rift, and Agnes had no idea what would flood forth from that. So instead they kept busy, fussing about kettles and clean towels.

Agnes sat on the back bench of the taxi with Shuggie packed between her knees. Leek and Catherine sat tight on either side, wedged amongst the boxes, their thighs pressed close to hers. She had ironed all their outfits, taking time to starch Catherine's work shirt, picking out Shuggie's blazer from the catalogue. She had bleached her dentures, and her hair was freshly dyed, a shade darker than black, closer to the saddest navy.

That morning she had tilted her head forward and asked Catherine what she thought of her new mascara. The mascara looked too heavy for her eyelids, like she was on the edge of sudden sleep. Now, as the taxi pulled out into the main road, Agnes made a show of looking back and waving mournfully through the rear window with a long, heavy blink. She thought it was a cinematic touch, like she was the star of her own matinee.

The hackney chugged up the Springburn Road and was past the empty Saint Rollox railworks before she turned back around in her seat. She ran through the hollow reasoning why she was going along with Shug's plan, but as she tried to fortify herself with this rosary, it seemed like the stupid fancies a love-daft lassie half her age might have. Agnes rubbed the pads of her fingertips as she counted off her foolishness: The chance to decorate and keep her very own home. A garden for the weans. Peace and quiet for the sake of their marriage. She dug deeper.

There was a chance that things would be different, she hoped, once she got him farther away from his women.

The windows grew foggy, and Shuggie drew a sad face in the condensation. With a flick of his thumb, Leek altered it to look like a swollen cock and then slumped down in his seat. Agnes drew her ringed hand over the drawing and saw through the clear glass that they were passing the big blue gas containers behind Provanmill, the guards at the northeastern gate of Glasgow.

They drove for a very long time in silence. Eventually the taxi chugged to a stop at some lights, and Shug opened the glass partition to tell them they were nearly there. He closed the glass again, and Agnes wondered whether it was from habit or something truer. She remembered when he had been courting her, how he would keep the glass open and try to charm her with his easy patter. He would lean back and rap his Masonic ring on the divider, a faint line on his left hand where his wedding ring should be. The air would be thick with his tangy pine aftershave and hair pomade. On weekday afternoons the taxi would smell of the sweaty stink of them, the glass misty from their lovemaking. She thought of the happy hours parked under the Anderston overpass, happy hours before they really truly knew one another.

Agnes looked at the grassy front gardens of the low bungalows and tried to feel excited again, but it was like trying to make a fire with wet wood. There had been a line where the houses had imperceptibly passed from council to bought. Shug slid the separating window open with a swish. "Look at they gardens, huh!" The houses were beautiful, with roses and carnations and smiling ornaments behind double-glazed windows. They pulled farther along, and the houses rose above them in a raised cul-de-sac, a manicured hump elevated above the noise of the road. Each private house had a garden, which had a drive, which had a car and sometimes even two. Agnes looked at Shug's eyes in the mirror; he had been watching her. The look felt as close to love as she could remember. "If you like this, then just wait. Joe's said it's like a happy little village. A real family sort of place where everybody knows everybody else. Nicest place you could hope to live."

Leek and Catherine shared a snide sideways glance. Agnes wrapped a hand around one of each of their knees and squeezed a firm warning. Shug shouted over the sound of the diesel engine, straining over his shoulder to be heard. "It's next to a big colliery and all the men work up at yon coal mine. The wages are good enough that the women don't even need to go out of the house for work. Joe said all their children went to the same school. Good for our Shuggie, get him out of the sky, have some boys his own age to play with." His eyes were flashing happily in the mirror, he looked pleased with all his planning. Agnes watched him stroke at his moustache. "It turns out there's no pubs out here. It's bone dry, except for the Miners Club."

"What, not a single one?" Agnes sat forward.

"None. You need to be a miner or miner's wife to get into that club."

Agnes could feel the sweat rise on her back. "What are you meant to do for fun?"

But Shug wasn't listening. "This is it!" he shouted, pointing in excitement to a turning on the road. The taxi tilted as Agnes and the children leaned over to see the turning that would take them to their new life. On the corner sat an empty petrol station. It had a wide forecourt but only one pump for petrol and one for diesel. Shug slowed the taxi and turned into the street beside it.

Agnes rooted around in her leather bag. There was a jangle of bingo pens and mint tins as she took out a lipstick and pulled a fresh line of blood red around her mouth. With her hand already to her mouth, she surreptitiously slipped a blue pill between her teeth, and with a single crunch she broke it in two and swallowed it dry. Only Catherine noticed. Catherine watched her pout her lips and wipe carefully at the side of her lip line. Then Agnes reached over and adjusted the buckle on her high black heels, and with her long painted nails, she smoothed her wool skirt and picked at the oose migrating downwards from the front of her pink angora jumper.

Catherine narrowed her eyes. "How come *you* aren't dressed for flitting?"

"Well, there is *flitting* and then there is *moving house*." Agnes spat on her comb and dragged it through Shuggie's hair. He squirmed, but she held his shoulders and kept combing until the hair sat in neat rows and she could see the clean pink lines of his scalp.

"*Pfft*. How do I look?" asked Leek, rumpling his hair over his face. His big toe was bursting the seam of his white trainers, a dirty sock starting to poke out.

Agnes sighed. "If anyone asks, you are with the movers."

They slid the windows all the way down, and the taxi filled with a rushing breeze that carried the scent of fresh-cut grass and wild bluebells. Underneath the bright green tones was the dark brown of untended fields, mounds of cow dirt, and the dark places at the bottom of wet trees. The beaded sleeves on Agnes's pink angora jumper danced in the wind, and she twinkled like a rabbit dipped in rhinestones. Shuggie reached up and ran his fingers through the glass beads. His mother's mouth was set in a wide white smile, her teeth not touching, like someone was taking her photo. She would have looked happy if her eyes hadn't kept anxiously flitting back to Shug's eyes in the rear-view mirror. Shuggie sat playing with her sleeves and watched as her back molars came together and slowly started to grind back and forth.

The road narrowed again, and the last of the manicured gardens dropped away for good. There was a spit of dead yew trees and then flat, open marshland sprang up on both sides. Small brown hillocks and clumps of brush and gorse broke the endless emptiness. Dirty copper burns snaked through the open fields, and the wild brown grass grew right up on either side of the enclosing fences, trying to reclaim the rutted track, the Pit Road. The road itself was covered with a settled layer of charcoal dust, and the taxi pulled lines through it as though it were the photo negative of fresh snow.

The taxi shuddered around a lazy bend. In the distance lay a sea of huge black mounds, hills that looked as if they had been burnt free of all life. They filled the line of the horizon, and beyond them was nothing, like it was the very edge of the earth. The burnt hills glinted when they were struck with sunlight, and the wind blew black wispy puffs from the tops like they were giant piles of unhoovered stour. Soon the greenish, brownish air filled with a dark tangy smell, metallic and sharp, like licking the end of a spent battery. They curved around another corner, and the broken fence ended at a large car park. At the back of the car park sat a high brick wall with an old iron gate set into it, held tight with a heavy padlock and chain. The guard's booth at the side was tilting at a funny angle, and a thick layer of weedy grass grew on its roof. The mine was shut. Someone had painted *Fuck the Tories* on the plywood barrier. It looked like it was closed for good.

Opposite the gates was a low concrete building. Dozens of men were spilling out of its windowless structure and stood in dark clumps on the Pit Road. At first it looked like they were leaving chapel, but as the diesel engine roared nearer, they turned as if they were one. The miners stopped their talking and squinted to get a good look. They all wore the same black donkey jackets and were holding large amber pints and sucking on stubby doubts. The miners had scrubbed faces and pink hands that looked free of work. It seemed wrong, these men being the only clean thing for miles. Reluctantly, the miners parted and let the taxi go by. Leek watched them as they were watching him. His stomach sank. The men all had his mother's eyes.

The housing scheme spread out suddenly before them. Ahead, the thin dusty road ended abruptly into the side of a low brown hill. Each of the three or four little streets that made up the scheme branched horizontally off this main road. Low-roofed houses, square and squat, huddled in neat rows. Each house had exactly the same amount of patchy garden, and each garden was dissected by the identical criss-crossing of white washing lines and grey washing poles. The scheme was surrounded by the peaty marshland, and to the east the land had been turned inside out, blackened and slagged in the search for coal.

"Is that it?" she asked.

Shug couldn't answer. From the roundness in his shoulders she could see his own heart had sunk. Agnes's back teeth were powder. As they drove towards the little hill, they passed a plain-looking Catholic chapel and a huddled group of women still with their housecoats on. Shug searched the street signs and turned the taxi a sharp right. The street was a uniform line of modest four-in-a-block houses. Four families lived in one squat block. They were the plainest, unhappiest-looking homes Agnes had ever seen. The windows were big but thin-looking, letting the heat out and letting the chill in. Up and down the street, black puffs of coal smoke came out of chimneys, the houses were incurably cold even on a mild summer's day.

Shug stopped the taxi a few houses down. He leaned over the steering wheel to get a clear look at the building. There were hardly any cars parked on the street, and the ones that were looked like they were not in working condition.

While Shug was distracted, Agnes rummaged around in her black leather bag. *"You three keep your mouths shut,"* she hissed. She lowered her head into the cavernous bag and tilted it slightly to her face. The children watched the muscles in her throat pulse as she took several long slugs from the can of warm lager she had hidden there. Agnes drew her head from the bag; the lager had washed the lipstick off her top lip, and she blinked once, very slowly, under the layers of wasted mascara.

"What a shitehole," she slurred. "And to think I dressed up nice for *this?"*

1982
Pithead

Eight

By the time the back doors on the Albion van were open, there were people standing in the middle of the road openly staring. They held wet tea towels and bits of half-finished ironing, things they hadn't bothered to put down in order to come and look. Families came out from the low houses and settled down on their front steps as if there was something good on telly. A tribe of sooty weans, led by a trouseless boy, crossed the dusty street and stood in a semicircle around Agnes. She politely said hello to the children, who stared back at her, rings of a red saucy dinner still around their mouths.

The tight formation of the miners' houses meant the front doors faced one another, each building separated by a low fence and a thin strip of grass. The front doors opposite Agnes's were all thrown open, and women stood watching, a half dozen children milling about each one, all with the same face. It was like the photo of her Granny Campbell and her Irish dozen that Wullie had once shown her. Agnes, standing on her stoop, smiled across the low fence and waved, her beaded rabbit sleeves glinting in the light.

"Hello." She politely addressed the general congregation.

"Ye movin' in?" said a woman from the door beyond her own. The woman's blond hair curled back on dark brown roots. It made her look like she had on a child's wig.

"Yes."

"*All* of yeese?" asked the woman.

"Yes. My family and I," corrected Agnes. She introduced herself and held out her hand.

The woman scratched at her root line. Agnes wondered whether the woman spoke only in questions, when she finally answered. "Ah'm Bridie Donnelly. Ah've lived upstairs for twenty-nine years. Ah've had fifteen downstairs neighbours in aw that time."

Agnes felt all the Donnelly eyes on her. A skinny girl with dark round eyes brought a tray of mismatched tea mugs through the door. Everyone took one. They didn't draw their eyes from Agnes as they supped.

Bridie nodded over the fence. "That there is Noreen Donnelly, ma cousin. But no ma blood, ye understand." A grey-coloured woman rolled her tongue in her head and nodded sharply. Bridie Donnelly went on: "That lassie is Jinty McClinchy. Ma cousin. She *is* ma blood." A child-size woman next door to Noreen took a long drag on a short doubt. Her eyes narrowed from the smoke, and right enough she looked like Bridie in a headscarf. They all looked like Bridie, even the boys, only they looked less masculine.

From out of the side of her eye, Agnes could feel another woman crossing the dusty street. The woman stopped and talked to the semi-circle of raggedy children; she nodded like they had given her grave news and marched on through the front gate to the new house. Agnes had no escape. Behind her Leek came sullenly out of the house for his next load.

"Is that your man?" said the newly arrived woman without intro-duction. The meat of her face was a taut as a leathered skull. Her eyes were deep pockets in her head, and her hair was a rich wild brown but thinning, like the coat of an uncombed cat. She stood in bagged-out stretch pants, the stirrups stuffed into men's house slippers.

Agnes stumbled over the absurdity of the question. There were twenty-odd years between her and Leek. "No. That's my middle wean. Sixteen in the spring."

"Oh! In the *spring* is it." The woman considered this for a minute and then jabbed a sharp finger out at the vegetable van. "Is that there your man?"

Agnes looked at a mover struggling with the old television she had tried to wrap for discretion in a bed sheet. "No, he's a friend of a friend who's lending a hand."

The woman thought on this. She sucked her gaunt cheeks into her skull head. Agnes made a half wave and a half turn to leave. "What's that on your sleeves?" asked the thin woman.

Agnes looked down and cradled her fluffy arms protectively, like they were kittens. The rhinestones shook nervously. "They're just wee beads."

Shona Donnelly, the tea girl, exhaled slowly. "Oh! Missus, I think they're lovel—"

The thin woman interrupted her. "Do ye even have a man?"

The front door opened again, and Shuggie came out on to the top step. Without addressing the women he turned to his mother and put his hands on his hips; he thrust a foot forward and said as clear as Agnes had ever heard him speak, "We need to talk. I really do not think I can live here. It smells like cabbages and batteries. It's simply unpossible."

The heads of the audience turned one to another in shock. It was like a dozen faces looking at their own likenesses in the mirror. "Wid ye get a load o' that. Liberace is moving in!" screamed one of the women.

The women and children howled as one, high squeaky laughs and throaty coughs full of catarrh. "*Oh!* I do hope the piano will fit in the parlour."

"Well, it's so nice to meet you all," said Agnes with a thin grimace. She clutched Shuggie to her hip as she turned to leave.

"Oh, dinnae be like that. It's nice to meet you an' all, hen," wheezed Bridie, her hard face softening around the eyes from the good howling. "We're all like family here. We just don't get that many new faces."

The skull-faced woman took a step closer to Agnes. "Aye, well. We'll get on just fine." She sucked as though a piece of meat was stuck between her teeth. "Just as long as ye keep yer fancy sleeves away from our fuckin' men."

For the rest of the afternoon Shuggie walked the edge of the new scheme while the men unpacked the moving van. Women in tight leggings dragged kitchen chairs to their windows and sat watching, empty-faced, as box after box was unloaded. They had taken to greeting the boy with extravagant waves, doffing imaginary caps and then cackling to themselves.

In his new outfit he walked to the far end of the street. There was nothing out there. The street stopped at the edge of the peatbogs like it had given up. Dark pools of boggy water sat still and deep and scary-looking. Great forests of brown reeds shot up out of the grass and were slowly inching over the scheme, intent on taking it back from the miners.

Shuggie watched shoeless children playing in the stour. From the edge of a clutch of council bushes he pretended he was cataloguing some small red flowers, studying each for its size, while he waited for the children to ask him to join them. They were riding bikes in circles round each other and ignoring him. He popped the white berries between his fingers, trying to look casually disinterested, and then he tried to wipe the shine off his good shoes with the sticky juice.

The miners' tackety boots made sparks on the tarmac. The men slowly started drifting one by one along the empty road. There was no colliery whistle now; still the men were pushed along by the muscle memory of a dead routine, heading home at finishing time with nothing being finished, only a belly full of ale and a back cowed with worry. Their donkey jackets were clean and their boots were still shiny as they jerked along the road. Shuggie stepped back as they passed, their heads lowered like those of tired black mules. Without a word, each man collected a handful of thin children, who followed obediently, like reverential shadows.

* * *

Agnes stood behind the front door and closed the large glass draught
door ahead of her. She couldn't think. In the small pocket between the
two doors she finished the can that she'd secreted in the bottom of her
bag. She pressed her face against the wall, cold and soothing; the stone
was thick and damp, and she could tell it would be slow to heat up.

She stood in the hiding place for a long while before she walked the
length of the hallway, past two small bedrooms. Catherine was standing
in the middle of the first, moving neither here nor there. The wild miners' weans were resting their elbows on the outside ledge and looking in
the bedroom window at her like it was a zoo. Dumbfounded, she could
only stare back. The wood-framed windows were poorly fitted, and the
chipped glazing putty warned of cold nights and wet walls. Agnes could
hear the weans talking as clearly as if they were in the room with her.

Leek had found the other room. He had opened the bag that kept
his drawing supplies and was lying on the bare floor drawing a charcoal
picture of the black hills. He took the edge of the pastel and drew the
figures of the dark-jacketed men who had watched them as they arrived.
They lined the mound of the hills like trees with no leaves. She watched
her son, jealous of his talent to disappear, to float away and leave them
all behind.

There were no more bedrooms after that. The third that they had
been promised was clearly the living room, and as she retraced her steps,
two and then three times, she knew all the children would need to be
put together in one single room again.

Shug was standing at the end of the hallway looking blankly at her.
His comb-over had been dancing in the wind, and he caught the waving strands and with a lick of spittle tried to smooth it back down over
his head. He stepped back inside the open kitchenette and motioned
for her to follow. The kitchen had a large clothes pulley hanging from
the ceiling that looked like a torture rack. At the far end hung a set of
miner's working clothes, neatly arranged to dry, from socks to white
underwear to a blue polyester work shirt, all stiff with age. Would the

man who they belonged to ever be back from the mines? Maybe they had the wrong house after all.

The facing of the chipboard cabinets was peeling in places, and Shug stood working his pinkie finger under one of the laminates. Behind him, in the corner above the cooker, sprawled a vine of black mould. Without looking at her he simply said, "I can't stay."

At first she barely looked up. She had thought he meant only to go out on a shift and make money. He did that often, came home from a shift only to stand up again and announce he was heading back out. He had never been a man given to sitting at home.

"What time would you like your dinner?" she asked, already worrying about chip pans and bread knives.

"I don't want your dinners any more. Don't you get it?" He was shaking his head. "This is it. I can't stay any more. I can't stay with you. All your wanting. All that drinking."

It was then she saw that the brocade cases were settled amongst the packing boxes but the red cases were not. She must have had a look of profound confusion on her face, because Shug met her eyes and was nodding slowly, like you did when a child swallowed medicine, goading it on, waiting for the *ick* of it to reach the gut. Agnes looked away. She didn't want to understand. She didn't want his medicine. She stopped looking for the chip pan, started rearranging the beads on her jumper so that the shiny, faceted sides were uniform and facing outward, stalling for time, unsure of what to do now.

"This is it," he said again.

There was a single chair in the room, a broken-backed kitchen chair, covered in paint splashes and used for reaching high cabinets. Agnes closed the kitchen door quietly; out in the hallway the children were already complaining, aware now that there were not enough bedrooms. She put the broken chair in front of the closed door and sat down. "Why am I not enough for you?"

Shug blinked like he could not believe what he was hearing. He shook his head, and as he spoke he prodded himself in the chest. "No, m'lady. Why was *I* not enough?"

"I've never so much as looked at another man."

"That's no what I meant." He rubbed at his eyes like he was tired. "Why did you no love me enough to stay off the drink, eh? I buy you the best of gear, I work all the hours God sent." He stared at the wall, not at it but through it. "I even thought, maybe if I gave you a wean of my own, but no. Even that wasn't enough to keep you still."

Taking her roughly by the elbow, he tried to lift her from the seat. Agnes shook herself free and sat back down like she was in a peaceful protest.

She was in the dangerous in-between place. Enough drink to feel combative but not enough to be unreasonable yet. A few mouthfuls more and she would become destructive, mean-mouthed, spiteful. He stared at her as if he were reading the weather coming down from the glen. He took hold of her and tried to shift her again, before the great rainclouds inside her burst.

She wrenched herself from his grasp, sat down again, and drew herself to her full height. She regarded him coldly for a long while. She could still not believe what was happening. "No. Not good enough. This doesn't happen to women like me. I mean look at me. Look at *you*."

"You're embarrassing yourself." He pulled on the front of her jumper.

Shug moved her by force then. She did not cry out as he took her by the hair and pulled her to the floor. Agnes pressed herself against the bottom of the kitchen door as though she could keep him inside forever. He slammed the door into the back of her head, like she was only a loose corner of carpet. As he stepped over her, his right brogue caught the underside of her chin, splitting the pearl-white skin clean open.

"Please, I love you. I do," she said.

"Aye, I know that."

By the time the hackney had turned on the Pit Road, her children were in the hallway and Agnes, sparkling and fluffy, was lying like a party dress that had been dropped on the floor.

The red leather cases never made it into the miner's house. Shug did not come back to see her for several days, and when he did he didn't have the cases with him. He had taken them to Joanie Micklewhite's and slid them into the space she had cleared for him under her bed. Agnes did not know that at first. Shug simply reappeared one night, gently kissed the gash on her chin, and laid her down on the fold-out settee in the living room.

Shug started coming in during his night shifts and using her in this way. He waited until the small hours, when the children would be in bed, then he whistled nonchalantly up the hallway in freshly pressed shirts. As she undressed him she could tell his underwear was clean and boil-washed by another woman. When they were done, he would lie there for a moment until Agnes wrapped her arms around him, and then he would stand up and leave. If she cooked for him, he would maybe stay a little longer. If she started in on him with question or complaint, he would leave, and he would stay away for several nights in punishment.

After he'd gone, Agnes would lie on the fold-out settee because she could not take to their bed without him. She lay awake the rest of the night staring at the ceiling while the boys slept in their bedroom next door. All that first autumn Catherine would climb on to the mattress with her mother, and they would lie there together under the damp and the growing mould.

"Why don't we just go back to Sighthill?" Catherine would whisper. But Agnes couldn't explain through the hurt. She knew he would never come back if she returned to her mother's.

She was to stay where she was dropped.

She was to take any little kindness he would give.

Eventually Guy Fawkes Night arrived, and the air was thick with bonfire wood and burning tyres. Leek and Catherine stood at the window and watched home-made pyres burn across the boggy blackness. Weans launched fireworks at each other like they were whistling missiles. It seemed like rare fun.

The television was still half-unwrapped from its bed sheet and placed on the floor in the corner, not yet a full commitment. Catherine sank into the settee, her wet hair wrapped in a turban towel. It'd be the late news and then another night of listening to her mother weep in the dark.

Agnes waited in the back, in the kitchen. With the lights turned off, it was the room with the best view of the Pit Road. Every night she watched for the hackney and got her hopes up with the approaching hum of any diesel engine. She'd been drinking all the day away, but it wasn't helping any. She walked between the window and her stash below the kitchen sink. From the click of the latch, the children could count the times she opened the cabinet and snuck a drink.

"Mammy, what's for eating?" Leek shouted from the settee.

Agnes stopped picking at the scab on her chin. She looked at the pot on the electric cooker. "I could heat you some of this soup."

"The one with the peas in it?" Leek asked.

"Yes."

"Well, not if it's got *peas* in it," said Leek, a little hurt that his fifteen-year war against green vegetables went unnoticed.

"Uh, hullo, its *pea* soup, ya big dafty!" mocked Catherine.

Leek dug his foot into her side and pulled the towel off her head, ripping some of her hair along with it. He threw it in the far corner for spite. *Get it up ye*, he mouthed silently. They had agreed, without ever discussing it outright, to tread as lightly as they could around their mother.

Catherine stood up to fetch the towel from the other side of the room. She had held on to her virginity as Lizzie had warned her to, so now it wouldn't be long till she was married to Donald Jnr, and then she wouldn't have to share a bedroom with either her brother or her mother in this cold damp. The thought alone stopped her from leaving; she was on her way out anyway.

Catherine rewrapped her hair and flicked her brother the finger. She went through to check on her mother. Agnes was distractedly circling the kitchen like a toy train; every so often she stopped and opened the cabinet under the sink, filled a mug from a container within a plastic bag, and took a long drink. Catherine nudged the cabinet door open with her toe; with relief she saw it was not bleach Agnes had been pouring into the mug.

Catherine wrinkled her nose at the congealed soup pot. "Mammy, how about phoning in a wee Chinese?"

"Guid idea!" Leek chimed in from the other room.

Catherine had said only Chinese, but Agnes had heard Shug. She had the strange power to tie anything back to him these days. Her eyes came into sharp focus. "I could phone the rank and see if Shug's coming round the night?" she offered brightly. "Mibbe he'll bring a Chinese over?"

Catherine groaned. Agnes had been warned not to phone the rank any more. Shug had added it to the long list of things she had to stop if she ever wanted him home. It was his emotional ransom. Perhaps though, if he knew the children were hungry, he'd come over and things would be OK for a few hours. She could fix herself up nice, and maybe he would spend the whole night with her on the fold-out settee. Agnes took a mouthful from her mug and thought through her script: sound normal, sober, non-committal; keep it easy and smile down the phone. It hadn't worked any night before, she didn't know why, but she wanted badly to try again.

Agnes sat at the little pleather phone table and lit a cigarette for her nerves. When she finished dialling she turned her engagement ring back around, as though the person on the other end could see. The gold of her wedding band had turned a dirty-looking yellow.

A woman's voice on the phone answered with an annoyed crackle. "*Northside Taxis!*" It was Joanie Micklewhite. Agnes knew her only casually.

"Hello, Joanie, is that you? It's Mrs Bain."

"Oh, hullo, hen. Whit can I do ye for?" Joanie sounded flat, like when you turn the corner and run into someone you'd rather never see again.

"Can you get a message out to Shug, to please phone home," Agnes said. She wondered then whether Joanie knew he had left her. She wondered who at the rank knew he wasn't sleeping in her bed.

"Let me try. Can you haud on, hen?" The phone went quiet as Joanie put the line on hold and tried to contact Shug's taxi over the big CB radio. It took an eternity before Joanie came back on the line. "Ye still there?"

She caught Agnes mid-puff. Agnes exhaled the smoke above her head. "Still holding! Did you get through to him?"

Joanie paused slightly, and Agnes stiffened for rejection. "Aye. He said he'd give you a phone in a while."

Agnes brightened up, something like hope caught in her chest, and she looked forward to seeing him, her own husband. She thought about the velvet dress she would wear for him; she wondered if she had time to shave her legs.

Then Joanie added, "Agnes. I know he hasn't told you everything, hen." She stuttered on: "I . . . I just wanted you to know that when you do find out, I'd never meant for anything like this to happen. I have seven weans of my own. And, well, I'm sorry."

The last of the bonfires were dying by the time Shug arrived. The children were in bed, sullen and hungry. Agnes couldn't touch any of the Chinese. She watched his hair fall from his bald head as he shovelled great mouthfuls into his gullet. Through all this he hadn't lost his appetite, and that killed her. Agnes rubbed at her temples and sat amongst all the unpacked unpacking. There were still no red cases. "Does she keep a nice house?"

"No' really," he said, without looking up.

Agnes drank as much lager as she could in one go, before she needed to lower the can to take another breath. When she was done she asked, "So, is she good-looking?"

"I told you on the phone. I don't want to fuckin' talk about her." He ripped a slice of white bread in two. "Let me eat my dinner in peace. I didnae drive out here to fight."

Agnes was quiet for a long time, thinking carefully about what to say next. Her left hand worried her knife. She was caught between wanting to start a fight and stab him and wanting him to stay a little longer. When she spoke again she tried to keep her voice even and calm. She found it helped not to look at him. "It's not going to happen is it? Our new start?"

Shug stopped chewing. He shrugged. "This is a new start Agnes. I couldn't cope anymair."

She cupped her hands over her face. The polish on her nails was bright, as if still wet. "Why the fuck did you bring me here?"

Shug pushed his plate away. His moustache was heavy with a congealing pink sauce. "I had to see."

"Had to see *what?*" she asked, her voice cracking in anger. "I thought this is what *you* wanted."

"I had to see if you would actually come."

Agnes took hold of the neck of his jumper then. Shug picked up his money belt and kissed her with a forceful tongue. He had to squeeze all the small bones in her hands to get her to release him. She had loved him, and he had needed to break her completely to leave her for good. Agnes Bain was too rare a thing to let someone else love. It wouldn't do to leave pieces of her for another man to collect and repair later.

Nine

Agnes had to sink three whole lager cans before she could go out the front door. A group of women stood in a cluster by the fence, their arms folded like car bumpers. It was like they had been waiting there since she had moved in four months prior. The cold didn't seem to bother them. The ground was littered with cigarette doubts, and there were dirty tea mugs stacked on the fence posts. They stopped talking and turned as one when she came out the front door. Holding her head high, Agnes made sure the clicks of her black heels were sharp and clear on the pavement. She smiled haughtily at the women in their leggings and slippers. She passed them by, heading up the road to the Miners Club, to forgetfulness.

The women looked on silently. She was almost out of earshot before one of them spoke. "We've no had a falling out already, have we?" said Bridie. Her streaked hair was still unbrushed, her thick trunk wrapped in men's jogging pants and a housecoat.

Agnes didn't turn around. "What gave you that idea?"

"Ye've no invited us to yer party. Are we no pals?"

"What party?" Agnes half-turned.

"Well, where else are ye gaun dressed aw nice like that?"

"The Miners Club. I wanted to see what you lot did for fun."

The women all looked one to another. They twisted at their Saint Christopher's medallions nervously. "Don't be botherin' about that," Bridie said. "The men don't like it when we show our faces up there. Stay here with us, and we'll hae a wee welcome drink to oorsels." Bridie drew a large, clear bottle from behind one of the fence posts. She tossed the contents of her tea mug into the street and shook the vodka bottle. "Why don't ye come over here and tell us all about yersel?"

Agnes stepped closer and watched the bitter liquid eat the ring of tea scum. She held her hand up in moderation as the pure vodka neared the top and gave a prim giggle. Bridie glanced at her sideways and filled the mug to the very top. "Gies peace. Ah cannae have ye thinking we're cheap."

Agnes took the mug with a polite thanks. The women ran their eyes up and down their new neighbour: the strappy heels, the hard-set hair, the beautiful fur coat. Agnes glanced up and down the empty road and let them drink it all in. The nights were gathering in again. The street lights were on, and a gang of collarless dogs wandered from stank to stank, sniffing the rotten drains. One pissed, and the others took their turns and marked the same spot. She turned back to the women, and they were smiling hungrily at her. "Well, cheers then." She chinked the tea mug against theirs.

Someone took a pouch of rolling tobacco out and passed it around. Jinty licked some fag papers and tenderly poured a thin line of golden tobacco in. "Put that away!" said Agnes, seeing a chance to repay them for the vodka. She reached into the deep pockets and pulled a pack of Kensitas out of the mink coat.

Bridie looked at the glossy gold packet, at the gold-plated lighter. "Jeezo. It's like the Queen of England has moved in."

"It makes a right difference when you don't have to pick the baccy off your teeth," Jinty agreed.

The women took one each and lit the cigarettes. They all took long greedy draws and savoured the taste in silence. They held the cigarettes between the thumb and forefinger, as if gripping a pea-shooter. They studied Agnes, her painted nails dancing in front of her face like so many red ladybugs. Between delicate fingers, she took light shallow puffs as they sucked their cheeks thin. Then she lifted her other hand and took deep greedy mouthfuls from the mug.

"Where ye frae then?" asked Jinty, reaching out to touch her emerald earrings.

"Originally? Germiston. But I suppose you could say all over the East End. I've moved a fair bit."

"All ower the East End, eh?" echoed Bridie, nodding sagely. "A Good Catholic wummin then. What brings ye out here to our wee scheme?"

Agnes faltered. "My man heard it was a nice place to live, safe for my weans." She paused. "*Good Neighbours.*"

"Aye," said Bridie, with a laugh. "It's no Butlin's, but that sounds like the good auld days. That mine has been dying for years. There's hardly nae work there for naebody anymair. Every year we've got mair men sat at home, wanking in the daylight."

"There's a couple who've still got jobs. Mainly filling in the holes to make sure no kiddies fall in," added Noreen. "Don't want any mair accidents, see."

"Accidents?" asked Agnes.

"Aye, it's always been a gassy seam. They used to have to pump the methane out just to work it. Mind, the men knew this; they knew what they were working against and respected it best they could, but one day it just fell in on the poor souls. Pure collapsed. There was an explosion that burnt them all up. Left some weans wi' no daddies." Jinty was still staring at Agnes's earrings. "It made a lot of lonely women."

They turned and looked at the house that belonged to the woman with the skull face. Bridie sighed. "Don't worry about Colleen McAvennie. Her bark's worse than her bite."

"Is she your cousin as well?"

"Oh, aye, but no blood, ye see. She's just protective of her Jamesy. Used to be he was a good-looking fella. He was a big burly banksman; used to ferry them up and down in a cage lift in that shaft. Got burnt in that mine, took the skin all off his shoulder and the side of his neck. Red as a July sunburn." The women bowed their heads, almost as a sign of respect. "A fine-looking man nonetheless."

"Anyways, where did yer man go off tae wi' them fancy red cases?" asked Jinty suddenly.

"He's a taxi driver; sometimes he needs to take his stuff with him," she lied. It was thin. "He works the night shift."

Jinty sucked at her teeth. She laid a sympathetic hand on Agnes's. "We wurnae born yesterday, hen. He looked to me like he was leaving for longer than that."

Bridie waved her cigarette at Jinty. "Och, never mind her. Don't sink to her level. All we are saying is, we've aw got men and we've aw got men trouble."

The women puffed on their fags in empathy. Noreen looked worried. "How you gonnae feed yersel if he disnae come back?"

Money was always on her mind, her heart was gnawed with the worry. "I don't know."

The women looked from one to another. Bridie spoke first. "We'll have to get ye on benefits. Ye can go up the office on Monday morning. Ye'll have to tell them ye're needing disability allowance, otherwise they'll have ye up the dole every Thursday."

"Will they sign me on to disability?"

"Ah widnae worry, hen. They'll take one look at yer address and give it to you easy. Look at this place." Bridie waved her hand into the empty street. "It's no like there are any new jobs coming here. Disability is the only club we've got, and Monday is club day."

Agnes lifted the vodka mug again and stared down into the faint clouds. The tea must have been very milky.

Bridie topped it up to the brim with a smile. "Aye, ah took ye for a drinker." She drew on her fag. "Aye, the minute ah saw ye, ah spotted it. They thought you were the big *I Am*, all done up in sequins, like some big dolly bird from the city. But ah could see through it. Ah could see the sadness, and ah knew ye had to be a big drinker."

The women nodded and cawed, "Aye," like a murder of crows. Agnes froze with the mug on her lips.

"Do ye drink anything and everything?" asked Bridie.

"Pardon?" said Agnes, lowering the mug.

"Is it a *very* bad problem ye've goat?" clarified Bridie.

"I don't have a problem."

"Look, hen. Ye're standing out here drinking vodka in the middle of the street. Ye'll have no problem signing on the disability looking like that."

"You have a mug of vodka as well." Agnes was affronted.

Their mouths turned downwards unkindly as they tilted their mugs towards her in the orange street light. The filmy whiteness of milky tea showed in each one. "No, hen, we're drinking piss-cold tea," scolded Bridie. "It's only ye who's neckin' vodka like it was tap water."

Agnes's face smarted red. The women smiled pityingly through tight lips. The pupils of their eyes, hooded by their lids, looked black in the orange street light. Agnes looked into the mug and threw the rest of the vodka down the back of her throat.

Bridie held up her hand. "Listen. *One day at a time* and aw that shite. Ah've had a wee problem maself. Six weans and a husband out of work? You better believe ah drank." She squashed the finished cigarette doubt into the dust with a sandalled toe. "It was the blackouts that did me in though. Ah couldn't take that first five minutes of every day waking up and wondering who said what to who and what bastard ah'd had a fight wi'. Ye'd go into the kitchen scratching for a cup of tea, and they all look at ye side-a-ways. Then ye'd look around and one of them would have a black eye. Then ye'd go to the mirror and ye'd have one an' all." The women all nodded in empathy. Nobody laughed.

Jinty added, "I've stood up at Dolan's shop talking about *Dallas* with women ah'd dragged along the street by the hair the night afore." She curled her hands into fists, her thin body animated by the scandal. Then she pointed at skull face's house across the road. "Do ye a'member the time Colleen felt Isa was making eyes at Big Jamesy?"

Bridie tutted. "That was a nonsense. They're blood. Everybody always forgets that."

"Well, there was no telling Colleen about *that*." Jinty turned to Agnes. "Now oor Colleen disnae take a drink. She's right close to the Baby Jesus, takes him everywhere in her heart. But this one Monday morning, she took a drink, a right good hammering. She's gone up the post office and done in her Monday Book, spent every fuckin' penny and swilled it down her neck. Her weans were greetin' and starvin', and she drank every drop. She gets a plastic bag and goes up and down that road scoopin' up dog shite. White ones, black ones, runny and hard, near fills the bag to the top. She took this bag of dog shite and staggers up the road there." Jinty pointed towards the slag hills. "She puts on a yellow marigold glove and she starts throwin'. Ah mean *absolutely* covers the front of Isa's house. She was throwin' that shite and screamin' for Big Jamesy to come out there and face her like a man."

"What happened?" Agnes asked.

"Aye, ah'm getting to it." Jinty slung a sly look over her shoulder to Colleen's gate. "She showers the place in dog shite, you could smell it for miles. It goes on the windows, sticks to the pebble-dash. Drenched. Lord knows ah'm no a big fan of Isa—her man took early redundancy from the Pit, and she spent it at the bingo and won a pretty penny—*bu-ut* I do not condone throwing shite in the street like a savage."

Bridie took up the tale. "Anyway, turns out Big Jamesy wisnae diddling Isa. He was working. *Working!* Of all the things to be doing. He got himself a part-time job hauling scrap and couldnae tell anyone for fear they'd shop him to the disability."

Jinty kissed her Saint Christopher. "Here Colleen thought he was at it, and the man was out trying to make a bit of extra money."

"Thank God for blackouts." Bridie crossed herself solemnly. "Look. Ah know why ye drink, hen. It's hard to cope sometimes. Ah steer clear of the drink, but ah still need a couple of these every day." She took a baby's aspirin bottle out of her pocket. "Bridie's little pals."

"Aspirin?" asked Agnes.

"Naw!" Bridie licked her top lip, she leaned in closer. "Valium. If you want just try a couple. A wee taste that's all. If you want more, I'll look after ye. *Special price*." Bridie pushed down and unscrewed the lid of the small plastic bottle with a smile. She tipped two into Agnes's palm like they were sweeties. "Here, just try it, and welcome to Pithead."

Ten

His mother was nowhere to be found. He cupped the bone-white tooth in his hand; the little incisor floated in a pool of spittle and blood, and he was sure he might die. Was this what happened now that he was seven? He was afraid to probe his teeth with his tongue should they all come loose. He needed to find her to ask. But his mother was gone.

Shuggie stood with his face against the rusty metal gate and watched a pack of pit dogs roam by. Five male dogs harassed a small black female dog. They made a high yipping noise as they prowled past, and Shuggie pushed his lips between the fence slats and sang along with them, *yip yip yip*. He listened to the dog's song, and it was as if they were calling him outside. He wasn't allowed out the front gate without telling her, but then she wasn't here.

Keeping his plimsolls planted firmly inside, he stuck his head out and looked left and then looked right. He played a game of holding his breath and then darting out and darting back, all the while stealing glances up and down the short road to try to see her.

She wasn't there.

The pack of dogs called him out of the gate. Shuggie picked up his dirty blond dolly and tossed her out on to the pavement. Daphne landed with a raspy crack and made a snow angel in the dust. He leapt out and grabbed her, darting back inside like a little bony fish, closing the gate with a loud metal clang. He looked over his shoulder, no one came to the window and no one came to Bridie Donnelly's window. There was no one watching. She wasn't there.

Shuggie opened the gate again and followed the dogs. There was a clutch of women standing in men's slippers on the corner. They had been talking animatedly about something, but he saw how they lowered their voices as he approached. One of them turned and curtsied towards him. Trying to look casual, like he didn't care, he made a show of dancing along the dusty road past the chapel on the hill. He made a great game of kicking plumes of dust into the sky and danced farther and farther from home. He came to the Catholic school and watched children play at their morning break. He stood in the shade of a horse chestnut tree and wondered why he wasn't in school himself. There hadn't been cartoons on that morning, so it hadn't been Saturday, he knew that much, but she hadn't laid his clothes out like she sometimes did, so he hadn't gone, and she hadn't said anything.

The boys were mercilessly kicking a bladder into the corner of the playground, and they saw him before he noticed them watching. "What's that ye've got?" shouted the smaller of the brown brothers, the sons of the skull-faced woman, Colleen McAvennie. Shuggie instinctively hid the Daphne doll behind his back.

"Hello," said Shuggie with a polite wave. He mimicked the swishing curtsy of the miner's wife and gracefully extended his left leg out behind himself.

Open-mouthed, they peered through the peeling railings and drew their eyes up and down the length of him. "How come ye're no in school?" asked Gerbil, the younger one, picking flakes of green paint from the iron.

"I don't know," Shuggie admitted with a shrug. The boys were only a few years older than him but were already thick-built and brown from summers spent outside, exploring marshes and throwing cats into the

Pit's quarries. He had seen them easily move heavy loads of their father's scrap from the back of his lorry.

Francis McAvennie narrowed his dark eyes and said, "It's a'cos your mammy is an auld alky." He watched Shuggie's face to see the sting of the words.

Gerbil McAvennie put a flake of iron paint between his lips. "How come ye don't have a daddy?" His voice was already deep like a man's.

"I d-do," Shuggie stuttered.

Gerbil smiled. "Where is he then?"

This Shuggie didn't know. He had heard he was a whoremaster and that he was raising another woman's weans while he fucked every bastarding thing that sat in the back of his taxi. But it didn't seem right to admit this. "He's on night shift. Making money for our holidays."

The break bell went, and Father Barry came out to line up the playing children. Gerbil reached his hand through the fence, his long fingers snatching at Shuggie's doll. Francis gurgled like a happy baby and joined in the game till they were both grabbing wildly. Shuggie stepped back into the shade of the horse chestnut tree. "I'm telling Father Barry on ye! Ye should be in school," they screamed.

Clutching Daphne to his chest, Shuggie turned on his heels and ran away as quickly as he could. He was out of breath by the time he came across the Miners Club, but he could still hear the McAvennie boys calling out for Father Barry.

The club was run-down and empty-looking. Shuggie pulled himself up and hung from the bars on the windows. Then he idled around the forecourt, where spent lager kegs bled out puddles of flat ale. The dirty lager mixed with petrol and made lochans of shining rainbows. Shuggie knelt down and pushed Daphne's blond hair into the iridescent puddle. When he took her out, the shiny yellow hair had turned the colour of night, and he tutted. Where were the beautiful rainbow colours? He pushed her down again and held her under the surface longer this time. Her eyes automatically closed, like she was sleeping, but she was smiling so he knew she was OK. When he lifted the doll out of the puddle, the black liquid rolled off her face and down on to her white woollen dress. Her cheap yellow hair had turned matte black. He stared at it and realized that for a minute he had forgotten about his mother. Daphne smelled funny.

For a while he weaved in and out of the lager puddles. He peered out on to the road, and when he was absolutely sure Father Barry was not looking for him he darted across the road and into the mouth of a wooded lane he had not seen before. The lane backed a row of older-looking miners' cottages that were joined at the back with a communal garden. At the near edge of the garden sat a large brick bin shed. It was flat and rectangular, with no windows and a dark opening, where a painted green door now hung open and broken. At the side of the bin shed lay a washing machine, the kind used in hospitals or government buildings, solid and big as a wardrobe. It was too heavy for the bin men to take away, so it lay rusting next to the shed, and fat lazy flies dipped in and out of its shadow.

Inside the machine sat a boy, with his legs above his head, curled around the drum like a broken-backed cat. "Want a spin in my carnival ride?"

Shuggie was startled to find him in there.

The boy swung inside the drum and rocked in semicircles, in one second his feet were above his head, the next his head were above his feet. "Look, it's dead fun!" he coaxed.

Shuggie held Daphne out to him and offered her up for first go. The boy uncurled from inside the drum, pushing out his long brown legs, like a spider through a keyhole. He arched his body out backwards; straightening, he was almost as tall as the metal machine. He was a good year older than Shuggie, at least eight or nine, starting the long stretch already.

"Hiya. Ma name's Johnny. Ma maw calls us *Bonny Johnny*." he said with a tight smile. "It's supposed to be like a wrestler's name, but I think it's pure shite." He slapped his own forearm like the wrestlers on television did before a fight. He chopped at the empty air. "Whit's your name, wee man?"

"Hugh Bain," he said in a shy voice. "*Shuggie*."

The boy was watching him, peering through half-lidded eyes the same way Shuggie had seen the miners' children squint when he raised his hand in class. It was a blend of disbelief and disdain. He had often seen his granny look at his father this way. Shuggie turned his left knee-cap inwards.

Then Johnny smiled. His face changed so quickly it made Shuggie take a step back. It was like a flick of a light switch, and his face brightened like a bare bulb in an empty room.

"Is that a dolly ye've got, Shuggie?" The boy was using his name like he had known him a long while. Without waiting for an answer he added, "Are ye a wee girl?" He stepped into the long grass, flattening it as he came.

Shuggie shook his head again.

"If ye're no' a wee girl then ye must be a wee poof." He tightened his smile. His voice was low and sweet, like he was talking to a puppy. "Ye're no' a wee poof, *are* ye?"

Shuggie didn't know what a poof was, but he knew it was bad. Catherine called Leek it when she wanted to hurt his feelings.

"Do ye no' know what a poofter is, wee man? A poof is a boy who does dirty things with other boys." Johnny was up against Shuggie now, nearly double his height. "A poof is a boy who wants to be a wee girl."

Bonny Johnny was a dirty white colour, like he had been steeped in tea. He had sepia skin and honey-coloured hair and eyes like amber lager. When Johnny smiled he had all his big boy teeth already. Shuggie worried the gap in his own smile with his tongue. Johnny snatched the doll from him and tossed her into the drum. "See! She wants a ride."

Johnny pressed himself into Shuggie's back, put his arms around his waist and lifted him up into the mouth of the machine. Shuggie climbed up into the drum, and he felt a helping hand give him a final push as he tumbled in. Clutching Daphne, he looked back out into the daylight, his bare legs chilled by the cold metal.

Johnny grabbed a raised ridge inside the drum and moved it slowly from left to right, rocking it as gently as a baby's crib. Shuggie fell over and scrambled for ballast against the swinging, he tensed all his muscles and bared his teeth, like a scared cat. Daphne slid away, clanging around the cylinder.

Johnny kept on rocking gently. "See it's no' *that* bad, is it?"

The motion came to remind Shuggie of the pirate ship ride that sat outside his grandfather's favourite bakery. He gurgled with involuntary laughter.

"Haud on," said Johnny. He gripped the metal ridge tighter, and bracing his body against the machine for purchase, he rocked it harder. Shuggie's head and knees travelled in semicircles as Daphne hit the roof. The muscles on Johnny's neck stood out as he pulled the drum round with all his might. Shuggie spun head over heels. He spun over and over, again and again, his head cracking on the metal paddles, his foot hitting him square in the back.

The drum slowed and Shuggie crashed into an upside-down heap. A thick arm grabbed one of the metal bars and stopped the centrifuge. A siren wail rose in Shuggie as the pain shot down through his crown, his split knee, and his bruised shins. From behind his waterfall of tears he could see a large hand come down again and again on Johnny's head, the boy ducking for cover to protect his face. The attacker was too tall for Shuggie to see a face, just the angry lashings of a tattooed arm, slapping the boy's bare neck and shoulders.

"Whit in the name of the wee man have ah telt ye about playing with that fuckin' washin' machine?" scolded the headless torso. With his fat thumb, the man jabbed towards the drum. "*Get. That.* The fuck out of there, afore ah really gie ye something to greet about."

As swiftly as the figure had arrived, it disappeared again. Johnny stood in the opening looking like a battered dog. His smile was gone, his ears were pinned down. He reached in and plucked Shuggie out of the drum. "Listen. Ye stop that greetin', or I'll gie you something to greet about."

Out of the drum the daylight was almost blinding. The pain in his head stole the colour from his sight.

Johnny looked the boy up and down. There was blood on Shuggie's leg from where the metal had burst the skin, and bruises were already showing on his arms and legs. Johnny whipped him around the corner through the black flies and into the cool darkness of the bin shed. It smelt sour as curdled yoghurt.

In the dark, Johnny spat on his hand and rubbed it over the boy's wet face and then down the length of his bloody leg. It made everything worse. The blood became a spittle wash, smearing further instead of wiping away. The boy grew panicked, his eyes wide in fear. He ripped a handful of large green docken leaves out of the dirt and scraped them up and down Shuggie's leg. He scrubbed until the blood lifted off and was replaced by a thick trail of mushed green plant mucus. The chlorophyll stung the cut. Shuggie started to girn again.

"Haud still you poofy wee bastard." All the tones of his earlier friendliness were gone. Shuggie could see his father's red hand marks blooming across Johnny's sepia skin.

It was quiet in the bin shed but for the buzz of fat bluebottles. Johnny rubbed and rubbed the little boy's leg until his breathing calmed. His rubbing turned Shuggie from white to red to a deep green. As the panic left Johnny's eyes, slowly the fake smile returned to his tanned face. It was very dark in the bin shed.

Bonny Johnny stood up again, a wiry silhouette against the bright daylight. He handed Shuggie the pulped green leaves and then he took down his gym shorts. "Stop girning," he said, through his big boy teeth. "Now you rub me."

By the time Shuggie had limped back to the Miners Club the sun had nearly dried up the rainbow puddles. He'd left Daphne in the machine. He didn't ever want to go back.

As he climbed the stairs to the hallway he could hear her on the phone. "*Fuck you, Joanie Micklewhite. You tell that whoremastering son of a Proddy bitch that he cannot have his cake and eat it too!*" Each filthy syllable was enunciated with the alarming clarity of the Queen's English. "*You shitty, dick-sucking bastard. You are as plain and tasteless as the arse end of a white loaf.*" The receiver went down with a clang, and the bells tinkled with the impact.

Shuggie reached the end of the hallway and turned the corner. His mother sat cross-legged at the little telephone table with the mug on her knee. She looked at him like he had risen from the carpet itself. She didn't notice his missing tooth or the leg, stained with blood and spit and docken.

Plastered on her face was the glassy grimace that came from under the kitchen sink. She took her earring and threw it across the room before she picked up the phone again. "Now I'm in a mood to tell your granny where to fucking go."

The house was only a stone's throw from the bus stop, but Leek walked home very slowly. His legs were heavy from the day's graft on the Youth Training Scheme, his insides heavy with the dread of what might lie at home. He only hoped for a peaceful hour so he could draw, but it had been a year free of peace since they had moved to the Pit.

He knew Catherine would not come home again tonight. She was getting adept at sneaking around under Agnes's nose, holding her secret life with Donald Jnr away from their disintegrating mother. Instead, Catherine blamed her boss for all manner of slave-driving and told Agnes she would be late at the office and would need to stay at her granny's. Leek saw how his mother worried over money, how she worshipped Catherine's weekly pittance, and so she said nothing. Leek knew Catherine really was at Donald Jnr's, lying on the blow-up mattress in his mother's spare room and trying to keep her hand locked over her modesty until Donald finally married her. After all his years of practice, Leek was angry that it was Catherine who was disappearing first.

It was still daylight, but there were harsh lights on in every room, and the curtains lay open in a shameful way. It was a very bad sign. In the front room Shuggie was idling between the net curtain and the glass. His palms and nose were pressed flat against the window, he was rocking his head back and forth in a soothing way, and no one was telling him to stop. When he saw his brother he mouthed *Leek* and left a grease smear on the glass.

The net curtains fluttered to life. A shadow fell across the window, and Agnes appeared behind her youngest. Leek raised his hand in a half wave and put his other on the gate in a gesture that said he was coming home. Agnes smiled out at him, the too-toothy grimace that telegraphed a thousand messages. Her eyes seemed dull to him, unfixed, and instantly he knew she was gone.

She disappeared again, back to the telephone table, back to the drink.

Leek picked up his tool bag and turned away from the house. There was an insistent *chink-chink* on the glass. Shuggie's lips were wide as he overenunciated dramatically: *Where. Are. You. Going?*

Leek mouthed silently, *To Granny's.*

Shuggie tried to steady his lips. *Can. I. Come?*

No. It's too far. I can't carry you.

What he never told Shuggie was that he had once found his real father's address. Brendan McGowan. It was there, in Agnes's phone book, circled in many different colours and thicknesses of ink, as if she had gone back to it, again and again, over the years. Leek had walked to this address the winter before and had sat on the wall opposite the broad Victorian tenement. He'd watched a man come home from work, a man he didn't recognize, but who shared the same tired stoop. A man with eyes of the same light grey. The man parked his car in front of the building and then walked past Leek on the street with nothing more than a polite nod.

As the door opened, three small faces had raced down the close to greet him. Leek had watched the happy, rowdy family sit and eat at a dining table pressed against the front window. He'd watched them talk over the top of each other, the children standing defiantly upright on the dining chairs as the man laughed at their excitement. Leek had watched for a long time before he folded the address and dropped it between the slats of a storm drain.

Leek picked up his tool bag and headed out of Pithead. He turned his back to Shuggie and dared not look again at the pleading face in the window. It was going to rain and it would be a long walk to Sighthill. He was tired, he had been tired for a long time now. All he wanted was a rest.

Eleven

Colourless daylight poured through the net curtains. It poked her in the face, and with a snort she thumped back into consciousness. Agnes opened her eyes slowly and found herself staring at the cream Artexed ceiling with its icy stalagmite texture. Her lips wouldn't close over the sticky film on her top teeth as the dry boak rose inside her. Under her right hand she felt the slippery damask fabric of the armchair. Her fingers traced the familiar fag-burn holes. She was vaguely upright, cradling a dead phone receiver.

She sat still awhile, her head tilted over the back of the chair, like an open pedal bin. She closed her eyes again and listened to her brain thump loudly. Like a tide, the blood flushed in and out, in and out of her skull. Over the ebb she could tell the house was empty. It was early, but the boy had taken himself off to school again. He had already missed too many days. Too many days sat at her feet, just waiting and watching. The school didn't like that. Father Barry had said that the Social Work would have to be notified if he did not start having a regular attendance.

Some mornings she would wake up with a fright and find Shuggie staring at her. He would be dressed, dwarfed by the bag slung over both shoulders, his face washed and his wet hair parted and brushed in the front only. She would lie there, fully dressed, trying to pull her dry lips over her teeth, while he would say, "Good morning," and then quietly turn and leave for school. He hadn't wanted to leave without letting her know he would be right back afterwards. He took her pinkie in his and swore it.

The house was quiet. She tilted her head forward into her hands, and the blood filled the back of her eyes. Shuggie wasn't standing there as usual. On the table in front of her was a mug of cold tea, the top already congealed with a milky skin. Next to that a slice of white toast poked through with a clumsy knife, littered with lumps of butter too thick to spread. With a hand over her eyes she scanned the low coffee table for something to calm the shakes. She tilted mugs towards her and looked inside for a mouthful of beer. The mugs were empty. Agnes reached for a cigarette and with a sorry whimper pulled the last one out of the packet. She lit it with shaking fingers and took a long drag.

Feeling no better, she got up and shuffled around the couch looking for hidden quarter bottles or half-finished cans. She stoated around the empty house, tipping out all the hiding places that might hold a forgotten drink: the laundry basket, behind the vinyl video case covers that were made to look like encyclopaedias. On her knees, she pulled all the empty grocery bags out from underneath the kitchen sink till she knelt waist-deep in a cumulus of blue and white plastic.

The panic set in. From room to room she wandered, making shrieking, sucking noises of frustration through her front teeth. She had to keep stopping to spit gobbets of rising boak into sinks and old tea mugs. She dug out her big black leather bag and rifled around inside for her purse, sprang the metal clasp at the top, and opened it. Saint Jude rolled around at the bottom in a bed of fluff and grit. It was Thursday, and all the Monday and all the Tuesday benefit money was already done in.

On the Monday prior, she had lain awake through the night waiting for the radio clock to turn to eight. In high heels and uneven eyeshadow she had fairly run up the Pit Road to cash what the miners' wives called the "Monday Book." Standing at the back of the benefit queue, her head held high, her hands shaking in her pockets, Agnes had tried to ignore the women in their thin nylon jackets that made dry swishing noises. She stood there separate and aloof, as they rattled with their smoker's cough, grumbling with sticky phlegm.

Thirty-eight pounds a week was meant to keep and feed them all. It made mothers stand in the little shop and look at pint cartons of milk like they were a luxury.

Agnes cashed the Monday Book with the air of a queen. She walked directly past the milk to the front of the shop, and promptly bought twelve cans of Special Brew. She talked cheerily about the good weather they had been having, but the Indian man said nothing. She was sure the blue elephant thing hanging behind him was giving her the hairy eyeball. She reclasped her purse demurely as he slid the cold metal tins into a plastic bag. The women behind her did sums out loud, their lips moving as they counted, adding bread to oven chips to cigarettes and then, defeated, putting the bread quietly back on the shelf. Agnes slipped back out into the street, and behind the low sandstone shop, she crouched in the broken glass and popped open the first cold can.

On a Tuesday morning she went back to the shop already with a drink in her. She glided up the dual carriageway, her knees dipping elegantly with each step. Agnes cashed in her Tuesday Book of eight pounds fifty in child support. Fortified by the Special Brew she told the shopkeeper that his blue elephant gave her the "heebie-jeebies."

But it was Thursday now. She looked down into the purse, empty but for Saint Jude and the oose gathering in the creases. Sad, selfish tears of the poor me's welled in her eyes. She raked a finger through the dirty ashtray. She needed to think what to do next.

The alcohol leaving her body made it hard to watch the television, so she ran a hot bath. The water would make her feel less cold, less sore. She rinsed the sweat and flatness out of her hair. She took the flannel cloth and began wiping the taste off her teeth and lay back in the scalding water and thought how she could get some money. Across her soft middle ran a deep red welt where, after she had passed out, her black tights had dug in, bruising the flesh. She stuck her finger in the welt.

It ran across her spare tyre like a train track and that made her think of the Glasgow train, Paddy's Market, which lay underneath its arches, and the pawnshop that sat there.

Without drying herself she ran about the house in a wet house-coat looking for something to pawn. In the daylight everything looked cheap and worthless. She turned every Capodimonte ornament in her hands and even tried picking up the black-and-white television, but she would never be able to hump it by foot into the city. In the bedroom she considered her jewellery, all the odd pieces that were lying loose in an old penny-bank bag: the Claddagh rings her mother had given her, her granny's locket, Catherine's christening bangle. It took effort, but she reluctantly put the bag back in the drawer.

She did a sly amble past Leek's heavy toolbox. She nudged it with her toe. It was empty, he had taken all the tools with him to the YTS job site. He had carried it all, even the things he would surely not need. He had learned his lesson the last time she had been itching for pawn. Agnes scratched at her palm. She kicked the empty toolbox and went to Catherine's wardrobe. She was surprised to find so little inside, it was like Catherine was a lodger who hadn't committed to a new place. She turned a pair of high suede boots in her hand, but they had long been ruined with rain and mud.

Losing hope, she opened the little linen cupboard that held the good towels. There, folded away in a bin bag, was the old-fashioned mink coat she had bought on Brendan McGowan's good tick. She took the plastic bag out of the cupboard and pushed her hand inside to the furry pelt. It felt like pure money.

Within the hour she had her hair set, the long mink coat on, and was walking up the main road the long miles to Paddy's Market. She walked against the traffic, her head high, with a knowing smile on her face. The Pit grit pushed into her open heels as if it were beach sand. She straightened her back to look like she enjoyed letting the rush-ing traffic blow through her hair and tried to ignore the fine dust that rasped between her toes. Passing cars slowed at the odd sight. Her face burned with the flying grit and the shame, but she tilted her head back and walked on. She felt like she must have looked mental.

Every time she neared a bus stop she lingered like she was waiting for a bus, making a grand gesture of looking up her sleeve at a watch she did not own. Then she waited until the traffic thinned a little and walked on to the next one, her head thumping, her heart burning. Four miles or so from the scheme, a bus slowed and actually stopped for her. Looking the other way she took one hand from her mink pocket and waved it away, like she was too good, as miners' wives gawped out the window at her.

By the time she reached the outskirts of the city it had started to spit. It was a light sprinkle at first that hung on the tips of the coat and glistened like hairspray. Agnes was exhausted from walking in the high heels, but as she crossed the narrow streets of her first marriage, the fear that she could meet someone she knew made her walk faster. The spit became a downpour and soon the drenched coat slapped off her bare legs like a wet dog tail. She took refuge in a tenement doorway and watched the buses push dirty waves on to the pavement. For a moment, she missed the good Catholic.

Black mascara ran down her cheeks. She had a crumpled wad of toilet paper, and folding the sour boak stains into the back she wiped the lines beneath her eyes. The coat was sodden and matted in places where the water had pooled and sat. She took an ornament out of each pocket and rubbed the glass faces of the ballerinas till they were dry.

Across the road sat a long grey building. On the left hand was a taxi garage of sorts, where parts of broken black hacks and minibuses lay around like dinosaur bones, and somewhere in the back a radio played. Beyond this sat a small office, and through the dirty window Agnes could see that the walls were lined with new fan belts and hubcaps, tins of grease, and bottles of engine oil. It was a heavy service garage, not for the casual motorist. There were no packaged sandwiches, no maps of things to see.

A little bell rang as Agnes went inside. She was making a puddle on the floor as a man in overalls came through at the bell's command.

Red-haired, stocky, and flat-faced, his head joined directly to his body as if a neck were an unnecessary luxury. He looked up from his dirty hands, surprised to see a beautiful lady in a fur coat standing there.

"I'm really very sorry to bother you," started Agnes, in her best Milngavie accent. "But I got caught in the rain and I wondered if you had a toilet I may use. *You know*. To tidy up a little." She pointed at the wet coat.

"Well . . ." He rubbed his stubble. "It's no really for customers."

Agnes pulled at the coat; it shook big globs of water. "Oh, right," she said, her eyes falling to the dirty floor.

He studied her for a minute and with a scratch of his thick arm declared, "Well, ye dinnae look like a customer either, so ah suppose that mibbe it wid be alright."

He led her through the garage. Taxis lay in states of disrepair, leaking motor oil that made the floor difficult to walk on in heels. She watched the coat drip on to the greasy cement and the water bead and run away like little tears.

"Um, wait there just a minute," said the man. He darted nervously inside a thin red door. She heard the *rrshhhh* noise of canned air freshener, and he appeared a minute later with rolls of magazines and newspapers under his arm. "It's a bit basic, but ye'll find all ye need." As he held the door, a blonde with big tits peeped out with a saucy wink from under his arm.

Agnes went into the filthy bathroom and closed the door tight. She stood for a long while looking at the melted old hoor in the mirror. In the toilet there was no automatic dryer, so she took a handful of paper towels and started grabbing fistfuls of the wet coat, pressing the towel into it like she had spilt something on a carpet. As much as she could grab and squeeze, the coat kept giving out more and more rainwater.

It took her a long time before she felt composed enough to step back out into the garage. The man was right outside the door, frozen to the spot, with two mismatched mugs. "You looked like ye could use a warm cup of tea."

"Do I look that bad?"

"Oh, naw."

She took the mug; it was only slightly oily. "I must look like a drowned rat," she said, in the hopes he would disagree.

"Drowned mink, really."

As the man looked around for a clean seat, Agnes studied him closely. He had washed his face since she came in. There was a ring of oil round his neck and sideburns where the cloth had missed, and the front of his fair hair was still wet against his pink face. He was hand-some, she thought, in a solid, Shetland pony sort of way. He pulled out a bar stool, and she noticed his left hand had only two fingers and a thumb, the other two gone like he had chewed them down when he was nervous.

He met her eyes and moved the hand behind his back. "It's a long story."

Agnes cringed, embarrassed to have been caught staring. "We've all got a couple of them."

"Missing fingers?"

"No," she laughed. "Long stories."

"Like how youse are off to pawn that coat?"

She laughed again, too sharply this time, and then she stopped. He wasn't laughing with her now. She brought that Milngavie voice out again, the one that said, *I am a woman with a rich man and a big house*. "I am not off to pawn this coat. What on earth gives you that idea?"

Without hesitation the man said, "Oh, ah'll gie ye one better. Ye're off to pawn that coat, ye've walked here aw the way frae Ballieston or Rutherglen." He looked off to the side. "No, wait! There's a pawnshop in Rutherglen." He went quiet for a minute. "You've walked here from . . ." he snapped the fingers of his good hand. "Pithead!"

Agnes blanched.

"Am ah right?"

"No."

He paused for a minute and looked at her over the top of his cracked mug. "God, ah'm sorry, Missus. Ah mean, how fuckin' rude of me. Ah thought ye were off to pawn that coat. Ye know, for drink money like."

Agnes lowered the mug from her cold lips. Her eyes found his. "Well, you're wrong."

"Aye, well now, is that right?"

"Yes."

"Well, that's for the best then, int'it?"

"Why?" she asked, despite herself.

"Cos the Gallowgate pawnshop is shut for gasworks, that's why." She scowled at him to see his bluff. He only raised an eyebrow. "Look, ah wisnae trying to be rude. Honest Injun. It's just that it takes *one* to know *one*, eh?" He held up his bad hand in testimony and wiggled his two good fingers.

Agnes sat the mug down with a slosh. "Thank you for letting me use your toilet, but really I'd better go. My husband will be worried sick."

"Aye, ye do that. It's a long walk home in the rain. Still, mibbe ye'll find that wedding ring ye've lost."

Agnes had gone right off of him. She lifted her head high and pushed her black curls away from her face. "What do you want with all this?"

He turned his mouth down in disappointment. "Nothing. Well, not what *youse* think anyway. Look, Missus, ye just came in here in a right sorry state, and from the look o' ye, there was a thing or two ah could easy tell." He slowed himself slightly. "Ah could tell because ah'd been through it maself, that's all. Don't get your knickers in a knot. Finish your tea, won't ye? Ah used a new teabag for that cup and everything."

Agnes took up the tea again, using it to hide her shock, to fill the silence, to stop the bubbling inside her gut.

"So, have ye been to the AA yet?"

Agnes stared at him blankly.

"Alcoholics Anonymous?" He started singing, "*Wan day at a time, sweet Jee-sus*?" Agnes shook her head.

"Well, are ye at least willing to admit ye have a problem?" He tilted his head like a tired schoolteacher. "Ye came in here wi' the level-five shakes."

"I . . . I was wet . . . and cold."

He laughed. "Look, when ye are wet or cold yer knees knock and yer teeth chatter. Ye know, like *this*." He made a cartoon impression of a frozen lunatic. "BUT! When ye are scratching around looking for a bottle of lighter fluid to drink, ye shake like *this*." The man shook like a reanimated corpse.

The shame rose in her again. "What would you know about it?"

"Ah know that yon mink will only get you about six bottles of vodka and mibbe a hot fish supper." He picked at his teeth. "Well, at least my mammy's did when I robbed it off of her. I also know that six bottles of vodka, a fish supper, and three nights spent sleeping in the gutter will gie ye septicaemia." He waggled his half fingers again.

They were quiet for a while after that. He opened a packet of cigarettes, and after taking one from the pack with his teeth, he offered the pack to Agnes. Agnes lit the cigarette and drew on it like she was famished. Her shoulders fell, and catching her breath she gazed around at the black hack graveyard. "Do you know a taxi driver named Shug Bain, by any chance?"

"Cannae say that ah do," said the man, studying her face.

"He's a short, fat, balding pig. Fancies himself as a Casanova."

"That could be any one of them," he laughed. "What rank is he wi'?"

"Northside."

"Naw, they put their motors in at yon garage on the Red Road. Probably never met him."

"Well, if you ever meet him could you fix his brakes?"

The man smiled. "For you, beautiful, *absolutely*."

The man finished his cigarette and went on studying Agnes. "He's no the reason you're headed down the plughole, is he?" Agnes didn't answer. He began to howl meanly: "Ah-ha, ya daft eejit. Doin' yersel in for a man."

Her shoulders pulled up proudly again. "What if I am?"

"Do ye know what to do, if ye *really* want to get yer own back?" He paused.

So like a man, she thought, to have an opinion on everything. "What?"

"It's quite easy. Ye should just get the fuck on with it." He slapped his hands and threw them open in a wide *tah-dah* gesture. "Get on wi' yer fuckin' life. Have a great life. Ah promise that nothing would piss the pig-faced baldy bastard off more. *Guar-rant-teed*."

Twelve

In the end, Catherine twisted Shuggie's wrist and dragged him down Renfield Street. The boy had stopped at nearly every corner to silently lodge a protest about how much he didn't want to go. Without a word he would stand on his laces, and with a sleekit eye on her face he would gently let the knot unravel.

"You are bloody doing that on purpose!" seethed Catherine, bending to retie the school shoes for the fourth time in ten minutes.

"Am not," said Shuggie with a satisfied smile. He took one of his mother's romance novels out of his anorak pocket, and opening it, he rested it on the top of Catherine's head as if she were a hallway table. He started to read. Catherine stood up and snatched the book from him, an angry devil boiling inside her, and she lashed the thick book across the back of her brother's legs. She seized him by the wrist again. "If we miss this bus there won't be another for ages, and when you start complaining, '*I'm Hun-gry, I'm Thir-sty, I'm Ti-red . . .*'" She mimicked his whine. "Well, you needn't think I'm going to take pity."

"I don't sound like that," huffed Shuggie, his legs windmilling to keep up with his sister's stride. He twisted his arm from her grasp. She halted and spun her brother to face her. "Shuggie. I thought we were to be pals. You and me." Her face didn't look very friendly.

He huffed, "I don't want to be *your* friend."

She cupped his chin and turned his head gently back to face her; his eyes followed reluctantly. She ran her fingers through his neat parting and separated the thick black hair the way Agnes liked. The boy had grown so much over the past two years in Pithead. It was hard to describe, he had grown taller but he had also sunk somehow, like bread dough stretched much too thin. She could see he had slid deeper into himself and become more watchful and guarded. He was nearly eight now, and often he could seem so much older.

"Now when we get there I want you on your best behaviour." Catherine smiled a polite hello to an older couple passing in colourful rain cagoules. "Please, do this for me? I'm caught in the middle of a big, big mess, and I'm only asking for a little help." She looked at his small face, his lips pursed, he looked like a stubborn old wummin. She let her hands fall defeated to her side. "OK, you win. As always. But I want you to know that if you *do* tell Mammy where I took you today, she will *die*. Do you hear me? Die!"

Under sullen lids, his eyes swung back to meet her face. "How?"

"Shuggie, if you tell her she will take more and more drink, and she won't ever be able to stop." Catherine stood up and unclipped her coin purse; it was cognac-coloured with a painted camel and had been given to her mother by Wullie once. She counted out enough silver coins for two bus fares. "She will drink so much she will wash all the goodness out of her heart. *T'chut.* If she does that, I don't think Leek will ever speak to you again." She closed the old leather purse shut with a satisfied click, and her face brightened. "Oh, look! Here comes the bus."

They sucked on soor plooms and pressed their noses against the front window of the top deck. The bus swung across the river, and Catherine pointed at the bones of the Clyde, the cranes that were out of work for good. She told him about how Donald Jnr had been let go from the shipbuilders, how he wanted to go to Africa for work.

"Say a prayer for me, Shuggie . . ." she pleaded.

"I have a long list. I will add you," he lisped, his cheek bloated with the sour sweetie.

Catherine could believe her brother had been praying his very hardest for lots of things. She picked the raw skin around her thumb and worried again that she was doing the wrong thing. Since Shug had left her mother, she had told herself that it was not her fault. It rarely worked, but the selfish part of her would not be dissuaded. It wasn't fair: just because her mother had lost her man, why should she give up hers?

When they got off the bus, they passed rows of identical brown houses, all with fenced-in gardens in the front. None of the houses had any flowers. Catherine walked up a narrow path and through a heavy brown door without knocking. She stepped on to a stranger's hall carpet and waved at her brother to follow. Shuggie had never seen this house before; he was suddenly scared at how familiar it all was to Catherine.

The house was warm, like there were plenty of coins in the meter, and it smelled rich and sweet with the scent of roasted potatoes and meat gravy. Catherine sat on the carpeted stairs that ran to a second floor. She unzipped his anorak and hung it on the banister. Shuggie could hear televisions roar different channels from different rooms. The Old Firm match was on in the front parlour, and cartoons were honking and tweeting from somewhere upstairs. Catherine fixed his tie and kissed his cold cheek. "Best behaviour, right?"

She led him through to the back of the house, where a warm dining room was connected by a serving hatch to a thin kitchenette. As they came in, six or seven adults Shuggie didn't know turned at once and smiled. Catherine dropped her brother's hand and went to a man who looked like Donny Osmond. She kissed him lightly on the mouth.

"We were wondering where you had gotten to," said the man, rubbing the back of his fingers gently over her cold cheeks.

"*You* should try dragging him through a packed town centre." She turned to her brother, who was standing in the doorway. "Shuggie, don't just stand there, come over here and say hello to your Uncle Rascal."

Shuggie stepped into the dining room, the heat and the smell of roast ham made him feel light-headed. He wrapped one arm around

Catherine's legs as she introduced him to the adults who were huddled around a sliding door, smoking cigarettes and making a great show of blowing smoke carefully out into the back garden. He didn't recall most of their names as soon as they were said. She turned him towards an armchair in the corner. "This is your Uncle Rascal." She gave the boy a light push. Shuggie held out a polite hand and shook the man's paw.

So vague was his memory of his father that for a moment he thought the man could be him. There were the same ruddy flushed cheeks and a thick, manicured half-moon of a moustache. The man looked like a photo Shuggie had seen once, hidden underneath his mother's underthings in a drawer, but instead this man still had a thick head of hair, which was dyed a gravy brown but real and thick and all his own. Rascal pumped the boy's arm till it hurt. "Been too long, wee man! Terrible situation that it is." The man smiled. There were happy stars in his eyes.

Catherine introduced him to the Donny Osmond who had kissed her. "This is Donald. You remember, don't you? Well, Donald and I are getting married."

The boy glanced up at her. "Will I get cake?"

The man stepped forward and shook Shuggie's hand. He looked like he had brushed his brown hair from the underside, so that it curved like the cap on a shiny button mushroom. He was pink and thick and friendly-looking. He pumped the boy's hand too. "I *see* it. I can. I can see the resemblance now," he roared.

"I'm sorry there are no more big boats for you to hammer," said Shuggie earnestly.

"No bother, wee man," said Donald. "Will you come visit us when we live in Africa?"

Catherine scowled at Donald as she lifted her brother and nearly pushed him whole through the serving hatch into the kitchenette. There was a mess of bubbling pots, and a deep-fat fryer full of roast pota-toes was crackling in the corner. Catherine introduced him to Donald's mother, his Auntie Peggy. Everything about her was small and pointed, from the happy corners of her eyes to the pink tips of her ears. Catherine whispered into Shuggie's ear, and the boy repeated: "Thank you. For. Having me. To dinner. Auntie. Peggy."

"So, where is he?" asked Catherine, lowering her brother. "I've lied and lied and dragged this boy through the town for him. Are you to tell me he's not showed up?"

Shuggie felt a flick on the back of his bare neck, a thick flat fingernail welt like the ones Gerbil McAvennie gave when Father Barry was not looking. "Oww!"

"Don't stand there with your back to me, son." The man in the black suit filled the doorway, not in height but in breadth. Shuggie eyed him with caution. There again was the thick moustache and the quick eyes from the photograph. This man was flushed-looking, his head pink and scrubbed clean under long thin strands of brown hair that were combed over the top. His nose was small and delicate, not like the Campbell bone, and his brows were straight and dark and hid the darting of his clear eyes. Shuggie watched him and wanted to touch his own face, to feel it and see whether he had the same rosy round cheeks, the same thick hair on his lip.

Behind the man was a woman, waiting to be introduced, her hands clasped demurely across her front. Shug twisted the ring on his pinkie finger. "Are you not going to give your old man a hug?"

Shuggie had not seen his father in a long time. Anytime Shug had come to the Pit he had made sure the children were in bed first. Shuggie held on to his sister's leg. Catherine spoke for her brother. "Shug, he's shy. And no wonder with you flicking at the wean like that."

"It's the Bain code. Hit them afore they hit you." He crouched, and Shuggie could hear the heavy swing and clash of many silver coins in his pocket. "I like your tie, very dashing. Are you breaking hearts yet and taking after your old man?" There was movement behind him as the woman who had been waiting came through.

"I swear, travelling on an Old Firm day is a bad idea," the woman said. She was worn-out looking, the sides of her eyes puckered as she pulled a tight, reluctant smile. She was shorter than his father, which made her very short. Her hair was clipped close to her head, and Shuggie could see the grey untended roots throughout. She wore a simple V-neck jumper with a large Pringle lion on the chest, and under that she wore a pair of women's trousers. She looked like one of the dinner ladies at school when they smoked by the bins after lunchtime.

Catherine stepped forward without a smile. "It's nice to meet you, Joanie." She didn't look like she meant it. They shook hands, then collided in a clumsy, nervous embrace.

Shuggie's head nearly snapped on his neck, and his lips must have been hanging open because Catherine pulled her *quit it* face. His father, still crouched, never took his eyes from his son's and was smiling like he was enjoying himself. Shuggie pulled on Catherine's blouse. She leaned over, and he cupped a hand over her ear. "*Caff, that's bad Joanie. You are not supposed to like her. That's the hoor who stole my daddy.*"

"Say hello to your new mother," baited Shug, still grinning. "Go on, give your new mammy a hug."

"No. Some of us know what side our bread is buttered on," said Shuggie, leaving the safety of the traitor's leg. He didn't know where he had heard that before, probably from her, screaming at her phone table.

"*Pfft*. You're gonnae need a new mammy, Shuggie. That old one you've got is for the knacker's yard." Shug stood up with a click of the knee and a wince. "Or the Eastern Hotel, more like."

Joanie waved a small hello to the boy. She held out a paper shopping bag. "You never mind him, son. Sometimes I swear his heart is as empty as a Fenian's cupboard on a Thursday." She came forward with the shopping bag, it looked very heavy. "Listen, you don't have to call me anything but Joanie." She peered into the bag. "Our Stephanie has outgrown these, but they are so new-looking I hadn't the heart to throw them out. Would you like them?"

He shook his head no, but his lips said, "What are they?"

She came closer and set the bag between them like she was feeding a cautious beast. Then Joanie the Hoor took two steps back. "Ye'll just have to look and see."

His father came out of the kitchenette with a tall glass of milk, there was already a rich line of cream on his bristles. He leaned against the wall and watched the boy hug the safety of the corner. Shuggie wanted to step away from the bag, wanted to pretend like he wasn't interested, but it was calling to him, and he found himself stepping towards it. He tapped the bottom of the bag with his toe and it was heavy. He used a finger to push it open. At the bottom were eight bright yellow wheels. His eyes were wide as saucers as he took out the first roller boot.

"I still don't know why we couldn't have given him Andrew's old bladder fitba," said Shug to Joanie.

They were a bumblebee-yellow suede with white stripes and white laces. The laces were fed through a dozen holes, and the boots went up nearly to his knee. He loved them.

"What do you say to Joanie?" prodded Catherine.

He wanted to pretend he did not care. He wanted to put the boots back in the bag and tell Catherine that they had to leave. He felt like a traitor. He was no better than his sister.

Auntie Peggy's high voice came out of the kitchen hatch. "Shug. You'll never believe what the Prodigal has gone and done."

Shug smirked at his nephew and then smirked at Catherine in a way that made her want to fold her hands over her chest, over her belly.

Donald Jnr spoke first. "No! It's no *that*, Uncle Shug. I've got an offer of work, good high-paying work where I get to be lord and master over four dozen men."

Shug finished the last of his milk. "But I was looking forward to seeing you on that rank."

"You might see him on the Renfrew Street rank yet," said Catherine, as she helped Shuggie into the new boots. She turned her head, spoke to Donald Jnr over the small bones of her shoulder. "I have a career of my own, you know. I can't just up sticks and follow you around like a shadow."

Shug watched her try to master his nephew and laughed. "Donnie Boy! You thought you were on to a sure thing, but look how the Catholics are revolting."

Donald Jnr turned to his uncle. "It's a good job in the palladium mines. Out in Transvaal, I think it's called. They telt us they will take nearly all the Govan riveters, fly us out there, find us somewhere to live. Even give us a month in advance. *Yasssss! Soooth Efrika. Boyeee.*"

"Youse gonnae be a Kaffir master!" said Shug, his bottom lip stuck out in genuine pride.

"Don't use that horrible word in front of the boy," Catherine said. She helped her brother on to his feet and turned him towards the door. "Go play in the hall. Make sure and shut that door behind you." They watched him go, his arms stretched out for balance, his fingers splayed upwards like pretty bird wings. Shuggie pushed off each step into a gliding graceful swoosh, but each boot embedded soon enough into the deep pile carpet. They watched him clomp out into the hallway, his face split from ear to ear in a smile.

Shug sucked his teeth in disappointment. "I don't think that boy is mine."

Shuggie lowered his arms. He stopped gliding across the carpet. Suddenly he could feel just how heavy the old roller boots really were.

Shug turned to Catherine and asked, "What do ye think she'll say when she hears I've seen him?"

Catherine looked at Shuggie, she could see the scalding in his cheeks. "*Oh no.* We can't ever say he's been here."

A mean smile broke over Shug's face. He spoke in the pushing voice that bullies in school used when they wanted to see a fight. "Go on. Let him tell her."

With a shove, Catherine closed the door between them. Shuggie could hear his father roar with laughter. He heard Catherine ask, "Why on earth did you ask me to bring him if you are going to be such a bloody bully?"

Shuggie spent the afternoon wearing lines in the hall carpet, trying as hard as he could to ruin it. He listened to the adults fight about something he thought was called Joanna's Bird that lived in the south of Africa. He heard Catherine say she would be settled there by Christmas. He wondered what black people were like and why they needed Donald Jnr to make them work better. He wondered why his big sister had to go off and leave him.

Thirteen

The black slag hills stretched for miles like the waves of a petrified sea. The coke dust left a thin grey coating across Leek's face. It hollowed out his already gaunt features, outlining the thick horse bone of his nose, and darkened the fine hairs of his scant moustache. His feathered fringe had stopped bouncing up and down and lay heavy and grey against his forehead. He looked like a man made of graphite, like one of his own black-and-white drawings.

It was slow-going, climbing up the crumbling black hill. It sucked at his feet and with every step it ate him nearly to his knees. The fine jet dust found every opening and filled every space. It poured over the top of his slip-on loafers, their braided tassels swinging up clouds of black like the tail of a dirty cow. On the downward slope the loose slag raged after him like a hungry wave. Although there was nothing to him, his hollowness still brought the crust of the hill pouring down. The slag shrugged as though it were turning itself inside out, clearing him off and revealing a darker, untouched blackness beneath. Each time the hills wiped him away he felt more unnoticed, more like an unseen ghost than usual.

Crossing the black sea was best when it wasn't windy or wet. When the wind licked the dry hills they took to the air like the inside of a burst Etch A Sketch, like the lead dust from a million shaved pencils. If it caught in his mouth, he could taste it for days. When it rained over the colliery, the hills felt tired and beaten. They solidified, as if they had given up and died.

Leek climbed to the top of the highest bing and sat down. He lit a short doubt and looked out over the dead colliery and the dying scheme that lay beyond. Like a diorama, it sat orderly and uniform in the peaty marshland, the way a model maker's collection of toy houses sat on a balding brown carpet. Even from here Leek thought it looked petty and small.

He took his sketchbook from inside his anorak. His sooty fingers left smudges as he tried to capture the horizon with the broad side of a soft pencil. If the Pit scheme had been made by a model maker, then what a miser he must have been. Where were the miniature tin cars, the farm animals, or the green fluffy bushes that looked like spiny sea coral? Leek watched the black-jacketed figures loitering around the men's club and wondered whether the model maker didn't like colourful, happily painted figurines.

He looked out over the scene, past the pipe-cleaner trees and the carpet of dead marsh. The Glasgow to Edinburgh train seemed like a toy in the distance as it charged through the wasteland that separated the miners from the world. It created an unseen boundary, and it never ever stopped. Years ago the council had ripped out the only station, for big savings in stationmaster wages. They laid on a single bus that came three times a day and took an hour to get anywhere.

Now, in the evenings, the eldest of the miners' sons stood at the train tracks with beers and bags of glue and watched with sadness and spite the happy faces roar by every thirty minutes. They fondled their cousins' tits under baggy Aran jumpers and ran across the tracks in front of the speeding train, their soft hair whipped by the near miss. They threw bottles of piss at the windows, and when the driver let fly his angry horn, they felt seen by the world, they felt alive.

Since the colliery had closed they had taken to laying branches across the tracks, thick brown limbs that they had to bounce up and down on to rip from the dying trees. When the trains severed them easily, the boys left stones and then later red builder's bricks. A boy not much older than Shuggie had lost an eye from the flying, sparking rocks. So instead, armed with cans of lighter gas meant for sniffing, they started to set fires in the reeds. Leek had watched as they set the brown marsh on either side of the tracks ablaze. Still the Glasgow trains would not stop.

Leek scored his chewed pencil through the desolate view. He didn't realize it, sitting there alone, but while he drew his hunched shoulders fell from around his ears.

It was getting harder to get up in the mornings, to let the day in, to come back to his body and stop floating around behind his eyelids, where he was free. He was turning up later and later for his apprenticeship. The gaffer was giving up, Leek could see it. They floated by each other with equal disinterest.

At first the gaffer, a sinewy, pragmatic man, had given the well-practiced speeches. As the apprenticeship went on, and Leek kept staring through him, the speeches slowly filled with bitter bile. Leek nodded like a metronome through the spit-stained lecture on how his generation was ruining the country. The gaffer, fair frothing at the mouth, reached out and pushed Leek's fringe away with a rough palm. The young man's eyes were empty as two dull marbles. The man had seen it all in his thirty years in the building trade: generations of weans dragged in on government schemes, lazy and disinterested or mouthy and fly. Over time they would break and fall into their place, grow up into men who got lassies into bother and needed the steady wage. In all his years he'd never met a soul like this boy before.

Angry, the gaffer drew his short pencil from behind his ear and with a set jaw stabbed it a half inch from Leek's face. Leek never flinched, he'd practiced that for Agnes. He locked the door that lay behind his eyes and walked away, leaving the body, the plaster dust, the flask of cold tea, and the angry gaffer behind.

The gaffer might have let him go, but this was a YTS, and as long as Thatcher was subsidising his wages the man would let him stay on.

They would always need a tea maker. The older joiners took to sending Leek to the store for tartan paint. They made him check boxes of half-inch nails and sort them into ascending sizes. Leek just shrugged his shoulders to their laughter and went on his way, happy to be losing his body in their monotonous, fruitless tasks, his mind floating free about the world.

Now, in the silence, he turned the pages of the sketchbook and drew two envelopes from the back leaf. The first envelope was a thin, colourful airmail letter, neat sky-blue paper that folded on itself, and was sent with a row of springbok stamps from Catherine in Transvaal. He turned it in his hands and wished it didn't make him so heartsick to read it. He wished her excitement for patio furniture and biltong sausages didn't make him feel so much like a discarded thing, something so easily left behind.

Still, Leek thought this new sadness was better than the anger he had felt at first. Sadness made for a better houseguest; at least it was quiet, reliable, consistent. When Catherine had first married Donald Jnr, they had all been angry. Agnes, soaked through with vodka, had dragged Catherine's mattress out to the kerb. She had managed it single-handedly, and the boys could only stand back as the last of their sister was set amongst the black bags.

Leek took up the second letter. It was dirty now, creased at the corners from hours spent reading and rereading. The envelope was a thick cream paper, mottled, like expensive watercolour stock. Someone had written his name in black calligrapher's ink, *Mr Alexander Bain*, taking the effort to level it off with a neat ruler line. Leek opened the envelope and unfolded the typed letter. The paper snapped with quality. His dirty fingers traced the familiar crest at the top of the page; he could have read it with his eyes closed.

Dear Mr Bain,
I am pleased to inform you that after careful review of your application and your portfolio we are happy to offer you an unconditional place on the BA (Hons) Fine Art course . . .

Leek folded the letter and slid it carefully back into the envelope. He knew it said that they would send him more information, that he had to contact the registrar of the fine-art course to accept the coveted space. He knew it said he should start in September. But that was already a September two years ago. He thought back to the time when he had received the letter. He saw Shug leave. He saw Catherine watch the door and his funny little brother, hungry and fearful, while his mother sat with her head in the gas oven.

It was cold and quiet on the petrified sea; that was why he liked it. Lost in his daydream, he ignored the sound at first, until it got closer and grew more insistent, the horrible farting of sucking wellies. Shuggie appeared, red and flushed, on the crest of the slag bing. The usual creamy colours of him were muted by a layer of dust, but there were wet pink circles around his eyes and mouth. Leek hid the letter in the sketchbook and carefully tucked it all back inside his jerkin.

"I asked you to wait!" moaned Shuggie. His bottom lip was a pink bubble in the grey dirt.

"If you cannae keep up, then don't ask to come." He felt sure they'd had this conversation before; he felt like they were always having it. Leek stood up and took off again. He looked like a daddy-long-legs trying to glide on the surface of inky black water, his blue nylon anorak as shiny as the shell of a beetle. He tried to lose his little brother by bolting down the steep sides in large jumps. He had hoped the boy would stop and turn for home. Still Shuggie kept on.

Leek listened to his brother panting like an asthmatic at his back, it was breaking his peace. He should have told him that he couldn't come, but his brother was a notorious grass. Shuggie had learned this skill well but was clumsy at using it. He would spill the worst information for the littlest reward, and he almost always went too far. Agnes, when provoked, could chase Leek round the house with a heavy Dr Scholl's sandal; the flat rubber sole left purple welts floating in red slap marks, which got Shuggie grinning like butter wouldn't melt.

Leek had wondered why his mother even cared if he wandered the dead mine. He was sure it wasn't the danger of the slag or the bottomless black water in the old quarry. It was the dust that bothered Agnes. It was what the neighbours must think when they saw him come back covered in soot and dirt. How she could no longer pretend that she was nothing like them, that she was better born and stuck only temporarily in their forgotten corner of misery. It was pride, not danger, that made her so angry.

With a flick of his loafer Leek sent a shower of slag backwards and listened to the small cough and whine. Shuggie made a growling sound like an angry badger, and Leek laughed and resolved to make him do it again on the way back home.

Leek galloped down the last of the hills and waited for his brother at the bottom. The tide of slag moved like a landslide. Shuggie took large windmilling leaps, and on his second or third step the slag suddenly solidified. His legs moved too fast, and with a sharp shriek he pitched forward on to his front and slid the rest of the way on his face. He came to a rasping stop, and the slag rose silently around him, swallowing him like a hungry grave. Leek reached down and with one hand lifted the boy clear of the coal by the strap on his backpack. A small black face with two white eyes blinked up at him in confusion and fear.

Leek couldn't help but laugh. "What have I told you? You have to take it lighter on the way down, else you'll set the whole side of the fucking thing moving."

"I know, but it starts sliding and I get a fright that I might get buried." Shuggie shook the slag from his black hair. "Mammy would burst you if I died."

Leek set the boy down. "Do you have to be so annoying? Why can't you just be normal for once."

The boy turned from his brother. "I am normal."

Leek thought he could see the pink rise on the back of Shuggie's neck. His shoulders shuddered with the start of tears. Leek spun his brother back around. "Don't turn away from me when I'm talking to you." Leek studied his face closely. It hadn't been rising tears; Leek knew the flush of shame and frustration well enough. "Are the kids at school *still* battering you?"

"No." He twisted free from Leek's grip. "*Sometimes.*"

"Don't let it bother you. They see the one thing that's a bit more special than them and then they just pile on."

Shuggie looked up. "I told Father Barry on them. I asked him to make it stop." Shuggie straightened the pleat on his trousers. "But he only made me stay behind after bell. He made me read about the persecuted saints."

Leek tried not to smirk. "What a useless old bastard. That's just the way of the Chapel: '*Stop complaining, it could be worse.*'" He kicked off his tasselled loafer and, bending over, emptied it of slag dust. "You know when I was at school they said there was a Father that was diddling this one quiet boy. Can you imagine that?" He lifted his eyes and met Shuggie's face. "Has he ever touched you, Shuggie? Father Barry, that is."

A cloud passed over Shuggie's face, dark enough to make Leek stop ridding himself of coal dust. "No," he said quietly. Then the words started tumbling out quicker than he could organize them. "But they said I did things to him. They said I did dirty things. But I never. I promise. I don't even know what those things are."

"I believe you, Shuggity. They are just bamming you up." Leek took his brother in his arms, and in a great crushing hug he mashed the boy's face into his ribs. "Anyhows, how old are you now?"

Shuggie didn't answer right away, he was happy to be suffocated. Then he spoke in a very considered tone, like he was reciting some fact in front of a dusty blackboard. "July sixteenth. Four twenty in the afternoon. You were a difficult birth, Leek, a *very* difficult birth."

"Fuck's sake!"

Shuggie buried his face deeper into Leek's side. "I just think we should know things like that about one another." Then he added sullenly, "Eight. I'm nearly eight and a half."

"Sakes! Why couldn't you just say *that*? Anyway, you're big enough. It's time you tried to blend in more. You have to try and be more like those other wee bams."

Shuggie turned his head and gasped for air. "I am trying, Leek. I try all the time. Those boys let their shirt tails hang out like they have no shame, and all they do is kick that stupid bladder about. I've even seen them put their fingers down the back of their trousers and then smell it. It's so . . . It's so . . ." He searched for the word. "*Common.*"

Leek let him go. "If you want to survive, you need to try harder, Shuggie."

"How?"

"Well, first, never say *common* again. Wee boys shouldn't talk like old women." Leek hauched a wad of phlegm. "And you should try to watch how you walk. Try not to be so swishy. It only puts a target on your back." Leek made a great pantomime of walking like Shuggie. His feet were pointed neatly outwards, his hips dipped and rolled, and the arms swung by his side like there was no solid bone in them. "Don't cross your legs when you walk. Try and make room for your cock." Leek grabbed at the bulge in the front of his corduroy and strode back and forth in a half strut, half lazy amble. "Don't bend your knees so much. Take longer, straighter steps."

Leek walked around in easy natural circles. Shuggie followed in his wake like a mimic. He was trying his hardest to hold his arms tight. It was hard to make it look natural.

They strutted like two cowboys across the flat upturned earth. On the face of the mine sat the main colliery building. As big as Glasgow Cathedral, the abandoned building sat like a lonely giant on the moon. Large broken windows were set in simple arches, too high for a view but high enough to catch all the day's light for the cavernous inside. The windows that remained intact were blacked out with coal dust. At the far end of the building a large smokestack towered into the sky, and on wet days you could barely see the top for the soaking clouds. Pipes and rods lay scattered on the ground, the hurried tearing of hacksaws visible in the ends, looters taking what they could strip before the mine was officially dismantled for scrap.

"I want you to wait here." Leek marked a cross in the dirt. He reached over his brother's head and, grabbing the handle of the backpack, spun him around. He unzipped the little zippers, and Shuggie buckled at the weight of him rooting through the bag. "You are to keep lookout, right? If you see anybody then come and get me right away." Leek drew bolt cutters and a crowbar from the backpack.

The little boy nodded, feeling lighter already. "Why have we got to do this anyway?"

"I've telt you a thousand times. I need to save money. I've got plans. I can't be a YTS apprentice forever."

"Am I in your plans?" asked Shuggie.

"Don't fuck about." He pointed to the colliery. "It's getting harder every time, cos there's less and less for the taking, so I might be gone awhile. Do you hear?" With a loud zip Leek closed the empty backpack and spun his brother back around. "Keep your eyes open." Leek slid into the darkness of the colliery building. Shuggie watched him cross the pools of dim daylight, and then he was gone into the dark corners of the coal cathedral.

For a while Shuggie drew in the dirt. The stour was deep and soft. He drew a horse and then he drew Agnes. He liked to draw curly hair. He drew it on everything. It looked cheerful.

Leek crossed to the very back of the building, intent on stripping the copper from the far wall where the cables met the lighting generator. Closed for less than three years, the mine was sealed and slowly being dismantled, the owners selling it for scrap. The miners and their eldest boys had been trying to beat them to it. The copper in the wires was worth its weight, so they stripped junction boxes, ripped up the cables, and gnawed it all bare like mice. Leek saw the rubber casings were already pulled from the wall and what lay on the floor was empty, like marrowless bones. He followed the cable outside to where the wires started to run underground towards the main shaft. A hundred feet from the back of the colliery building the cable stuck up in the air. The last salvager had pulled all he could and left it sprouting like a ruptured artery. Leek bent and with the sharp end of the crowbar began to break the hard dirt.

He was at it for an hour or so and lifted his head only when he could smell the house fires come on in the scheme. The smell of the burning coal told him it was getting late in the afternoon. They were safer back across the black sea before it got dark.

As he hacked and sawed he wished Shuggie was bigger, wasn't such a whiny runt, that way he could have carried more. The copper itself was heavy but the thick rubber casing was a killer. It wasn't clever to strip the wire there in the open face of the colliery. A couple of the younger Pithead boys had been caught stealing the copper and been done for it. It cost them more in fines than you'd make from stripping the whole Pit of its wiring.

Leek wrapped a disappointing length of rubber wire around himself several times like a climbing rope. Swinging his crowbar, he crossed the grey pools of light and emerged into the dark winter afternoon. He cheered himself with thoughts of the room he would rent one day, at the very top of Garnethill near the Mackintosh Art School, with the extra copper money he'd been setting aside. There was even enough for a wee bribe for his brother, the grass. He almost smiled as he stepped back into the daylight, but it was too quiet. The grass was gone.

Shuggie would have liked to have thrown stones. That was fun. Last time he had spent an hour trying to reach the high windows and finally put one in. It made a loud crashing sound in the silence. Leek came hurtling out of the darkness and leathered him for that.

Instead he was walking in wide circles, he stopped every so often to grab at the empty front of his trousers and kick his legs a little wider like a cowboy. He was deep in concentration, trying to imagine a normal body like Leek's, which hardly seemed to have any graceful or usable joints at all, when he finally saw the man. By the time he registered the danger, the strange man was running with plumes of slag dirt dancing at his heels. By the time Shuggie realized he should also run, the man was past the massive winding towers and almost on him.

Shuggie was supposed to warn Leek. He was supposed to keep watch and run into the colliery when the bogey was up. The man was coming down on him, and Shuggie looked at the darkness inside the building and he ran the other way.

The empty backpack danced from side to side as Shuggie bolted. He took the first hill at a run, attacking the side of it, sinking knee-deep, wellies farting indecently. By the time he reached the top he saw that the man was scaling the side of the hill in long strides like Leek did, digging each foot in and flying over the loose slag. Shuggie turned along the crest of the black dune and ran for his life. He could feel the stranger's determination, he could almost feel the man's hands on his legs. As he flew down the far side, the earth roared after him, and with a grainy splash he fell into the valley between two hills. The man appeared at the top. Shuggie watched him stand there against the darkening sky, his shoulders spread and fell, and his hands balled into frustrated fists.

Shuggie ran through the black valley, but the man followed like a kestrel on a mouse.

The slag hills were ending, only the hummocky peat fields lay beyond. The man could sail down the slag and catch him easily, so the boy ran faster, across the shale and weedy slag, past the point where the grass won the battle and the brown fields began. He stumbled through the weeds, listening for the flattening of grass behind him. But there were no more footsteps.

Shuggie reached a thick tuft of yellow grass and threw himself down in a heap. The man stood at the top of the last hill, his shoulders rising and falling as he cupped his hands to his mouth and hollered: "I'll get ye, ya wee thieving bastard!" Then he was gone.

Shuggie lay still in the clump of long weeds until he was sure the man was truly gone. He lay there so long that his front was wet through, as the peat happily released the damp from the last rain into his clothes, dead earth having no use for it. The slag sea lay between him and the scheme, and the man lay between him and home. What the man would do to him flowered in his imagination, a montage of cartoon bogeyman violence. Shuggie didn't want to be buried forever in the slag sea. He wanted to go home. The ground flushed warm as he pissed himself.

The winter afternoon was dying quickly, the sunless sky was a solid blanket of fleecy greys. Shuggie began walking around the slag hills, keeping to the fringe of marshland that encircled it. It was slow-going, and his legs were red raw from the indigo dye leaching from his trousers. He came to a wide crater in the ground, a sunken frying-pan-shaped stretch of dark grey mud that collapsed into the earth like the centre of an underbaked cake. The walk around the outside would take too long. If he could cut across the middle he would be home in no time. The dim glow of the scheme lay on the far side, warming the low-hanging clouds like a bedside lamp. Shuggie crudely blessed himself and climbed down into the crater.

The sunken ground was only ten or so feet below ground level, but the sides of the earth were steep, and as he slid down the slag he wondered if he would be able to climb back up. With a wet thud he landed at the bottom. From the safety of the crumbling edge he stretched his leg out and tapped the surface of the crater. It was wet and sticky, but like a slimy bar of soap it was more or less solid. He took one foot and tested it on the smooth surface. It held. He lifted it and looked at the wellie footprint, it lingered for a moment, and then like magic it disappeared.

Boldly he took a quick couple of steps on to the smooth surface, stopped, and ran back to the rocky edge. He watched the ghostly footsteps disappear. It was like he was being followed by his shadow, and here, fading in front of him, was the proof. A smile caught fire on his cold face, and for a moment he forgot about his chafing thighs. With airplane arms he made sweeping circular patterns in the wet grey mud and danced with his invisible ghost partner. He started to sing gently to himself.

To the far side it would take less than a minute at full wellie-boot run. With a jump he started out on the glassy mud. As he took quick little steps across the crater the red wellies made a *slap-slap*, *slaaap* sound, like a fat hand hitting a fat thigh. The footsteps bounced off the sides of the crater and echoed around the pit. It was the change in tone he noticed first.

It got slower. It got deeper. From a tight *slap-slap* the sound changed to a wet slurp, like the back of a spoon on cold porridge. By the halfway point he was getting tired. The mud started shifting and sucking at his wellies. As his knees were pumping higher, his legs were moving slower. His feet were being pulled free of the wellies. He spread his toes and gripped the rubber like a desperate claw.

In a sudden panic he veered off course. He was the length of four Leeks from the crumbling bank when he could no longer pull his foot from the hungry mud. He released himself from the wellies and jumped from the little red boots. Now barefoot, he realized how stupid he had been; the mud felt as wet as bathwater. He took two or three steps farther and stopped. He felt the mud sucking on his feet like a greedy mouth on an ice lolly. It started eating him again. He would not make it.

If he was to die, he would die in the boots. He thought only of her face when they found him without the wellies, and her Dr Scholl's sandal and the welt it would leave on his corpse. He struggled back to the red boots and stepped into them. Clutching the top of one, he tried to free himself, but as one leg moved higher it drove the other deeper into the wet mouth. The mud rose up to the buckle, well past his calf, almost to his knee. It started to soak his trousers. He watched it spill in over the top of his boots and felt it between his toes. He let go, finally, straightened up, and then, because he did not know what else to do, he started to sing again.

"*Ah buhlee that chi-hil-dren are our few-ture. Teach em we-e-ll and let em lead the-he way.*" Shuggie watched the coal mud fill the other boot, the chance to abandon the red wellies gone. "*Show em all the bew-ty they possess in-si-hide.*"

Louder now, he sang on, mimicking all the notes in the way he had heard on the radio. "*Ah decidet long aglow ne-er to wa-halk in anybody's sha-dow. If ah fail if ah suck seeds at least it been as ah buh-lee. No matter what youse tek from me. Youse ca-hant take away ma dihig-ni-tee.*"

There was a muffled voice in the dark. "The fuck? Haw you. Whitney Houston. Up here."

Shuggie hadn't seen the shadow on the edge of the crater; even now it was hard to pick out Leek against the coal-coloured sky. "What the fuck are you doing in there?"

Shuggie screwed his eyes shut. "*AAAAH, YOU BLOODY FANNY BALLS BASTARD SHITTY SHIT, HURRY UP! GET ME OUT OF HERE, YOU FUCKING FANNY FINGERER!*"

In the dark there was a scrabble of dirt and heavy feet on the wet mud.

"*FUCKING MOVE IT.*" He listened to feet strike the sucking slag. "*GET ME OUT OF HERE, YOU CUNT.*"

The wet slapping sound got closer, he heard a familiar sigh, as Leek started to swear under his breath. Leek grabbed his brother by the back-pack and with a grunt plucked him like a skinny garden weed. Shuggie felt himself pulled free of the mud and then plonked back down on its surface. Leek took hold of the back of Shuggie's anorak like a set of reins and dragged him towards solid ground.

"Aaah, no! Wait! NO!" They stopped short. Leek brought his face close to his brother's, peering in the gloaming to see what the new fuss was. "Leave me. *Leave me!*"

"Are you stupit or something?" Leek dragged him to the edge and cuffed him hard on his ear. He seemed angry at Shuggie. He seemed in a great hurry to be gone.

"I can't go home again," the boy flailed dramatically. "Not without my wellies. She'll kill me! She's still paying the catalogue."

"Jesus Christ!" Shuggie felt the hand relax on his hood as his brother slipped back into the crater. In the dark there was a grunt and the sound of frustrated tugging as the mud sucked and belched again. It was quiet for a moment, till he heard the slap-slapping of Leek's boots and felt the hand on his shirt neck again. Leek dragged Shuggie away from the crater, and only when Shuggie started to whine about the jagged rocks did Leek stop and let his brother put the wellies on. As Shuggie slowly put on his boots, he watched his brother pace with nerves, his eyes on the far horizon, peering back towards the colliery over the distance they had come. He seemed itchy with adrenaline.

"Hurry up!" Leek shook Shuggie by the shoulders, his long fingers meeting in the middle of his back. Shuggie blinked up at his brother. He noted for the first time how Leek's eyebrows had grown together in the centre. He found it oddly distracting and was going to say so.

But there was something wrong with Leek's voice; it was garbled and distorted. He was scaring Shuggie. There was a spray of darkening blood on Leek's face, sticky as syrup. The side of his left eye was blackening into a bruise that looked like a deep hollow in the gloaming light, and his bottom lip was swollen and split. Leek rubbed at his jaw like it was very sore. He put his hand inside his mouth and took out his bottom set of dentures with a pained wince. There was a tooth missing, another one was cracked, and the pink ceramic plate was split clean in two, like someone had struck him hard in the jaw.

"Are you OK?"

"*Fuuu-uck*," moaned Leek. "I told you to keep a fuckin' lookout. You were supposed to warn us about that watchie." There was no skin on his knuckles as he rubbed at his jaw. His eyes shone scared in the dark. "I hurt him bad, Shuggie. I had to. This is all your fault."

Leek put the cracked ceramic in his pocket, and Shuggie saw now he had no copper cable, no crowbar in his hands. Leek started them at a jog and kept checking as though they were being followed. Shuggie's boots were not on correctly, his damp socks bunched between his toes and rubbed the skin from his foot, but he dared not ask his brother to slow down.

When they reached the edge of the scheme they were both grateful for the safety of the sickly orange street lights. When Leek spoke without his bottom teeth, his face half-collapsed. It was hard to understand the soft, mushed words, but Shuggie could read the fear and disappointment in his eyes clearly enough.

Fourteen

Leek never went scrapping for copper again. The Pit watchie was hospitalized, his skull cracked open by Leek's crowbar, his mind scattered like a pile of dropped playing cards. The polis went door to door, looking for the young man who had done it. When they came to their door, Agnes made them wait on the bottom step. She fiddled with her gaudy bauble of an earring, did not need to feign annoyance, and huffed like they were insulting her by darkening her door. She turned them away easily, and never before had Leek been so grateful that his mother kept herself immaculate.

Agnes never even asked Leek if he had done it. It never even crossed her mind. Bridie Donnelly had stood smoking by the fence post while the polis went up and down the street. She only seemed surprised it wasn't one of her own brood. Bridie said it was the best thing that could have happened to the watchman's family. His security contract would have been ending soon, and now he was guaranteed disability for life. She said he had never been a big talker anyway.

All that winter and right through the spring thaw, Leek's teeth hurt him. The National Health Service was slow to replace them, and so he wore the cracked bridge only when he was outdoors, keeping his mouth clenched shut because the dentures slipped free any time he spoke. At home he did without and sloped about the house with the overbite of a cartoon turtle. When he saw Shuggie he sat on him and pinched his skin till it came out in welts. Shuggie felt it was owed and did his best not to cry out.

When the NHS finally replaced the false teeth, Leek's bite struck the top set at an odd angle and the ceramic plate pinched at the back and brought his gum out in raw sores. Like an apostle, Shuggie followed him with slices of white bread. He tore off a small hunk, balled it to a pillowy mush, and handed it to Leek to put under the ceramic and sooth the blisters. Shuggie carried bread in his pocket for Leek up until the summer. Many times, when Agnes washed his school trousers, she would find a forgotten slice of pan loaf, stiff and blue with mould.

It turned to the summer holidays, and the road was hoaching with McAvennie children and their cousins and their cousins' cousins. They were making the most of the two weeks of good west-coast weather, bouncing footballs off kerbs or riding bikes and screaming as they sent great mouse-coloured clouds of slag dust into the air.

Shuggie wilted away from them.

He felt something was wrong. Something inside him felt put together incorrectly. It was like they could all see it, but he was the only one who could not say what it was. It was just different, and so it was just wrong.

He loped into the shadows of the house and clambered under the chain-link fence, out into the peat marshes that ringed the scheme. He walked away from the council houses a good while. The rare sun beat down on his back, and through his thick jumper, his skin started to feel prickly from the heat. Turning off the flattened path, he crushed a new road through the tall reeds. He stomped around in circles until he trampled a large oval section completely flat. The dead grass made a thick brown carpet. Shuggie slipped off the heavy wellies and began to practice as Leek had shown him.

He stood at one edge of the circle and walked to the other side. The first crossing was a quick nipped walk, short sharp steps with swinging arms. In frustration, he dug his clean fingernails into the palms of his hands and turned around and started again. He took slower, more deliberate steps, made room for his cock, swung his feet out, and pressed each heel firmly into the soft earth. Shuggie took off the wool jumper and wiped the sweat from his forehead. He scolded himself, turned around, and did it again.

He did this back and forth all afternoon, each time willing himself to go slower, to stop swinging his arms so expressively, and to be more like Leek, like a real boy. It came so naturally to those boys, without any thought, without any apology.

Agnes sat upright in the chair by the window and watched the street. Packs of weans roamed at play, but Shuggie was not amongst them. At half past ten her house and her make-up were already done, and although she wasn't leaving the house she put on her low-cut jumper and a fitted grey skirt. She sat drinking the dregs of old lager and wondering where exactly her boy was hiding from his childhood.

From boredom, she picked white flecks of sock oose off the arm of the chair; she made a neat pile in a square of toilet paper and then folded it and put in her pocket. It made her sore that she was still paying for this old three-piece suite and her boys wouldn't respect it. She would bleed five pounds a week for the next eight years to pay for it, and they sat on it upside down and sideways, shoes off and shoes on.

The broken gate across the street opened, and she sat up. The ragged bunch of McAvennies began wheeling salvaged bikes out into the dust. They were beautiful children, she had to admit. The slovenly ways of their mother made them look like little wild lions. Their long hair was thick and animal-like, and their eyes the beautiful gypsy brown of their father's.

She had taken the middle girl once. She hadn't intended to, but she had been washing the windows in vinegar water and she couldn't concentrate. The children had been playing in the street, in the dip of the road where the stour collected. She couldn't enjoy cleaning her windows while watching them sat in the filth there. She beckoned the one they called Dirty Mouse over and lured her around the back of the house by giving her half of an apple. For an hour or so she ran a hard-backed brush through the wild tangles of the girl's hair and carefully cut the knots and dreadlocks from the nape of her neck. When she was done, Agnes was surprised to see how straight it was, how shiny and silken, the colour of caramel and tabby cats. Together they did it up in a neat ponytail, then in braids, in French knots, and then in big French plaits like the ones Catherine used to wear to school. It was a lovely afternoon.

Colleen had done the nut when she found out. She was screaming at the top of her lungs before she had even left her house. She crossed the road like a coming storm and rapped hard on Agnes's door, screaming, *"Who in the name do ye think ye are? Parading around here like ye are the big* I Am. *Ye should focus yersel on that poofy wee boy of yers."*

Then there was wild spitting. But Agnes, numbed with lager, didn't blink an eye. She turned the hard brush over and patted it reassuringly against her leg. *Keep it up*, she thought, *and you'll see how well I can use the back of a brush as well.*

Some days, not many, Agnes thought it was shame they could not be civil. There was so much the women held in common, although Agnes would have bitten off her own tongue before she admitted it. Agnes had heard from Jinty that there was a time when Big Jamesy had spent the last of his redundancy on junked cars and BB guns for the boys. It had sent Colleen out to steal their Christmas dinner from the Fine-Fare supermarket. They both knew the keen edge of need. The women could have been closer then. Separately, they had both gazed hungrily at the pages of the Freemans and lain awake in the quiet of the night, wondering how to make a pittance stretch around. If *he got this* and *she got that*, then what would they themselves do without? It was a mother's math.

Separately, the two women had spent whole afternoons hiding behind settees from the Provident man. It was like an odd synchronized swimming, the way the Pithead women all sank to the carpet and crawled across the floor. The Provvie was a thin man in a big suit. He would peer through windows unabashedly. He had spent years watching curling fingers of cigarette smoke billow inexplicably from behind the settees in empty houses.

Colleen, indirectly through Bridie, had even taught Agnes how to trick the electric meter, how to open the box with a hairpin without damage to the lock. One Sunday every month she reclaimed her coins and her boys sat eating runny ice cream sandwiches in front of a roaring hot, three-bar electric fire. Silver coins sat in her hand like a pile of jewels, and Agnes would pump some of the coins back through and get double the month's electric allowance. The meter man's books never added up. Agnes could picture him down the pub with the man from the Provident, wringing their hands at the industrious mothers of Pithead.

As Colleen clutched Dirty Mouse to her chest, Agnes wondered why Colleen hated her so much. Agnes coveted what Colleen had. She was thick with family. They were close, and they were close by. Her children were young and strong and still needed her. Most important of all, she had her man, her only ever man, and he was still there. She also had her God, and by her own account He had chosen her to be superior, to bear moral witness on those around her, and she did, like a middle manager carrying out the Big Boss's bidding. To Colleen, diddling and shoplifting were one thing, necessary sins. Black tights and high heels were altogether more mortal.

As Agnes finished her lager she watched the wild McAvennies bicycle towards the Pit Road. She watched Colleen come out her gate with her message bag and follow their plumes of dust out of the scheme. It was then she took a notion.

Colleen's man, Big Jamesy, was under a rusted Cortina shell. He was dirty already or dirty still, Agnes could not tell. With a sharp *clip-clip* she crossed the narrow road. He lay flat on his back, a stain of dark oil spilt around him like a pool of treacle. Agnes rapped her big ring on the metal car shell.

"What's it noo?" His sigh was so gruff that she felt the heat of it on her ankles. Metal tools fell to the concrete, and the man did a crablike shuffle to get out from under the wreck. It seemed to take him forever.

Her face practiced a series of uneasy, casual-looking smiles. By the time he found his feet, he stood a good two heads taller than her. He was the colour of the black Irish, so honeyed that the dirt and oil almost suited him. The side of his neck was burnt and puckered from the Pit explosion, his hairline at the back oddly asymmetrical. Still, he was handsome. She hated that.

"Is your Colleen home?" she asked.

Jamesy eyed her warily. His eyes stopped on her low V-neck jumper. "Don't try and kid a kidder," he said flatly. "What is it ye whant?"

Agnes dropped her eyes. His hands were thick and calloused. "I had a favour to ask you."

"*Oh, aye.*" Now he smiled like all the men she had known. His sharp teeth pointed inwards, in to the back of his throat, like a trap.

"I'm at my wits' end," she said. "I'm having a bit of bother with my boy, the wee one."

His face was stone again. His eyes were on her body. "Aye, he's no right. Yer gonnae have to watch that one. Always has too much to say for himself. I saw him skipping a rope the other day. Ye'll be whanting tae nip that in the bud."

"That's why I'm here." Agnes folded her arms, but he kept his eyes on her chest.

"Do ye whant me to get my boys to gie him a slap?"

"No!"

"Just a wee tap. Toughen him up."

"*No!* It's not his fault. It's hard growing up without a man around."

"Whit about yer Leek?" The filthy man considered his own question for a moment; the way his lip curled sourly said he thought little of her eldest boy. "So. Whit the fuck do ye whant frae me then?"

The wind blew out of her. "I just see you doing all these lovely things with your boys."

There was no pity in the man. His hardness, even with his own, was legendary on the scheme. "Aye, and whit do ye whant me to dae about it?"

"I thought if I gave you a couple of pounds maybe you could take him with you the next time you went fishing, or maybe teach him how to kick a ball?"

The tight movements of his face told her he was considering it. "Agnes, I'm no whanting yer money."

Agnes felt like a fool. She wanted to get back to her drink, to douse her anger and embarrasment with it. "Right. Of course. I'm sorry I bothered you. I just thought. Never mind." She stiffened her spine, ready to walk her shame back across the road.

"*Haud on.* I'm no saying there's nothing ye can do for me." Big Jamesy smiled then, and his teeth looked sharp as knives. He pushed an oily hand up his manky vest. He ran it across the meat of his belly.

The smell of grease and motor oil stayed with her for a long time after. His cock had been considerably darker than his body, like it was grimy or, she hoped, like it had grown tough and discoloured from overuse. It was dark like the thigh meat of a chicken, and it struck her as odd that it was not as honeyed as the rest of him.

Jamesy was still turgid as he re-zipped his fly and pulled Agnes back to her feet. It was over so fast, and he ushered her out of Colleen's house all sleekit and shameful. He acted like a sore loser, like a customer who regretted a purchase but couldn't return it to the shop. He grumbled that he would pick her boy up that Sunday, that he would take Shuggie fishing at a canal that was clogged with garbage and fresh pike.

At first Shuggie had recoiled and looked like he had never heard a worse idea. She had cried in the bath later that night, trying to dig the oil out from her skin and feeling like a fool. Shuggie had heard her there, sat in the cold water, crying to herself. She had been mostly sober, and to him it was different from the drunken poor me's. He resolved to show an interest in the fishing, anything to make her happy again.

He fixated on the planning of the day, the organizing, the list making and the list checking. He planned the lunch and the clothes, the things he would put in his school bag and the little things he would put in each pocket: tomato sandwiches, a toy robot for sharing, a little plasticky pair of sunglasses, and a Christmas cracker whistle. When he had laid out all the preparations and put everything neatly in its place, he sat on the edge of his bed like a patient little dog.

After Sunday breakfast the house across the street started to come to life. The long-limbed McAvennie boys burst out the door and started loading bags and rods into the back of their father's scrap lorry. Francis carried an old plaster bucket full of maggots and heaved it over the side. Agnes heard the noise and came around the corner into his bedroom. She made an excited face to the sweating, plastic-wrapped boy.

"See, I told you!" She sounded more relieved than he was.

Shuggie kept his eyes on the truck across the street. He touched each of the cagoule pockets in turn, like the Father during mass. "I'm going to catch you the biggest fish ever."

"I know you will," said Agnes, smacking her lips.

"Sh-should I go across the street now?" he asked.

Agnes thought about it for a moment. Then the pride in her answered. "No, you wait here. Mr McAvennie will come to you."

Big Jamesy stepped out into the road. "Shall I go out now?" asked Shuggie again.

Leek had been trying to sleep the morning away. A week of manual labour made him look forward to a long lie. He had been listening to them dither and let out a muffled scream from under his bed sheets. "Yes, for *God's sakes*, GO!"

Agnes swatted at the lump of Leek. "No! I said Mr McAvennie will come to us." She watched the dark man take wide steps down the path; with a thick foot he kicked loose car parts back under the Cortina, which was mounted on bricks. She rubbed the side of her thumb raw as he moved some of the bags in the back of the truck, securing them under cords, and then he passed behind the truck and stepped out into the road.

Shuggie was wringing his hands in anticipation. She fixed the neck on his cagoule. "Listen, you mind and be a good boy for Mr McAvennie. Do as he tells you. Try not to be a burden, all right?" She kissed him on his small hot mouth, there was a bead of sweat on his top lip.

The hillock of Leek's bed sheets spoke again. "Don't drown fuckwit. I'd never get over it."

There was a sound of the old lorry engine starting, it took them both by surprise. They saw the beast rise and lurch as the handbrake was released. With a look in the wing mirror, Big Jamesy pulled it out into the road. Panic cracked across the boy's face. The truck had been facing the wrong way, towards the end of the road instead of its mouth. The end of the road was a dead end; stumped in by the reedy marshland, it widened like the head of a spoon, and cars often had no choice but to continue up to the very end of the spoon to turn and come back out.

Agnes bit her lip. "I think he's just turning the truck around." She tried to believe it. "But maybe let's go wait at the door."

The boy nodded, his face red hot. They stood behind the front door and adjusted themselves as though they were making a grand entrance on the stage. Holding hands, they stepped out and went and stood by the edge of the road. In the distance the green lorry had turned and was rumbling back.

They stood on the kerb, erect and proud, as other people might stand on a grand train platform. She held his hand, and with his free hand, he held out the soggy tomato sandwiches. Agnes fluttered her ringed fingers. *"Right, dry your face and mind what I said."*

The truck didn't slow. Big Jamesy didn't even look down on them. The soot dust whipped into the air as the truck chugged past. They stood for a long time watching it recede.

When the dust settled, there was a rapping sound, a high *chink, chink*, from the window opposite. Colleen McAvennie lifted the stubborn sash and leaned out into the street, a look of suspicion on her face. "Wit are the pair of ye stauning there all glaikit fur?"

Agnes could only smile, as if the bus she had run for and missed was not the bus she had wanted. Her dentures were gleaming white in her red mouth, stour already sticking to the fresh paint on her lips.

Her boy sat in the coal bunker at the back of the house flicking the warm tomato out of his sandwiches. He hadn't cried like she had expected him to. Agnes had burst the electric meter and emptied it of all its shiny coins. With that she had gone up to Dolan's shop and bought a handful of chocolate bars and a small fish fillet. When she handed him the little fish fillet, he hadn't gurgled with laughter like she had hoped he would.

He just wiped the soot dust from his hot face and shrugged his shoulders. "I didn't want to go anyway." There were tears of frustration on her cheeks as she said she was sorry. He looked up at her and asked, "Why?"

"I'm sorry you have a prick for a father."

Leek, under duress, kicked a ball in the back garden with Shuggie. Agnes watched them from the window, and it was clear neither of them wanted to be there. She found some cans of Special Brew hidden under the sink. She rolled the cold bronze in her hand and thought about calling forth the demons inside her. If she drank to get drunk, then she would be fighting in the street before the end of the day. She sat on the edge of the clean settee with a can of courage and hissed it open.

Colleen brought her rubbish bin in from the roadside, stopping to gossip with the housewife who lived on the left of her. She was twisting her crucifix in a girlish way. Agnes could tell she was feeling pleased with herself. All morning women flitted around Jamesy's disembowelled Cortina. Agnes could tell they were feeling social, because they all waddled quickly, in that clenched-arsed way they got when they were anticipating good gossip. Bridie Donnelly picked the leggings out of her crotch. It made Agnes feel better to look at their dirty skirts and tea-coloured tights, at their baggy leggings and housecoats.

Agnes was strategic in drinking the lager. She wanted to time it for Big Jamesy to be home before she swung through that rusted gate. She wanted him to watch as she told Colleen what he had done to her with his oily fingers. If her blood rose in drink too early she would peak, her mind would slow, and she would slur as she spat the truth.

Agnes was feeling the first flush of the drink when a strange woman came along the road. The woman was checking an address on a piece of paper, counting the identical houses as she passed. It was easy to tell she wasn't from the Pit because her hair had been expensively cut and set. She wasn't a Catholic cousin, because she had a bright red handbag, and it matched perfectly her bright red shoes.

The flash across Colleen's face told Agnes she didn't know this woman either. The woman approached the group, said something to Colleen, and Colleen nodded slowly. Stubbing out her fag, she picked up her cold mug of tea, and looking backwards over her shoulder, she led the stranger inside. The gossiping crows scattered.

Agnes sat forward. She thought the woman must have been the Social Work, and she wished she had called them herself. They were cracking down in Pithead, catching the dole dodgers who were working part-time and the disability claimants who were up ladders wiring in television aerials. But the woman didn't stay long enough for that; she left with the beautiful red bag still under her arm. Agnes watched her step through car guts and close the broken gate politely. She took a pair of expensive-looking sunglasses from her bag and used them to push her hair from her face. It tickled Agnes, for she knew it would make Colleen livid. *Sunglasses? Who in the name of the Holy Father does that bitch think she is?* With her head held high, the neat woman walked up the empty street and out of view.

Agnes waited, but Colleen never came out again.

When they were hungry the three McAvennie girls floated up the street like ghostly brides. Their golden hair was matted and blown about their faces like a veil, and their long summer dresses, once a delicate blue, were washed out with age. Agnes had only closed her eyes a moment, but when she looked up the bulk of Big Jamesy's scrap truck was mounted on the kerb opposite. It was still daylight outside, but the big lights were already burning in the McAvennie house. In the bare bulb light she could see people moving quickly from room to room. Agnes hissed open another can and gulped it down quickly.

In the bedroom she changed her skirt for something that would let her kick, and donned the angora jumper with the rhinestone beads, the impractically fluffy one that Colleen had been so suspicious of. She took some time going through her box of jewels, picking the largest gemmed rings, which were papal in scale. The glass gems were so poorly set they ripped tights and caught on tea towels. Some mornings after a bad bender, she woke up to find cuts on the side of her face or the inside of her forearms. Agnes looked at her bejewelled hands, a sparkling weaponry, knuckledusters of peeling, plated gold. The last of the lager curdled in her empty stomach, and she knew the time was now.

Agnes stumbled outside and leaned on the broken fence. She took a deep breath and felt a little light-headed and a little discouraged again. Then the screaming started.

The McAvennies' door flew open, and the youngest boy started running at full tilt out into the scheme. With the door open, Colleen's voice rang clear across the low houses. "James Francis McAvennie! Ye are no better than a Proddy dog carrying on lit that." Agnes stood stock-still in the middle of the empty road. Up and down the street, children stopped playing and windows quietly opened a narrow crack. She knew women were turning down televisions and twitching behind curtains.

"Whut? Aye, go on then, *hit us*. Ye think ye are a big man around here, don't ye? Ah'm gonnae get my brothers round here, and we'll see who is the big man now, eh? Ah should have listened to ma mammy. Ye dirty Orange fucker."

A man's voice said something sharp but inaudible, and Colleen shrieked louder. "Ah will *not* keep ma voice down. Ye've broken yer vows and God will never forg—" Agnes imagined Big Jamesy must have taken her by the throat, because the street fell silent for a moment. Then Colleen's voice wavered back, this time with less anger. "Where do ye think ye are going? James? *To her?*"

Big Jamesy McAvennie burst from the house, the neck of his T-shirt ripped, as if Colleen had been hanging from it. He was still dressed in his waders, and he had a black bin bag full of what looked like clothes and bed sheets tight in each hand. There were sore stripes of red sunburn and fresh claw marks across his face and burnt-up neck. He climbed up into his truck and started the engine.

Agnes was swaying in the middle of the road; he couldn't have missed seeing her there, drunk but proud, with her clenched, gemmed fists. He rolled down the window of the truck with a furious pump and shouted at her like a frustrated man looking for directions. "Whit the fuck dae ye want, Hoor?" He used it as though it were her name. "Come to pick the fucking bones clean? You are a bit quick, aren't ye? Ye're s'posed to let the meat cool first."

With that the truck roared away. By the time he had reached the end of the street and turned, Colleen was at the front door, looking wild. *"James! Jamesy!"*

Agnes stumbled back to the kerb, clumsy with drink. Jamesy swerved deliberately and narrowly missed clipping her with the back tyre. The road filled with the usual cloud of soot.

Agnes was blinking on the opposite kerb, but Colleen hadn't the peace of mind to see her. In her thin face was a wildness and an emptiness, alive and dead at the same time. She fell with a crack to the tarmac and lay, loose-legged and blank-faced, in the dust.

Agnes looked up and down the street like a person who wanted to stick the boot in sleekitly, or a person who wanted to run away from a car crash. She was unsure which.

There was a faint breeze fluttering all the curtains, but no one came to help, no cousins, no other Pit women. Silhouetted at the McAvennie window stood the four remaining children, lined up in descending heights like little Russian dolls. All with the same sad, beautiful face. One day she would give them all a deep hot bath to really stick it to Colleen.

From the gutter there was the loud *rrrip-rip* noise of hair being pulled from an old brush, a sticky tugging sound, like old gummy linoleum being torn up. Agnes stepped closer to the flailing woman. The belly full of flat lager, the dust, and the tangle of limbs made it hard for her to understand what she was seeing. At first she thought Colleen was ripping her football top into shreds, but as she stepped closer Agnes could see the clumps of matted hair the woman was ripping free in each claw. *Rip. Rip.* It came out in wild handfuls.

Agnes flitted around the fallen woman. Before she knew it, she was kneeling in the dirt, using her ringed fingers to try to tame the younger woman's furious talons. She wrapped herself tightly around Colleen. "Here, what's all this, then?" She said it in a voice so kind it shocked even her. She hadn't come to help.

Colleen went limp in her arms, and Agnes gently lowered the woman's claws into her lap. Agnes prised open the fists, which were still clutching the ripped-out hair. She began pulling the thick strands from between the thin fingers as if she were cleaning an old comb. Colleen's hollow eyes stared into the dirt for a long time before she spoke. "Ah should have left well alone instead of getting on at him while he was down. All ah said was ah didnae want any more mouths to feed." Colleen's hands were shaking. "Since that mine shut he was coming at me night and day like a teenager on the boil. He was never any use at all that *pulling out* nonsense."

Agnes was staring at the bald patches on Colleen's head; there was already dust on the blood-pricked scabs. "Five weans is enough for any woman."

Colleen snorted. "He would have had a hundred if he could. But ah jist thought, *fuck ye, McAvennie,* and to spite him ah shut the shop." Colleen started to cry again. The tears came out in long thick streams, almost as if she had a leak. They poured down her bony nose, dripping off her chin. Colleen turned her eyes towards Agnes and looked at her then as if for the first time. "That must be when he started fuckin' around."

Agnes was conflicted. She would have told any other woman that it would get better in time, even though she knew it would sit on her chest for the rest of her life. She offered no such salve to Colleen. It occurred to her that they were equals now, and she couldn't be ashamed at how her insides lifted at the thin woman's bad news. She bit her lip to stop from smirking.

Miners' women were pacing in the street now. Cousins and the wives of cousins, circling nervously, as if Colleen had turned into an animal they were unsure of how to approach.

"She walked up to me as nice as ye like. *With they sunglasses.* Big fancy ones in two shades of brown. She said her name was Elaine. Asked if she could have a word in private. Ah thought she was from the catalogue, thought she was trying to sell me some shite for the weans' Christmas."

Colleen then let out a groan. She uncurled her fingers and took the hem of her skirt. With a single tug she spilt the thin fabric in two from hem to belly. Then she fell listlessly back to the pavement.

"For the love of God." Agnes grabbed at the shredded fabric for modesty. Colleen had no underwear on; the frizzy hair of her cunt was shocking against the sallow smoothness of her belly. "We've got to get you in the house. Up. UP!" Agnes tried to lift her, but she was too uncoordinated with the drink. They toppled over together into the stour, and Agnes tore the skin off one of her knees. She tried to drag Colleen inside, but the wasted woman, nothing but a pile of bones, slackened all her muscles and slid back into the dirt like an unruly child. Agnes stood over her, sweating and spitting. "You can't lie here like that."

With her eyes closed Colleen moved her hand across the dirty pavement like she was caressing fine sheets. The words came out slower and thicker now. "Ah don't fuckin' care. Let Jamesy McAvennie hear. That his. Wife died on the. Road. With her old cunt out."

There was nervous laughter from some of the weans on bikes. Agnes gave Colleen a hard shake; she found she enjoyed it, so she did it again. "Madam, have you no pride?"

Colleen's eyes opened wide and then closed. Her breath grew lighter.

Agnes pinched her. "Here! What's gotten into you? What have you taken?"

But the soft pile of bones did not answer.

The fences were hung full of women squawking like big nosy crows. The news had spread fast. Colleen's cousins were screaming blue murder, and Jamesy's sisters were throwing their fists in defence of his good name. Jamesy's mother, eighty if she was a day, was spitting and swinging a balding mop like it was a scythe.

Not knowing what else to do, Agnes drew off her tights and then her own knickers from beneath her skirt. She did it with a brass neck, stumbling half-cut, right there in the street. She struggled to put them on Colleen. It was like dressing a life-size dolly whose limbs, instead of being stiff and rigid, were limp and heavy with slow blood.

By the time the ambulance came, Colleen wasn't talking any more. Agnes sank to the dust beside her. She regarded her expensive white underwear, luminous with good bleach. They hung on the thinner woman like a lacy nappy, and they were, Agnes thought, more kindness than she deserved.

Fifteen

He reminded her of the colour of sausage casing, except it was less of a colour, more of a watery tint that has been spread too thin. He looked worn through. Lizzie had to use both of her hands to cradle one of his, and as she laid her cheek on it, she could feel the raised cobalt veins that traced the top of it. These were hands that had loaded grain trucks for twenty years, hands that had laid pungent tarmacadam, hands that had killed Italians in North Africa.

Now Wullie was having trouble even breathing. The air in his lungs sounded as if it was being run over a grater, it would catch on the prongs and stop, only to rattle and rasp back out of him. Lizzie wiped at his face with the hanky she kept up her sleeve. His mouth was always open now, the corners caked and dry. She wanted to kiss him once more, she wanted some last memory of the fine man that he had been, that he still was.

The old men in the other beds were dozing. She had watched the nurses give them all a drop of liquid morphine, and now they looked like they slept an uneasy sleep. Lizzie unbuttoned her coat and drew the scarf off from around her hair. She lifted Wullie's hand and drew down the bed sheets. At first she thought to climb in beside him, lie against the stone wall of his body and cry. Instead, as she mounted the hospital bed, she had a change in her heart. She clambered on to the bed and then, still in her good coat, she straddled him.

Anyone else might have missed it, but Lizzie was sure she saw the lids of his eyes flutter, the corners of his mouth pull tight in a cheeky smile. She rocked back and forth gently. It wasn't meant to be as dirty as it looked. She only wanted to feel him pressed against her, warm and alive through the cotton of his pyjamas, through the clammy poly blend of her underwear. She only wanted to give him a little comfort against the pain. Didn't she owe him that?

Lizzie lit a fresh cigarette as she rocked and rubbed on top of Wullie. She took a deep lungful and then leaned over and blew it into his face. She could only imagine how much he would be missing his Regals.

"Are ye alright, Mrs Campbell?" asked a voice from behind her. There were hands gently but firmly holding her elbows. "It's alright now, darlin'," the voice said, as it guided her off the bed. "It's alright, ma wee china."

Wullie didn't stir as the Sister helped Lizzie down. His pyjamas were wrinkled where Lizzie had creased them, otherwise nothing had changed. Without any judgement, the nurse snuffed the doubt in Lizzie's fingertips and pulled her skirt back below her knees. Lizzie felt herself guided back to her seat, and she felt the cold glass of water at her lips. The whole time the Sister soothed her, in a gentle, calming voice, she petted her like a cat, and it made Lizzie want to tell her secret things. Lizzie took the Sister's hands in her own and said, "Please, God, don't take him away. *Please*. No' again."

Agnes's face was very thickly made up, and it looked to Shuggie like the paint had been layered over several other faces she had forgotten to take off first. The boy followed her at a discreet distance, stopping now and then to gather up things that fell from the pocket of her matted mink coat.

As Agnes stoated through the infirmary's automatic doors, a concerned nurse ran over, thinking she was in need of attention. Shuggie watched the girl try to corral his mother and slip her gently into a tatty wheelchair. Agnes pushed past the nurse and went in the direction of the oncology wards. Shuggie heard the nurse say to a male attendant that she thought for sure Agnes was a working girl.

"She is *not*," said Shuggie, quite proudly. "My mother has never worked a day in her life. She's far too good-looking for that."

The matted mink coat gave her an air of superiority, and her black strappy heels clacked out a slurred beat on the long marble hallway. The rubber tip had worn away from around the right heel, and although she had coloured the shoe in with an old black bingo marker, the sharp metal nail scraped the floor with the screech of hard times.

Gaunt faces looked out from white beds as she scratched her way past. A large, friendly-looking Sister came out of a booth and stepped directly into her path, a green clipboard clutched to her chest like a shield. She was as wide as a small wall. "Scuse me. Can ah help yeese?" said the nurse with a tired smile. "Ah'm Sister Meechan." She pulled at the official-looking badge on her blue uniform.

To Agnes, she seemed kinder than the nurses Lizzie had worked with years before, great hulking Glasgow women able to hold grown men down on a Saturday night and pull broken bottles from between their ribs. They had granite faces, cold and hard, from watching the endless soap opera of mindless violence. Sister Meechan was clearly trying her best. Agnes looked down at the stocky nurse and looked at her small badge. The letters were moving. She took a deep breath and tried to sound sober. "No, thanks. I know where. I'm going."

Sister Meechan didn't break her well-trained smile. "Do ye, aye? It's the back of nine. Visitin's done for the day."

With a heavy blink Agnes drew her eyes over the officious woman. The end of her nose was pitted like a small strawberry. Agnes let her eyes linger and tutted in sympathy for it, letting the Sister know she had clocked it. Then she put her ringed fingers on the nurse's thick arm in an entitled way, each finger falling on to her flesh as if she were playing scales at the piano. "I'm here to see my father."

Agnes's breath was yeasty and sour on the nurse's face. "And what is your faither's name?" said the Sister without flinching. Glasgow routinely presented her with all sorts.

"Wulli . . . William Campbell."

The nurse made to check the name on her green clipboard but stopped. "Och, ah *see.*" Her practiced face cracked, and underneath, several real emotions played across it. She hugged the clipboard to her broad chest and took her free hand and placed it gently on Agnes's arm. Agnes found herself staring at it.

"Oh, hen," she said tenderly, breaking all the formality of her training. "Ah'm dead sorry for the state of your daddy. He's one of our favourites, such a big handsome basturt, and he's no been a single bit of bother." Then Sister Meechan stepped closer to Agnes and added conspiratorially: "Ah am worrit about your wee mammy, though. She disnae seem to be coping aw that well. The night ah was making sure aw the supper things had been tidied away, but when ah reached your faither's bed ah noticed the privacy curtain was still half-drawn. Ye ken it was far too late for that. So ah pult back the privacy curtain to find the poor soul atop of him gieing it pure laldy."

Shuggie would have said that the nurse was a kind lady. Agnes would have to disagree. If she had been sober she might not have laughed. If the kind nurse didn't have her hand on her arm and that pitiful look on her face she might not have laughed. However, she wasn't sober and she wasn't in the mood to be condescended to. So she laughed. It came at first as a guilty giggle but then it caught her with a shake, and she threw her head back in gaudy, haughty peals of laughter. Then she said, cruelly, "Were you jealous?"

Sister Meechan's fleshy jaws smacked together. "Dear God!" The strawberry nose twitched. "Do ah need to remind ye that this is a *communal* ward?"

Shuggie saw his mother's fists tighten. "Oh, give me a break." Agnes dropped her jaw, her eyes still bright with laughter. She leaned in close. "After nearly forty-seven years together that poor woman is mad with the grief." She extended a mink arm and pushed past the broad Sister as easily as drawing curtains back from a window. She clipped up the corridor to the door of the ward. As she turned, the bare nail made a shameful scrape on the floor. "And *my* Daddy is one fine-looking man."

Shuggie watched from the shadows and waited for his mother to push through the big swing doors into the ward. He came up silently behind the Sister, who was standing slack-mouthed and staring in the direction of the scraping heels. He was sure the Sister was feeling sorrier for the old woman with the dying husband, for now she also had a bad drunk for a daughter. Shuggie poked her fleshy arm, and she jumped at the silent visitor by her side.

"I'm sorry," he said, much like it was a calling card. "Please forgive her abruptness. She really is a good person." Then he added, "So. Is this where people come to get to heaven?"

Sister Meechan clutched her hand to her heart from the fright. The boy in the fitted suit was standing very close to her. He clasped his hands behind his back, like he was an old man, like he was the head of the hospital himself. She wanted to touch him back. She wanted to see if he was real. "Och, son. Ye cannae be sneaking up on folk like that."

"I take care where I walk. I don't *sneak*." He straightened his narrow tie. "Can you please answer my question?"

The Sister blinked. "Heaven? I suppose so. Sometimes."

Shuggie chewed his lip. "So can they go to hell from here too?"

She could have told him it depended on the shift, that most people admitted to the ward on an Old Firm game day should probably go *straight* to hell. She looked him up and down; the boy couldn't be more than eight or nine. "No, son. Not too often," she lied.

With curious fingers he started to stroke the metal watch chain that hung from her pocket. "Do they leave on a bus for heaven?" A patronizing smirk crossed her lips, and she reached out a scrubbed hand to pat him on the head. He ducked instinctively and tutted, "Please don't do that! I just had it parted." With a sullen look he came closer again and resumed twisting the interlocking links.

Sister Meechan's hand wavered awkwardly in the air, unaccustomed to not being in command. "Ye are a very tidy little boy."

"My mother says it doesn't cost anything to take pride in your appearance."

With a glance down the hallway she asked, "So was that wummin yer mammy?"

Shuggie nodded. "Uh-huh." He looped the chain around his fingers and stole a glance up at her kind face. "It's OK, though. You don't have to like her. Sometimes she drinks from underneath the kitchen sink. Nobody really likes her then. Not my daddy, or my big sister, or my big brother. But that's OK. Leek doesn't like anyone really. Mammy says he's a social spastic."

Sister Meechan closed her eyes, the clear grey eyes that had seen all manner of sins and sights. "Does she do that often?" she asked.

Shuggie dropped the chain. He looked up at her through his knitted brows. "I can manage. I can fetch messages and make sure she goes to bed on time. Besides, Sister Nurse. You never answered my question. My mother told me that my grandaddy would be going to heaven soon, and I wanted to know if he had to get a bus or if we could take him in a black hackney?"

The Sister's hand moved from her heart to her throat. "Och, son. It disnae really work like that. They don't leave on a bus. I mean sometimes they go in a big black car." She started worrying a tab of neck skin, twisting at it as though it were a necklace. "But when a person goes to heaven they don't take their bodies wi' them."

Shuggie stuck his bottom lip out in thought. His right eye closed in sour disbelief. "Do they not take their hearts?"

"Naw."

"Do they not take their eyes?"

"Well. Naw."

"Do they not even take their fingers?"

"Naw, son. They don't take their legs, or their arms, or their noses. They don't take anything, because it's not their bodies that go to God. It's their spirit."

Shuggie looked relieved somehow. The nurse could see a weight shift on his shoulders. He turned on his polished heels and followed the perfumed cloud of Agnes down the corridor. He stopped at the double doors.

"So if your body doesn't go to heaven, it doesn't matter if another boy did something bad to it in a bin shed, *right?*"

The door to the communal ward had swung open with a slam. The lights were low and drowsy; beige men sat propped up in white beds. On the far side of the ward Wullie's bed was ringed with orange visitors' chairs. Each of the empty chairs had a lonely pool of reflected light, and Lizzie sat alone, her grey coat, grey skirt, and tan tights fading away against the bright plastic.

Agnes threw her hands over her face in a wide arc of grief, something like a grotesque peek-a-boo. Backlit by the bright corridor light she performed like she were onstage at the King's. She crossed the ward and let her bag and coat slip off and lie behind her in a trail across the floor. In defiance of Sister Meechan she put an open-toe sandal on the bedrail and climbed up on the bed. Lizzie looked down at the foot on the bed, heartsick at the painted toes bursting through the worn black tights. Agnes mounted the bed and draped herself over her sleeping father like his widow. Then she began to hug him and wail like his mistress. Wullie didn't stir. Lizzie rose from the chair and without a word pulled her daughter's black skirt back down over her white nylon petticoat.

The ward door opened a thin crack, and Shuggie appeared, carrying a handful of her belongings. "You'd lose your head if it wasn't screwed on."

The dying men stirred again at the apparition of youth. A visiting lady in a lambswool twinset folded her arms across her chest, she pointed her suede driving moccasin towards him in disapproval. The suited boy walked across the floor and silently gathered more of his mother's things, dragging the discarded coat behind him like a wet towel. His granny was smiling at him. It was the smile she had when she was watching Sunday telly and not paying much attention. She didn't look sad at all, Shuggie thought, she looked peaceful, resigned. He sat on one of the empty chairs next to her and held her thin hand as they watched Agnes stumble down off the bed. In the dim light his grandfather looked the colour of condensed milk. His skin looked thin, like yellow flypaper, and was pulled so tight and thin over the bony Campbell nose it put Shuggie in mind of a chicken's wishbone.

Agnes sat in the other seat next to her mother and took her free hand. Lizzie said, "Visiting hours are over."

Agnes's head bobbed on her shoulders. "Mammy, this is hard for me. I just couldn't get up the courage to come."

"Aye, well, you look *plenty* full of it now."

"I just finished what I had in the house. As soon as it's all done I'm going to get better. I'll even join the AA." She was lying, and it rang hollow.

"I've never liked those AA places. They attract the lowest kind of people. God gave you a will. You should use it to save yourself."

For a good while the three generations sat in silence, their hands laced together in a chain. Agnes's cheap stone rings were as big and blue as Lizzie's knuckles. Agnes took a length of toilet paper out from up her jumper sleeve, wiped her eyes, and then handed it to Lizzie, who did the same and passed it to Shuggie, who folded it to a side free of mascara or phlegm. Agnes reached into her black bag and drew out two cans of lager. She popped them with a foamy hiss, dropping the pulls neatly back into the bag. "I don't think I can handle this. Are they all to leave me?"

Lizzie took the white toilet paper from Shuggie and modestly covered the half-naked pinup on the side of the lager can. "I feel like he's just back from that bastarding war. It's too soon for him to leave again."

Shuggie watched the lambswool woman twist her mouth in disgust at the open lager. He turned to tell his mother, but he could see Agnes wasn't there in the room with them. She hadn't even heard a word her mother had said. Shuggie straightened the buttons on the front of his granny's wool coat, turning all the plastic flowers the right way up, leaves at the bottom, the petals at the top. He waited as the women talked and talked and talked and did not listen to each other.

The old man lay in the bed taking his shallow breaths. The air made a wheezing sound as it squeezed around the tumours in his lungs. Agnes clenched her jaw in anger so tightly that the porcelain dentures shrieked like two supper plates rubbing together. "I should never have left with that bastard Shug." She lit two fresh cigarettes and handed one to her mother. "I'll tell Daddy that when he wakes up, eh."

It was this that brought Lizzie's mind into focus. Lizzie took a draw on her cigarette and blew it carefully into Wullie's face. "Your faither is never going to get any better."

Agnes patted the bed. "Not my daddy. He'll be right as rain in a few days."

"*Agnes!* The doctors have said he's never going to get home again."

Agnes took another drink from the can. Shuggie watched the layers of old mascara dissolve and black tears start to migrate down her face. "Why do we have to just lie down and take everything in life?"

Lizzie shrugged. "Oh, what guid are the poor me's now?"

They were silent a good long time after that. It grew so late it became early. The lambswool woman eventually left, and shortly after Sister Meechan brought them opaque mugs for the lager and cleared the offending lager cans. The nurse said nothing more, and Agnes knew then it must be getting close to the end. The Sister gave Wullie more morphine, gave Lizzie an ice cube for his lips, and then she pulled the heavy curtain closed around the four of them. Shuggie's legs went numb from the hard seat, but he knew better than to make a fuss.

In the quiet, Agnes slowly sobered. She read the Freemans catalogue to steady the shakes. She had been dog-earing certain pages, starting in early February, to get ready for the next school year in August, Shuggie stretching and growing like a weed. She refilled their mugs, slower now, and asked her mother, "How will you manage without him? For money and that?"

Lizzie shrugged. "How have *you* managed?"

Agnes glanced at her father. "I wouldn't like to say."

Lizzie let the boy doze against her, she lifted her arm and pulled him into her side. She checked he was sleeping before she spoke again. "I need to tell you something Agnes. I don't want you to pass remark on it. I couldnae bear it if you judged me."

Agnes sat forward. "What is it? Are you all right?"

Lizzie shook her head. "I've been hard on you. I know I have." Lizzie paused as though she was waiting for Agnes to disagree, but Agnes did not disagree. "I was never a fan of Big Shug. But I was harder on you than I should have been."

"It's OK. You were right to be hard."

"No, I've been in your shoes. I suppose I just hoped for better shoes for you."

Lizzie checked the sleeping boy again before beginning her tale. Shuggie had his eyes firmly closed, but he was not asleep. He listened very closely to what she said next.

Lizzie took a deep breath and held it as long as she could before she spoke again. "Whatever it takes Agnes, keep going, even if it's not for you, even if it's just for them. Keep going. That's what mammies do."

She'd been pulling a grey-headed mop over the tenement stairs, stopping her dance every so often to wring its head with her bare hands. The acid tang of bleach and pine resin nipped at her eyes as she chased dirty water from stair to stair and pushed the last little wave out of the close mouth. Lizzie dragged the heavy tin bucket into the street and poured the brackish water down the hill. Half-dressed weans jumped and danced over this new river, screaming with delight.

She spent the rest of the morning washing sheets in Agnes's tin baby bath. She would never have admitted it, but she missed the steamie. She used to love the ritual of it; it was a place free of men, free of weans, a place where the women could share the bits of themselves that they couldn't talk about at chapel. She would pay her money, get her sink, and put her curtains and work dresses in to steep in the deep boiling water. As the dirt loosened from the cloth, the women would stand around in a half-circle and work the gossip into a lather. Nothing happened in Germiston that the steamie didn't know about.

Now, she knew, they were talking about her. Now they waited for her to finish on the wringers; they would say happy goodbyes, and when she was gone they would pluck her good name to bits like a bit of old ham bone.

As she choked the dirt from the clothes, great tides of water lapped over the side of the tin bath. She cursed at the mess, but at least she didn't have to wash his things any more. At least she didn't have to wash for Wullie Campbell. She couldn't imagine one of his granary overalls fitting in the little bath anyway. There would be no room for the water.

Lizzie had been red-faced and thumping down into her laundry when she noticed Agnes twirling, her frilly white socks sucking up the pooling suds. Lizzie lifted her from the damp floor. She dropped the child in a kitchen chair and redid the velvet bow in her hair. "I suppose you're hungry again?"

Lizzie's brow furrowed as she ran her fingers over the cabinet shelves. There was nothing there to eat: a handful of pockmarked potatoes, a stick of gritty lard, and a poke of flour that was so used up it looked like it might blow over from emptiness. She reached behind the empty bread bin, took an old box of soap flakes off the bottom shelf, and tipped it gently. Three hidden eggs rolled out of the box. They were brown and plump, with not a speckle on them. With a spoonful of lard she cracked them into the black pan, and they rolled and spat luxuriously in the bubbling fat. She turned to Agnes and put her finger across her lips in a secretive way. The bairn looked up at her with fat cheeks, and she put her little pink finger across her bud of a mouth and made the motion back to her mammy.

Agnes sat on Lizzie's knee, and they ate the hidden eggs from the same plate. The yolk was so deep and fatty that Lizzie could feel it coat her teeth, and she could see it gum together the child's lips. Happy and full, she dawdled Agnes on her knee for a while, listening to the weans play Injuns in the street, listening to the siren at Provan Gas Works call the men back to work. Lizzie wondered whether a man who was still walking back to the gas towers felt any shame, any shame at all. She remembered how Wullie had felt before the day he told her he couldn't take it any more.

It was a mild day. From the open window Lizzie could hear the huddled concentration, tiny hushed voices and the whoops and shrieks when the little Injuns snuck up on the dim-witted cowboys. Then the tone changed suddenly. The weans were excited about something different, they were gasping and cheering now, and something was travelling up and down the street faster than it could ever be carried by foot. Many voices were sharing the same words, passing mouth to mouth, like a rudimentary telegram. Lizzie moved discreetly behind her net curtains to catch a sly peek; all the other women were hanging shamefully out of open windows. Weans were shouting bits of news up at their mothers, and the women were turning around and sharing it with the darkened rooms behind them.

There was a sudden knock at her door. Lizzie looked at Agnes, the child had a thick ring of yellow yolk around her mouth. She wiped it, hiding the evidence. She knew the door was not locked, it never was. This was a good close, full of papists. Whoever was outside now must be a stranger to her. Lizzie stopped at the hallway mirror and tried to push some life back into her hair. In her head she ran down her list of debts, checking their good standing; she looked in on the empty shelves one more time in the scullery, and feeling fairly secure, she opened the front door.

The greenish-cobalt light that poured in through the landing window settled on him like a fine dust. The man said nothing. He was half-smiling as he slipped a bag from his shoulder, a tall heavy cotton bag, so full of things that it stood up on its own and nearly came to the bridge of her nose. She didn't know why she said it. Perhaps she could think of nothing else to say.

"That better not be full of dirty clothes."

He laughed, and she had been grateful of that later: to only laugh at her and not let her confusion steal the joy from the day. "Can I come in?" He doffed his side cap.

She had the sensation of not being able to place him, this stranger. His face was like a face she would see on the Royston Road, and she would return the half nod out of politeness instead of deep recognition.

Still, Lizzie stepped backwards into her hallway, and the stranger stepped over the threshold. He dragged the heavy canvas bag behind him and closed the door. He was folding and unfolding his field cap when he saw the eyes looking at him from beside the table.

"Is that her?" he asked.

Lizzie could only nod. The last time he had seen her, she had been pink as a ham hock, and wrapped in an embroidered blanket that Granny Campbell had handworked. Of course, there had been christening photos and Easter cards, but it was not the same. It seemed like this was the first time he had seen her with his own eyes. He drank in the thick ebony hair, the glass-green eyes, and best of all, the chubby legs. Wullie knelt, and he was crying, slow rivulets of relief that she should be a happy-looking and healthy wean. He opened the mouth of his tall bag, and very gently he took out a beautiful doll wrapped in hand-painted fabric, brightly coloured wonders, one after the other, beaded ribbons from Africa and wee paper crosses from Italy. There were penny sweeties in striped wrappers and more dollies, all different colours and patterns; they had faces with skin colours and eye shapes Lizzie had never seen before. Everything Wullie laid down in front of her, Agnes took up, till she was dropping things from the overflow in her arms. As Agnes leaned against his knee and turned the riches in her hands, he buried his nose in the crown of her hair and drank in the sweet soapy freshness of her.

As Wullie knelt, Lizzie had been touching him gently, *almost* not touching him. The back of his neck was a syrupy brown like she had never seen, it was the colour of burnt sugar tablet, golden and sweet. She could see a little down the back of his shirt neck, and she could see how the line changed sharply from this dark burnt tan to a healthy golden tone. She had been gently considering a lock of hair that curled behind his ear; it was free of pomade and a horn-brown colour so alive with the sun, so different from tip to root, that she didn't recognize it, she didn't recognize him. She wondered, where had the flat ebony gone that she knew and loved. She let the fine hair run through her fingers, and then she tugged it, hard.

Wullie looked up at her then. He closed one eye and smiled his lopsided grin. He was real. He was home.

The papers had never said; she checked them every day, sometimes twice, sometimes ten times. When she came back from the hospital, she would go to the shared cludgie in the back green and sit on the warm bowl and read the paper auld Mr Devlin would sometimes leave there. The papers had spoken of how the boys in North Africa had won a great victory, but they also told of the many sons from Glasgow, from Inverness and Edinburgh, who had sacrificed and would never be coming home. Lists and lists of names. Even the wee few streets of Germiston had lost that many. Every week it felt like families came with heavy heads out of the close mouths having been down at the chapel saying prayers for their lost sons. There had been so many she had lost count. Mr Goldie, young Davie Allan, the Cottrell brothers, who were only twenty-two and twenty-three and had left behind seven fatherless children between them.

In turn, all these poor soldiers had each been declared dead, and Wullie had not. She had told her mammy Isobel how that gave her hope, but Isobel had travelled a long hard road in life. She held her youngest daughter in her arms and told Lizzie to put aside hope, to give her attention to practical things, her new bairn, her wee job, and feeding the pair of them. "*If ye hope*," said Isobel, "*Ye also mope.*"

None of that mattered now. Wullie Campbell was home, and Lizzie was moving around the room before she knew what she was moving for. There were happy voices in the close; she could hear them sing his name, and she knew they would be coming for him soon. She gathered Agnes into her arms and took her to the drying cupboard. She parted a stack of towels and took out a hidden sewing tin; she opened it quietly, and the air was thick with the sweet smell of buttery Madeira cake. The shelf also held a greasy ham hock, and Lizzie ripped a hunk from the bone. She put the whole Madeira tin on Agnes's lap and into each hand slid a hunk of greasy flesh. "Mammy needs you to stay in here awhile." She closed the door gently on her daughter.

They would be coming for him.

Lizzie quickly stepped out of her underwear, she didn't kiss him, she still had not thrown her arms around him. None of that would be enough to fill the absence she had felt. She doubled herself over the back of the wooden armchair and gripped the turned armrests for support. She felt him appear behind her, his presence was faint at first, like he was merely following her on the street, but then he touched her, he kissed the back of her neck, and she felt him push roughly inside. She watched his brown hands as his strange fingers curled around her pale forearms. He pushed into her slowly, and then he went faster, and soon he folded on to her, covering her as if he were a blanket, as if they were one.

They would be coming for him.

He didn't smell as she remembered. There was an overripe orange tang to his hair, and his breath, though sweet, smelt more like molasses than she liked. Lizzie turned her neck to look back at him, his eyes were open and concentrating on her, and she was sure it was him. That green and copper colour, the colour of a golden sun bursting through thick green beech leaves, was still the same.

Once, long before Agnes, Wullie had taken her on three separate buses and up to the Kelvingrove Hall. She had never been inside such a fine building before, and she was shy to follow him through its grand halls. She felt her shoes were too loud, too squeaky, and the hem of her good dress hung too long out of the bottom of her coat. Wullie hadn't minded. With his thick arms he separated the crowds for her. He acted like he had the same right to be there as any doctor from the Byres Road. Only later did he confess to her that he knew of this grand place just because he had repaired the tiles on its roof.

It had been a rare afternoon. At the top of the sandstone staircase there had been a painting on exhibition; a beautiful oil painting of a stand of beech trees sat at the side of a lazy river, the autumn wildflowers still golden and bracken-coloured on its bank. Wullie had been smiling at her then, and she had forgotten all about her chapel dress. His eyes were speckled the same colours as the painting, the same faded green colour of uncollected hay and deep umber of a red deer. Now, as she searched these eyes for the man she loved, she knew the green of the painting was the same, even if the frame they sat in was something different.

There was a faint noise. She had forgotten. How could she have forgotten when she had lost so much sleep worrying over it?

Wullie stopped pushing into her. He straightened and was staring into the corner as if he was seeing something approaching in the distance, something he didn't like the look of. Lizzie felt him slip out of her. He tidied himself back inside his uniform and was moving towards the far corner. He was tiptoeing with his palms wide open, as if the thing hiding there might spook and try to rush past him. The infant cried out again. He was girning as Wullie pulled back the tented curtain of the crib.

She would never forget that look on his face. He was staring at her over the wide bone of his shoulder when the front door finally gave. Nobody bothered to knock, and there were footsteps and cheering as the union men and their wives spilt in with plates of sandwiches and half-bottles of Mackinlay's. She had only enough time to let go of the arms of the chair and straighten herself before the first cans of sweetheart stout were burst. As he made a pantomime of hugging his pals, his green and amber eyes never left her face. All she could do was mouth across the happy crowd to him, *I'm so sorry*.

Later they had pulled the heavy curtain across and climbed into the recessed bed before the last well-wishers had left. He said he was tired, but Lizzie could feel the heat of the drink radiate off him as he lay awake beside her. She wondered if her shame burned outwardly in the same way. They didn't talk. They lay there not touching, and he felt farther away from her now than he ever had in Egypt.

When she woke in the morning, he was already dressed in his good wool suit. The trousers were wide-looking now, a little old-fashioned, and she could see that the jacket hung on him more loosely than it had in the past. He had found the secret tins of Spam and hidden ham hock and the last of the Madeira cake that the grocer had given her. He was trying to feed his daughter a mouthful of fried Spam, and each time she refused he would laugh and spoil her with a bite of Madeira.

She didn't like to see him with that dirty food. She could imagine Mr Kilfeather, the bow-legged greengrocer, but she could not rightly remember how it had all started, it had all been so insidious. Had it just been an extra handful of eggs? A little more than the ration book would give? Had it been the spare arse end of a loaf? How could she tell Wullie any of it?

The infant, this other little Kilfeather boy, was gently cooing to itself in the corner. Wullie's back was to it, like he couldn't hear it.

As she stepped from behind the curtain, Wullie rose without looking at her. He rebuttoned his jacket and kissed Agnes goodbye, then he removed the bundled bag of clean sheets from the old pram. Lizzie was watching him as he lifted the little boy from his crib; the baby's pink arms reached out to him, like it knew and trusted the deep well of goodness from which Wullie Campbell had sprung. Lizzie watched Wullie place the baby in the proud carriage and tuck the knitted blanket tenderly under his chin. He turned for the door.

Something made her step forward. She put her hand on the carriage handle. "Where are you going?"

"Out."

"Will you be back?"

"Of course." He sounded surprised at the question.

She felt like if she cried she would never stop. Lizzie let go of the handle. "I'm so sorry," she whispered. "I got bits of meat. We ate well. I didn't know. I. I just didn't know if you would ever come home."

"I know," was all he said.

She was pleading now. "When I found out I took every Askit powder I could get. Great big handfuls of it. It was just. It was just too late."

"I don't need to know, Lizzie." He took her face in his hands and kissed her then. It was the first kiss she had been given since he had kissed her at Saint Enoch's on the day he left. She had never let Mr Kilfeather kiss her, she felt she had to tell him that.

He said, "I'm sorry I was away so long." Then Wullie took the pram, and the strange baby, and went out into the mild spring morning.

It was the longest day she had ever known.

Wullie was back before the street lamps were lit. Lizzie had been at the window all day, and she could hear him whistling all the way down Saracen Street. Mrs Devlin told her later that he had given her a fright, because at first she had thought it was one of yon Indian fellas, seeing how dark and golden he was. Then, she said, he had danced up the stairs, singing and swinging on the banister like he was Fred Astaire himself.

When he came in the door, there was no pram, there was no blanket, there was no strange little boy. He gathered his girls into his arms, and Lizzie could smell the cold fresh air on him, like faraway open fields.

Wullie ate his dinner with an appetite, two big bowls of pea soup thickened with cream and salty with stripped mutton. Lizzie couldn't tell him where it had all come from, how it had been paid for, and she was relieved that he didn't ask.

That night, as she cooried into him behind the curtain, she stroked the thick hair on his arm. She turned to him and asked where the baby boy was.

Wullie pulled her closer to him and looked at her with those speckled green eyes, and all he said was, *"What baby?"*

Sixteen

Agnes thought about what her mother had told her, she thought about it constantly in the days leading up to her father's death. The lung cancer eventually took him. He rattled all the way to the end.

They buried Wullie Campbell on a damp day in March, on a gentle slope at the back of Lambhill Cemetery. On the days she was sober, Agnes cried for her father. Then she cried for herself, jealous that Shug had never loved her the way Wullie had loved Lizzie.

When she was in the drink, she phoned her mother and railed at the old woman for having spoilt her memories of her father. What man takes a baby and just makes it go away? Then, within a month of her father's death, her mother died, and there was no one left to scream at any more.

Elizabeth Catherine Campbell had died in her slippered feet.

By the time Agnes had pleaded with a Glasgow taxi rank to drive all the way to Pithead and take her to the hospital, Lizzie had been with the angels for an hour and a half. Agnes, in her state of distress, had walked out and down the centre of the lonely Pit Road to meet the taxi. When she finally saw the headlights she threw herself prostrate into the dust.

When she arrived at the hospital, the polis had told Agnes that the bus driver was devastated. "He's a good man," they said, "with many years of clean devoted service to the corporation." It was just he never expected the old woman to step backwards off the kerb. He never meant to kill her, but in stepping backwards she must have been determined to kill herself. That's what they said.

Under the shaded brims of their police hats, Agnes knew the constables were running their eyes the drunken length of her, as though this ruin of a woman would drive any mother to the same. Their cold eyes and their warm words did not match. "It happened often enough," they said then, as though Lizzie had chosen this cowardly way to end things. Her mammy would *never*. She was a good Catholic. Agnes knew better.

Later that week, when the undertakers finally released Lizzie, Agnes set the body up for a viewing in her mother's bedroom. Leek helped her lift the double bed and lean it against the wall to make way for the trestles and the small coffin. Their mattress lay propped there, and she knew it would never come down again. From the linen closet she took a wide sheet and draped it over the bulk of the mattress like it was a ghost of good memories now dead. She hadn't yet paid her father a month's mind, and already here she was, stood at the foot of her dead mother. Her bones cried out for drink.

Agnes sat alone at the side of Lizzie's open coffin. She covered her hair in the most sombre headscarf she owned and wore the same black knitted dress for the second time that month. The Sighthill flat held no good memories for her now. First it had been her daddy and now it was her mammy. She laid no cardboard over the carpet this time; let the mourners ruin it.

Lizzie looked tiny in the coffin. The undertaker had applied thick make-up to the gouges on her forehead, and hidden her mangled hands under the band of silk trimming cloth. Agnes arranged her Bible and coiled her medallion of Saint Jude on top of the silk. She was done with all that.

Agnes had asked that Lizzie be dressed in her olive Sunday suit and that the roots be dyed out of her hair. The undertaker had asked her to bring a hat to cover some damage to her mother's head, and she gave him a photo that showed how her hair should be set into tight rosette curls and how it should frame her face on the sides. The man did his best to return her to a look of peace, but there was a thick waxiness to her face that denied Lizzie her true likeness. There was no happy tint to her cheeks, no light rose flare at the end of her small nose. Agnes kissed her then. She cried for her forgiveness.

When she ran dry, she sat upright again and listened to the hum of the television in the flat next door. She took off her last pair of unpawned earrings and gently inserted them into her mother's lobes. "I know they don't match." She pulled a tight curl over the left one. "At least Daddy will have a good laugh when he sees you."

Her hands turned Lizzie's good brooch upright, the beautiful tin pressing of the Virgin and Child that Nan Flannigan had brought back specially from Lourdes. "Poor Nan. She should have kept a closer eye on you." She exhaled. "Why did you have to do such a stupid thing?"

Agnes spat on a piece of balled-up toilet paper and wiped at the bone of her mother's cheeks. The heavy paint barely shifted. "I was going to make tinned salmon sandwiches instead of cheese this time. Is that all right? I didn't like the way the edges of Daddy's pieces went hard as they sat out all day. I could see those ingrates roll their eyes. I saw that bisim Anna O'Hanna and her curled lip. I even heard Dolly say to her John, 'All they people in from Donegal and *no* even a slice of meat for the bread.'"

Agnes pushed out her bright lipstick and drew it across her mother's thin lips. Rubbing a little on her thumb she smoothed it into her gaunt cheeks as rouge. She wanted to straighten the emerald-green cloche but was afraid to touch the back of Lizzie's head, so instead she licked gently at the auburn curls on her crown with the end of a pick comb. "There, you look better for a little life in your cheeks." The words stuck in her throat.

Agnes stayed by her mother's side for the night. In the damp of the April morning they laid Lizzie's coffin in the open space above Wullie. The ground was sodden. The grave needed to be pumped out of water before they lowered her in on top of her husband.

After the burial, Agnes wrapped sandwiches in paper towels and sent Shuggie three times around the room, until black handbags were bursting and fragrant with hot salmon and butter. Even when people turned the boy away Agnes sent him back around, and around, with pretty plates heavy with thick meat.

It was dark when they got home from the reception. The miners' women were still leaning on sagging gates, taking advantage of the break in the spitting rain. She was sober, for fear her mother had been watching, but now, as she stood over Leek, she let the amber sweetness of Special Brew soak her heart.

Agnes stood over him as he opened his sketchbook. From an envelope at the back he unfolded a long piece of paper with what seemed like an endless amount of numbers on it. Sleekit and embarrassed, he covered the rotary from her eyes and slowly dialled the long African number. Here it was then, the number that Catherine never wanted her to have. It was the loneliest feeling.

She tried to listen for as much information as she could glean, but he was laconic with his words. She strained to hear Catherine's voice. From the damp hallway in Pithead it sounded to Agnes like there were beautiful canary birds in the very air. She wanted to imagine Catherine surrounded with lush carpets of tropical flowers, with pretty names she might never learn, from books she would never read. In her heart she hoped her daughter was happy. She hoped Catherine would call out to her, that Leek would pass the telephone and she could tell her for herself how much she wanted her home.

"Catherine, it's me. It's Leek," he said. "I'm sorry. It's Mammy's phone. Yes. She's here actually, she's standing right next to me." He looked Agnes up and down suspiciously. There was a pause. Agnes could hear Catherine raise her voice in agitation. "Don't worry, I never. I promised you I wouldn't."

"Do you like South Africa?" There was a pause. "Oh, he's fine. Nearly died up the Pit but he's fine. Still a bit funny. You know, *funny* funny." He held his wrist out and lisped into the phone, "Gerald Fitzpatrick and Patrick *Fits* Gerald. Like."

There was laughter on the other end. Agnes prodded him. "Right, anyway, Catherine, is Donald there? No, I *wasn't* checking. It's just, I've got some bad news. It's just, well, Granny is dead." There was another long pause.

Agnes mimed, *Is she crying?*

Leek waved her away. "Last week. She was hit by a corpy bus. It was fast. Her mind was going. Well. Fine. No. Look, I didn't know how to say, but Granda is dead too. It's no joke. I swear. We didn't want to upset you. Three weeks or so." He started to talk through gritted teeth. "Well, it was my decision not to tell you, actually, that's the thing about being left behind in all the fucking shite, you get to make all the shitty decisions." There was a long pause. Agnes thought she could hear Catherine cry or apologize or both. "So, are you coming home, then? Oh. Oh. OK. Oh. Fine. Well, congratulations, I suppose."

Agnes mimed, *Is she asking for me?* and tried not to look too desperate.

Leek sighed. "Look, Caff, do you want to speak to Mammy? Sober. *Mostly*. Sad. I suppose. OK. I will. OK. No. I understand. Suit yersel. Thanks." With that, he hung up the phone.

Agnes's hands were out in front of her; she hadn't realized she had been grabbing until the line went dead. Leek just shrugged and spoke mostly into the carpet. "She was too upset to talk." He rubbed at his sore jaw. "They had South African boerewors for dinner. On a stick with bits of fruit. How boggin' is that?"

Seventeen

Her body hung off the side of the bed, and by the odd angle Shuggie could tell the drink had spun her all night like a Catherine wheel. He turned her head to the side to stop her choking on her rising boak. Then he placed the mop bucket near the bed and gently unzipped the back of her cream dress and loosened the clasp on her bra. He would have taken off her shoes, but she wasn't wearing any, and her legs were white and stark-looking without the usual black stockings. There were new bruises on her pale thighs.

Shuggie arranged three tea mugs: one with tap water to dry the cracks in her throat, one with milk to line her sour stomach, and the third with a mixture of the flat leftovers of Special Brew and stout that he had gathered from around the house and frothed together with a fork. He knew this was the one she would reach for first, the one that would stop the crying in her bones.

He leaned over her and listened to her breathing. Her breath was stale with cigarettes and sleep, and so he went to the kitchen and filled a fourth mug with bleach for her teeth. He tore a page from his "Popes of the Empire" homework and wrote in soft pencil: *DANGER! Teeth Cleaner. Do not drink. Don't even sip by accident.*

He heard the front door close gently. Leek would be late for work again. He was always reluctant to leave the protective cocoon of his bed; under the covers his day still had an unspoilt quality to it. Shuggie peered through the crack in the curtains and watched his brother's sloped shoulders inch along the road. The first of the miners' children started milling towards the school. The boys who arrived early to play football in the concrete playground were the same ones who made rings around him and shoved him when they got bored. Shuggie found her blue biro and went through his homework jotters like a bookkeeper, adding her name in a flourish, *Mrs Bain*. It looked odd now.

The clock radio was still flashing plenty of time till he could slip in unnoticed to morning Mass, so he turned back around on the stool, clasped his hands, and waited patiently. The dresser was neat and orderly, as she liked it. When she didn't have the shakes she would empty the little jewellery box and make sure she wiped each piece, regardless of its worth. Sometimes she lay all the trinkets out on the dresser table and they played jewellery shop. She would let him make up new combinations for her, lay out selections of earrings with complementary necklaces. It had been easier before she had pawned the loveliest things.

He watched her reflection in the mirror, her sleeping back heaved up and down. Shuggie uncapped a bottle of mascara and rubbed the black ink into the grey cracks in his school shoes. Then he took the wand and drew it under his eyelashes. The fine lashes stood out beautifully from his face. Agnes rose from the bed like a fairground skeleton. He tried to push the brush back into the tube, but it wouldn't go, and so he slyly slid the mascara down the back of the dresser.

But Agnes wasn't looking at him. The ebbing drink had made her bounce to her feet, and she was standing stock-still at the side of the bed with one breast half-hanging out of the black bra, which itself was hanging out of yesterday's clothes. Then she sank to the side of the bed, like she was kneeling for bedtime prayers.

Her boy must have left for school. She knew he had been standing there watchful as a trapped ghost, but when she opened her eyes he was gone.

Lifting herself, she sat on the edge of the bed, the pail of water between her knees, and tried to quiet the pulse that was beating in her flushed face. The boak rose in her chest, and she strained over the bucket, arching her spine like a choking cat. She pulled the thread of memory tentatively towards herself and began gently looking at all the pictures her mind had tied to it. She saw the chair, the clock, and the empty house. She saw herself walking from the kitchen to the living room to the kitchen again and then on her knees scraping dust from the skirting board with her fingernail. She saw the clock again and then the lights of the scheme came on, the curtains were undrawn, and the boy home from school.

Beyond that, her mind jumped like washing flapping on the line. There was the telephone and a taxi, there was the bingo and sitting alone. There was drink and drink and no win and drink and no win and the woman next to her asking if she was OK and Agnes asking her if she had any weans and the woman saying no and turning away. There was a taxi home, not with Shug, and stopping at the dark mouth of the closed pit. She could almost see the taxi driver's face, and then she was screaming and choking on his aftershave, and then there was only panic.

The boak rose; it came out in a violent, red-faced torrent. Spittle covered her hand, the side of the bed, and the black leather bag on the floor. Holding the sticky hand off the edge of the bed, she lay back on the pillow and pulled in gasping breaths like she was drowning. Timidly and tenderly she slid her dry hand across the sheets and down between her legs. She pressed lightly on herself and felt the new soreness there. Then she was sick again.

It was a while before she could summon enough strength to sit up. How badly she wanted a scalding bath, but a half-empty meter meant the bathwater was only tepid. There in the shallows she could see the red bruises on the insides of her thighs and the black, pancake-size welts that looked as though the flesh was dying underneath the cream of her skin. The water soon chilled, and she was shivering as she dried herself and put on a clean jumper. It was all she could manage to put hairspray through her hair and some blue powder on her eyes, and then she sat down in the armchair, frozen as a regal waxwork.

She still didn't move when there was a light cheerful knock at the door and the sound of long nails clawing a desperate greeting. "Ag-niss! Ah-g-niss. It's only me." Jinty McClinchy was already standing by her chair by the time she asked, "Can I come in?" She looked down at the frozen woman and sucked in through her teeth with a squeaky laugh. "Oh, hen. You look like ye've taken a good soaking. I have *be-en* there. Ah can tell ye."

Of all the Pit cousins she was the only one who smelled of heavy night cream and Elizabeth Arden perfume. She donned a knotted heads-carf in the sun and liked flat comfortable shoes for her child-size feet. Jinty wore a Saint Christopher medal, and she always swore on the Bible when she was judging you. If the drink made Agnes melancholy and regretful then it made Jinty sharp and needling. She liked to sit and put the world to right, telling people where they went wrong. Two lagers down, and her little eyes would narrow like those of a fussy judge in a jam-making competition. She was a shrew, and it was said she had been papped from every house in the scheme.

Jinty was shaking her head pitifully at Agnes. "Shall ah put on a wee bit o' dry toast?" She was taking off the floral headscarf.

Agnes nodded in silence, the edges of her mouth unable to hold a polite smile for long. Jinty took herself into the kitchen, and although the bread was laid out next to the toaster, Agnes could hear her nosing into every cabinet looking for drink. When she couldn't see the top shelves she would jump, jump, jump, like a giddy little dog, her flat sandals slapping on the hard linoleum.

After some time, Jinty came back with a single piece of hard brown toast. "Was it a bad night, hen?" she asked, in her high, childlike voice, her eyes already scanning the room.

"*Yes.*"

"Aye, well, hen. Ah cannae stop long. Ah cannae stop long. Ah just came round for a drop of tea. Things to do, ye see." She took off her coat and sat down expectantly.

Agnes tried to set the plate at the side of her chair, but her hand shook and the dry toast fell to the floor.

"*Dear, dear, dear.* Look at the state o' ye. That's a terrible state to get yersel into."

Agnes lifted her hands to her face. Her head was sore, her arms were sore, and her body felt like it was bruised all over.

"Well, now. Well, now. Ah hate to see ye suffer." Jinty looked at her out of the side of her eyes and sniffed. "Ah don't suppose ye have *any* in, do ye?"

Agnes knew that Jinty already knew the answer from her search of the kitchen cabinets. "I think there is a last can under the kitchen sink. In a bag, behind the bleach." Her head was swimming.

Jinty sniffed. "Shall we have a wee taste? You know. Just to get ye right?"

Agnes nodded, and Jinty, with creaking knees, sprang from the settee and near skipped through to the kitchen. She found the can as easily as Agnes knew she would and returned with it and two rinsed-out tea mugs. She put the mugs on the table and with a little finger pulled the ring on the Special Brew. The can bubbled foam as she expertly poured half in each of the mugs. She took a white finger and ran it around the lip of the empty can and then popped it in her mouth as though it were whipped cream.

"Oh, that's nice," she moaned quietly. "Ah suppose we could just skip the tea and have this." Her eyes slid to the side. "Ah wouldn't be doing this, mind, but ye look like ye are in a right state, and ah hate to see any of God's creatures suffer."

As if it were a dolly's tea party, Jinty lifted a mug with two little hands and offered it to Agnes. Agnes took the mug, put it to her mouth, and took a small sip. The boak groaned inside her. She took another and out of habit set the mug down on the far side of the chair, hidden and secret.

Jinty lifted her mug and took a mouse's mouthful. She made a happy sound and took another and then another. The two women didn't speak again until the mugs were almost drained. Agnes felt the lager push the boak back into her belly; the shaking in her bones grew quieter. She ran a hand over her tender thighs and started to feel angry.

Sip-sipping away, Jinty could see the empty bottom in sight. "Aye, well, ah cannae stop long." She took out her hanky and wiped her lipstick off the edge of the empty mug. "Would another wee one make ye feel any better?" she sniffed.

Agnes nodded feebly.

Jinty's scheming eyes narrowed. "Ah didnae see any more under that sink of yours. You've no got another secret planking place, have ye?"

Agnes thought about the usual places, behind the immersion heater, the top of the tallest wardrobe; she shook her head.

"Oh! Well, ah cannae stay anyway," said Jinty sadly, the fine lines around her mouth pinched. "*But just look at ye.* Ye look like you might die if ah left ye now. Do you have a couple of pound, mibbe? I suppose ah could run up to the wee shop."

Agnes reached down the side of the seat and took out her purse. It was empty but for chewing gum wrappers. Her mind went to the driver and the taxi and the dark Pit, and she felt the bile rise in her again.

"No' even a wee bit left from your Tuesday Book, hen?" asked Jinty sadly.

Agnes shook her head.

Jinty McClinchy shifted nervously in her seat like she had the itchy piles. She looked at Agnes and looked at the empty mug. Finally she sighed, and then she sniffed, "Well, let me see what's in ma purse, eh?"

With a heave the tiny-boned woman lifted her big leather bag off the floor. She sat it on her small lap and almost climbed in it. Agnes heard keys and coins moving around at the bottom, and then there was a sweet watery thud, as Jinty drew out three cans of warm Carlsberg. "You can pay me later." Jinty opened a can and repeated the delicate pouring and the waiting and the licking of the foam from her small white finger. Only when they were starting the third can did they start to feel like themselves again.

"I was at ma daughter's last night. You should have seen the state of that house." Jinty wiped the end of her nose with her old hanky. "I look after an idle bastard with a rotten liver, and ah can still keep a clean house."

"How is the new baby?" asked Agnes, only half-interested.

"Aye. Fine, ah suppose. She loves the thing as much as you could," Jinty said dispassionately. "She'll get more off the benefits now of course. Ah telt her she should set a little aside and hire a cleaner. *Filthy*. Honestly, ah look at her sometimes and ah don't know what ah have raised." Jinty was getting worked up. "There was dust that thick on her skirting board. She looks to me as if to say, 'Mammy, can you *no help*?' and ah just turned to her and said, '*I have* raised my children. *I. Am.* Done.'" The woman made a cutting motion in the air.

Agnes nodded sadly. She would have loved a house full of grandchildren. She would have loved a house to be full again of her own children.

Jinty went on. "Gillian's eldest called me *Granny* the other day. I nearly had its wee tongue out. I wouldn't mind, but his other granny makes him call her Shirley, so ah wasn't going to be the only old bitch at Christmas." She picked up her drink and studied Agnes over the top of her mug. "Here, what are ye so quiet for?"

"Me?" asked Agnes. "Nothing."

"Agnes, ah might be a lush, but you are a bloody liar."

The women sat in silence and tanked the rest of the can. Eventually, Agnes asked quietly, "Jinty, if I tell you something, would you keep it between us and not tell a soul?"

The woman's eyes shone like beads. She crossed her heart with a finger, except she missed and crossed the wrong side. "On my life."

"I had a bad blackout last night." Agnes then told Jinty the story of the bingo and the taxi and the driver pulling over into the Pit mouth. She lifted the sleeve on her jumper and showed Jinty the finger marks the rapist had left in her white skin.

The little woman tutted and shook her curly head. "Bad bastard. To do that to a defenceless wummin. What is this world coming to? The way people take advantage of each other. That widnae have happened in our day. They would have caught the swine and ridden him through the Trongate on a fence." With a knuckly finger she motioned the sharp fence rail going right up the man's arse. Jinty took her hanky out and wiped her nose. Then she took it and wiped the shop dust from the top of the last can. The women looked at it mournfully. "Is there no way you could get a couple of pounds?"

Agnes watched the last of the golden liquid pour into the mugs. In her mind she shook the telly meter, the gas meter, and the electric meter, and they were all empty. "No," she said sadly.

"Is there one of your men friends ye could phone?"

Agnes thought about the bruises on her body. "No."

Jinty sat quiet for a minute savouring the last of the golden liquid. "How about giving that fella a phone?" she asked. "Ye know, the wee fella with all the long hair in the back." She mimed the curly mullet that was popular with footballers and pop stars. "Ah heard he's no short of a bob or two and that he likes a good drink."

"Who?"

Jinty thought for a moment. "Lamby. Aye, that's it. We could gie him a phone."

The cousins of Pithead told everyone that Iain Lambert was a coal miner whose wife had left him high and dry just before the closing mine delivered the final blow. With no woman to spend the pitiful severance on, he had kept it hidden under his bed. When the other miners drank it away or used it to feed and clothe their growing broods, Lamby still sat on his nest egg and went out and got a part-time job repairing rented tellies. The cousins said Lamby was a lonely and dull man who was not made for the romance novels. He had got himself a trendy footballer's mullet but still looked like an undernourished teenager. Despite his being nothing in the looks department, these same women brought him plates of burnt potatoes with grey meat and bowls of frozen broth. The cousins said he was a good man who kept himself to himself and that after the mine shut he proved himself to be a worker still. They fed him bits of leftovers, knowing that his Pit severance could have fed their weans for a year or more.

Jinty chimed in again. "We could have a wee party. Just the three of us."

Agnes looked at the emptying mug and felt the panic rise. She nodded.

Jinty was up on her quick feet like a startled cat. She pulled the phone book from the vinyl telephone table and, licking her little fingers, flicked till she came across the *Ls*. She read aloud. "L. L. Lambert. Mister C." Jinty checked the address and, sure it was Lamby, went and dialled his number. She cleared her throat as the phone rang. It was lunchtime on a Thursday, but a man's voice came on the phone.

"Oh hello, Lamby," she said, in her best accent. "It's wee Jinty here. Aye, that's right . . . I live on the other side of the scheme. You will know ma John. I used to go around with Mhari McClure. Aye, that's right." She paused. "Mhari? She got into a terrible state on the Valium, aye. Ah know, it is a right shame. She was a lovely lassie as well. Last time I heard she was working Blythswood. Aye, well, but for the grace of God, eh? But you know there is a big difference between enjoying a quiet drink and selling yourself for a prescription, don't ye think? Sad it is. I was there when she started that Valium nonsense. Aye, awful it was," Jinty sniffed.

"Anyway, ah was giving youse a wee phone because I wanted to see if you wanted to stop by ma pal's house for a wee drink," she paused. "Aye, it is a bit early, it is. It's just she is a lovely lassie, and I have been dying for the pair o' ye to meet. Aye, *Agnes Bain*. Aye, that's right, puts you right in mind of Liz Taylor, a bit paler though." Jinty smiled excitedly into the living room; she motioned for Agnes to paint her face. "So, will ye come? Guid! Lamby, I hate to ask. Do you think you could be a real pal and bring a wee carry-out with ye? Aye. We're a wee bit short. Aye, she is *lovely*. Keeps herself immaculate, smart talking . . . Aye, we'll have a wee party. Just bring six cans and a wee half-bottle. Oh, and then whatever you would like to drink for yourself. Remember, it's the house near the corner."

Jinty finished the phone call and told Agnes he had said he would be there in the hour. She started tidying up the empty fag packets and ring pulls. "You know, hen, if ah were you ah might run a wee brush through ma hair. Cover they bruises. Try and make yersel look a bit more appetizing."

They waited over an hour on frayed nerves until Lamby arrived. Jinty showed him in. He sat on the edge of the settee and fidgeted with his trendy bomber jacket like a teenager. Agnes could see that everything the scheme had said about him was true. Jinty made the introductions and slipped the heavy plastic bag out of his hand.

"Nice to meet ye, Agnes," he said through a row of neat teeth.

Agnes mustered as much of her charm as she could. "It was nice of you to come visit with us. It's hard to make your own fun in this desolate place."

"Aye, well, it isnae every day a fella like me gets an offer from two beautiful wummin such as yersels," Lamby said. Jinty squealed with filthy delight.

Agnes had heard better patter. She sat back in the armchair. "So, you are not related, then?" she asked, "I don't think I have yet to meet someone from this scheme who was not tied right back to Jinty by blood or marriage or weans."

"No, ah think my ex-wife had something to do with the McAvennies. Ah'm an O'Hara; we tend to live over on the burn side of the scheme . . . in the flat-roofed houses."

"It's a wonder some of the weans develop bones at all."

Lamby smiled kindly at the insult. "Aye, well. That's probably why ye've been the talk of the town. Fresh blood and all."

Jinty took a half-bottle of Smirnoff from the bag and poured a big finger into each of the three mugs. On top of the vodka she poured in some bright, fizzy Irn-Bru. It bubbled and hissed and looked as innocent as ginger ale. "Oh, ah cannae stop long," she sniffed to herself, taking a big mouthful.

Lamby smoked rollies, and he sprinkled the paper with tobacco and ran his pink tongue along the sticky edge. "Besides, ah've seen ye afore," he said to Agnes. "Ah always thought ye *must* have had a man. Lookin' as well as you do." He licked the first cigarette closed and passed it to Jinty.

"It doesn't cost to take pride—"

"She's a happy divorcee," interrupted Jinty. "She's the lucky one. Any wummin can do fine without a fat sack of meat snoring next to her every night. Isn't that right, hen?"

"Spoken like a true wummin," said Lamby.

Agnes thought how he looked too young to know what a true wummin was but said nothing. She took a long mouthful from the mug. The vodka tasted clean, like bleach. Lamby licked the next cigarette very slowly. Agnes saw that his nails were very clean and his ears and neck looked flushed pink, as though he had just taken a hot bath. "Ah mean, come on! There has to be somethin' men are still good for," he said lasciviously.

This tickled Jinty. She swung her little legs and cackled like a girl. "Absolutely bloody nothing," she squealed. "Agnes, do ye hear the cheek o' this filthy wee bugger? He thinks we were born yesterday." The heat of the vodka brought out a split-veined sanguine in her cheeks. "Have ye been seeing anyone lately, Lamby?"

"Aye, a couple of birds," he said, looking at Agnes. "Ah'm playin' the field. Tryin' to keep it casual-like." He gave her a wink.

"Och, men are all the bloody same, eh, Agnes? Even as babes they lie on their backs fascinated by their little *thingy*."

"How about you?" he asked Agnes. "Have you been seein' anybody?"

Jinty rolled her knees in an excited circle and answered for Agnes. "Her!" she squealed. "That one is practically on call for the Greater Glasgow Taxi Livery."

Agnes felt the sting of the words push into the bruises on her body. She lifted her mug anyway and nodded a sad acceptance of the award.

Jinty pulled the plastic bag from between her small feet and added, cruelly, "If you're not a taxi driver, then this one's not interested."

"Is that right?" said Lamby. He looked at Agnes directly again and with a hurt frown asked, "How's that working out for ye?"

Jinty interrupted again. "It's not a choice she can help. It's a curse! She hears the thrum of a diesel engine, and it's knickers off and *whoosh* the meter's running."

The room got colder. There was a slow sucking in of air, and Agnes's face hardened to glass. The drink soaked into her now, and the words escaped her in a low, threatening hiss. *"You are one low, backstabbing little cunt, Jinty McClinchy."*

The little shrew stopped her mindless laughing. "Och, calm yersel. I didnae mean anything by it." She greedily tipped the mug to her face, but her little eyes were sharp daggers peering over the top of it.

Lamby stiffened, looking from one woman to the other. The room was silent. "Eh, look, mibbe ah should head, eh?"

Jinty crossed her ankles demurely over the bag of carry-out and shushed him. "Oh, don't mind her. She was just a bit unlucky in love last night. Ye have to stay. Ye have to help and cheer her up, eh."

Agnes sat quietly for the rest of the afternoon, drinking whatever Jinty put in front of her and smoking whatever Lamby rolled. He tried to talk to her about all sorts of things, but when she got the chance to answer for herself she could only manage a yes or no. By the time they were well into the cans, Jinty had seen enough.

"Lamby, son, I don't know what's gotten into her," she moaned sourly. "She's normally the life and the soul."

"That's alright." His cheeks were flushed the same red as Jinty's, and he still sat in his nylon bomber jacket. Agnes thought he must have been uncomfortable; she wondered whether he was embarrassed because he had no one at home to iron him a clean shirt.

"Aye, but ah don't want ye leaving here thinking ye've spent the day at the old folks' home. Put one of they tapes in, would you. We'll have a wee party."

Lamby reached over and opened Lizzie's old stereo unit. He lifted one of the tapes from a pile and slipped it in the player. "My wife used to like this," he said, mostly to himself.

"Och, what a voice that wummin has. What. A. Voice!" said Jinty between draws. She twirled her small white hands in the air to the melody. "Lamby, for God's sake, would you get that miserable sod up."

He eyed Agnes nervously. "No. Leave her be. She disnae want to dance." After a quarter bottle and six lagers he was feeling only slightly less timid.

"Lady Bain!" Jinty scolded like a headmistress. "This is a party! This man has brought us drink! Now give him a dance!"

Agnes looked at Lamby, as itchy as a young lad at a school disco. She gave him the best half-smile she could manage to let him know it was all right. On uncertain legs Lamby rose to his feet. He took her hands and tried to tug her from the chair the way plumbers pull a stubborn clog out of a drain. Agnes hadn't stood since she had sat in that chair earlier; the drink and the inertia made her legs go soft, and as she rose he caught her in his arms as if they had been lovers for a long time.

"There you go, eh," squealed Jinty, pouring herself a sly top-up behind their backs. "Keep a good haud of her."

The two of them did a sort of end-of-the-night dance, a clumsy waltz, old-fashioned and slow. They held each other up purely by the way their sweaty bodies were mashed together. Agnes's face was inches from his, and for the first time she noticed that he had shaved for their little party. His neck was covered in sore gooseflesh, and there was a smell of pine about him, from the kind of aftershave that smelled like bathroom cleaner, not a trace of sex in it.

"Ye're a great wee dancer." He spoke to her kindly. She tried to be attentive and listen. But only her body was in the room.

Jinty drank the mug dry. "Gie him a wee kiss!"

"Ah havnae been up the dancin' since ma divorce came through," he said.

"Don't be ungrateful! He bought ye all that drink! Kiss him!" shouted Jinty.

"Maybe ah could take ye one night?"

"He'll no be back!" Jinty warned.

Agnes was nearly two inches taller than the younger man. With their age difference, it could almost have been her own Leek she was dancing with. She saw now the far side of his face had a knife scar running from ear to chin, a common enough chib mark, but on such a young man it seemed a shame. With a clumsy hand she reached out and touched it.

"Ah. So ye noticed that, did ye," he said shyly.

"You look like my eldest boy."

"Gie him a wee kiss, for God's sake!" squealed Jinty, cracking another can.

Agnes let her hand linger on the young man's face and thought how she missed her eldest boy. Even when he was there in the room she missed him; he had the way of always leaving her feeling lonely. Lamby, this man, put his hand to her face and his lips on her mouth. Jinty crowed with delight. Agnes felt his lips open, felt him suck, felt his tongue probing there. His hand slipped lower down her back.

"Now don't you two do anything ah'll have to confess for." Jinty McClinchy was fanning herself giddily, relieved to have earned her carry-out.

The hands that had been gentlemanly started the sly creep across her arse. With kneading fingers he pressed the bruise she had earned at the top of her tail bone. The boak rose in her. She turned her head, but it was too late. She vomited the sour contents of lager and vodka and Irn-Bru down the front of his trendy jacket.

"Oh, for fuck's sake!" screamed the man, dripping in the watery bile.

"Mammy?" Shuggie stood in the doorway.

Agnes fell back into the seat and put her face into her hands as the hot drunk tears started to burn out of her. The man looked from the broken lady to the little boy in his school clothes to the woman tucking the last of the plastic bag into her big leather handbag. As he pushed past Shuggie, Jinty shouted down the hallway after him: "Lamby, son! She's no usually like this! Ah'll gie ye a wee phone another day, and we can have another little party!"

The little woman sighed as the front door shut with a slam, and then she looked into all the open fag packets on the table, consolidated them into one packet, and slipped this into her bag. The woman shook each of the open cans on the table and when she heard the swoosh of remains she poured it into her mug until she had emptied them all. Jinty downed the mug in two or three big mouthfuls, and then she drew her floral scarf out of her bag again.

"Right, ah cannae stop long."

Eighteen

Shuggie stood as far away from the bladder ball as he could. When it rumbled across the playground he made a show of running towards it but was careful to always let the other boys beat him there. He was happier to stand in the shade of the goal corner and watch the girls play a line of skipping elastics, the best of them twisting gracefully down the rainbow-coloured lengths.

There was a damp bursting sound in his left ear. The bladder caught him unawares on the side of the face. It stung like the flat of a hand. The ball rolled to the feet of the opposite team, who sent it into the goal.

Francis McAvennie stopped at Shuggie's side. As he was the eldest McAvennie, the trouble between Colleen and Big Jamesy had the deepest repercussions for him; the promotion to "man of the house" was instant, and he found himself caring for his siblings as Colleen numbed herself on Bridie's blue pills. He leaned over as close as he could, so close that Shuggie could feel the shower of his warm spittle. "*For fuck's sake. Stop being such a poofy wee bastard.*" The other boys gathered round like pit dogs, their eyes greedy.

"Do you want to be a girl?" Francis grinned, his arms wide for the crowd. Shuggie shook his head; he only wanted to put his hand to the welt on his face. "Would you rather put on a wee skirt?"

"I don't," mumbled Shuggie.

"Don't talk back to me, poofter." Francis, a clear foot taller than Shuggie, pushed him in the chest. "You're a poofy little fairy. You and Father Barry are going to burn in hell for the things you do."

There was a chorus of giggles, then the laughter changed to a chanting chorus of *hit him, hit him, hit him*. Francis lifted his left hand to slap the red side of Shuggie's face. The boy flinched to the other side, but Francis stopped short and with his other hand made a fist and crashed it into Shuggie's temple. He turned to the cheering boys. "My da calls that the Ratcatcher."

Shuggie lay on the ground with his head ringing on both sides. A pair of bare legs with slack white socks appeared over him. The girl was spitting like a cat, her long hair making a stream of frothing lemonade. "Stoppet, Francis, ye fuckin' bully! Go ahead an' try that shite on me an' ah'll get ye battered. Ah've got plenty mair cousins than you have." The girl whirled on her heels to tend to him. Shuggie could see the boys give her the finger behind her back, but they were stepping away regardless.

There were scabs on her bare knees, and Shuggie couldn't stop looking at the burst elastic of her socks. As she put a hand under each of his armpits and hoisted him to his feet, he could see the floral gusset of her underpants from underneath her skirt. "You should hit him back," she said. "Ah bet if ye hit him the once, he'd no pick on ye again." Shuggie didn't know which side of his face to rub at first. "Do you want to cry?" asked the girl. Shuggie nodded. "Well, don't yet, haud it in until we round the corner, and then ye can cry. Ah won't tell."

She led him out of the playground as the boys climbed the railings to spit on them. "You two away to play dollies?" said a ginger-headed boy. The girl was on the fence in a flash. She grabbed the boy's school tie and pulled his face into the thick metal railings. There was a clang as his bony forehead rang off the rusting iron. "*Run!*" squealed the girl.

They left a cloud in the dust, and there was no stopping until they were halfway up the side of the low hill to Pithead.

When they caught their breath the lemonade-haired girl started roaring with laughter; there was a pinkie finger's space in the middle of her front teeth. She had a line of freckles across her nose, and her eyes were as shiny and blue as a cat's-eye marble.

"Do you really have enough cousins to fight the McAvennies?" he asked, still trying not to cry.

She shook her head. "Naw. It's just me and ma da. He'd fight you for the telly remote, but that's about it," she shrugged. "Ah'm Annie. Ah'm the year above ye."

"Oh. I've never seen you before."

"Ah've seen ye. Everybody's seen *you*." Annie pointed to the top of the hill, where a makeshift cul-de-sac of mobile homes had been set up. "We live in they caravans. Ah'll walk ye home. They'll not dare touch ye when ah'm here." She puffed out her thin chest. "Where do ye live?"

Shuggie made to point along the low miners' houses and then lowered his hand. She would be drunk. She would be on the phone to the taxi rank raging for his father. "I don't want to go home just yet."

"It's Thursday," Annie said sagely. "Surely all the drink money is spent by now?"

Shuggie squinted at the girl. "How do you know that?"

She hooked her hand over his arm. "Ah've met her once. Your maw. She was sat on our settee one day after school. Ah've never heard a person talk so nice before."

"I really hope she was no bother."

"Naw, not at all. She smelt lovely. She showed me how to put a French plait in ma hair." Her face darkened. "Ah just feel angry for the bad things they say about her. You should fight for her."

"I do fight for her!" he said. "Mostly with herself, but it's still a fight."

The girl made a rasping noise of resignation. "Ah just let him get the fuck on with it. If ma daddy wants to drink himself to death that's his business. He's lost, ah think. He misses ma maw."

"Is she dead?"

"Aye, sort of. She lives in Cambuslang with ma wee brothers and a semi-professional football player." They walked to the field that held the caravan cluster. "But really, ye two should fight back. Ah've heard people say she is a right hoor for the drink, that ye need a daddy and it's her fault ye are the way ye are." The girl looked wistful then. "But ah've never met a more beautiful lady. Ah'd be right proud if she was ma maw."

The twelve caravans made a neat semicircle, and someone had lined the uneven mud path with heavy field boulders. Every manner of personal belongings poured out of the tin homes, the path was littered with plastic toys and sodden furniture. The immodesty of it shocked Shuggie. Annie stepped up two breeze blocks to a beige-coloured caravan. A large brown German shepherd lay across the open doorway. Shuggie cautiously followed her inside, stepping carefully around the watchful dog and holding his school bag to his chest. The caravan was narrow and long, the kitchenette in the centre and a horseshoe dinette at the far end. There was a colour television hanging from a bracket in the ceiling; it was blaring the horse-racing results in a fast, shorthand voice. The shallow sink was heaped with dirty plastic dishes. Shuggie watched some ants weave industriously amongst spilt cornflakes.

"Da. It's me," said Annie.

Shuggie could barely see the man sitting in the darkened dinette. He was hunched over the day's paper, running a biro pen under the name of horses. "Have ye eaten anything?" she asked. "Ah could make you a bowl of cereal. Ah can even heat the milk if ye want?"

The man with the rheumy eyes didn't answer. Shuggie watched him drink from an old tea mug and go back to scoring the horse races. He tried not to picture his mother here.

At the back of the caravan Annie opened a thin door and pushed the boy through. The bedroom was a pink palace. There were two single beds crammed in the neat space, on each was a Disney princess blanket, and around the walls were thin shelves, each housing a dozen bright rainbow ponies. The room was immaculately clean.

"Ah'm sorry about the mess," said Annie, sinking on to the three feet of pink carpet between the beds. "Ah try to keep on top of it, but it's hard when he's that determin't to sit in his own filth all day." She patted the floor beside her, and Shuggie squeezed down into the tight space. "What does yer maw do on the drink? Does she mong out like that?"

"No, she gets very drunk and then she gets very angry," he said. "I worry that she'll hurt herself."

"Like do hersel in?"

"I suppose. Sometimes before school I hide all the pills in the bathroom. I know my brother takes his razors to work every day." He twisted his finger through a loop of pink carpet. "But most of the time I just worry that she will make it worse for herself. She loses her pride. People don't really want to know her any more. My sister lives with black people a million miles away because of her. My big brother is trying to save enough money to leave."

Annie reached under the bed and opened an old colouring book. He was disappointed to see that she had matched the colours well enough but that she hadn't stayed in the lines. "When the mine closed ah had to stay here tae look after ma da," said Annie. "Ma old maw didnae gie two hoots." She flicked through the pages. "Do ye want to do some colouring in?" she asked abruptly.

Shuggie shook his head. His eyes couldn't help but flit to the shelves of rainbow-coloured ponies looking down happily on them.

"Do ye want to play with ma horses?" asked Annie. She was watching him closely, but he shook his head and tried to look disinterested. "Ma maw sends me them at Christmas and Easter. Sometimes she keeps sendin' the exact same one, that's how I know she's not payin' any attention."

Annie bounced up on one of the thin beds. "Here, yer maw plaited this one's hair for me." She handed Shuggie a raspberry-pink horse. It had a long, purple plastic mane and tail, both of which had been plated neatly and finished in a bow made out of a plastic loaf tag. Annie gathered a handful of other ponies and bounced down off the bed and back to the caravan floor. They were all kinds of coloured plastic, each painted with long eyelashes and cheerful smiles. "You be Butterscotch,

Cottoncandy, and Blossom. Ah'll be Bluebelle a'cos she's ma favourite. The others want to steal her pretty hairclips, but she's too fast."

The plastic ponies looked like puffy dog toys, but to Shuggie they were magical. Annie let him play with the ponies for the whole afternoon. They talked in high, animated voices, racing them across the face of the bedspread. They ran tiny brushes down their manes until the plastic hair shone with static.

Eventually Annie grew bored by the ponies, she seemed restless then, itchy. Her thin arm searched the darkness beneath her bed. From underneath the flounced pink ruffles she pulled out an oyster shell ashtray heaped with cigarette ash. There were two or three half-smoked doubts embedded in the ash. Annie pushed open the caravan window, she lit a crooked cigarette, took a shallow puff, and blew the smoke through the crack. She inclined her head in the direction of her father. "Sorry, he gets my nerves up that bad."

She offered the damp doubt to Shuggie. He pursed his mouth and shook his head primly. Annie shrugged and slid back to the floor with a bump, the cigarette clamped tight between her teeth.

Shuggie was making Cottoncandy chase Bluebelle over a cassette-tape gymkhana when Annie asked abruptly, "Shuggie, have ye really touched Johnny Bell's wee-man?"

The sore sides of his face flushed red again as he remembered Bonny Johnny, the washing-machine boy. Suddenly he wanted to drop the girl's toys, push them away from him like they were evidence of the dirty things he had done. "No," he lied.

"What was it like?" she asked, regardless. The cigarette was hanging from the corner of her mouth as she covered the pony's flank in star-shaped stickers. She did it all with an air of routine and boredom, lethargic as any unionized workie.

"I said I *never*."

Her left eye was shut tight against the sting of rising smoke. "Well. Ah would say 'I never' too. But ah've touched a wee-man before. Ah've touched the O'Heaney boys' and Fran Buchanan's."

"But you are only nine!" said Shuggie. He sat away from the ponies now. "Those boys are in the big school."

"Ah'm ten and three-quarters," Annie exhaled a long plume of smoke, and blew a perfect, elegant circle. "Anyway, they took me up by the old Pit winding machines and let me have some Buckfast."

"Did you not tell Father Barry? The police would jail them for that."

"No." She stubbed the doubt and laid her head on the bed, calmer now. "It wisnae worth it, though. Buckfast's pure mingin'."

Shuggie was shocked at her nonchalance. He was thinking about his mother again, here in this tin box, with Annie's father and his nicotine fingers. He knew she would hate it here, but still she had come. A swift rage possessed him. "Why did you do that?" he spat out at Annie. "Why do girls *always* let boys do what they like?"

Her lilac-coloured pony had been prancing in dainty circles. Now Annie sat back from the playthings, and she was, for the first time that afternoon, lost for words.

Outside, the German shepherd started barking. Shuggie felt the whole caravan tilt as the dog rose and skittered off the front stoop.

"Oh, for fuck's sake. RAMBO! Rambo!" Annie bounced over the bed and out of the tiny bedroom. There was a great commotion in the caravan park as the dog met with another, and they fell upon each other with squeals and gnashing teeth.

Shuggie didn't want to be there any more. He didn't want to be pretending it was OK to be playing with girls' toys or touching the dirty bits of boys in secondary school. He didn't want to be anything like the lemonade girl. He didn't want to be like Agnes. He wanted to be normal.

He rose to his feet and picked up his bag. Annie was roaring at Rambo to let go of the other dog. He could hear the fast gibberish of the racing blare from the telly. Shuggie didn't want to think of Agnes here, he didn't want to think of the nicotine-coloured man pawing at her, and then her plaiting Annie's hair for a warm can of Special Brew.

It made him angry, so he unzipped his school bag and put two ponies inside.

* * *

Every weekday, before the last bell, Shuggie's guts would tighten, and he would raise his hand and ask most politely to be excused. Dough-faced Father Ewan would inwardly curse the little boy who seemed regular as clockwork. At first he would ask the boy to wait, just wait the extra fifteen minutes till the school day was finished. Shuggie, always biddable, would nod with a wince and sit cocked slightly to the side, looking to be in genuine, desperate need. His wincing and huffing would soon start to distract the other children, and the Father would acquiesce.

Later, in the staffroom, the soft-middled Father would joke about what this miner's diet of boiled cabbage and ground mince might do for the clergy. The polite little boy, the only one who clearly knew the difference between *May I* and *Can I* had been getting the cramps at quarter past three almost every afternoon of the school year. Father Ewan had come to set his watch by it.

So Shuggie would spend the last minutes of the school day sat on the low toilet. He would take his trousers down, only to be safe, but he came to know it was only indigestion. It was the burning bile of anticipation, the rising fear of what might lie at home.

Agnes had gotten sober many times before, but the cramps had never really, completely gone away. To Shuggie, the stretches of sobriety were fleeting and unpredictable and not to be fully enjoyed. As with any good weather, there was always more rain on the other side. He'd stopped counting a while ago. To have marked her sobriety in days was like watching a happy weekend bleed by: when you watched it, it was always too short. So he just stopped counting.

The boy could not remember the change in himself.

At what point the cramps died away and things became different was unclear. He could remember coming home from school one Friday in November and standing outside the house as he always did. Every small detail of the house told of what lay within. This evening the curtains were drawn tight against the cold and the lamps were on. His stomach lifted in hope. Shuggie opened the front door a crack, just enough so he could hear the hum of the house. He knew what to listen for. Wailing and crying foretold a bad night; she would want to hold him in her arms and tell him bad stories of the men who had broken her. If there was the sound of country guitars and sad melancholy singing, then the warm moistness of shit would start to wet his underpants.

To hear his mother on the telephone was not always a bad sign. He had to creep in between the front door and the draught door to listen very closely to the tone of her voice, push his ear against the cold dimpled glass and hold his breath. She didn't have to be crying or screaming or slurring her words for the drink to be in her. It could still be there. It made her overly polite, a false Milngavie accent full of long-syllabled words. Her lips would pull away from her front teeth and she would use words like *certainly* and *unfortunately*.

These were the worst sounds to hear. Agnes was mourning her losses but still too far from unconsciousness. She would sit him down and tell him her stories, only this time she would be angry and not sad. With a packet of half-smoked cigarettes beside her she would glide her finger through the phone book and make him dial the telephone numbers that she read out.

"Five-five-four, six-three-three-nine."

Holding the receiver in his hand the boy would listen to the *chirp-chirp* and hope that no one would answer. He grew ashen as a voice came on the other line.

"Hello?" said the stranger.

"Oh. H-hello. I'm terribly sorry to bother you." Agnes would nod her approval from the armchair. "I am looking for someone called Mister Cam McCallum."

"Who?" asked the voice.

"Cam McCallum," repeated the boy. "He lived in Dennistoun between nineteen sixty-seven and nineteen seventy-one. He was a bus conductor in the East End, going between George Square and Shettleston. He had a sister named Renée who married a man named Jock."

The voice, confused at this oddly detailed information, would say, "Sorry, son, there's no Cam McCallum who lives here."

"I see. Thank you very much, sir. I am sorry to have bothered you." Agnes would hiss with disgust from the front room and make him phone the next McCallum in the book.

It was worse when they found who Agnes was looking for. The man on the other line would say, "Who is this? Ah'm Cam McCallum. What do yeese want?"

The boy's heart would sink. "Oh, I see. Could you please just hold on for a minute, Mister McCallum. I am transferring your call."

Agnes's eyebrows raised incredulously. *Is that him?* The boy would cup his hand over the receiver and nod. "Right," she said, taking up her mug of lager and a fresh packet of cigarettes. He would hand the telephone to her like an obedient secretary, and Agnes would arrange herself as if Mr McCallum could see her through the phone. With a fresh cigarette between her long fingers she would lift the receiver to her mouth.

"*Youu baaaastaaard,*" she hissed as an introduction.

"Hello? Who is this?" answered the man.

"*Yoouu Diirty Fuuucking Whoremaster of a Baaaaastard.*"

The man would hang up eventually. He always did. Agnes would take a long draw on her cigarette, then a long pull on the old tea mug. She would stab the redial button on the telephone and smile as it quickly connected her.

"Don't you hang up on me. Don't you dare fucking hang up on ME!"

"Who the fuck is this?"

"Did you think you could get away with it? Eh? The things you did to that young lassie. You bad bastard. There's not a bleeding heart in you, is there?"

Cam McCallum would hang up again, and if he were wise, he would wrench his telephone from the wall. Agnes slid her finger through the phone book like it was a menu, looking for something to fill her hunger. She moved on alphabetically, to the very next man who'd wronged her. *Brendan McGowan.* "Now wait till I tell you about this scunner." She turned to Shuggie with the receiver crooked under her chin. "Losing me was the biggest mistake he ever made."

She could sit at the telephone table until it got dark, then she could sit there in pitch-blackness. The end of a lit cigarette was her only light. Shuggie sat next to the electric fire listening to her roar. He was afraid to switch on any lights, hoping the dark would make her sleepy, worried the light would draw her to him like a moth.

All this in mind, Shuggie crept home from school and listened carefully at the draught door, hoping that she would not be crying or listening to country music or sitting ready for battle at the telephone. Even the hum of silence could set his guts twisting again. He had heard it once and had believed in it, the deafening hiss of nothing. He had crept into the house to listen closer, believing it was good news, and had let his hands fall from his tight sides. Agnes was there on the floor, in her tight black skirt, in her good winter coat. She was kneeling like she was praying, but the backs of her hands were soft against the linoleum, her head fully in the big white council oven. The sound of nothing had been a trick. The hiss of silence was only the thick gas carrying her away.

After that, he'd learned not to trust the quiet.

As far as the good signs went, the sounds of a busy kitchen were the best to hear, the slurp and shake of the washing machine, metal spoons in the sink, and the sound of soup bubbling in big pots. On these days he would stand happily in the hallway and wipe the condensation from the Artex walls till she found him standing there, half-stupefied with contentment, his fingers drawing wet patterns on the white plaster.

Other than the McAvennies, the worst bullies at school always seemed to come from houses where fathers still had work. Their food was microwaved or breadcrumbed, foil-wrapped, and individually sized. Their parents were younger and let their children eat what they liked and when they liked. They teased the children who ate stovies and mince, they would hold their noses and tell them they smelled like rotten cabbages. When they said this to Shuggie he buried his face in the arm of his school jumper and breathed in deep. The boiled cabbage and ham hock, the potatoes and lamb mince, to him it was a comfort, and he felt lucky to have it on him.

There were days when he would come home and hear another voice in the house. He would need to creep along the hallway till he could be very sure who it was. Nice people had stopped visiting a long while ago. The longer his mother had stayed in Pithead the more likely it seemed the visitor was a bad person.

Amongst the worst were the Pit uncles, nervous, jerking men with thin hair that always seemed wet. They would come to see how she was coping without a man. They would bring bars of chocolate and plastic bags full of lager cans, and they would keep their jackets on indoors.

Shuggie knew being home from school was a disturbance to their bad plans. Occasionally an uncle, if hopeful of getting his feet under the drop-leaf table permanently, would feign an empty interest in the boy while pushing chocolate bars across the ash-covered table to him. The man would ask: *How was he doing at school? Did he not like to play outside?*

As the boy got older they stopped doing this, stopped smiling at him with the face of Fagin. Now that he was ten, they saw him almost as another man, and they sat with petulant scowls that said Shuggie was ruining their dirty plans.

If there were unopened lager cans, then Agnes would make Shuggie sit next to the men on the couch. She would lean back and squint through the cigarette smoke, watch them shift uncomfortably. Between mouthfuls of lager, she would study them as if they were curtains and a bedspread and she were trying to find a matching set. She told the men how bright her Hugh was or how well he was doing in school. They would listen and nod and see their plans to jump his mother in the afternoon slip away. Some had spent quite a lot of money getting her just the right level of pliable. Now they were blocked from a clumsy, sweaty fuck in front of the after-school cartoons.

The returning uncles wised up; they would bring cheap footballs, plastic kites, all toys meant to take Shuggie outdoors. The truly desperate would hand over a greasy pile of coins, suggesting to Shuggie, "Take yourself to the pictures for an hour." Shuggie would look blankly at the clammy men and drop the greasy coins in his school bag, like a bus conductor, say thank you politely, and turn on the noisy television.

This happened only if they were still in the living room by the time Shuggie came home. If they were already in her bedroom, then the boy didn't get any money, and no one bothered to ask him what he wanted to be when he grew up.

As bad as these uncles were, they were interested only in his mother. To Shuggie, the aunties who came to visit were often worse. It was like Agnes's worst qualities went out and found a friend. He would be forced to babysit both women as they descended noisily into drunken oblivion, huddled over ashtrays sharing the last of the doubts and cursing the men that had brought them so low. Unlike the men they would talk and talk and talk.

These sunken-faced Pit aunties appeared at the door most mornings like feral cats. Even after a five-day stretch of sobriety they had the power to drag Agnes back into the drink. It was like they could hear her shakes from the other side of the housing scheme and would oblige at nine in the morning with a cheap carry-out. If that day Agnes had the conviction to be sober they would sit down and drink in front of her anyway. Misery loved company, and her eyes were soon greedily on the plastic bag by their feet.

If Shuggie was home from school, he wouldn't let the women in. Even before the first postman had come, they were there with heavy bags in hand. At the front door they looked almost like good people, but he knew better. He tried to politely push them back down the stone stairs many times. He would lock the door, and they would call through the letter box, "Is your mammy no home?" and plead, "I've just come over for a wee cup of tea." He wanted to stick forks through the opening into their thin faces as Agnes lay broken inside the house, her bones shaking, guts calling out for a taste of warm lager.

Like a cold draught, they always pushed in.

They waited till they heard the morning bell, to be sure he would be gone. When he crept back through the door at four o'clock they smiled triumphantly at him.

Auntie Jinty was the worst of them. She would pester Shuggie for a kiss as he came in the door from school. The boy could feel her warm tongue against his cheek like a piece of fatty stewed beef. On damp days Agnes made him rub the little woman's hard feet. Years of the drink had eaten her features, but they spread even thinner in grimacing pleasure as her sour little feet wriggled in her brown tights. She never gave him money.

Jinty hated Shuggie because his presence guilted Agnes into periods of dryness. If it wasn't for him they could have left the shores of sobriety behind and forever sailed a sea of Special Brew.

"What class are ye in now?" she asked once, her feet in his hands.

"Primary five," said Shuggie, keeping his eyes on Jinty.

She turned to his mother; she still had her headscarf on. "Well, it's a bit late, Agnes, but ye know, ah think there would still be time to make a difference."

"Time for what?" he asked, rubbing at her bunions.

"To get ye into oor Louise's school."

The boy flashed a startled look; he flicked his eyelashes at her and drew his brows down. "Your Louise is a right spazzy." As soon as he said it he knew it was unkind.

Jinty pulled her foot from his hand and leaned forward in the soft chair. She uncurled a long knuckly finger and shoved it into his chest. Her face was sore-looking, and Shuggie knew her husband hit her. Agnes had said as much. As she spoke, her bottom lip looked like it might burst. "Oor Louise has special needs, and her school has donkeys. Does yer school have donkeys?"

"No."

"Well, ah think ye should go to her school because it has donkeys." She took a satisfied tug on the foamy beer.

"Mammy, tell her I'm not a spazzy. I don't need donkey school." His voice was whining and threatening to break. He did not take his eyes from Jinty.

Agnes's eyes were closed, and a lit cigarette was slipping from her hand. Beer sloshed on to her lap in big raindrops. Jinty saw her opportunity and went on with a false smile. "There will be lots of other children just like ye. Ye'll make lots of friends and get good hot lunches and hot dinners."

"I have friends," he lied.

"It's a big adventure because ye get to stay overnight and come home on Friday nights just for the weekend."

Shuggie had seen the special bus drop Louise off on Friday night. He had seen the McAvennie boys throw stones at it as it drove by. He knew Louise vaguely, she was quiet like Leek. He had also seen how she looked happier on a Sunday than she did on a Friday.

"Look, it'll be guid. Ye won't be so *different* any more." Jinty turned to Agnes, who was slipping into the noisy sleep of an old man. "That's it set, eh, Agnes?" She nudged his sleeping mother. "Tomorrow ah'll call the school, and Shuggie can go straight into oor Louise's class." Jinty lifted her foot again and thrust it back into his lap.

Shuggie knew in truth that Louise was only a wee bit slow; neglect had made her shy and withdrawn and that made her always a half beat out of step, which the Pit took to be funny-acting. Bridie Donnelly had said that Jinty was just selfish. The special school got Louise away throughout the term and allowed Jinty to dedicate more time to raising her favourite child, Stella Artois.

Agnes said later that by the time she realized what was happening, Shuggie had Jinty on the floor and her Saint Christopher medallion was broken at the lock. When Leek later asked him what had happened, the boy could only remember twisting her big toe till it cracked; he had wrenched and twisted until her knee buckled and she fell screaming for mercy out of the chair. After that, Shuggie said, everything just fell away; it was like when you look through binoculars but from the wrong end.

Shuggie listened at the front door out of habit. As he walked up the long hallway, he could feel the walls wet with cabbage sweat and the condensation from tea kettles. He slipped like a ghost deeper into the house till he saw her standing in the kitchen doorway rewrapping a block of soft white lard. Her hair was soft, white roots shining below the black dye, her face was free of make-up. As she wrapped the lard she was looking out the little window above the sink on to the miles of marshlands. She looked peaceful.

He straightened tall at last, and the pain went from his bowels. She saw him then in the shadows of the hall. He went to her, and she placed her arms around his head and pulled him close to her soft stomach. Shuggie wrapped his arms around her, and she buried her face in his soft black hair. "*Mmmm*, you smell just like fresh air," she said, cupping his cold cheeks and kissing them gently.

"You smell like soup," he said.

"Charming! Away, take your uniform off. I'll bring you some tea."

"You *will?*"

She chased him from the kitchen. The living room was cosy and smelled like hot hoovers and lemon furniture polish. The electric fire was on, and the big curtains were drawn against the cold scheme outside. He turned on the TV, and the meter at the top flashed that they had six hours left before they needed more fifty-pence pieces; it was pure luxury. Standing on the back of his shoes he kicked them off, shook out of his school trousers, and unbuttoned the white shirt. The clothes fell about him on to the floor, where he left them in a melted pile. He sat in the middle of the big square coffee table in his clean underpants and stared open-mouthed at the afternoon shows.

Agnes came in with a mug of hot tea and a small plate, which she set in front of him.

"What's this for?" he asked.

"It's for you," she said.

Shuggie looked at the golden apple turnover and slowly reached out a single finger to touch it. He could feel the heat come off it. She had put it and the tea plate in the oven to warm them through. The pastry was brown and flaky, and all over the top were little white crystals of hard sugar that had melted and made a crispy, sweet-looking shell. On each side of the pastry was hot, sticky golden apple sauce, oozing out on to the plate in bubbling clumps. The turnover made a happy, crisp crackling noise under his finger.

The boy looked down at the plate blankly. He worried he could hardly eat it, as his stomach was doing something that felt like the fear cramps. This time, instead of the choking sourness, something bubbled inside him like yellow sunshine. A smile broke inside him, and lifting his stocking feet he rocked back on his tail bone and spun and spun and spun on his backside until the little tea table was shiny with delight.

Agnes had chosen the Dundas Street meeting in the hope that she would not know anyone there. She had tried AA meetings from time to time, but they had never taken. She would be looking around the fellowship at the broken men and women as the shame rose inside her. In the daylight she would have crossed the street just to avoid these people.

Even though her attendance was spotty, the East End group she sometimes went to had started feeling small and overly familiar. Agnes had made a mess of it. Most of the older men had visited her in Pit-head, and she was starting to see familiar parts of herself in the faces of the drawn, nervous women. It was getting harder to deny she was like them. So one night Agnes stayed on the bus, passed the familiar meeting rooms, and continued on to Dundas Street. It was a fresh start, she had thought, and hopefully a better class of alcoholic.

The Dundas Street meeting was in the city centre between the Queen Street train station and the Buchanan bus station and as such pulled in a fairly wide congregation. The sandstone building had been a once-grand trade merchants' office, but through changes in the sixties came to resemble a poorly run primary school. It was long ago stripped of its ornately carved mouldings and suffocated under dowdy brown council paint, strip lighting, and peeling linoleum. To Agnes, it looked very *anonymous*.

The Dundas Street AA had a cheap, long-standing lease on a high-ceilinged meeting room. A slightly raised stage at the front of the room was set with a folding table and six plastic chairs lined up behind it. To the left were a smaller antechamber and a thin corridor where an urn and biscuits were kept. It felt transient, but the regulars tried to make it homely and comfortable with calendars and postcards sent from Lourdes, from Rome, from Blackpool.

Agnes put Shuggie to bed early and then caught the bus into town, not sure whether she would make it to a meeting or, as she had done before, turn herself towards a bingo hall on the Gallowgate. It took all she had to climb the Dundas stairs, and when she walked through the door she was relieved not to see a familiar face. The air was thick with cigarette smoke. People shifted nervously in their seats, each a respectable distance from his or her neighbour. There was an almost constant chorus of racking coughs and sticky wet phlegm. It felt less cosy than the other meetings. People nodded and smiled politely to each other, but there seemed to be less connection, more of the anonymity she craved. She sat an unobtrusive distance from the front and could feel the eyes burn on the back of her head. She was overdressed in her long mohair coat, but she was more comfortable that way.

A group of people who had been talking quietly in the corner took to the six chairs at the table on the stage. A handsome silver-haired man stood up from behind the table. His eyes were deep and brown, and his brow stood out in a thick, pronounced line. Despite the nerves and shakes within her, Agnes could not help but feel a thrill.

"Hello," he began, in a booming voice. "Thank you for coming to the Tuesday night group. For those of you who don't know me, my name is George and I am an alcoholic. I have been at Dundas Street for, oh, well, nearly twelve years now. I am encouraged by the amount of familiar faces I see tonight in the crowd, and as always I am also saddened by the amount of new ones."

He rested his thick knuckles on the table. "We also have some old friends on the top table the night and one or two new ones." The people to his left and right shifted and smiled. "Afore I introduce them to you let us start by taking a moment and asking the Lord for help." The man lowered his head, his hair shone like Christmas tinsel. Agnes squinted at him then for a better look. The room moved as one as heads rolled forward and eyes closed for the Serenity Prayer. Agnes knew it by heart, none of it had seeped into her head.

The meeting started, and she listened to the top table discuss the matters of the meeting and pass out news and condolences. A friend of the group had died; from what Agnes could tell, it was the drink that had gotten her. George introduced the newest faces on the top table and asked them to share their story with the group. A thin man with a flat Weegie accent stood up. "Hiya, ma name's Peter un ah'm an alcoholic." His eyes misted as he spoke about how he'd lost contact with his wife and then how his sons had fallen into first the drink and then the drugs as well. Agnes listened to the man flattening his vowels, spitting out the story as if he were angry, using short familiar words that the Glasgow people had made up. She felt she knew him down to his particular tene-ment because of how he spoke. She didn't wonder at his circumstances, and by the end she felt sorry for him: he would never have been able to escape the weight of his own accent.

As they kept talking, she drifted miles away, her insides hurting for a drink. A voice called out. "*You*. The black-haired woman in the purple coat." George was pointing directly at her. "Would you like to share anything with the group?"

Agnes made to shake her head *no*, but instead she found her legs tightening, and almost involuntarily she stood up. She had done this before, a dozen times at a handful of different chapters. She turned to the left and then her right and gave a small smile. All the faces turned to her, but their features were only blended featureless smudges. A passing worry that the back of her lovely coat was creased from sitting distracted her a moment, and she stumbled over her first words. "H-Hello, my name is Ag-Agnes, and I am. I suppose I am. An alcoholic."

The room made a sound of tepid support. "Welcome, Agnes."

Agnes made to go on, but she found now that the words left her. Her hand ran over the back of the coat trying to smooth any wrinkles. Except for some chronic coughing the room went silent.

"I am in flames, yet I do not burn," boomed the man's voice.

"Sorry?" said Agnes.

"*Ego sum in flammis, tamen non adolebit*," George said. "I am on fire. I do not burn. It's Saint Agnes's lament."

"Oh." She was unsure whether she should sit down.

"Never a truer word spoken, eh?" he continued, finding his footing, addressing the broader fellowship. "I am in flames, yet I do not burn. Well, let that be hope for us all. Every one of us here tonight has been ravaged by the flames." He cleared his throat and spread his arms, like a fairground huckster. "Haven't we all burnt for another drink, burnt up with the fever, with the sweat and panic, our throats on fire, our hearts burning in our chests?" The crowd made an agreeing murmur. "Then you have it." He made a satisfied *ahhhhh* sound. "That glorious drink you have wanted so badly, and it burns through you, as sure as petrol. Like petrol it fuels the demons in you, it burns you away to the very devil. You go up in flames, and everything you touch you destroy; everyone you love steps away, steps back from the fire. Money burns, families burn, careers burn, reputations burn, and then when it's all burnt, *you* still burn."

The crowd was rapt. "Aye, I cannot tell you how I have watched the flames burn everything I ever had. Even when I was trying to be done with the drink, standing there crying out for help, it was like I was still alight, the great untouchable." The crowd tutted in sympathy. "As I reached out for help, everyone shrank back from me; they pulled away from fear that the fire would return. 'Don't help him,' they said. 'He's no worth it,' they said. 'He'll never change, he'll just pull you down as well.'"

The handsome man shook his head. The room was quiet now. "Still, at the end, it was true, eh? I am in flames, yet I do not burn." He wiped the spit from the corners of his mouth. "That's what Saint Agnes had to teach us. How even in the darkness there is still hope."

Agnes blinked blindly around the smoky room. She tucked her skirt and coat under her and made to sit down again. The man raised his voice again and pointed at her. "Flames are not just the end, they are also the beginning. For everything that you have destroyed can be rebuilt. From your own ashes you can grow again."

Agnes smiled demurely, she resisted the urge to roll her eyes.

The speaker had tried his best to inspire. The meeting went on, and all the fellowship turned to face the front again. Agnes let out a long, low breath; it felt like the first of the evening.

There was a comforting hand on her shoulder then, a woman's hand, fine and pale, but the back of it already puffed with the thick blue veins of age. The woman leaned forward to whisper into her ear. She came so close that Agnes could not turn, she could not see her face.

"Aye, right enough. The bastards couldnae burn Saint Agnes, so they beheaded the poor lassie instead. Fuckin' men! Eh?" The old woman patted her shoulder once, and then, with a cough, she sat back in her seat.

Nineteen

Agnes stepped out of her own ashes in time for Shuggie's tenth birthday. She was off the drink for three months before she took up the night shift at the colliery petrol station. She had spread Christmas over four different catalogues, piling the tree with presents and filling the table with four kinds of game and meat with no way of paying for any of it. As Leek and Shuggie lay fat and full in the glow of the television, she did not realize she need not have bothered. They were happy with her alone, with her sobriety and the peace it brought.

The catalogue bills started to come in, but more than the money there was something else about the job that she needed then. The job helped with the loneliness. It kept her busy, gave her something to do on the long, empty nights. Without it she would have sat at home, wondering what she would do until sleep finally came. Most of those nights she would sit there thinking about Shug, thinking about the friends who never called any more, about Lizzie and Wullie and about Catherine in South Africa. The night shift helped keep her from the drink.

The petrol station doubled as a small shop, the only place for a mile that sold cigarettes, sugary ice lollies, and bags of oven chips. It was the centre of nothing. She pulled a drawer towards herself and lifted out the dirty coins that rattled there, dropped in the change, and pushed packets of fags and pints of milk back through the safety-glass partition. It was a social life of sorts, and she was glad for it.

Four nights a week Agnes sat behind the safety glass staring out into the empty darkness. At long intervals taxi drivers would pull in and fill their black hacks with diesel. Some would ask for the key to the dank little toilet, and some would ask her for a paper and a cold can of Irn-Bru. On either side of the safety glass they would have their banter, about the strikes out at Ravenscraig, about the death of the Clyde, about the shared things in their lives. Taxi drivers were used to being behind glass; their own nights were partitions and windscreens. Agnes grew glad of their company.

Over time a couple of the men became regular, and a few started to have their breaks there with her, eating sandwiches on either side of the glass. The late-night business at the petrol station improved after she started. Some hackney drivers went out of their way to call by, to spend five minutes with the beautiful woman who laughed at their stories, this doll who seemed always pleased to see them. They moved on only when the next driver pulled up.

Sometimes, if she was occupied in conversation, a few of the taxis circled the station until she was free. They watched her like shy weans gawping at a plate of biscuits. She could see them criss-crossing up and down the empty road, waiting for their ten minutes of peace with her, turning petulant when they saw her laughing with some other driver.

Some of the older drivers asked only for the things that were on the low shelves. It was a game for them, to kill the time. Agnes didn't mind. They gabbed away and watched her glide around the small shop, collecting their orders of sugar and starch. They felt less lonely as she bent over to get the day's paper, savouring the tightening of her skirt as she crouched to reach the bottom shelf. They appreciated the way her jumper hung low and the black of her bra was visible against her rose-coloured skin. Agnes knew what a horrible thing it was to be lonely.

After a few dark winter months of working in the station, things started coming to Agnes. At first it was small things, like boxes of potatoes or extra jars of pickled onions from the cash and carry. One morning she was given a shipping box of panty liners. Soon a couple of the drivers started bringing bigger presents, like a used fridge, an old portable television, and other electronics that had come off the backs of lorries. Shuggie had come home from school and found the cracked draught door reglazed. He had come home and found the mouldy kitchenette freshly painted.

Towards the dead end of the night shift there were whole stretches of time when no one would stop in at the garage. Agnes would sit and stare out at the Pit Road, counting the hours by watching the back and forth of the lonely night bus. These nights she would sit behind her safety glass and slowly flick through her Freemans catalogue, spending wages before they were earned. The sun would creep up, and she would get ready for the shift to be over, slipping a bar of chocolate into her pocket for the wean's school and helping herself to a fly packet of cigarettes. She'd open the lock on the door and let the morning shift in. As she walked the road back to Pithead, the morning sun would set the slag hills on fire before the heavy sky had a chance to roll in and cover the scheme in its usual grey blanket.

On the way home Agnes would sing a polite *good morning* as she passed the tired bones of the women with cleaning jobs in the city. The cleaners would rub the gold crosses that hung around their necks and mutter a quiet *aye* without looking at her. What a respectable Catholic was doing coming home at that ungodly hour, these thin women could not fathom. They were suspicious of this woman, who wore lipstick in the early morning and unchipped nail polish the colour of sex. The men who were lucky enough to still have jobs would look up and smile as they passed Agnes. They tried to hide the wrapped lunches that their wives had made as they wished her a good morning, gave her a sly wink.

When she got home she would slip the stolen chocolate bar under Shuggie's pillow, and with a kiss and a cup of milky tea she would wake him for school. At the foot of Leek's bed she would leave his overalls, clean and washed from the night before. The boys would lie in separate beds, silently facing each other, listening to the sound of her singing along to the morning radio. Neither of them would blink, scared to be the first to break the spell.

Agnes had been working the night shift for only a couple of months when she first met him, the red-headed ox. He was different from the others. The other taxi drivers had taken on that familiar shape of men past their prime, the hours spent sedentary behind the wheel causing the collapse of their bodies, the full Scottish breakfasts and the snack bar suppers settling like cooled porridge around their waists. Eventually the taxi hunched them over till their shoulders rounded into a soft hump and their heads jutted forward on jowled necks. The ones who had been at the night shift a long time had turned ghostly pale, their only colour was the faint rosacea from the years of drink. These were the men who decorated their fingers with gold sovereign rings, taking vain pleasure from watching them sit high and shiny on the steering wheel. This could not help but remind her of Shug.

When the redhead first stepped from his taxi, she tried not to stare. He must have been new to the driving. His shoulders were still straight, and the pink in his face was from daylight and fresh air, not dark pubs and golden pints of stout. He was a tall, broad man, and as he filled the taxi with diesel she watched how he stood straight and proud. He rocked the taxi side to side with one thick arm, his red curls shining under the flickering fluorescent lights. He didn't flinch when he saw her, as the other men sometimes did, but he didn't smile either. She was sat behind her glass, her arms folded, as if she was waiting for a lover who had forgotten to come and pick her up. She pushed his change towards him in the little safety drawer, and he mumbled thanks and went back to his taxi.

It was a few weeks before he turned up again. This time she was talking to him before he had even reached the window. "You've not been driving long, have you?" she said, with a lipsticked smile, the drawer pushed out towards him invitingly.

"Scuse me?" he said, shaken from his thoughts. "I cannae hear ye frae ahind that glass."

Agnes took in the broad Scots, the soft song of Strathclyde in his voice. She went on in the Queen's best. "I was just asking if you are new to driving taxis."

"Whit makes ye ask a man tha'?" he asked pointedly, his breath warm on the cold glass.

Agnes's smile cracked. "It's just, I get a lot of taxi drivers pass through here. You seem more . . . cheerful than the rest." He looked at her much as he might a talking dog. She fumbled on. "You know, you just seem less jaded by it. All that driving. All those difficult passengers."

"Do ye think ye are a good judge o' character then?"

The question took Agnes by surprise. It was her that was silent now. The redhead dropped some coins in the drawer with a loud tinny clang. "Gies a pint of milk and a white loaf. Pan bread, not plain. Make sure it's fresh, and don't squash it flat in yer contraption." He pointed at her security drawer.

It took her a moment to recover and get up out of her chair. She was halfway across the little shop before she looked back to see whether he was watching, but the redhead was staring at his feet as though there were a story written on his shoes. He breathed in through his horse-like nose, and she watched his shoulders rise and spread and then fall again. He looked tired, sick and tired. Returning to the window she placed the small milk bottle in the drawer and slid it through to him. He took it up in his big paw. She dropped the loaf in the drawer, and it was only then that he spoke again. "Ye'll squash ma loaf." Agnes looked up at him, dumbstruck. The loaf would fit with a push, but he protested again, his cheeks turning pink, "I'm tellin' ye, don't shove that through there."

"It'll be all right. The bread's springy." She pushed her fingers against the moist loaf, and as if it were an advert for freshness, the loaf sprang back.

The man was silent.

Agnes smiled coyly. "Well, there's nothing I can do about it. I can't open the security door." She placed her hand on her chest and opened her eyes wide. "You see, I'm here all by myself."

The redhead moved from one foot to the other, his cheeks flushed red. He blinked and looked at his feet and took a hard lungful through his big nostrils.

"Look, do you want this loaf or not?" asked Agnes, leaning close to the glass. The front of her jumper shifted, and she knew the black strap of her bra would be on her shoulder. She smiled through half-lidded eyes.

He slammed his thick fist on the glass. It made her leap back as if she had been slapped. "*Mother of God.* Can an honest man no get a flat fucking bit o' toast."

This brought out the demon in Agnes. It did her morale no good to feel so invisible. To be ignored like this made her want a taste of the drink. With a painted fingernail she slipped open the glued end of the loaf and drew out the doorstep slice. She dropped it into the drawer pan like a dead fish. She pushed the single slice towards the big man.

He looked down into the drawer at the loaf slice like she had shat in a box. "Well, take it then," she warned, the smile and the bra strap were gone. The redhead drew up the slice and held it tenderly. With a metal zip the drawer drew back inside, Agnes deposited another slice and pushed it through to him. The man drew it up. They went on in silence, Agnes dropping slices of pan loaf into the drawer and the man gathering them up delicately, like china dishes. She was sure he hadn't breathed since the first slice had slid towards him. Somewhere inside him the air hissed out like a burst tyre, and he looked down at the half loaf in his arms. Agnes kept working the drawer.

"I used to work down the Pit till they shut it," he said quietly. "How could ye tell I wisnae a driver?"

"I could just tell," said Agnes. "I've had experience."

"Aye?"

"I could write a book." She slipped another slice into the tray.

"I don't know how they do it," said the red-headed man. "And the people you meet? Every manner of scoundrel."

"It takes a certain kind of person to be out here at night. Have you been on the night shift long?"

"About a month."

"It's awful lonely, isn't it?" said Agnes.

The man looked at her for what seemed like the first time. "Aye, it's very lonely," he said, his eyes were tired.

She slid the last doorstep slice towards him. "Well, come by tomorrow night. I'll feed a box of cornflakes through this drawer to you."

The man smiled for the first time. His teeth were big and straight and white. "OK."

"Mind and bring a plastic bag 'cause I'm giving it flake by flake."

Since Shug there had been other men, but there had been no nights out. All day she had waited for the taxi horn. She had taken her bath by lunchtime and still had to wait until eight o'clock, when he said he would call for her. The clock radio blinked its neon numbers like a countdown. Agnes swung all day from feverish to despondent, and now, waiting in front of the vanity mirror, she felt increasingly stupid. In her mind she made a list of all the things she mustn't tell this new man. The bad things better left untold made her throat feel choked. It called out for a drink.

Shuggie sat in thoughtful silence next to her, his hands patiently on his lap, his ankles crossed neatly, with the same look of pained nerves on his face. Agnes tried to tidy her life into a narrative and felt increasingly dull and flat. The things she shouldn't speak about left her with yawning gaps. They shaped her into a woman who had been asleep since 1967, the year she had met Shug.

The red-headed ox was called Eugene. It was a good name, both old-fashioned and plain. It was a name mothers chose for firstborn sons, the ones that were to be solid and true, mother's pride but not her joy. It had always seemed to Agnes that it was the name Catholic mothers gave to the sons who were for the priesthood, the children marked like a tithe offering.

Eugene pumped the horn of the black hack, and Agnes jumped with nerves. Small perfume bottles tinkled lightly on the night table. She looked down at the boy, who had crossed his fingers for good luck. He held them up and shook them at her with a hopeful smile. Leek leaned in the doorway, his arms folded across himself. She asked him for a kiss for luck, and Shuggie watched as she put her arms around his neck. At first Leek didn't move, and then very slowly he unfurled and held her in his arms. He showered her cheeks with kisses until, giggling like a schoolgirl, she had to push him away and check he hadn't ruined her blush.

Outside, in the soft evening light, she saw again how handsome the man was. In a wide-lapelled suit and with his thick hair combed wet through, he made the old hackney seem like a Rolls-Royce. Eugene opened the driver's door and stepped out. Agnes saw his thin bolo tie, his tiepin gleaming proudly. This was, she realized, the first time they hadn't been separated by safety glass. He opened the back passenger door for her, and without looking up she knew the Pit women were all stewing at their front windows. She felt the breeze of a thousand net curtains twitching. With a ringed hand she pushed her hair from her face and threw her head high. She could almost hear the angry slapping of gums.

"Did you find it OK, then?" she asked, as he closed the door behind her.

"Aye, no problem at all," he said, starting the engine. "Did I keep you waiting?"

"No, no. I was in a real rush to get ready, the day just flew by." She tried to sprinkle her words with a light casual laugh.

"Well, you look the part." He eyed her approvingly in his mirror.

"Oh, that's a relief," she said, lifting her arms and letting the leather tassels on the sleeves shake. "I had no idea what to wear."

Agnes had never been to the Grand Ole Opry before. It sat on the South Side of Glasgow, on the Govan Road, an old converted picture hall in a decaying part of town. Couples went for the country-music nights, with line dancing and gunslinging matches. It might have been the good craic of the country music or it might have been the guns, but somehow the Opry appealed deeply to Glaswegians. Any night of the week it was ram-packed. For a few hours Edna McCluskey from

Clarkston could become Kentucky Belle, while her man, wee Stan, would slip into a leather waistcoat and a big, tasselled Stetson and become Stagecoach Stan the Bounty Man.

Eugene parked and helped Agnes down from her carriage. The Opry's Old Western sign lit up the street and shone off the wet tarmac. People jostled at the door to get in, and Agnes had the impression of being at a fancy premiere. Eugene cut to the front of the queue, gave a flash of his shiny silver sheriff's badge, and they walked right in.

Inside, it barely resembled the picture house it had once been. It was laid out over two levels, with a big stage at the front. On the stage was a band, the singer in tan-coloured leather chaps, his hair swept up into a rockabilly quiff over his pockmarked face. He held the mic stand against his legs as if it were the girl he was in love with. He sang with a thick Johnny Cash twang.

In front of the stage was a small dance floor, where some older couples were doing a hurdy-gurdy version of a hoedown. Old men in tight denims swung thick-armed housewives around, and they looked like they were having a rare time as they locked arms and two-stepped in time to the band. The Opry women wore either cowgirl outfits with Stetson hats or big flouncy harlot's dresses with lace trim and feathers in their hair. Agnes looked down at her tight black skirt and leather coat. It had cost a fortune from the catalogue. She had sent it back twice to get the fit just right. Now she looked around the room at the denims and the ruffled dresses, and she hated the outfit.

Eugene led her through the crowd. He had leather boots on, and under his tan suit jacket he had a gun belt with a decorative tooled holster holding a shiny pistol in each side. Heads nodded familiarly at him, and he nodded stiffly back. Around the dance floor were small round-top tables where the younger couples sat, not yet drunk enough to take up dancing unabashedly. Eugene pulled out a chair and sat Agnes down in the dead centre of the room, not tucked away in some corner. He took her coat, and she let him linger, his thick hands on her shoulders, just long enough to breathe in the perfume of her hair.

The place was alive with the infectious rattle of the band and the stepping, bouncing dance. The air was thick with the warm smells of golden whisky and leather. It was early still, but the crowd was already carried away. Agnes thought it was funny how a bit of cheap dress-up could be so liberating.

"What do ye make of it then?" asked Eugene, his face wearing a wide, proud grin.

"It's marvellous, isn't it?"

"It really is. Glasgow was the original Wild West, ye know. Ye can still get scalped out on Maryhill Road on a weeknight." Eugene was relaxing into his element. "I'm glad we could finally get to dae this."

"Me too."

"I realized tonight wis the first time I'd could be sure ye had actual legs," he laughed. "That ye wurny just some petrol-station stool from the waist down."

"I hope you are not disappointed."

"Naw, naw." Eugene laughed and held out his paw as way of a formal introduction. "Nice to meet you. Tell me a wee bit about yersel?"

"Not much to tell." Agnes lifted a wet beer coaster and started to spin it nervously. She unfolded the narrative she had practiced in her head. "Glasgow papist born and bred. It's been a quiet life."

"Aye, me too."

"I'm a divorcee," Agnes added quickly, liking the way it sounded better than, *My man left me for a plain-faced dowdy hoor.*

Eugene paused; it felt to her like a second too long. "Could ye not make it work?" asked the Catholic.

Was he disappointed? Agnes couldn't tell. She shook her head and was relieved when, with a jangling of spurs, a waitress appeared at the side of their table. She was a pretty enough woman, dressed in tight light-coloured jeans and a big rattlesnake belt, the snake's head still attached, its rattle rammed in its own mouth as a closure. "Why, hello thure, Sheriff, how's life been-a-treatin' you?" She spoke in a broad Texan twang by way of the sharp end of the Gorbals.

"Hiya, Belle, cannae complain." Eugene held his hand out towards Agnes. "This is my friend Agnes; this is her first time."

Without smiling, Belle nodded her big hat in Agnes's direction. It was a cold greeting. "So, Sheriff, you riding that new stagecoach of yours around this wild city?"

"Aye. Unfortunately."

"Well, a-one of these days I'm a gonna persuade you to come and rustle me up," she went on, in pure Hollywood Texan, leaning close, her shirt splitting open at the chest. "Maybe we could take a little run out to Burntisland. My niece has a caravan by the watter."

Agnes wondered whether they had seaside caravans in Texas. She giggled. She couldn't help it. The waitress looked down at her like she was a pest.

"Maybe another time, eh." Eugene shifted in his seat.

Belle sighed and stuck a thumb in her belt loop. "Well, what'll it be, pal?" Her accent was now flat South Side.

"I'll have a pint and a hauf." He looked over to Agnes.

"Um . . . I'll just have a Coca-Cola," said Agnes. She was dry-mouthed over the moment she had dreaded all day.

"Is that eht?"

"And some lemon?" added Agnes, as breezily as she could.

"Comin' right up." The woman sighed and jangled away, taking care to swing her arse like a fattened heifer.

Agnes watched Eugene's face. She was glad he didn't steal a glance. "Well, she seems *nice*."

"Aye, I suppose," said Eugene unconvincingly.

"That's a very pretty name, Belle."

"Aye, it is. Shame her real name is Geraldine."

Agnes laughed. "Is that right then, *Sheriff*."

Eugene let her laugh at him, it was generous, and it made her relax a little. "Aye, that's Geraldine from Gartcosh, and I'm not entirely sure she didnae kill that snake and make that belt hersel."

"I better watch myself then."

"Aye. That wummin could make new boots out of an old husband."

The drinks came, and they sat watching the line dancers swing each other around and around for a while before he turned back to her. "So, why are ye no taking a drink?"

Agnes scanned the story of the cleaned-up version of her life. "Oh, you know. Drink doesn't agree with me. It gives me a terrible head in the morning." She scratched the back of her neck nervously.

Eugene seemed as if he was not going to accept the lie. The flicker of recognition flashed between them. "Aye, well, maybe later."

"Maybe." She tried to change the subject. "So anyway, how come the town's sheriff is still single?"

"I was just going to ask ye the same thing."

"That's a long story. You remember those boots made out of husbands?"

"What? Should I be careful then?"

"Well, some say I'm a divorcee looking for a matching purse." She sucked on the little straw. "So go on. Answer my question."

It took a while for him to answer. He took a sip of the lager and a mouthful of the whisky. "Well, I was married for a very long time, up until last year actually. The big C. Quite sudden."

"I'm sorry to hear that." She laid her hand on his. "Same thing did my father in."

He only nodded and took another mouthful of each of the drinks. The sweat on the side of his lager looked refreshing.

The country music wound down, and the band told the crowd they would take a break. A sweaty couple came over, the woman in a brothel dress and the man in a standard cowboy rig. "Hiya, Sheriff, how's eht gaun?" said the woman, as honky-tonk as you could get from Glasgow. Eugene introduced the couple as Leslie and Lesley, a couple of regulars.

Leslie said, "If ye see my wife, don't tell her I'm here with my young burd." The little man smiled a ferrety grin.

"Gies peace. Like ah've no heard that afore." His wife rolled her eyes, bored after years of the same nonsense. "We jist wanted to come over and see how you were doing, Sheriff." Lesley folded her mutton arms under her big chest and took her crucifix between her fingers. "How are you bearing up?"

"Well enough." Eugene looked a little cornered.

"We're still praying for you up the chapel," said Lesley. "Feels like yesterday, doesn't it?"

"Aye," said Eugene. He glanced nervously at Agnes.

"God love her and keep her." Lesley twisted her cross.

Eugene lifted his whisky in salute but didn't drink.

Agnes watched Lesley. The woman was studying Eugene, her eyes moving from his hair to his mended waistcoat buttons to the collar of his shirt, bleached clean and starched. She was one of those women who lived in details. *Who was ironing his shirt? Who was feeding him?* "How's yer sisters?" she asked finally.

"Aye, fine enough." he said. "I might be the eldest but ye wouldnae credit it to watch them in action. They could patronize Methuselah."

"Och, they'll only be worried about ye. Tell your Colleen I was asking for her and they weans, will ye? Terrible mess wi' her Jamesy. Tell her I'm sending some old clothes over for them. Our Gerald's taken another stretch, growing like a weed. I don't know how your Colleen clothes five of them since that Pit shut."

Eugene sat stock-still, his whisky glass still half-raised. It took Agnes a moment, but when the penny dropped, her smile began to crack.

"That place is going to the dogs since that colliery shut. I heard all about the Valium nonsense. Oh, *and* I heard all about that alky hoor that's moved in across the street." She turned to Agnes, expecting some solidarity between women. "In my day the Chapel would have moved someone like that along. It's no right, having a wummin like that amongst guid families."

At that, the ferrety cowboy rolled his eyes and took his wife's pillowy arm. He half-dragged her back to the dance floor. "Aye, well, cheerio then," said the woman brightly, and she turned to Agnes. "Lovely to meet you, darlin'."

Agnes nodded, but her eyes were already glassy, black eyeliner threatening to return to liquid form. After the Leslies left, she and

Eugene were quiet a long while. Then Agnes spoke: "So, are you *all* laughing at me?"

"No." Eugene shook his tangle of red curls like an earnest child. "Not me."

"Everyone is laughing at me," she said, mostly to herself. "I must be a big joke to you."

"No," he said again. His broad pink palms lay face up on the tabletop, like Shug's always had, a con artist trying to appear sincere.

Agnes watched the hands rest there and gulped down the poor me's that wanted him to hurt her, the part of her that longed for the expected. "So, what exactly is Colleen McAvennie to you? You all loop around so much I wouldn't be surprised if she was your cousin, your sister, and your milkman at the same time."

Eugene sighed. "You asked me if I found your house alright and I said *yes*. Well, ah wisnae very clear." He took a slow mouthful of the beer, a quick mouthful of the whisky, and lay his palms open again. "Colleen McAvennie is ma baby sister."

The happy noises in the room stopped. Agnes could feel the Leslies surely looking at her. Their thin eyes branded her with the familiar burn of shame on the side of her face, on the hem of her skirt, on the rings on her fingers. She let the words sink in. The amber lager called her name. It said it would make it all better.

She realized that Eugene was talking again. "Our Colleen is only one of eight of us, all livin' on that scheme. Good Irish stock. Ye know how it can be. Our Granda was one of the first miners, and we all grew up and sort of stayed on. They didn't think much of imagination in they days." He tried a warm smile. She was not to be thawed.

"So. What does she say about me?" asked Agnes, straightening her spine.

"Och, don't you worry about her. She says too much about every fuckin' thing." His open palms closed into balls.

"Well, anyway, I can imagine . . ."

"It's just a small place . . ." soothed Eugene.

"*I'm a bad drunk . . .*"

"and there's nothing to dae . . ."

"*and I'm a bad mother . . .*"

"where everyone knows everyone's business . . ."

"*I make a right show of myself . . .*"

"and should mind their own."

"*and I am a filthy hoor.*"

At that last word he shifted awkwardly in his seat. The good Catholic, the firstborn, solid and true.

"I see," she said quietly.

"I have to ask," he said, after a moment. "I mean. *Ah'm very sorry to ask ye this.*" She watched his thick neck twitch. "But did ye ever sleep with her man? With Big Jamesy?"

Agnes waivered over the answer. Years of drink made you uncertain. Years of people asking *Do you remember the night you did this?* made you lose your own sense of truth. The things she had forgotten in blackouts could be small and insignificant, but they could also be epic and they could be wretched. The truth was she had not slept with Jamesy, not willingly anyway. He had conned his way inside her and then he had welched on their deal. That made it something worse than sex. She didn't know the name for it.

"No. I never slept with Jamesy." She said it in as certain a tone as she could manage.

Eugene lifted the glass to his lips again, glad, it seemed, to put something between them. Agnes sat bolt upright, her head tilted high to the point of looking uncomfortable. "You know the things they say about me are not true. I keep a lovely house. It's immaculate."

A thin man took to the stage. Ragged and pinched-looking, he had long white hair in the style of Willie Nelson, the front of it fouled yellow with years of nicotine. He rattled into the mic much like he was calling a Scottish jig.

"Gather round folks. It's that time again. It's H-high Noon. Which for you—good old Irish cowboys amongst us—means it's half past ten at night." The crowd laughed kindly. "It's the gunslingers' ball. So line yersels up. An' we can get started wi' the first round."

Glad of the distraction, Eugene downed the rest of the amber liquids in one. "Right ye! On yer feet." He rose and, not waiting for her answer, lifted Agnes from her chair. He drew back his coat, exposing his two silver pistols. He drew the holster from his waist and encircled hers with it. He tightened it, but it still hung loose. "Right then. Watch me."

"The cowboy onstage is gonnae count to three." He held his arms stiff by his side. "Only when he gets to three are ye allowed to go for yer gun. Right? When he gets to three, draw yer pistol and then aim and pull the hammer and then fire." Eugene drew one of the guns up and with a quick motion palmed the hammer back and mimed squeezing the trigger. "Don't worry about being too guid an aim. Just be as fast as ye can on that trigger."

"I can't. I'll make a fool of myself."

"We left our pride at the door." Eugene pointed to the shiny plastic badge. "Ah'm the sheriff in this town, and ye're my lady. Nobody will mess with ye."

Agnes only heard the part where she was *my lady*.

The thin man onstage called out the women's round, and women started to line up. Agnes hadn't noticed all the guns before, but there they were, long and shiny and fake-looking. Eugene deposited her in line. "I can't!" she hissed.

"Look, jist pretend it's our Colleen, and ye'll surely get her right between the eyes."

The first two women squared up, twenty feet apart across the sawdust-strewn floor. The thin man introduced them as the Anniesland Angel and Delta Deirdre. With his hand in the air, he counted loudly into the mic. "Ah One-ah . . . Ah Two-ah." On three, each woman reached for the pistol at her waist. She drew it level and palmed the hammer and pulled the trigger. It made a loud smoky crack, like a wean's cap gun. Delta Deirdre got the clear jump on the Anniesland Angel. She blew the smoke from the top of the gun. The room let out a roar.

"Oh, aye," said Eugene. "I forgot ye'll need a stage name." He slipped away with a wicked smile. She watched him sit back at the table and order another round. He gave her the thumbs up, his fingers meaty and pink.

By the time Agnes reached the front of the line, the air was thick with sulphur like it was Guy Fawkes. A woman at the front asked Agnes her name and writing it down handed it to the man on the microphone. Agnes was led across the floor and turned to face another woman, the one she would have to shoot. Unfortunately, she looked nothing like Colleen. Wearing pigtails, frilly white socks, and a short kind of gingham pinafore, she was easily sixty and looked like she made school dinners for a living.

The thin man onstage announced the gun fighters. On the left was Arizona Ann. The crowd clapped as the dinner lady lifted the hem of her dress and curtsied. On the right, the man said, pointing to the newcomer, was Phoenix Rising. The crowd clapped again, and Agnes was sure they had clapped a little louder for her.

The man started the count. "Ah One-ah . . . Ah Two-ah—"

"Sorry. Wait, wait!" shouted Agnes, sinking to the ground and tucking her clutch bag between her legs. The crowd laughed. Agnes crimsoned.

With a sigh the man started the count again. In concentration, Agnes put her tongue in front of her teeth. The men were all watching her. "Ah One-ah . . . Ah Two-ah . . . Ah Threeeee . . ."

There was a bang, and then shortly after there was another bang. Agnes opened her eyes. The dinner lady had raised her fist in victory.

In his round, the sheriff made it through to the semi-finals, and Agnes sat most of the night alone at the table and nursed a warm glass of cola. He shot the other men easily, and in a funny way she felt proud; she sat in a daze and let herself think about what a good-looking couple they could make. Then she thought about Colleen and all the other tight faces that had judged her and might be his siblings.

The sheriff was eventually put out by the singer, who went as the Singing Plumber. The pockmarked man looked like he was really into it, like he practiced in his bedroom with his Kenny Rogers records on. He had a scowling face, which he pulled into a cheap Clint Eastwood gurn that he'd proudly perfected.

The plumber went on to win; he got some tokens for free drinks from the bar and then climbed back up onstage, and the band started again. More couples, greased by cheap drink, took to the wooden floor. The sheriff led Agnes into the centre and held her close, in the formal way that young people didn't bother with any more.

"I liked the name ye picked for yersel."

"Thanks, but you didn't give me much warning." He was warm and sweet-smelling and his breath was hot. She allowed herself to be pulled into him and let her body press against the barrel of his chest.

"Ye did great." He looked genuinely proud. It made her happy.

"*Hardly.* I was shot dead in three seconds."

"Did picturing Colleen no help?"

"I had my eyes shut."

Eugene roared in laughter, his eyes shining with the drink. "Well. Ye definitely win the prize for bonniest."

"*Shush.* Besides, just you wait. I've got some old curtains at home, and I'm going to make me a big dress for the next time."

He looked thrilled. He shook her slightly. "Will there be a next time?"

"Go on then, I suppose so, now that I have the outfit planned."

"I can't wait to see it. Will it be one o' they big flouncy hoor's dresses?"

At that word, Agnes flinched as if he had stepped on her toes. He felt her straighten in his arms. Agnes shrank back into herself, and cold air filled the spaces where she had pressed her body against his. The band played a new song, a sad, broken-hearted tune, one that made women dance with other women and sing along.

"So how long have ye been off the drink?"

"Maybe you should ask your Colleen." It was Eugene's turn to stiffen.

"Is it hard. Not drinking?" he asked earnestly.

"Yes, and it gets harder, not easier."

"How come?"

"Well, you get a little bit stronger every day, but the drink is always there waiting. Doesn't matter if you walk or run away from it, it's still just right behind you, like a shadow. The trick is not to forget."

"Forget what?"

"All sorts of things," she sighed. "How weak you are, how bad you were on the drink. You think sometimes that you can control it. That you'll have mastered it."

"I bet ye can master it," he said plainly.

She looked up at him. "That's why going to the meetings is important. You'll *never* master it."

"I hope ma drinking doesnae bother ye?"

It took her a moment. "No."

"Does it?"

"Oh, no. Just wish I could have one with you. To feel normal."

"Och, ye look normal enough to me."

He had answered so plainly, so quickly, that it struck her. "Believe it or not, that's one of the nicest things I've heard in a long time."

They danced on, and she tried to feel better. She tried to cut off her doubt and her shame and let the daydreams from earlier reignite. He could be the one to help dig her out of her emptiness, a friend, a lover, a father. She could keep him clean and fed; she would keep herself neat. He could give her money. They could have holidays. He would buy her messages in a big trolley from a big, name-brand supermarket. She would love him. This was how her daydreams ran.

The spaces of cold air were closing between their bodies again, when something inside her pushed her to ask, "If Colleen told you that I am such a disgrace, why did you come tonight?"

He didn't answer for a while; the wait made her embarrassed, and when he did answer it was clear he had thought about this before. "Ah have been lonely fur years now. Lonely long afore ma wife died. Don't get us wrong. She was a guid wummin, a guid wummin jist like our Colleen, but we were jist stuck in our wee routine." The music didn't match the soft sadness of his words. "When ye think about it, ah've been under the ground most of ma life. There wasn't much in me for sharing at the end of a day. After twenty years, what do you talk about? But she *was* a guid wummin. She used to make me these big hot dinners, with meat and gravy, the plate scalding hot cos she'd warm it up all day in the oven. We ate big hot dinners because we had nothing left to say. Nothing worthwhile anyway."

He went on. "Ah'm forty-three. That's four years older than when ma own father died, so I should've been done. I should've been retiring from the pits, living the rest of ma days out with her and with nothing to say."

She heard his throat catch, "When I saw ye I wasn't looking. I didn't know of you then, hadn't heard our Colleen lift your name. That's wummin's stuff, isn't it? They don't talk to the men about that. Gossip. Telling tales. Chapel. That's their club. All I know is when I saw you sat behind glass, I saw someone lonely too, and I hoped we might have something to say to each other." His lip trembled. "I realized then. Ah don't want to be done."

Agnes kissed him then. Eugene, solid and true. His lips were hard but tasted sweet.

Twenty

Agnes was sat on the bedroom carpet with her back to the door. Soft love songs played on her bedside clock, and she was on her knees, with the pink buds of her toes wriggling behind her, happily humming along. Shuggie watched her head lowered in concentration as she sorted through piles of her own underwear. She was sorting it all, the black from the white, and then separating the whites into fresh bright whites, almost whites, and at the end a discarded pile of used-to-be-a-very-long-time-ago whites. Shuggie came up behind her; he spread his own toes and interlaced them with hers, pushing each joint tightly between his mother's. He put his arm around her shoulder and watched her work.

She held a lacy pair of underwear out to him, it had a sateen gusset in the front, but the sides were all lace. She was pinching the side seam. "What do you think of these?" she asked. "I think maybe they are too low on the hip, a bit old-fashioned maybe?"

They reminded him of something. Shuggie glanced from the underpants to the white lace curtains hanging over the window. She followed his gaze. "You cheeky sod!" But she wasn't angry, she leaned against him and threw the knickers in the discard pile. "That settles that!"

Shuggie picked up an old white bra. He stretched it and listened to the elastic groan and snap. "I bet Leek could make a catapult out of this. I could put in all the McAvennies' windows with five lumps of coal."

Agnes uncurled his fingers from it and threw it back into the discard pile. "I'd never be able to live it down."

"What are you doing this for, anyhows?"

Agnes held a negligee up to her face, suspending the silken fabric just below her eyes, and moved it back and forth, like one of Sinbad's mysterious harem. "I just need to get organized."

"Why bother? Father Barry taught us that the only person that should see your underwear is you."

"That Father Barry, he's a right good time. If you must know, I'm having a night out"—she leaned into him conspiratorially—"except in the daytime."

"With the taxi driver? You're not going to let *him* see your underpants are you?"

She laughed and flicked the small button of his nose. "Aye, with my big gingerbread man. And for your information, *no*, I'm not going to let him see my underpants."

He had been so excited to show it to her. Since he had picked her up in the hackney he had alternated between saying, "you're gonnae love it" and "I hope you're gonnae love it," every few minutes. Eugene drove them down roads Agnes had never seen, and at first she had been sad to see they were angled away from the city. She had been hopeful that they were going for a nice lunch in the town or, better still, an afternoon show at the King's, and so she had dressed for that.

Now they stood looking at the deep gouge in the earth, and Eugene scratched the back of his neck in consternation. "Fuck, I'm gonnae have to carry you."

The mud crept over the black heels, she threatened to topple at any moment. "But what if you drop me?"

He peered into the deep gorge. "Och, don't worry. Ye'll die quick." He lowered on to one knee in the muck, like a knight, and presented his back for her to climb on to. Agnes delicately hoisted up her skirt, as high as it would go, not minding that he should see her thighs but careful not to expose the clumsy, thick gusset of her black stockings.

She wrapped her legs around him, and he lifted her easily. It was very dangerous going down; there were some slick steps embedded into the earth, but deeper down the steps eroded and the path was blocked with collapsed boulders. Eugene held on to the side of the gorge and took it slowly. Several times he had to put Agnes down and climb ahead and then help her over some obstruction. They were both breathless and filthy when they reached the bottom.

The gorge that they stood in had been carved from thousands of years of slow-moving water. The lazy river that ran there was rust red, the water collecting millennia of red sandstone sediment. It looked almost like watery blood, and it made Agnes uneasy. The red walls towered overhead, undulating and twisting with the slow will of the river. In the centre was a large sandstone deposit that stuck out into the water like an altar. Although the gorge widened at the bottom it narrowed towards the top and was overhung with trees and moss. When she looked up she could hardly see the sky. Eugene was beaming.

"The devil's pulpit," he said proudly. "Smashin', int'it?"

Agnes stood on the balls of her feet. Her heels pitched and stuck into cracks in the rock. "Well, I can tell you were a miner."

He was running his hand over the sandstone and moss, caressing it like he had missed it. "The first time we came here was with ma faither. Hardly anybody knew about it then. He'd set up a wee deckchair, open a few cans, and let us spend hours laughin' and roarin'." Eugene was looking around, remembering the good times. "The water is freezin', but our Colleen used to love swimming in it. She had such long legs, she could easily beat any of us in a race."

Agnes frowned at the blood-red water, she tucked her evening bag under her armpit. "She must have looked like Carrie at the end of the day."

Eugene bent over, he scooped a handful from the burn. "No, no! You can drink it, fresh as anything. Look."

He held the water up to her lips, but she put her hand to her chest and shook her head. Almost instantly she wished she had just drunk the water. Eugene looked crestfallen then. He wiped his wet hand on his trousers. "That was stupid of me, eh. What was ah thinking bringing a wummin with your manners to a place like this?"

"No. It's just not what I had expected." She ran her hand across the red sandstone, trying to pull from it the warmth of his memories. "I suppose it's been a while since either of us were at the courting?"

"Does it show?" Eugene rubbed the dust from his brogue on to the back of his trouser leg. He dug a piece of red rock out with his thumbnail. He squeezed it tight, till his knuckles blanched white. "I was only a lowly miner, but ah bet if we squeeze this long enough it'll make diamonds."

Agnes laughed. She unclasped her evening bag and tilted it towards him. "Why didn't you say so? Now you're talking!"

When two German tourists came down into the glen he carried her out of the earth again. This time she wrapped her whole self around him and deliberately held her lips close to the pink skin behind his ear. Eugene had a plan for the day, and whatever form it took, she was determined not to spoil any more of it.

He drove them to the Campsie hills, it was a boggy walk to the far side of the hills, but this time she did not complain. They sat on the far side of the green slopes and looked out over the distant city. He had packed an old tartan blanket, and without her needing to ask, he sat between her and the howling wind and unfolded the food he had prepared.

It was a simple spread, hearty and plain. There were thick cheese sandwiches, in which the cheese was cut in a width equal to the bread, a whole farmer's punnet of large red strawberries, and a catering-size tub of sausages he had grilled at home. What it lacked in flair it made up for in bulk; he had prepared enough food for an entire shift of miners.

"How much did your wife used to eat?" she asked.

"Aye, I suppose she had a fair appetite." He let her laugh at him, and Agnes was reminded again of his goodness. Eugene pulled a noose of lager from his sports bag. "You don't mind, do ye?"

She picked mud from her skirt. "Please. Be my guest."

He offered her a choice between a pint of milk that looked warmed through and a party-size bottle of fizzy juice. She pointed at the fizzy ginger, and he decanted it into a thermos cup. "What do you drink when you dinnae drink alcohol?" He looked truly perplexed. It was a general question, not meant just for her.

But Agnes took it the other way. "Mostly the tears of my enemies, and when I can't get that, tea or tap water."

At that, they had a high-spirited *slàinte!* From where she sat, she could tell the lager smelled that familiar loamy, curdled smell, and she suddenly regretted letting Eugene sit upwind. She picked at a cheese sandwich; the cheese was good, a bright tangy cheddar. Agnes had to pick at it in birdlike pieces in case the thick butter would lodge the bread behind her dentures.

"Is it no good?"

"No, it's delicious," she said. "I was just thinking, I can't remember the last time anyone made me something to eat."

"Oh, my, how they've been neglecting ye."

She held her arms out wide and laughed. "Dear God. Thank you. That's what I've been saying!"

"Well, I can make cheese pieces, and ham with salad, when ye have it in. I can open a tin by maself, and ah can even boil a soft egg." He tilted his chin with boyish pride.

Agnes crossed her heart and swooned. "Mister McNamara, where have you been hiding all this time?"

Maybe later he would tell her how he had snuck the food for their picnic into his own house like a teenager with a bag full of contraband. He would tell her some other time how that morning he had made the thick sandwiches on a cutting board he had taken into the locked bathroom. He would tell her about his daughter Bernie and her prying ways, but later, much later. It could all wait, he didn't want to spoil her lovely day.

Agnes covered her mouth with the back of her hand and yawned. Eugene laughed, and then he did the same. "Aye, the night shift'll get ye like that."

"Look at us in the daylight. Creeping about like a pair of nocturnal creatures."

Eugene took a mouthful of lager. "Well. Ah'm just glad of the work. Even if ah have to stoat about like a, *like a . . .*"

"Well, like a *stoat*," Agnes offered.

"Missus, did ye just call me a weasel?"

"Other men, yes. But no, never you. Mind you, I absolutely love ermine. You can probably make a lovely coat out of stoat fur." Agnes yawned again and turned to face Glasgow. It seemed far away now, a clustered grey mass sitting in a verdant valley. They watched the afternoon sun rake the city from between low clouds. "Can we stay out here long enough to see the lights?"

"If ye don't freeze, aye, why not."

As if the weather had been listening, a cold wind blew over the fells then, and it made her wince as it buffeted her hair. Eugene opened the wall of his body and patted his big chest like it was where she belonged. She was too elegant to crawl. So Agnes stood, teetering on her black heels, and crossed the blanket to lie against him.

She closed her eyes as he folded his arms around her and held her safe. They sat that way for a very long time, not speaking, as they watched the slow gloam fall over the city. She was warm in his embrace, and she leaned back and trusted in the solidness of him. He rubbed the coldness from her shins, and she watched the freckles on his fingers as they slowly traced the sharp bone in her knee.

When he kissed her neck gently, she closed her eyes again and happily forgot all about the promise not to show him her underwear.

"Wake up!" She shook him violently. The boy peeled his eyes open. She stood over him with an armful of dark clothes. She leaned in and whispered excitedly, "Get dressed! We are going on a grand adventure."

He was still half-asleep as Agnes dragged him along the Pit Road and out of the scheme. Here, in the middle of the night, the peatbogs were pitch-black, and everything was silent but for the low gurgle of burn water and the song of bog toads. Since Eugene, it all seemed less ominous to her now, less of a sucking black hole meant to keep her stuck. Now she laughed as Shuggie whined, and she marched, cajoled, and dragged him along in the darkness, never breaking her happy song: *Ah beg yar parhdun, ah never promis't yo-hoo a rose garh-dun.* In her spare hand she swung a half dozen black bin bags. In one of them something metal and heavy clanged noisily about, something like tinned lager.

When they reached the fast road to Glasgow they snuck past the petrol station until they were under the shadows of the oak trees that lined the motorway. She watched the wide road for a break in the traffic, and then they darted out to the island in the middle of the carriageway. Like fugitives they crouched under the cover of some thick, jagged bushes. Agnes was giggling as she tipped up the black bin bags and out fell a shovel and a set of small gardening spades.

"Right, we have to be quick," she whispered, hacking at the soft mulch with the little spade. "We are not leaving till we get Every. Single. One."

Shuggie lay on top of his bed still dressed in his burglar's best. He chewed his lip as he thought about the red-headed man who had been kissing his mother and had put a song back on her lips. He wanted to ask Leek about it, but his brother had disappeared under the hillock of his bed sheets and the boy knew better than to rip him from his dreams. He padded across the carpet and pulled back a flap of curtain.

What he saw made no sense at first. Outside the window the grubby council garden had been transformed. The small plot that was once brown dirt and waist-high grass was a waving ocean of colour. Dozens of healthy, fat flowers waved in the breeze: peach, cream, and scarlet roses, all dancing and bobbing like happy balloons.

He went outside into the clear morning and gathered up any petals that had already fallen from the roses. When he stood up, the five McAvennie children were already hung on the wooden fence like windblown carrier bags. They gawped, slack-jawed, at the sea of pretty flowers, breathing heavy through open mouths. "Where'd ye get them?" screeched Dirty Mouse, the middle of the girls.

"I don't know," Shuggie lied.

"Well, they wurny there last night." A ring of chocolate cereal scum already framed her mouth. Her mousey hair was matted at the sides and pointed westwards down the road like it was giving directions on a windy day.

"Maybe they just popped up," he answered. "*Like magic.*"

The mouth-breathers laughed, a deep slow laugh. Francis, the eldest, stuck his hand over the fence and plucked a whole head off a white rose.

"Hey!" shrieked Shuggie, sounding more like a shrew than he would've liked. "Please, don't do that."

The boy climbed higher up the fence, until the topmost railing stuck in his thin belly. "Who's gonnae fuckin' stop me?" he threatened.

"It's just, they're not yours to ruin!"

"They're no yours either, fuckwit," spat Dirty Mouse, giddy with the promise of a fight. She was half Shuggie's age and already had the better of him.

"Ye think they just grew overnight?" asked Francis.

"*Maybe.*"

"Jesus Christ, you're a wee poofy dafty," said Dirty Mouse, baring her sharp baby teeth in a grin. The McAvennies laughed and bounced on the fence, shouting in chorus, "*Wee poofy daft-eee, Wee poo-oofy dafty.*" Their voices rang down the quiet street louder than any ice cream van chime.

"Ye like willies and bums," said Francis. "Ma mammy said to stay away fae ye, in case ye try and put yer finger up my arse!" The children bounced violently on the fence and clawed at him. They took turns spitting into the garden, arching high and spraying the boy and the plump flowers. One by one, they peeled off the fence and laughed all the way back across the street. Once inside their gate, Dirty Mouse turned and then waved quite happily.

Shuggie watched them soldier in through the front door. He pulled the arm of his black jumper over his knuckles and wiped the spit from his face. As soon as he did, he regretted it. Colleen McAvennie was at the window smoking, her arms folded across her thin body and a sharp smile plastered across her sunken, tea-coloured face.

* * *

All the windows were thrown open, and the cassette deck played on the sill. Agnes stood amongst her roses in cut-off denims and an old cotton top, whose straps she had pushed down so as not to ruin the lines of her sunburn. That summer had been unusually hot, with a series of long, dry days all strung together and a clear sun that rewarded enthusiasm with the threat of heatstroke and blisters.

Agnes whirled as though dancing with an imaginary partner. "Get your wee arse outside and dance with your mother," she called too loudly, her voice bouncing off the miners' houses.

Inside, in the shade of the cool bedroom, Shuggie scowled on the edge of his bed. He had been skulking since that morning. "Look, you can't sit inside all day," Agnes had coaxed. "The sun will soon be away for another year, and then you'll be sorry." She'd spun around, swinging a trowel, like she was mental. She'd looked as happy as he could ever remember, and he was surprised how this hurt. It was all for the red-headed man. He had done what Shuggie had been unable to do.

Agnes looked like the goddess of all roses. Her shoulders and face were flushed bright pink from the summer sun. Her rosy spider veins, from the years of winters and drink, shone on her happy cheeks. It was like Disney himself had coloured her and brought her to life, a fleshier, smokier Snow White.

Agnes pushed the top half of her body through his window and rested her melting boobs on the window frame. At least this was mildly better, he thought, for at least she wasn't spinning and dancing like a maddie for all to see. He had never been embarrassed by the sober her before. It was a new and unwelcome feeling.

Shuggie sat on his hands to keep himself from clenching his fists. He dreamt of throwing frustrated punches. Some were for the stupid roses, some for the stupid McAvennies, but most were because he had waited so long for this happiness and now he couldn't seem to enjoy it.

He looked up, and she was still smiling, dementedly, but it was contagious all the same. Her arms had been scratched by rose thorns but she didn't seem to mind. "You can't sit inside like an auld wummin. Meet me round the back garden."

Agnes disappeared from view, and Shuggie sulked for a while longer. A single white hand appeared from the cocoon of Leek's bed sheets. It pointed threateningly at Shuggie and then, with a jerk of the thumb, pointed threateningly towards the back garden. Shuggie knew his brother had been staying up later now that their mother was sober. He had been drawing, on large rolls of graph paper, schematics of woodwork cabinets he planned to build for his side of the bedroom. The first was a complicated unit to hold his stereo and LPs. Next to that he planned a low pine desk with covered shelves, so that he had somewhere comfortable to draw and a place to lock his imaginings away from his brother. Shuggie had spent hours poring over the drawings while Leek was at his apprenticeship. The units screwed directly into the stone walls. Shuggie ran his hands over the drawings and liked the sense of permanence.

Shuggie could still hear his mother singing. There was a loud metal clang that made Leek kick at his bed sheets and turn over violently. Shuggie took the warning and moped out of the dark house and into the sunlight. He turned the corner into the back garden and found her bent over with a garden hose in her hand, filling a white metal box with water.

She had pushed the Donnelly's worn out fridge-freezer over on to its side. For a year it had sat dirty and mouldy in the shadows of the house, waiting for the council to cart it away. The council wouldn't take it till it was put on the front kerb, and despite the four strapping teenage boys in Bridie's house, the fridge had sat and sat and sat. It smelled sour and milky in the summer and dank and foustie in the winter. Agnes had pulled out all the wire drawers and was filling it with water. The heavy metal door swung open like the lid to a coffin.

There was a tangle of emotion. The desire to jump into the cold fridge and shut the lid on himself wrestled with the need to tell her he loved her and that he was glad she was better. He wanted to crush her with his secrets the way she had once done him with hers.

"What's wrong with me, Mammy?" he asked quietly.

Agnes crossed the garden and wiped his hot face with a cool hand. "Feel that? You are burning up. Ten, it's just a funny age. I think mibbe you just have a bad case of growing up." Without any negotiation she slipped the black jumper over his head and pulled his trousers down. "Underpants or no underpants?" she asked.

"Underpants, obviously," he tutted and folded his arms. "We're not all in Africa."

The inside of the fridge was full to the top with cool, running water. Once on its side it was a topsy-turvy world of knobs and vegetable compartments. With all the wire shelves removed it was as big as a bathtub but twice as deep, with a flat bottom and straight sides. He sank slowly into the cold water and it ran over the sides. He shot to his feet again and looked at Agnes with panic.

"Are you getting my grass wet?" she laughed.

Shuggie pulled up his legs and dropped like a stone into the cool water. With a loud slosh it cascaded over the side and on to the grass. Under the water the world stopped. A wrinkly face appeared above the surface and smiled down on him. The tangle of anger inside him vanished, and he farted big bubbles.

He sat in the fridge for most of the afternoon, long after his skin looked like the top of old porridge. Agnes sat on the edge, smoking her cigarettes, drinking actual cold tea from the mug that used to house the secret drink. The overflowing water made the denim of her shorts turn a deep wet blue. He liked that she didn't get angry about it.

She stroked his inky hair as he made faces like a little fish for her. "What kind of man are you going to be when you grow up?"

"What do you want me to be?"

Agnes thought for a moment. "Peaceful." She pushed at his wet hair again. "Less worried-looking."

His face screwed up in a thoughtful knot. "I dunno. I just want to be with you. I want to take you away somewhere we can be brand-new." Shuggie slid down into the water, sending another wave over the edge. He reappeared, and his mouth was at water level. "Do you love that big ginger man?" he asked suddenly, sinking lower. "Is he to be my new father?"

She didn't answer.

"He's a McAvennie, and they're a bunch of dirty bastards."

Agnes drew in through her teeth, "Well. They're not *all* bad."

"They bloody are." He relaxed and let out another bubbly fart. It wasn't that funny, but they both tried to laugh.

She had been smiling, but then the clouds came back over her face. "It's been me and you too long."

Shuggie watched her mouth stiffen. She exhaled deeply as she stood up and gathered her cigarettes and lighter. She didn't look down into the fridge but out over the brown peat fields. "It's been me and you too long," she sighed again. "It's not right."

Agnes ripped open the envelope meant to pay the catalogue. Flush with petrol-station wages, she handed him a big blue note and let him take the whole crisp fiver out to the ice cream van. Across the scheme gas meters were cracked open, bronze pennies were counted, and all of Pithead spilt out into the street, trying to be first in line for a mouthful of sugar. Dirty, happy weans ran at a gallop, and housewives did a funny rolling speedwalk.

The ice cream van made it through one jangly round of "Flower o' Scotland" before there was a jostling crowd threatening to tip it over. It was a big, white tin trap of a box, and it looked like it had been home-made from a toddler's drawing of what a van should look like. It had seen better days: holes had been smashed in the side and later covered with bits of tin and wood that had been flat-screwed in place. It was set high on its wheels, and children stretched on tiptoes to reach the sliding-glass window. If sweeties weren't pushed up against the glass they could never see what was for offer. Gino, the Italian who drove it, liked it that way. It was braw for looking down young lassies' tops.

Shuggie stood at the back of the jittery queue. He stood behind Shona Donnelly, who lived above them, Bridie's youngest and her only girl. She turned and winked at him and pulled her top lower to reveal the rosy bow that lay in the centre of her training bra. When you had four brothers you were made sharp to the ways of men, and when you were the only girl you always got sent to Gino's ice cream van. Shona made a funny face like a gurgling toad and rolled her eyes.

Jinty McClinchy was an age ordering her rolling tobacco and peppermint chocolate. The weans after her had no money but a good stash of old ginger bottles that were each worth ten pence. They hoisted them up to the window with a clatter and then took their time spending their winnings. Penny chews and sherbet dabs, cheap chocolate mice and pink marshmallow mushrooms—all counted out one by one. At the back of the queue Shuggie stood with his hands on his hips; he silently corrected Gino's arithmetic every time he deliberately short-changed someone.

They spent the evening sitting on the couch watching soaps, eating their way through all the chocolate bars. They finished one and instantly opened another, carelessly ripping the shiny wrapping paper with happy moans. It felt nice, like they were suddenly millionaires. Shuggie lay on his back, stuffing chocolate into his mouth and looking up into his mother's face, watching the telly reflected in her big hexagonal glasses. Agnes was sucking the chocolate off the mint-fondant centre, making judgy faces at the drama on the telly. To Agnes, Sue Ellen Ewing was like her reflection but maybe in a funhouse mirror. She could relate to the alcoholic character, and every time she was drunk on the screen Agnes would make a tutting noise and say to Leek, "Oh, that's just like me, isn't it!" Then she would giggle through chocolatey false teeth. The fake glamour of Sue Ellen's tragedy made it look almost enviable. Agnes would tell the TV, "It's a disease, you know," and "The poor lassie cannae help it." Shuggie watched the actress tremble her bottom lip with fake emotion. The whole thing was a pile of lies. Where was the head in the oven and the house full of gas? Where were the tears and the half-dressed uncles and the sister who would never come home?

The curtains lay open, and the orange lights came on all over the scheme. *Dallas* finished, and the street began to empty of weans. The chocolate ran out, and they sat in silence, feeling sick and rotten and only half watching the adverts with talking chimpanzees on them.

"Dance for me, Hugh," said Agnes, out of the blue.

"Eh?" answered Shuggie, rolling over on the carpet.

Leek groaned, he didn't like it when she made a pet of his brother. What good was a soft boy in a hard world? He left them to their nonsense. They listened to him slam his bedroom door and knew he would be hunched over, his heavy headphones on, drawing again in the black book.

"Go on, dance for me. I want you to show me how the kids today dance." Agnes put a cassette in the deck of the rented stereo. As she pulled her beaded jumper down over her thighs, he could see her mind was elsewhere.

"Well, you stand a bit like this." He opened his feet to hip-width apart. "And then . . ." He started to wiggle his bum.

Agnes copied him. "Like this?" It looked more natural on her, on a woman.

"Then you have to shake your shoulders and move your hands just a little bit." He began a jerky shoulder shimmy, like one he had seen on the telly, done by a black singer with shoulder pads and a pineapple-shaped mohawk. "Then do this a little bit," he said, moving faster and faster, swinging his palms wide in opposite rotation to his hips, a bit like a skier, a bit like an epileptic.

"Like this?" she asked, looking like she was having a stroke.

"Well. Mibbe." He was not entirely convinced. "Do this next," he jerked like a robot and jumped forward and back like he was stamping out a fire.

Agnes tried it, and all the glass ornaments in the cabinet tinkled. "Are you sure *this* is how the young ones dance the day?" she said, already flushed from the routine.

"Oh, aye," said Shuggie, shimmying his shoulders lower to the ground, placing his hands on either side of his head, like he had a headache. He had just taught her the routine to Janet Jackson's "Control."

"I'm needing to rest for a wee minute." She collapsed on to the settee and picked up her cigarettes. "You keep dancing though, and I'll keep watching. I want to be a good dancer when I go uptown with Eugene."

Shuggie felt tricked. If he'd have known that, he would have taught her the zombie dance to "Thriller" instead. That would have shown her. The song changed, and Shuggie kept dancing. It was a self-conscious shimmy now, his hands burst open like fireworks, and his head flicked as if he had long sexy hair. He dipped and popped, using his hips too much for a boy. He emoted along with the song like it was a grand opera, not a three-bar pop-factory hit for thirteen-year-old girls.

"Brilliant! What a smooth mover!" she said. "I'm going to do all this up the dancing next week. Eugene'll just die. Just you wait."

He was enjoying her attention. Something inside him flowered, and he started popping his body like he'd seen the black boys on telly do. The self-consciousness left him, and he spun and shimmied and shook in all the telly ways. He was mid *Cats* leap when he let out a sharp scream. It was high-pitched and womanly, the same shriek he let loose when Leek leapt out of the dark at him. Shuggie stood with fingers outstretched, frozen in time. He hadn't seen them at first, and he would never know how long they had been there. Across the street, in the window of their front room, stood the McAvennies. They pressed against the large glass window, and they were gutting themselves with laughter. The window throbbed as they beat their hands against it with glee. Dirty Mouse did a little sexy, girlish pirouette, and Shuggie realized that was him.

He looked at his mother; when had she noticed? She only looked up at him and took a draw on her fag. Without looking out the window she spoke through clenched teeth. "If I were you, I would keep dancing."

"I can't." The tears were coming.

"You know they only win if you let them."

"*I can't.*" His arms and fingers were still outstretched and frozen, like a dead tree.

"Don't give them the satisfaction."

"Mammy, help. I can't."

"Yes. You. *Can.*" She was still smiling through her open teeth. "Just hold your head up high and *Gie. It. Laldy.*"

She was no use at maths homework, and some days you could starve rather than get a hot meal from her, but Shuggie looked at her now and understood this was where she excelled. Everyday with the make-up on and her hair done, she climbed out of her grave and held her head high. When she had disgraced herself with drink, she got up the next day, put on her best coat, and faced the world. When her belly was empty and her weans were hungry, she did her hair and let the world think otherwise.

It was hard at first to start moving again, to feel the music, to go to that other place in your head where you keep your confidence. It didn't go together, the shuffling feet and the jangly limbs, but like a slow train it caught speed and soon he was flying again. He tried to tone down the big showy moves, the shaking hips and the big sweeping arms. But it was in him, and as it poured out, he found he was helpless to stop it.

Twenty-One

Standing blue-legged in the middle of the football field, he was picked last, as was usual. He had expected that, but it never hurt any less. The fat boy, the asthmatic boy, the gammy-legged boy, and Lachlan McKay, with his love for toads, were all picked before him. In the November smirr they made his team take off their shirts. He walked up and down the pitch, rubbing at his chest, unsure whether it was frozen or scalding hot from the wind.

The teacher yelled that if he was cold, he should move more. His thin plimsolls squeaked in the wet grass, while wiry blue-legged boys tore patches of sod up as they flew past with their studded football boots. He made the lazy effort to be following the general direction of the ball but never made the mistake to come near it. The teacher gave up yelling encouragement and tried insults instead. He was an old man but a fit, flinty one, a Scottish shinty champion in his day. When they banned the cane a few years before he thought he might give up teaching altogether. In the end it made little difference; after all the years of peering into the dark corners of little boys' souls, he knew where real pain and motivation lay.

He cupped a hand over his mouth and shouted up the pitch. "Move IT, Bain! You little bender." It got a cackling laugh from the other boys. They were winded and tired but kept just enough breath to stop and to laugh at that one.

Shuggie hadn't expected Lachlan McKay to laugh, but he did. The day would have passed slowly like any other, but the dirty blond boy had laughed too. The snot and dirt around his mouth cracked, and he had laughed, open-faced with glee. Shuggie picked up his cold legs and ran up the pitch. Lachlan stood at the back, near his own goal, waiting for the ball. "Why did you just laugh?"

"Whit?"

"I *said*. Why did you laugh?"

"Cos I felt like it." He was picking some mud from his leg. The boy's clothes were well worn and fit badly. It was his brother's old shirt turned inside out and some borrowed gym shorts, the ones they gave you when you forgot your kit and tried to stay back and read a book instead. His legs were dirty, several layers deep, and his socks were black dress socks instead of name-brand sports ones.

"But . . . but," Shuggie stammered, drawing his eyes up and down the length of him.

"But fucking what?" The boy opened himself wide and squared around to Shuggie, moving his head like a fighting ferret.

"But what makes *you* think you can laugh at me?"

The ball sailed over them, and the other boys tore up the field like Shetland ponies, cantering as one and giving the impression they were scared to be separated. The teacher stopped at a trot. "Oi, you two ladies, when you are done having tea, how about you play some bloody fitba," he barked.

Shuggie might have said something back, might just have said something really cheeky, if the fist hadn't caught him in the side of the face first. He fell back, into the torn-up grass, the mud splattering up his bare back.

"McKay!" exhaled the teacher half-heartedly. "What have I telt you?" he said. The blond boy stood over Shuggie. Shuggie waited for the sweet revenge of punishment, the only true hope of the weakling. "*Never. Hit. Girls.* Now get back to the game." The pitch roared with laughter.

Lachlan had been shaking with anger. "Ye think ye ur better then me, fancy boy?" he spat. "Youse and me after school, square go." The excitement of the threat rippled up and down the pitch.

For the duration of the match, other boys would slow to be near Shuggie and tell him, "Oooh. Aaah. Ye're dead meat." One or two told him that they couldn't wait, how they wished it was three o'clock already. The McAvennie boys told him they were on his side and then ran over to the blond boy to stir the shit even more.

Lessons for the afternoon passed by in a sea of hairy eyeballs. No one was looking at the teacher, but instead all eyes turned and looked at the dead meat sat at the back of the class. Some of the girls smiled with real sympathy, but most were giddy with the glee of the spectacle. He had barely noticed the big clock above the blackboard before; now all he could do was watch the hands slide round much too fast. Even they looked excited.

The dirty blond boy was emerging unsteadily from a cocoon. He was intoxicated by the worship of his peers. The week before they had told him he smelled like he had shat himself. The week before that they asked whether his mother's benefit book covered the cost of plastic surgery. Now he sat in their false adoration as they jostled him around, and he grinned like a happy pet. He almost forgot what he was fighting for.

Shuggie watched him, and the hurt grew. He might have told a teacher and asked to stay inside. He might have waited until the other children were tired or bored before he ventured out and scuttled home. However, watching the blond boy smile, he felt at the very bottom of the world. The school bell rang. The tired teacher turned a blind eye as the children half carried the boys outside. The sea of bodies dumped them in the dark shadow of the school, a forgotten corner behind the prefab huts, next to the canteen bins.

Lachlan was smiling, the crowd were cheering for him like a gladiator. They made a semicircle as the two warriors looked at each other.

Hands jabbed into Shuggie's back, and he was pushed forward. The boy put his hands on Shuggie's chest and shoved him backwards, he smelled strangely of hay and caged rabbits. "Get the fuck away frae me, ye wee poofter," he lisped, looking round the crowd. They were loving it.

The crowd behind him caught Shuggie and edged him back in. On the edge stood Dirty Mouse and Francis. "How come ye don't do yer wee dance for us?" crowed Dirty Mouse. It made no sense, but the crowd laughed like it was the funniest thing they had ever heard.

Something exploded in Shuggie's chest. He felt his teeth grab the inside of his cheek as he ground them together. Before he knew what he was doing he was flying across the ground and sailing towards the blond boy. Lachlan's face changed from victory to panic in an instant, but it was too late. Shuggie caught him right in the face. It was an angry punch but a weak one; the wrist bent, and the fist made a slapping sound. The dirty boy stepped back, looked confused, and then grimaced with fury.

"You're no gonnae take that, are ye?" shouted Francis, smelling blood.

The boy answered, "*No.*" It was a rhetorical question. Shuggie tutted.

At first their bodies locked in a grapple, a struggle to turn the other one around and drop him to the gravel. Lachlan wrapped his arm around Shuggie's waist and kept trying to lift him up and put him down on his neck bone. Each time his legs came off the ground they went back down again, as if it were a clumsy dance. Shuggie lifted his arms above the hug and hit the side of the boy's face with all his might. It wasn't powerful enough; there wasn't enough swing, and it wasn't connecting right. They were evenly weak; the fight was boring even for bored children. It would have to be a fight of humiliation; the winner would have to embarrass the other to submission.

Francis's foot hooked the back of Shuggie's ankle, and the boys spilt like lovers to the ground. With the toe of his school shoe, Francis caught one sleeve of Shuggie's jumper, pinning him there. *One. Two. Three.* Lachlan hammered down his free fist into Shuggie's face. The blood ran backwards into his nose and bubbled into his throat; he turned his head to the side and it poured out on to the grey ground in a great crimson custard.

Shuggie couldn't move as the boy sat on his chest and Francis stood on his free arm. He lay there making some gurgling noises as the blood collected in his throat. At least the crowd was delighted. Only then did the tears come.

Black spidery lines of blood crawled over the left side of Shuggie's face. He stalked through the long peat grass, as the other children walked down the Pit Road talking excitedly, as if they had just seen a sky full of northern lights.

The sun was already low in the sky, the grass sharp and hard underfoot, a first autumn frost. He stopped behind the Miners Club and fiddled with some of the empty lager kegs. If you shoved your finger in the button just right they let off a yeasty belch. Some of the bigger boys would gather here and burp the barrels, licking beery dribblings off their fingers, turning in silent movie circles like they were drunk. They didn't know what drunk really looked like. Shuggie hated that he was no fun.

He waited in the shadows for a while, half-heartedly burping the barrels, and waiting for the Pit kids to make it home. Skulking through the long reeds he leapt from burn to burn, stepping on old TV's and upright prams to make it over the choked water. He stopped awhile at the downtrodden circle of grass. He thought about practicing. Instead he pushed big grains of dirt with his toe and started to cry again, sore grating gasps of tears, big angry self-hating poor me's.

By the time he climbed the chain-link fence into the back green, he had promised himself no dinner. Shuggie stopped at the upended fridge-freezer and pushed away the scum of dead midges. He pushed his whole bloodied head under the freezing water. He knelt quietly for a minute, holding his breath, but the burn of shame wouldn't go. He rubbed at his bloody face, and the water streaked and danced with light pink streamers. That's very pretty, he thought, then he regretted thinking like that.

Leek was standing over him, his hand on his collar. "Get inside! I've been waiting all bloody afternoon for you."

The house was full of activity; every big light was greedily burning. Leek and Shona Donnelly, Bridie's youngest from upstairs, were busy hanging handfuls of gold streamers. Hung across the wall was a pink baby banner that read *Baby's 1st Birthday*. Over the word *Baby*, Leek had neatly taped a piece of graph paper with *Agnes* written in coloured pencil. The wooden chairs from the dining set had been lined up against the wall and the settee pushed into the corner. Sausages were stuck on sticks, juicy pineapple chunks nestled next to sweaty orange cheddar cheese. On every surface lay bowls of salted peanuts surrounded by plastic litre bottles of fizzy juice, fat and refreshing-looking.

"What's all this for?" asked Shuggie, wiping at his damp face.

"It's her birthday," said Shona. She was unfurling a string of knotted fairy lights; she narrowed her eyes at him. "Is that blood on your face?"

"Just a nosebleed. It happens when your brain grows faster than your skull." He shrugged. It seemed plausible enough. "Anyhow, Mammy is only twenty-one! She told me herself." Shuggie slid slyly towards the pineapple sticks. "I think she might really be in her thirties, but please don't tell her I said that."

"It's her birthday for AA, you diddy, her anniversary for sobriety." Leek was balanced on a chair taping fat balloons to the edges of the veneer cabinets. He was smiling. It was so rare that Shuggie stopped to watch it.

Shona scoffed, "You've missed too much school, Shuggie. You talk lit such a wee posh boy, I thought ye would've been head of the class."

"Head full of shite more like," said Leek. "Probably why he gets the nosebleeds."

"Anyhows, your auld mother is forty-five if she's a day."

"Aye. I'm almost twenty-one, you retard."

It was hard for Shuggie to take in. "But she makes me buy her a happy twenty-first birthday card."

"What? *Every* year?" asked Shona.

"Yes."

Leek nodded at Shona, his point proven. "I know. *I know*."

"Look, I only do what makes her happy, alright? Anyway, why did nobody tell me about her alcoholic birthday? I would have made her a present." He was hurt; he fingered the peanuts, dipping his hand in all the way to the bottom of the bowl.

"Here, leave that you." Shona gave a sharp slap to the side of his head.

"Tell you? That's a bloody laugh. We couldn't tell *the Grass*. You can't keep a secret," said Leek.

"Yes, I can." Shuggie sank on to the sofa and ate the stolen peanuts one by one, savouring the salty taste, savouring the sight of abundant party food in his house. "I'm keeping like five hundred secrets right now."

"No, you can't, you are *the* number-one grass," mocked Leek.

"Shut it," *peanut*, "I know a million things," *peanut*, "that you don't know."

"Like what?"

"Aye, lit what?" said Shona. They stopped assembling the party and turned to look at him.

The temptation was sweet; the possibilities hung in the air like a thousand doors. He couldn't help himself. He ate some more peanuts and smiled.

"Well," *peanut*, "I know that Shona," *peanut*, "is taking money," *peanut*, "from Gino the Italian ice cream man," *peanut*, "in exchange for," *peanut*, "looking at his hairy willie" *peanut*.

Shona flew off the chair as fast as the tight pencil skirt would let her. Banners ripped free, but it was no use. Shuggie was up and through the door. Grasses needed to be skilled at fleeing.

"See, I telt you!" Leek called after him. "Number. One. Grass!"

The party was packed, and awkward strangers tried to cut out their own space in the small front room. Neatly arranged around the edge of the room were mismatched chairs that Shona had kindly borrowed from her relatives up and down the street. Sat on the chairs were the assembled members of the Dundas Street group. They arranged themselves in

tight clumps and sat chain-smoking, quiet but for the frequent chorus of bronchial coughs. Occasionally someone would speak, about the
weather or the misfortunes of wee Jeannie from Wednesday nights, but
the fellowship would soon return to sucking on their fags and looking
uncomfortably at their feet like it was a doctor's waiting room.

Shona Donnelly kept lookout for Agnes, her lithe legs sticking out
from under the drawn curtains. Her pale calf muscles were twitching
with anticipation, and some of the men in the room drew hard on their
short doubts and watched the calves go up and then go down as she
danced on her tippy-toes.

On the other side of the room sat a few neighbours: Bridie, some
of Shona's older brothers, and Jinty McClinchy, who looked sore that
there was no carry-out for drinking. They had heard it was a party, and
now they sat itchy in their clean shirts, lamenting the dry house. They
gawped openly at the subdued fellowship, who were still self-consciously
looking at the floor.

Shuggie washed the remaining blood from his face. He dressed
himself like a forties mobster in a black shirt with a wide kipper tie. He
pressed the shirt himself, leaving thin knife creases down the outside
edge of his sleeve, which made him look two-dimensional. He circled
the captive guests with paper plates heaped high with cheddar and
pineapple. Women delicately held up their half-smoked Kensitas, like
they were eating them, and said politely, "No the noo, son." He would
make a full rotation of the room, and then he would pick up the bowl
of peanuts or greasy chipolatas and circle the same route. To occupy
this busy waiter, the guests started taking food they didn't want and
piling it in pyramids on their knees. The grease stained through their
good trousers and skirts. They hoped he would stop, so they could go
back to looking at their feet in peace. Shuggie was having the time of
his life, and encouraged by the guests' politeness, he only circled the
hot room faster.

On a table in the corner sat two wrapped presents, odd-looking
because of the vast size of the table they sat on. Not everyone had
thought to bring one; not everyone understood why they were all here.

Of the two presents, which Agnes would open later, one was the complete set of *Jane Fonda's Workout* and the other a carton of two hundred Spanish fags that had been wrapped in baby's-first-birthday paper.

"It's lovely, isn't it?" said a Dundas Street woman, pointing her fag at the party decorations that covered the mantel over the electric fire.

"Do you like it?" said Shuggie, in earnest surprise. He was still unsure about the baby banners and the pink, girly balloons Leek and Shona had mounted about the place.

"Oh, ye've done her proud." Her face was cheerful; the rosacea of her cheeks made her look windblown, girlish, and she looked to the boy like she laughed a lot. Shuggie wondered if she was a real alcoholic.

"Leek was working all day," he said. "I've never seen him so excited."

"Aye? You've done a grand job. I think she will be over the moon," the woman beamed.

"Really?" He was still uncertain. "No. I know my mammy. I think she will go mental when she sees Leek has taped balloons to her good cabinets. That tape will take the veneer right off." He began to circle with the pineapple sticks again.

Shona's legs started twitching faster. "Right! Right! She's here! She's here!" She emerged from behind the curtains and drew them closed behind her. She wore a short skirt and all the make-up that her mother owned. "Right, now everybody, *shuuush*."

Everyone adjusted in the creaky chairs, and people who hadn't been speaking still put a finger over their lips. A few people practiced a smile; it flickered uncomfortably and left their faces. Leek switched off the overhead light, and the room was in sudden darkness.

Outside there was the sound of a black hackney mounting the kerb and the sound of the grumbling diesel engine being cut off. Heavy doors closed, and the gate was unlatched. Over it all was the happy *clack-clack-clack* of thin, proud high heels. The glass living room door opened and silhouetted a woman in the lit hallway. The room erupted with a hearty *SURPRISE!* and cut her off mid-sentence. Some of the older men had been taking a draw on their fags when she entered, and having missed their cue, they added a weak refrain of, "Aye, surprise right enough, hen."

Shuggie rushed straight up to her. "Mammy, do you want a pineapple stick? *They are to die for.*"

Agnes fell back against the door frame, and her hands shot to her painted mouth. She was dressed as though for a night at the opera, but in reality she had spent the afternoon playing the Buy One, Get One at the Ritz bingo hall. Eugene's blue eyes peered tentatively over her shoulder. There was Chapel in his stern face, and he couldn't help but look down his nose at the ragged band sat around the place. He stepped into the room and nodded solemnly, as though he were at a wake.

"What's all this, then?" asked Agnes. Her eyes were wide and swivelling, trying to take in the room. She had never seen some of these faces outside the old merchant's offices in Dundas Street. It was all somehow disconcerting.

"Happy birthday!" said Leek.

"What are you talking about?" Agnes was still turning about the room.

"It's your first birthday. Mary-Doll phoned to warn us. She told us it was important to celebrate on the road to recovery." Leek was beaming from ear to ear. He pointed at a tiny brown-haired woman sucking on a cigarette doubt. "It's been a *whole* year that you've been sober."

"It's true. Leek's been counting," added Shuggie.

"You've been counting?" asked Agnes.

"Yes," said both boys at once. Shuggie took a tattered paper calendar from the sideboard. Little pages hung below a watercolour picture of the Immaculate shrine at Lourdes. He leafed through a half dozen pages that Leek had marked off with small crosses.

People started to mill about the small front room, glad of the chance to get up off the hard chairs. Agnes swung from face to face, tearily receiving their hugs and letting them kiss her cheek with their blessings. Shuggie supervised the opening of the swollen bottles of ginger; he poured the sticky acid fizz into paper cups. Shona handed Eugene a bright green cup of limeade, and he looked down into it like it was very foreign.

"I've never heard of this Pithead place afore," said one of the Wednesday-night women. Mary-Doll was small and reedlike, as though the drink had whittled her away like a piece of soft carving wood. Her cheeks were sunken in under her big chestnut-brown eyes, and her dark hair sat on her rotted frame like a borrowed wig. Agnes had been silenced when she first learned that the woman was only twenty-four. She had touched her hand to her heart and heard Lizzie whisper that there is always someone worse off than you are.

Agnes cupped the little woman's hand in her own. "I've been praying for you. Any luck with your weans?"

Mary-Doll lit up, and the youth in her eyes became clear and new again. "Did I tell you already that ma youngest boy is just starting the school?"

"You must have been proud. Wee children look just smashing all done up in their blazers and tie."

A shadow crossed Mary-Doll's face. "Aye, he did that. I only managed to see a wee photograph, but I was sure and phoned him that night. He was so excited."

"Are they still with your granny?"

"Aye. She'll still no let me near them."

Just the thought of being separated from her boys made Agnes want to squeeze them close; it was enough that she had lost Catherine because of the drink. "There was a time I thought you'd never stop the shakes. Have faith, hen. Your granny will come around."

"Aye, I hope so," whispered the thin woman, not at all convinced. "It's a lovely photo right enough. I bought a nice frame for it and put it on the wall."

A man stood up from one of the borrowed chairs. Monday-Thursday Peter was the same age as Agnes but looked more the age of her father. He dressed in light bleached denims and a thick Shetland wool jacket that had gone out of style in the days when Agnes was first married to the Catholic. The man moved with an odd jangling gait, like he was made up of a pile of plates that threatened to teeter over. He had a gregarious, chatty way about himself, something he affected to cover his loneliness. "Haw, Agnes," he crowed. "How does it feel to be a born-again? A one-year-old."

"To tell you the truth I hadn't realized," said Agnes.

"Aye, well, it's nice to see yer weans so proud." Monday-Thursday Peter pointed to Leek. "They were keen to dae a little something. Ye know, tae keep the momentum gaun. Gie ye a wee boost over the hump of the first year."

Eugene had been standing at the mouth of the living room door, not committing to the room but unable to tear himself away from the spectacle of nervous bodies. Shuggie stood by the table of food, wiping the grease and sauce off the edges of the plates. He turned the plates just so, lining up fleshy chipolatas into neat arrangements and rotating the cheese so that the tops didn't dry out and crack. Eugene watched him fuss. The boy was making a decorative pyramid of paper cups when he finally looked up and saw Eugene silently watching.

"How's it goin', wee man?" asked Eugene, inching forward with his hands in his pockets.

"Fine, I was just . . ." Shuggie looked at his fussy pyramid of cups and drew his hand through it like a bulldozer. Paper cups spilt all over the floor.

They turned side by side, watching the party like it was a spectator sport and trying not to look at each other. "Quite the night, isn't it, eh?" said Eugene, kindly ignoring Shuggie's display of home-making and then home-wrecking.

"I suppose. I think Leek has lost his mind."

Eugene laughed. "No! It's a grand thing to love your mother. After all, ye only get the one." He smiled, then asked abruptly, "You know who ah am, right?"

Shuggie nodded and answered in a flat monotone. "You are Eugene McNamara. You are Colleen's big brother. You might be my new daddy." He was looking at his shoes. "But no one asked me about that."

"Oh?" It caught Eugene off guard.

"Well, I think it's bad-mannered of a person to claim a thing like that and not even ask the boy if he wants a daddy."

"You are quite right. A gentleman should properly introduce himself to another man." Eugene was holding his hand out for Shuggie to shake. "Ah'm Eugene. Nice to finally meet ye."

The boy shook it with trepidation. It was a bear's paw of a hand, one of the roughest things he had ever touched. "Do you plan on staying long?"

"Maybe an hour or so."

"No, I meant around and about, staying together with my mammy."

"Oh! I don't know. I hope so."

"Mister McNamara. I won't like you if you disappoint her."

For a while Eugene said nothing. The strange little boy had stunned him to silence. "You know, son, maybe it's time you thought more about yourself. Leave your mammy be for a while. I can take it from here. You should get out and play with some weans your own age, try to be more like the other wee boys."

From the pocket of his dress trousers Eugene drew out a little red book no bigger than a packet of cigarettes. It was thin and cheaply printed. He handed it to the boy, and Shuggie looked at the dog-eared cover. It read: *Free Gift with your purchase of the Glasgow Evening Times*. On the cover was a black-and-white picture of an old football hero; his socks looked thick and woolly. It was the *Wee Red Book Guide to Scottish Football History*.

Shuggie looked down at the book and flicked through the yellowed newsprint pages full of old football scores. *Scottish Premier League Results. Gers won 22, drew 14, lost 8, 58 points total. Aberdeen won 17, drew 21, lost 6, 55 points total. Motherwell won 14, drew 12, lost 10.* His face flushed with shame; any feelings of superiority left him. "Thanks," he said, and he slipped it quickly into his pocket, like it was a dirty secret.

Shuggie crossed the room to where his mother stood with the men from the Dundas Street chapter. They looked up at her like an adoring choir. The first man, Monday-Thursday Peter, supported another man by the elbow. This second man looked like he'd taken a stroke or like his motor functions had been addled by the drink. The third man was younger and broader, not yet a ruin or a shell, but his fingers were dirty with cigarette stains. This younger man was closer in age with to Leek. His hair was bleached at the tips, and he was dressed in a trendy nylon anorak, but it gave him the look of a jakey. He looked sly and light-fingered, like the Pithead boys who stood outside Mr Dolan's and used their Army pockets to shoplift. Shuggie was glad he had hidden his mother's Capodimonte ornaments. Then this young man smiled. His teeth were small but straight and white. His face was handsome and healthy and kind. Shuggie felt funny inside. The football book burnt his leg.

"Oh, this is my youngest, Hugh." Agnes was proudly stroking the top of his head.

"Hiya, pal," said the first man. He held his hand out to the boy. "I'm your Uncle Peter."

Shuggie looked at the hand without taking it and then looked up coldly at the man. "No," he sighed. "You're just *Peter*. I am very well aware of my family tree, thank you."

"Aye, he's a bright lad, right enough," said the man, straightening up. This close, Shuggie could see where his shaky hands had forgotten to shave; there were sore-looking patches on the underside of his chin.

Agnes gave Shuggie such a hard shake that his hair fell out of its neat parting. "What's gotten into you? Apologize to Mister . . . eh, Mister . . ." Agnes was lost for words, and Monday-Thursday Peter fidgeted uncomfortably. She shook her boy again. "Apologize to Peter!"

"I'm sorry, Mister Peter," he said, but his eyes were watching Eugene.

Mary-Doll crossed the room towards Eugene. "I've no seen you afore. Are you wi' the Dundas Street group?"

"Naw."

"Aye, I thought I didnae recognize ye." She pulled her shiny fringe down over her eyes, and feeling better she grinned. "I've been sober myself for nearly three months now. The council just gave me a wee flat. I was on that list for nearly four years, mind. I'm hoping to get bunk beds for the living room soon. Then my weans can come stay." She curled a tendril of her shiny hair flirtatiously around her finger.

Eugene tried a thin smile. She took it the wrong way.

Mary-Doll kept pumping out private details without a pause or concern. "I been saving up hard, and I've already bought myself a wee colour portable and a lovely new rug, bits and bobs, you know, this and that. I wish I had Agnes's touch, mind. She keeps a lovely house, doesn't she? She keeps herself lovely an all. Even at her worst she was always spotless."

"That right?"

"Aye. Even at her worst she was always neat as a pin." She changed course, tired of talking about other women. She placed her hand on his arm. "Listen, you didnae tell me which meeting you went to."

"Oh, well, I don't. I don't go to any meeting. I don't have a problem."

"*Oh, aye?* Lucky you. Do ye want mine?" She laughed, her gums were white and anaemic-looking.

"No, thanks." Eugene lifted his head and called over the music to Agnes. He thought she looked uncomfortable too and wondered what her boy was saying that made her look so. He nodded his big red head, and she made her way over to the door.

Eugene excused himself from the ghostly woman and led Agnes out into the hall. The hall was quiet and less smoky, and he finally let out a breath. Agnes watched as Eugene placed his hand on his money belt in a way that made her uncomfortable. "Listen, I better get back out there. You know, make a couple of fares before the clubs all shut for the night."

"Oh. Yes, of course. Are you all right?"

"Aye, aye," he answered too quickly. He scratched the line of hair at the back of his neck.

Agnes knew lying when she saw it. She leaned forward to kiss him on the lips, but Eugene turned awkwardly and caught her on the cheek. It was light and dry, like a casual greeting between French friends. As he pulled away, she realized she was still standing with her lips parted, ready for a proper kiss that never came. It was her sex kiss, and it was unwanted. It made her feel old and dirty. She could see Colleen in him now, and too late she changed her expression, from love to hurt to one of armour.

"Well, I'll phone ye, alright?"

"Yes. Please do." She sniffed airily, folding her arms.

"Well, you had better get back to yer. Eh. Yer . . ." He stumbled for words. "Yer *party*."

She watched the door close behind him, then the jiggle of the handle as he took care to make sure it caught in its lock, like he was sealing a box. She heard the gate latch on his way out and his voice call out to his nieces and nephews playing outside. It was a different voice than the one he had used on her. A life spent listening to the sounds of taxis told her he slammed the door of the hackney. She could hear the engine start with a growl and could tell he pulled away too fast. But, then, reading the taxis was the easy part.

From the living room she could hear the sugary hiss of more bottles of fizzy ginger being opened. She watched her friends in the room in their loose-fitting clothes. For years the drink had held them stuck, like they were frozen, robbing decades from them, spinning them out of the world and sucking the literal life from them. She felt ill suddenly, felt like she wanted them out of her house, to give her life a good bleaching.

Agnes looked down at herself and felt embarrassed for being so low as to be with them. Then she felt lower for being such an unchristian cur. Along the hall ceiling floated a thick wave of cigarette smoke. Someone put on a new top-forty record. Agnes had heard it before. The squeaky-voiced singer started singing, "Happy birthday, happy birthday." Agnes headed to the bathroom to fix herself up.

Was she broken and stuck, like them? In the mirror a facsimile of Elizabeth Taylor looked back at her, only now it was Liz, the vain and haughty version from the paparazzi photos on the yacht in Puerto Vallarta. Her hair was still thick, her make-up still feline. But now the hair was too black and the make-up was too heavy, the popular colours of a decade gone by. Even her eyelids were metallic green, like oxidized copper. She took out an old tortoiseshell pick comb and fixed the curls in her hair, flattening them into wavy layers and making them smoother, less bouffant-like, less old-fashioned. She took an elastic band and pulled a mean ponytail into the back, the first one she had ever worn. It lifted her face as she wiped the heavy lipstick from her lips, the metallic gleam from her eyelids, and the pink rouge from the burst red veins. Blank as a canvas now, she drew electric-blue kohl under her eyes, the way she had seen the young girls on *Top of the Pops* wear it.

When she lifted her head again, the woman who looked back at her was just the same. She was stuck like the others. It had nothing to do with the outside.

She was sick for a drink then, something, anything, to take the woman in the mirror away. Agnes drew the old gas-bill envelope out of her make-up bag and took out two of Bridie Donnelly's happy pills. Without water she crunched, tilted her head and swallowed them down, like a baby bird.

She took her time, finished her cigarette, and dropped it hissing into the toilet. As she watched it swirl down the drain she slowly forgot what had been bothering her. She looked in the mirror again and smiled. Now she was fixed up.

Twenty-Two

When Shuggie came home from school on his eleventh birthday there was a shoebox sat on the top step and a black hackney parked outside. Eugene had been cooler towards her since the party, so much so that even Leek had noticed. On the nights she didn't work at the petrol station Agnes had taken to chain-smoking by the phone and underlining pages from her twelve-step book. Shuggie and Leek had lain awake those nights. In the dark their eyes locked together as they listened to her sighing in front of the late-night television, knowing she wasn't paying attention to any of it.

Shuggie missed school for three days. He faked constipation cramps and followed her around the house reading aloud from *Danny, the Champion of the World*. He believed if he could fill her every moment with noise then maybe she would stay away from the drink. He had stood outside the bathroom as she peed and told her of the pheasants that Danny tricked with sleeping pills. He climbed into her cold bed at night and read non-stop as she lay awake. When she could take no more, Agnes filled him full of milk of magnesia and was relieved when he was loosened up enough to go back to class.

Shuggie sat on the doorstep and lifted the strange box on to his lap. Nestled inside, in clouds of white tissue paper, was a pair of black football boots. Shuggie slipped out of his shiny school shoes and into the studded boots. He clacked up and down the path. The boots were easily two sizes too big for him, but they looked like the same kind the boys at school wore. As he clacked around in circles he wondered whether they made him more normal.

The milk of magnesia grumbled inside, loosening his bowels. He pulled on the front door handle, but it was locked. He understood that well enough. As he waited in the shadows of the house he was just glad that Eugene had come back around; even a McAvennie for a father was better than his mother on the drink. He rested his ear against the door and prayed for Eugene to stay, prayed that his mother would find strength to stay off the drink and be at peace. Then he prayed for God to make him normal for his birthday.

His stomach flipped again. He was cupping one hand over his grumbling backside and with the other he pulled violently at the door. A key turned inside the lock, and the handle jerked from his grasp.

It wasn't Eugene. In the doorway stood his father. He was flattening his hair back over his pink head, and he looked down at the boy in shock. "You home from school already?" was all he said, after all this time.

Shuggie, wide-eyed, nodded like he was simple. He hadn't seen Shug since that afternoon at Rascal's three years ago. Shug tucked the back of his dress shirt into his strained trouser band and nodded at the boy's feet, "So, you like your present?" Shuggie looked down at his feet and realized the black football boots were not from Eugene after all. Before he could answer, his father grabbed at his face and said, "*Fuck me.* You're no half getting that big old Fenian nose."

Shuggie's hand flew defensively to his Campbell nose. He traced the little horse bone, the rudder-like bump that was growing there.

Shaking his head in disappointment, Shug pulled out the change dispenser he used in the taxi. With a flick of his thumb he slid out two twenty-pence pieces. "Here, mibbe if you take up the boxing somebody'll break it for ye."

Shuggie looked at the coins for a while, feeling more shocked than ungrateful. Shug took it the wrong way and reluctantly pumped out four fifty-pence pieces. "*Don't ask for mair!*" Grudgingly, he dropped the money into the boy's hand. "So, are you chasing the lassies yet?"

The boy had never been asked that before. He shrugged.

Shug thought of himself at eleven and took that as false modesty. "Aye, well, mibbe you're a Bain man after alls, eh?" His tongue wet his bottom lip. "It's a grand age to be sticking yersel into a lassie's bread bin, seeing as ye've got a couple mair years afore any real harm can come of it."

Shuggie could think only of Granny Lizzie's bread bin and the thick-crusted loaf she had always kept in there. The way she had cut away the crusts for him and then slathered them with butter and ate them herself.

"Well, I cannae stay talking aw day. You are spending my money quicker than I can make it." Shug stepped around his son and groaned as he got back into the hackney. The boy watched it sink and sigh under his weight. "Be sure and look after your mammy. Try and stop her from taking up with any Catholics, ye hear?" His father turned the engine over and drove off without a goodbye.

Shuggie turned towards the quiet darkness of the house. He stepped clean out of the new boots, and with a high kick sent them flying towards the peatbogs. He went inside and found her there, sat on the edge of his single bed. The covers were rumpled behind her, and at her feet sat a bag full of Special Brew. They looked at each other with the same dazed look, like they had both woken up from the same peaceful nap, like it would be a while before they felt like they had the will to form words and speak.

He had heard she was doing well, or rather, he hadn't heard anything, and that was the point. It had been over a year since she had called the taxi rank. Fourteen months since she had screamed blue murder down the phone at the dispatcher or since she had threatened to stick a knife in the boy and then gas herself. It had been over a year that he hadn't heard.

The boy's birthday was coming up, and that would be as good a time as any to see for himself. One of the other drivers had gotten a shitload of black football boots off the back of a lorry. They had pulled up a rental van next to the articulated truck, and while it was unloading, they stole six dozen pairs right there in the middle of Sauchiehall Street, as nice as you like, in broad daylight.

What boy didn't like football? If Agnes had a new man, he could just drop off the boots. No harm in that. If she didn't have a man then he wanted to know why she had stopped bothering him. She had hurt his ego in an unexpected way, so into the birthday bag he had slipped six cans of Special Brew.

Shug slid down the window of the hackney and leaned his arm on the hot black metal. He watched the light catch the gold of his rings and thought how his hands looked better after a week in the sun at Joanie's caravan. Everything looked better when he had a bit of colour on him. As he raced along the carriageway he wondered if Agnes was still as beautiful as he remembered. He appreciated Joanie, but she was no looker when held up next to Agnes Campbell. Joanie was peace and quiet. She was even and steady and not a bit of bother. She took a drink but never got drunk, and she never cared for the bingo or fancy carpets or dreaming. Joanie was a hard grafter and was content with her lot. She had little personality but was dirty and grateful in bed in the way that he knew plain women often were. Still, he had to admit that in the looks department Agnes Campbell was a prize mare and Joanie was only a scrapmonger's pony.

As he turned off into the colliery town he wondered if she'd ruined her looks with the drink yet. He'd seen it before. There was a type, especially in Glasgow, women who froze and withered at the same time. Their faces shrank, sucked dry by the drink, red lines bloomed on bony cheeks, sagging bags of sadness bloated under watery eyes. They tried to cover it all up, but they were stuck, and their faces became a museum to outdated hairstyles and heavy make-up. He wondered if she still had the light Irish eyes and the high cheeks, that soft pinkness that always smelled so clean and sweet. In the hot taxi he smiled and felt his blood rise for her. He found himself thinking about what he would say to be able to fuck her one last time. He was glad he had taken a bath the night before.

Shug had not been out this way in years. A look in the phone book confirmed it was still the exact same address. She still took his name.

Bain. He smiled, thinking her too proud to go back to being a dirty, common Mick. He found the house easily, the glorious garden of roses, too conspicuous and too showy for the shabby Pit town. The door was a different colour to the others, freshly painted in a red gloss; it looked confident, and it made him happy to see that. He knocked on the door and waited there for her to answer. From inside he could hear the roar of a hoover. He knocked again, and the machine went dead. He heard doors opening and cracked his best smile as the red swung inwards.

Agnes always kept the windows open in summer, and the opening door sent a wind rushing through Shug's long, thin hair. As she looked down on him, she caught him trying to hold it vainly back in place over his shiny skull. The lecherous smile slipped from his face.

There was no make-up on her face, and although older she looked as fresh as when they had first met. On her cheeks were thin broken lines, but the eyes still shone, and Shug thought how she looked as if she had just been out for a brisk walk. Her hair, dark as night, sat soft and curly on her head. It made him angry that she was looking down on his own baldness.

"There she is. The love of my life."

Agnes looked blankly down at him, her tongue rammed into the roof of her mouth.

"Well, don't look so bloody surprised." As soon as he said it, he knew he wouldn't win her over like that. He wanted to sound light and easy, remind her of what she had been missing. "It's been a while. Have ye no missed me?"

"You've gotten fatter."

His hand went from his hair to his belly. "Oh, aye, mibbe. She's a good cook, that Joanie."

Agnes winced. "A well-rounded hoor then."

"Look, I didn't come here to fight at your front door. I brought the wean a present for his birthday." He held up the cheap plastic bag. "Can I no come in?"

Agnes folded her arms across her chest like a blockade. Then she folded her face closed. "My boy needs nothing from you."

Shug studied her for a minute and worried he might have lost her forever. He wondered, how does a fish free itself of a hook? He reached into the bag and pulled out the football boot box. He held it out to her. She would not uncross her arms to take it, so he laid it, like an offering to the gods, down on the top step at her feet. "You know you've always been the love of my life." It was true, and it was a shame. "Here, this is for you." He offered the bag of lager as he retreated backwards.

"Those days are gone," she said coolly.

"Oh!" His lips pursed in admiration. "How long has it been this time?"

"Long enough to matter."

He gave her small round of applause. "I thought I hadn't been hearing from you."

"So you came for a look at the ruins. Just to check?"

"S'pose you cannae kid a kidder." He held his palms up in admission. "Can I no come in, *Missus Bain*?" He wielded her name as softly as he could.

She didn't say yes, and she didn't say no. She just turned and walked up the hallway into the kitchen. She heard the door close behind her, heard the key turn in the lock and the heavy footsteps of Shug at her back.

"I like what you have done with the place." Shug sat down at the little folding table; he was studying the corner where the damp still peeled the paper from the wall.

Agnes could see him looking at the fridge and the big freezer and wondering how she could afford any of it. Single parent with a raging drink problem. Without a word she put the kettle on and opened the bread bin. From the paper wrapper she took out two thick slices of white plain loaf and smeared thick yellow butter on them. She cut each in half and put it on a small tea plate. She slid the plate towards him, and he thanked her.

He took up a buttery slice and crammed the edge into his mouth; the butter was sweet and thick. "I hear Caff is enjoying South Africa."

"*Catherine?* So I hear." Agnes sounded tired.

"Do you no hear from her?" he asked.

"Not often."

"Aye, well, you're to be a granny now."

Her hand grasped the edge of the worktop. The air blew out of her. "So I heard."

"Wee Peggy Bain is flying out there, you know. To support her when the bairn comes. Times like this," he added cruelly, "you need your mammy, even if a mother-in-law is all you have."

"Where would I get the money for that?" Agnes turned to hide her face from him. She tried to busy herself in making two mugs of dark tea. She hoped he wouldn't see how her hand was shaking.

"Donald Junior is sure it's to be a boy. I telt him I'd buy the pram if he named it Hugh, after his favourite uncle."

When she could control the heat in her face, she turned and brought the stewed tea to the table. Into his she spooned three sugars and added a big splash of milk. "I was trying to cut back on the sugars, but what the hell."

"Your scabby heart?"

"Aye, still plays up from time to time. At least when it stutters, I know it's still there." He laughed and finished off a slice of buttery bread, folding the crust and shoving it under his moustache in one piece. "How is my boy? Is he anything like his old man?"

"Dear God. I should hope not."

Agnes got up from the table quietly and left the room. She wanted to process the news about Catherine in peace. She didn't say where she was going. Shug sat at the table and ate another slice of the buttered bread, and in his mind's eye he tallied the cost of the new appliances in his head. *She has a man*, he thought. He sat forward in the chair and craned his neck around the door to see if he could see her. Wiping his buttery fingers on his trousers he wondered if she had slipped off into the bedroom. With a grin he picked up the carry-out and started around the unfamiliar house looking for where she'd gone. Sticking his head round some of the half-open doors he noted how neat and clean everything was. He thought about Joanie, her cat-hair-covered couch, her dirty drawers on the bedroom floor, and he could picture her now, carelessly brushing toast crumbs off their mismatched bedcovers.

As Shug went slowly down the hall peering into rooms, her sad glass-eyed ornaments stared back at him. She wasn't in any of these rooms. He stopped outside one of the last doors before the front door and found her there with her back to him. It was a boy's room with two narrow single beds. On a low table by the door Shuggie had placed some robot toys, and in the spaces between them he had written out on neat little cards the names of those that were missing, ones that he didn't yet own. It reminded him of Agnes. He had forgotten how much she had wanted and wanted and wanted.

"Take a good look around," she said quietly, "and then go."

"Where are all the fitba posters?" he asked, looking at the empty walls.

"Hugh doesn't like football. Actually, he doesn't like posters much. He thinks they look common."

Shug looked at his son's side of the small, fussy room. The only sign of childhood was the neatly arranged robots. He looked at them and then realized what they were. They were a mantelpiece of sad glass-eyed ornaments.

"Seen enough?" Agnes seemed in that moment like a tired docent.

"I suppose." He sneered slightly.

"Good," said Agnes with a taut smile. She held her hand out towards the door. "Now you can fuck off."

Agnes was worried about her whites. All that summer the news was about Chernobyl and the nuclear explosion that had happened there. It had been a sad but distant worry until a man on the news warned about a light nuclear rain that was falling over the west of Scotland as it headed on to Ireland. As Shuggie helped her bring in the washing from the back line she asked him whether nuclear fallout might actually help get out stubborn stains. The boy shook his head; *no*, it wouldn't be like a bleach. He told her about the depressing nuclear war cartoons they had been made to watch by Father Barry, and he said it might just eat the bed sheet whole. They had just carried in the last basket of still-damp sheets when the smirr started. From the front window the bouncing drops looked like every other kind of Scottish spit. As it splashed off the empty street they made a great game of things they would like to see burnt away by it:

"*Double football!*"

"*Jinty McClinchy!*"

"*Dirty Mouse McAvennie!*"

"*This whole bastarding scheme!*"

"*Snap!*"

Shuggie lay in front of the three-bar fire and watched Agnes iron the last of the dampness out of the washing. The rising steam meant she had to keep wiping her face on an old piece of toilet roll she kept up her sleeve. She took out her top teeth and pulled funny faces at him through the hissing steam. It was unlike her to lower her vanity like this. But there, in the close heat of the fire, Shuggie dreamt of how he never wanted this burning rain to end. How it would be better if they were stuck inside alone, where he could keep her safe forever.

Big Shug had tried to bring her low. Neither of them spoke about his father or his sudden visit. To spite him, Agnes and Shuggie had made a grand gesture of delivering all the Special Brew to Jinty. They dressed in their matching best and slowly promenaded around to the McClinchys' door. Jinty had opened the door with a confused frown covering a thin veneer of disdain. They smiled up at her as if they were the most faithful of Jehovah's Witnesses. Only upon seeing the plastic bag did Jinty herself soften; at the dull clang of the lager bells she beamed in wonder like an apostle after the Resurrection.

Eugene had phoned on that very same day.

Agnes had heard from him less and less since her first AA birthday. Since he was a good man, she expected he would let her down gradually, very gently, and then she would never hear from him again.

Eugene called for her in the taxi. It looked shiny, as if it had been washed especially for the occasion. He honked the horn once, but when she went out into the street, he didn't get out and open the passenger door for her, as he had done the times before.

Colleen and the other women were lined up against the wooden fence opposite. Bridie held a half-dry potato pot and a grey tea towel. They looked as if they had been interrupted from their routine by the growl of Eugene's diesel engine. Colleen looked livid as Agnes left with her prized possession.

As the hackney pulled away Eugene didn't speak. They had just passed the chapel when he pulled the taxi off the Pit Road and stopped it a few feet from the wide iron gateway of the closed colliery. He turned off the engine, and like a living beast the taxi stopping shaking below them. It was pitch-black and silent outside. He reached up and turned on the little yellow interior light.

Agnes had been here a time before, with another taxi driver, a face she couldn't remember. It made her feel cold inside. She watched Eugene's kind eyes in the mirror. If she spoke first it would be clumsy and hurt-sounding, so she fumbled in her bag for her cigarettes and waited for him to say his piece and set the tone.

"I wisnae gonnae keep this going," he said quietly, without turning round in his seat. "I suppose I got a fright."

"I'm that scary?"

"It was all they alcoholics and their, eh, disease."

Agnes closed the neck of her coat defensively. "Well. Don't worry yourself. It's not catching."

She heard his lips open and close, and then eventually he spoke again. "I know it sounds stupid, right. It's just they people. The ones at your party. They were that. Ye know. *Pitiful.*"

She took the blow without a wince, and then she surprised herself. "Eugene, you should know that, 'they people,' well, I am one of them."

His face moved in such a way that she knew this wasn't at all what he had wanted to hear. "I didn't mean any offence. It's just that, well, ye seem so *normal.*"

"That word again." Agnes finished her cigarette and rolled her tongue around the inside of her teeth. "Eugene, listen, no hard feelings, OK. Just please take me home."

He was quiet for a long time, and then he slid the partition between them closed. The taxi shuddered to life. The bright headlights picked out the broken gates of the mine. Red paint, already faded, read: *No Coal, No Soul, Only Dole.*

The taxi swung out on to the road, but instead of the short distance back into the scheme, it turned in the direction of the main road, towards life. Agnes leaned forward and rapped her ring on the partition, from curiosity more than annoyance. "I asked you to take me home." He didn't answer, and sinking back into her seat, she didn't push. The thought of getting out of the house for even a single hour had hung before her like a sweet dream since he had telephoned.

They didn't go very far. The taxi reached the bright street lights of the main road and took a left on to the carriageway. Almost as soon as it picked up speed to join the faster traffic, it slowed again and pulled off on to a dark gravel driveway.

Agnes had seen the golfers' hotel before but had never been inside. It sat on the side of the dual carriageway, and because it was accessible only by car, it said it didn't want the likes of her. From her seat on the bus she would watch the Jaguars pull up, fancy cars from fancy estates, far away from here. She would watch the smooth-faced men take their golf clubs out of the car boots while their wives would stand by, with their small purses and low heels, wrapped in Scottish Woollen Mill jumpers.

It was true that the ring of green around Glasgow held the new slums of the urban resettlement, these forgotten, remote housing schemes. It seemed cruel to Agnes that these green fields also held some of the fanciest hotels and private clubs she had ever seen. The two different worlds didn't like to look on each other.

"We are not going here, are we?"

"How no?" he said, pulling the fat black hack between two fancy saloon cars.

Agnes gazed out at the garden lanterns leading the way to the white doors of the club. "Would you look at it? It's not meant for the likes of us."

Eugene laughed. "Ah'm offended by that."

The pride rose in her. Her hand pulled the hem of her skirt. "Oh, Eugene, I can't. I'm not dressed for it."

Without saying any more, Eugene stepped out of the taxi and opened her door. He had to reach all the way into the back of the cab to take her hand. In his warm paw hers was suddenly small and cold. She was proud, and she was frightened, and he was suddenly sorry for the words he had spoken before.

The dining room of the golf club was simple, but to Agnes it was the height of class. It was a big open room that faced a wall of glass doors that overlooked the green lawn of the eighteenth hole. The room was carpeted in thick paisley carpet the colour of gold and parsley, and the walls had panelling laid in to waist-height, and above this were photos of club members and famous patrons. Agnes didn't recognize any of them, and she didn't like to squint in front of strangers.

A young girl in a long tartan skirt led them to a seat in the back of the smoking section. Agnes almost died with shame when Eugene asked for a table nearer the glass doors and the lit fairway beyond. The girl only smiled and led them to a table closer to the front. As they sat down, Eugene said a loud hello to the tables on either side. The people politely nodded back.

It had a fancy Gaelic name, but she recognized it as chicken. Agnes was going to have only this chicken and chips, but Eugene wouldn't let the waiter take the menus until she ordered a starter, a main, and a dessert. She would have liked to have sat alone with the menu for days. She didn't know what all the things were, but to suddenly see it all laid before her and to know she could have her pick of it made her feel light-headed. It was like a Freemans catalogue, only better. She ordered what she understood, and then she sat there worrying about the cost.

"Listen, you have a wee drink if you want. Don't worry about me," she said, as the waiter brought them two fizzy colas. The glasses were tall, and each had a mixing stick meant for cocktails. "That's fancy, isn't it," said Agnes, examining the stirrer and unable to relax. "Honestly, I don't mind if you take a wee drink."

Their prawn cocktail starters arrived. The ice cream bowl was lined with a slice of lettuce and frozen pink prawns that swam in a sea of thick Marie Rose sauce. Around the edge of the glass were thick wedges of lemon. The prawns were still a little cold, not fully defrosted, which Eugene said wasn't very good of the place. Agnes didn't mind it, to her it tasted fresh, the ice a clean crisp stab against the sweet and tangy Marie Rose. "I've made this sauce before. But I've never thought about adding a lemon or the—"

Eugene stopped her mid-sentence. "Ah have to ask you about something."

Agnes set down her small fork.

"Ah don't mean to bring it up again," said Eugene awkwardly. "It's just, ah'm tryin' to understand, ah suppose. But, well, have they people, ye know the people at the AA, told ye when ye would get better?"

The waiter had come and cleared their bowls before Agnes spoke again. "I don't know what to tell you. They tell all of us that we will never get better. At least," she added, looking at him directly, "not in the way you mean."

"But ye know how ye telt me you are a different person now? You telt me yersel that it was him that drove ye to the drink. Well, all that's changed." Eugene tried to soften his tone. "If we made a go o' this, don't ye think that wid keep ye off it?"

"I don't think it works that way."

"Yer arse. Wi' me in your life, what would ye need a drink problem for? Drink is only for they sad pitiful bastards. Look at you now. Look at me, for fuck's sake." The pastel-jumpered couple at the next table made a distasteful cough. Eugene lowered his voice again. "Look, all ah'm saying is, ah like ye. I think you are that fuckin' smashin'."

Eugene was unwilling to admit defeat, and Agnes could imagine he was a man well used to being able to fix any object that was broken. It made her feel like an engine left corroding on a front lawn. "Well, I like you too."

The waiter brought the main dishes. He wrapped his hands in a towel and gently slid the hot plates in front of the couple. Agnes looked first at her roasted chicken, and then she cooed over Eugene's lamb and boiled potatoes like a wean at Christmas. Eugene ignored the spread and pointed his thick finger in the direction of the coal-mining estate. "You are the best-looking wummin in that whole scheme. Most o' them don't even run a brush through their hair, and look at ye. Any time o' the day, ye are spotless." He leaned in. "I just need to know. Afore ah really fall for ye. Afore we start something serious."

Agnes felt uneasy. She tried to change the subject back to the food. "That looks lovely. Big portions, aren't they? I thought it would maybe be a breast or thigh, not a whole half chicken."

The waiter coughed and asked if they had everything they needed. Eugene nodded yes. Then, on second thought, he added, "Pal. Bring us a bottle of your house wine, would ye?"

"Red or white, sir?" asked the waiter quietly.

Eugene looked at Agnes, who had gone stiff. He looked back at the waiter. "Would ye have white with chicken?" The waiter nodded that, yes, he thought that would be a good idea. So Eugene ordered a bottle of the white.

"You don't have to, if you don't want to," said Eugene softly. "Ah'm no forcing ye."

The chicken that had looked golden and juicy now looked dry and dead in front of her. The waiter brought the bottle of wine. He made to pour some for Agnes, and she didn't stop him. She remarked on how the wine was almost the light peach colour of the roses in her front garden. "You know, peach roses are meant to be the colour of sincerity, the colour of gratitude."

The two of them sat looking at the glass for a long time. Eugene raised his and toasted the two of them. "*Here's tae us. Wha's like us? Gey few, and they're aw deid!*" Agnes raised a half-smile and lifted her Coke glass. It was flat and watery now.

"You never told me much about your daughter." She pushed the chicken around the plate. "Bernadette, is it?"

"Aw, she's aw grown up now, ah suppose. She does wonderful things for the nursery weans at Saint Luke's. She's like her mother in that, and she was very close to her mammy when she was alive. They always did things together, guid things for the Chapel, charity work for the miners' widows." He sucked some gristle from between his back teeth. "But she can be at that stoup altogether too much. The pair of them were always at the fuckin' holy water. Back and forth like it was a dipping sauce."

"She sounds like a good person though." Agnes said it, although, knowing Colleen, she suspected otherwise. "Have you told her about me?"

"No," said Eugene flatly.

"Oh!" She would have liked to have sounded less deflated.

"Cos our Colleen did."

Agnes exhaled. "I'll bet she painted a pretty picture."

Eugene let his eyes float over the untouched glass of wine. "Ah suppose ye could say that."

They finished their dishes and talked about taxis and snack bars, South Africa and its palladium mines. Agnes pushed her fat potatoes under the half-eaten carcass. The waiter cleared the plates and brought the tiramisu out to the table. Eugene drank the bottle of white down as her glass of peach-coloured wine sat untouched, getting warmer.

"I don't think I could eat another bite." She was playing idly with the tiramisu. "It's lovely though. It's the best custard I've ever had."

"A wee whisky would finish this off lovely," said Eugene, scooping the last of the pudding into his mouth.

"You know, I would never have thanked you for a whisky. Not even on my worst days. I find it's like gin. It makes you sad. I didn't drink to get sad. I drank to get away from sadness."

"What did ye drink, then?"

"Oh, mostly only lager, and when I could afford it a half-bottle of vodka. On bad days it put the fight back in me." She paused. "It gives you the worst blackouts, though. Well, at least when you are drinking to get drunk."

"Ah can hardly believe that *you* and *her* are the same person." He paused, then said, "What do ye think would happen if ye took a drink o' that wine the now?"

"I'd probably want more."

"But maybe ye wouldnae."

"Maybe," she said, then trying to be lighter, "Eugene, you don't have to get me drunk to have your wicked way with me."

"Thank God for that!" He swept his hand over the debris on the table. "That would have been money down the drain, eh." He laughed, and his face grew pinker. "Look, ah'm no trying to get ye drunk. Ah'm trying to have ye try *a* drink."

"But why?" Agnes was suddenly very tired.

"Because . . . Because it's what normal people do." He moved the warm glass. "Look, just have a sip. To be social like. Ye'll be fine. Listen, if ye start any trouble, I'll have them put ye out and you can walk home." He pushed the glass towards her by its long, elegant stem. "Ye'll be fine. You're a different woman now."

Agnes took the glass in her hand and held the wine up to her nose. The glass was warm, and the wine smelled like sunshine. "I don't even really like wine that much," she said, pushing it away.

"Aw, yer shitebag scared."

She *was* scared; she was terrified even, but she wouldn't let him see. She lifted the crystal glass to her mouth, and a small mouthful ran down her throat. It burned in a way she did not remember. The wine tasted nothing like sunshine. It was bitter, like cooking apples and vinegar. "*See*," she said, putting the glass down.

"*Do you see?*" said Eugene, genuinely excited. He looked like he might rise to his feet. "You haven't burst into flames. You haven't grown another head." He lifted the dregs of his glass and swung it towards her in salute. "Cheers! Ah'm that proud of ye. Ah knew what ma sister said wisnae true."

He was right: she didn't feel any different. Colleen was wrong. Agnes felt a wave of relief. She slowly finished the glass of wine, hoping what he said about her was true, feeling like she had beaten the AA and that she could be normal again.

When the bill came, he paid in small notes, tightly curled from his nights out taxi driving. When they left the table, Agnes felt warm on the inside, and Eugene led her into the small members' bar. Eugene laced his thick arm around her middle, and she felt happy that people were looking at them admiringly. As they sat close to one another in the corner, Eugene kissed her earlobe, and Agnes ordered a vodka and tonic and then she ordered another and then another.

The taxi swerved back into the dark scheme. It was only good fortune that there were no other cars on the road. Agnes slipped around on the back seat, rolling in and out of a stupor. Eugene pulled the taxi over into the mouth of the closed colliery again. In the dark they tried to fuck, but it was clumsy and painful, and it made her rigid with a dark memory she couldn't quite remember. As Eugene fumbled on top of her, coins spilt out of his pockets and made her feel as if she were being paid for.

By the time Agnes had managed to scrape her house-key into the door lock, the lights were already on in the hall. As she fell in the front door, she felt her mohair coat catch on the jagged Artex plaster and heard her tights rip on its hooked spines.

She was sure she was smiling up at Leek, so she didn't know why her son would be so angry, why he was screaming down at her. All she understood was, he was hitting Eugene square in his thick neck with his fists. All she remembered was that another bedroom door opened, and there in the doorway was the little boy with the worried face of his own granny. His face was wet with disappointment. The front of his pyjamas was dark through with piss.

Twenty-Three

Christmas came and went, and Agnes started her New Year's celebrations early. By the time it had gotten dark on Hogmanay, she had done away with the surreptitious pouring of vodka, half-hidden out of view down the far side of her armchair. By the time the television started preparing for the festivities, she was opening cans of Special Brew with a triumphant hiss and crack and pouring them like waterfalls straight into her old tea mug. It was still hours until the Hogmanay bells and she was already listing all the men who had ruined her.

If Agnes had noticed that Leek was slowly disappearing, she didn't say. Leek had spent his Christmas week hiding inside sleep. At night he hitchhiked to the city and played his apprenticeship wages away in the puggie machines that lined the arcades under Central Station. He disappeared earlier than usual on Hogmanay, like a man who sees rain coming and tries to outrun it.

Shuggie stayed home, turning a drunk Agnes from the front door, keeping her away from the telephone. On Hogmanay, he sat by the window watching the Christmas-tree lights come on in the other front rooms as he pushed handfuls of white net curtains into his mouth. He stuffed them in until his mouth was full and he was less hungry than before. He soiled her good curtains in front of her and longed for her to tell him to stop, but she didn't.

While the McAvennies played with new bikes and enjoyed a visit from Big Jamesy, Shuggie sat by her feet like a quiet shadow. He watched without talking while she drank from the bottomless tea mug. She told him bad stories of his father again, picking up the tale like it was a book she had only set to the side for a year.

By the time the six o'clock news was finished she was sitting on her bed slurring into the phone to Jinty McClinchy. Shuggie slid quietly along the hallway and sat with his back pressed against her bedroom door. From there he could listen through the chipboard and could follow the bell curve of her worsening mood. He wondered how long it would be till she passed out, till he could have a rest.

There was music coming from her cassette player, and he could tell it was a bad sign. He slipped into the bedroom like a wary ghost. Agnes was smoking, dressed in nothing but her sheer black stockings and her black lace bra. Shuggie often bought new tights for her. Pride wouldn't let her leave the house in a laddered pair, so the boy learned the exact size and shade she liked. Pretty Polly jet-black, semi-sheer tights were in all of his memories of her, both happy and sad.

On her dark days, like today, the tights looked dirty and bad to him. They stood in contrast to her rose-coloured flesh and drew attention to the fact that she should have been dressed decently, like other mammies were. The tights left pink lines across the soft fat of her belly, where they pinched her skin. It seemed like something other people should not be able to see. He wanted her to cover it.

She had forgotten he was home. When she finally noticed him in the mirror, she smiled that glassy smile she did with her teeth closed. Reaching deep into her black leather bag she produced a single fifty-pence piece. "Look at the state of you," she said. "How can we celebrate the bells with you still in your pyjamas?" She gave him the coin and told him to fill a bath.

He didn't like to leave her like this. He could see she wasn't at home in her own body. She circled her arms around his waist, drew him to her and placed a kiss on his lips. He could feel the heat of her breath, her lips slightly parted and lifeless. "Clean yourself good now," she warned. "I want to start this year right."

When the bathtub was half-full of lukewarm water, Shuggie cautiously slid in. He worked the soap into his scalp and lay in the bath, listening to her shuffle from hiding place to hiding place, looking for the alcohol she had hidden from him and had now forgotten. He took out the little red football book that Eugene had given him and began to memorize all the teams and results of every match of the previous year's Premier Division. He was penitent with these Hail Marys, going over and over the meaningless scores till he had committed them to memory. It would be a new year, a new chance.

His Hogmanay outfit lay on her bed. It was the monochrome gangster get-up, the black shirt and the white tie. As they got dressed together in silence, they looked like an unhappy married couple who were headed to a very special party. He held his mother for balance and helped her pull on her skirt. "Let's have a look at you, then." She took a painted finger and slid it down his nose. "*T'chut*, look how handsome you are!" She shook her head in reverie. "Not a bit like your fat bastard of a father."

Agnes peeled off a can of warm Special Brew from its plastic noose. She looked at it lovingly and slid it solemnly into the boy's hands. "Here, take this to Colleen's. Wish her a happy New Year from me, and make sure she gets to drink in how smart you look." A bitter smile cracked over her lips. "Be sure and tell your *Auntie* Colleen a 'Happy New Year' from me and Eugene, eh?"

Every house in the street had its Christmas tree lit and proudly glowing in the front window. Dark-haired boys flitted down the street with bits of coal, excited and early to start the first footing. Shuggie took the short walk to Colleen's house at a slow pace. He travelled along the wooden fences that hemmed the thick white-berried council bushes. He had no intention of passing on the can of drink or his mother's message.

As he crossed the street he wondered what people were eating. He imagined them huddled together with full bellies, shut in from the cold.

He stood outside Colleen's house squeezing winter berries between his fingers and thought about the steak and butter sandwiches sober Agnes had made for the bells the year before. He thought about the way they had cuddled on the settee and eaten peppermint chocolate, watching the crowd in George Square bring in the bells with a song.

Shuggie wondered what to do with the can of lager. He hunkered in the darkness by Colleen's low coal shed and pulled the ring pull. It sliced away from the can with a yeasty hiss, and the familiar smell was heavy in the cold air. With a cautious tongue Shuggie licked the brew from the top of the can. The foam tasted harmless, fluffy, like bitter air, a little sour and metallic, like wrapping his lips around the cold kitchen tap. His belly stabbed with hunger and anticipation, it asked to be filled, for a little taste of anything. Crouching like an animal, he turned his back to the street and drank a small mouthful of the lager. It didn't burn. It tasted like flat ginger with a side of heavy seeded bread. He took another sip and another, and the grumbling in his belly grew quieter.

He was glad of the warmth of it and the way it made his heart feel dizzy. The hunger started to subside, and he was feeling a little lighter, when he heard a diesel engine draw up. He watched Agnes stumble down the uneven paving of the path, clutching her purple coat closed over her short skirt. She said something flirtatious to the driver and climbed gracelessly into the back of the hackney. The driver wore thick government glasses; it clearly wasn't Eugene. Shuggie panicked as the taxi pulled out of Pithead.

In the four months and thirteen days since Eugene had helped his mother back on the drink, the red-headed taxi driver had come by two or three times a week. Those mornings Shuggie listened for Leek to leave for his apprenticeship, and a few minutes later, Eugene would slip into the quiet house. Shuggie could set the television meter by it.

Since that night at the golfer's clubhouse, Eugene had had the good sense to avoid Leek. As Agnes had lain singing to herself on the hall carpet, Leek had howled, and in his boxer shorts he had huckled Eugene out of the hallway and into the street. Although Eugene could have easily resisted, his manners were such that he let himself be manhandled out the door and found himself apologizing all the way to the kerb.

That night Eugene had been sleepless with guilt. Early the next morning, away from his daughter's scowl, he had pulled the telephone from the hallway and snuck with it into the bathroom, locking the door. He had woken Agnes, and she had met him at the colliery gates. He apologized for pressuring her into the drink, and he promised he would help her set it right again. As they sat in the back of the cold taxi she had kissed him for reassurance. Her loose tongue felt bloated and lifeless, and Eugene hoped the lager on her breath was only the dregs of the night before. As her head lolled in the taxi, he had remembered then, she had not drunk any lager with him at the golf club.

After that night Shuggie had expected Eugene to flee. Instead, the boy sat in his school uniform at the telephone table and listened to them talk on the mornings Eugene came to visit. Shuggie unfolded his homework on his lap and signed her name carefully with the old biro. He remembered a time, in Lizzie's house, when he had played with one of his mother's Capodimonte knock-offs. The ornament was a romantic farm boy. He was wielding a blunt scythe and staring with such a strange wistful look that he must have been witness to the most glorious sunset. Repeatedly, Agnes had asked Shuggie to leave the boy alone, but he found he could not, and when she was in her Sunday bath he dropped it and the arm broke from the body and the scythe smashed from his hand. Shuggie had hidden the statue in the dark of Lizzie's airing cupboard. He sat next to the heat of the immersion boiler and tried to stick the arm back on with everything from Sellotape to congealing rice pudding. He visited the broken boy every day for a week and prayed for some miracle. When he wasn't in the airing cupboard he obsessed about it, and when he was in the cupboard he cried for what he had done. It was a whole week of torture before he panicked and just left it there, hidden between a set of old bath towels for someone else to find and repair.

Shuggie sat at the telephone table and thought about the broken ornament again. He listened to them talk in the quiet voices adults used in the morning, and he could tell Eugene was tired from his night shift. The man had a wallpaper book, and he was asking what pattern Agnes preferred, the happy field flowers or the bold bengal stripes with tiny fleurs-de-lis. From the telephone table Shuggie could tell his mother was hushed with a sore head and concentrating all her energy as she fried liver for Eugene's breakfast.

"It's nae bother," said Eugene quite happily. "Ah can do the whole kitchen in a day. My faither once taught me a recipe for that mould. Ah can scrub the walls in the morning and paper in the afternoon. It'll be brand new in no time."

"Yes, OK then," said Agnes in a tiny voice.

"Are ye alright?"

"Yes," she said. "Just a wee sore head."

Shuggie could hear Eugene close the heavy wallpaper book; he could imagine him laying his hands palm upwards and open on the top of it. "You know mibbe don't take a wee drink the day. How about if ye feel it coming on, ye could go for a wee walk or something?"

Shuggie listened to his mother struggle to keep her voice even and flat. Like a skelfy piece of wood, she sanded at it, to hone the roughness of sarcasm from it. "A wee walk. Yes. Maybe that would sort it."

A few weeks later, by the time the wallpaper was hung, Shuggie noticed Eugene had stopped saying things like this. He acknowledged instead that if Agnes needed to take a drink, would she at least please stop hounding the taxi rank for him. Shuggie sat at the telephone table again and took her dog-eared phone book on to his lap. He took the chewed biro, and finding Eugene's name, he changed the *6* in his telephone number to an *8*. Then he found the listing for his taxi rank and changed all the *1*s to *7*s as skillfully as he could.

When he looked up, Eugene was standing in the kitchen doorway with a Phillips-head screwdriver in his hand. Shuggie watched him go up and down the hallway and tighten all the door hinges till they shrieked against the wood. "Ah was just thinking," he said to her. "The taxi needs to go into the garage next week, so ah'll have a few evenings free. How about a wee night out, at actual nighttime, this time. Mibbe we could go back to the golf club and have that prawn cocktail ye liked so much. I was thinking this time I wouldnae have a bevvy. Mibbe this time naebody needs to have a drink."

Shuggie took his dirty tea mug and slid past Eugene into the kitchen. His mother was sat at the table, her head in her hands, her fingers scouring her skull, with a bucket between her knees. The new wallpaper was lovely, the yellow and blue field of flowers really cheered up the small space. Eugene had been very clever and neat in how he had lined up all the little bluebells. All the mould was gone, but now when Shuggie looked out the window, the brown marsh stood out like an enormous square stain in an otherwise pretty spring field.

Now Shuggie crouched outside the McAvennies and poured the remainder of the Hogmanay lager into the dead grass. He hid the empty can inside his shirt for shame. Half-stunned, he crossed the street and found the front door ajar and all the house lights still burning. He wandered from empty room to empty room in disbelief, still expecting to find her somewhere. He raked through the empty kitchen cupboards and found the last tin of custard. He opened it and dipped his spoon in deep. The sugary cream made the lager in his belly stop rolling around. He sat down on the low coffee table and greedily spooned the custard down as the happy revellers in George Square started to come on the television.

By the time the ceilidh band was in full swing he knew she would not be coming home. The revellers start to hug one another and break into song. He felt like a baby to miss his mother. It wasn't fair, the way everyone could up and leave as they pleased.

Shuggie searched the house for a note or a sign, a treasure map to where she had gone, but there was nothing. He searched her black bingo bag and found all the markers there. He went to the wee phone table in the hall and thought about whom he could call. The red leather address book by the phone listed all the people Agnes knew. She had been religious about keeping it updated, and some of the names in the book had been crossed out in what looked like anger. Next to her neat cursive she had scrawled in another hand, one that looked like another woman's entirely, a short comment. Nan Flannigan *still owes my mammy five pounds from 1978*, and Ann Marie Easton, *two-faced hoor*, and Davy Doyle *wore a navy suit to my daddy's funeral*, and Brendan McGowan *only wanted a slave and a housekeeper*.

There were many first-name-only entries in the book. Shuggie guessed that most of them came from the AA. Some numbers gave additional descriptive information, a way to tell one Elaine from another Elaine. Shuggie thought it was funny how AA members did this. Maybe it was to protect anonymity, family names being private, but more likely it was because people came and went, and descriptions were better than names. He flicked through pages of names he recognized: Monday-Thursday Peter, Big Bald Peter, Mary-Doll, Jeanette Mary-Doll's pal, Cathy from Cumbernauld, and Wee Ginger Jeanie, which was confusingly under *G* instead of *J*. That irritated him.

His mother could be anywhere, and he started to panic that he might not see her till February. He screamed at the thick book, "Where the fuck are you? *Tell me!*"

New Year's in Scotland was a legendary two-day party. New Year's in Agnes's Glasgow was endless. When they first came to Pithead the boy had seen a house party that had lasted for days. Agnes had still been drunk by the sixth. By the time Shuggie was getting dressed in his school uniform, ready for the spring term, Leek had decided enough was enough. Leek could bear a lot, but on the sixth of January he rampaged through the house with a black bin liner and pulled two ratty miners out on to the frozen street.

Shuggie wondered about Leek, about his screaming, flashing gambling machines, and his insides hardened. He was getting sick of playing "you touched it last" with his brother. Picking at his bottom lip, he idly lifted the phone receiver and sniffed at the sour smoke and the perfume of her lipstick that still hung on the mouthpiece. For comfort he held the beige handset and listened to the hum of the dial tone. He looked at the keypad, and finally noticing the red *redial* button, he pressed it.

The phone chirruped for a long time before someone answered. Shuggie could barely hear the woman on the other end for the din of loud old-fashioned music in the background. "Hullo. HULLO! Who is this?" she shouted, her voice thick with smoke and slow with drink.

"Um. Is my mother there?" he asked, now sitting erect.

"Who is this?" she sounded bothered by the interruption. "Who's your mammy, wee man?"

"My mother is Agnes Campbell Bain," he said. "C-can you tell her it's Shu—Hugh." He caught himself. "Can you please tell her I don't have any custard left."

The woman leaned back into the noise of the party. "Haw, does anybody here know an Agnes?" she asked of the room behind her.

There were other voices, and then she said, "Haud on a wee minute, pal. Happy New Year, OK." Before he could reply she had set the receiver down. He could hear men and women laughing in the background and could tell they were old because the melancholy Scots songs were already playing. Shuggie waited and listened a long time for the woman to come back. He was sure that she had forgotten him when a voice spoke.

"Sh-hullo," slurred the familiar voice.

"Mammy? . . . It's me."

The voice didn't speak for a while, and when it did it sounded confused. "What do you want? What time is it?"

"When are you coming home?"

"What time is it?"

Shuggie peered around the corner, and in the light from the telly could just about see the face of the little clock. "Half ten, um, no, it's almost eleven o'clock."

The voice went quiet. He heard the flare of a lighter as she sucked on her cigarette. "Well, then, you should be in your bed."

"When are you coming home?"

"Look, don't upset yourself. Doesn't Mammy deserve a party? It's been that long, Hugh." Her voice trailed off. "I've been promised that many parties in my day. Why are you trying to ruin my party." She was repeating herself now.

"Mammy, I'm scared. Where are you?"

"I'm up at Anna O'Hanna's. Away to your bed, and I'll see you when I get home." This part was ominously vague.

The line went dead, and it took him a while to replace the receiver. Shuggie thought about calling again, but she wouldn't come back to the phone. He sat there sniffing the receiver a while longer, and then he went to bed, still fully dressed, with the bedroom lights on and the Hogmanay celebrations still blaring on the television. There were happy voices out in the street; he could hear the McAvennie children run up and down the road shouting "Happy New Year" at the top of their lungs. They had a wooden football clapper that they were twisting into a roaring din.

He got up and went back to the phone table. Shuggie looked under *A* then under *O* and there she was, *Anna O'Hanna*. He had heard the name before. Anna wasn't from the AA, she was a childhood friend, who was or was not also a distant relative. They had once worked together in the STV canteens and gone to the Tollcross dancing together in their youth. She was, by his mother's own handwriting, *an old backstabbing slitty eyed gossip* and also *the best friend I ever had*.

Under her name was her address, marked as Germiston. He had no idea what Germiston was, but everyone Agnes ever knew lived in Glasgow, so he hoped Germiston would be there. Shuggie ripped a blank page from the back of his mother's phone book and copied the address as neatly as possible. Then he called a number he found in the phone book under *Taxi*.

"Hullo, Mack's Hacks," said the gruff man.

"Hello. Can you tell me where Germiston is, please?"

"It's in the northeast, pal. Do youse want a taxi?" he replied impatiently.

"Sorry to bother you again," said the boy politely, "but how much does a taxi to there cost?"

"Where youse comin' frae?" sighed the man.

Shuggie answered the man very specifically, giving the house number, the street, the town, and even the postal code.

"Ah, about eight pow-n, plus two fifty extra for being the New Year's."

"OK. One taxi, please," said Shuggie, hanging up the phone.

With a butter knife he pried open the gas meter the way Jinty had shown them. Carefully he counted out the fifty pences, lining them up neatly on the table in front of the telly. There were only twenty of them, which without counting on his fingers he knew was ten whole pounds. The boy got the long, flat bread knife from the kitchen and began prying the back of the telly meter open the way he had seen Agnes do it a hundred times before.

With practice he knew he had to jostle it, so that the coins would fall out without damage to the meter itself. If the telly man saw the meter was broken you would be in *big trouble*, but everyone on the street had so many years of practice that no one ever seemed to get into this *big trouble*. Shuggie had watched Agnes and then Leek raid the telly meter on a regular basis. You had to fill the meter with a fifty-pence piece for three hours' of telly watching. When the money ran out, the telly automatically switched off, leaving you in darkness. There was no negotiating till the end of a film or till the advert break. If your money was up, the telly went black.

Shuggie slid the butter knife into the slot and two lonely fifty pences rolled out. If the man had told the truth, that should be enough to get him to Germiston. But not enough to get him back.

When he heard the idling sound of the hackney, Shuggie went outside. All the house lights of the street were on, and happy families were spending the bells together. Colleen was alone at her window, watching her children run up and down the road rattling their noisemakers. Shuggie did as Agnes taught him, and so he waved and smiled as he got into the hackney.

The taxi driver was a thin fair-haired man. He was taken aback to see a child dressed as a Chicago gangster. "Are ye it, wee man?" he asked, puzzled.

"Yes." He handed the driver the handwritten address.

The driver lowered his head and peered at Shuggie's front window for a sign of an adult, a mother or father to appear at the living room window. Shuggie took the plastic bag full of coins out of his pocket and

placed it on his knee. All that silver made a sparking noise, and eyeing
the small boy and then the money, the driver finally took the handbrake
off with a huff.

The taxi pulled out of the small dusty scheme, and soon they were
up in the dual lane traffic and moving quickly. Shuggie knew this was
the road into the city centre. He made a note of the route, checking
off landmarks, preparing for the long walk back. First they passed a
secondary school, then some rugby fields, and finally the black void of
a silent loch. From there it all flew by unknown.

Instead of taking the low road the driver took a higher road, like he
was turning away from the city. It looked like back-country roads, like
the city had exhausted the edge of its sprawl. The road was undeveloped;
to the left were half-built Barratt houses with their backs facing the traffic and tall dark brown wooden fences keeping in their unplanted lawns.
On the right unfolded miles and miles of fallow fields, dark and empty.
The driver must have known the route well, because he kept glancing
back and smiling at the boy in the white tie.

"Ye look very smart. Are ye going tae a party?" he asked, smiling
in the mirror.

"Well, kind of. I also just think it's important to always look your
best."

The man laughed. "So where's yer maw, is she at this party?"

"I hope so," Shuggie muttered.

"Very grown up o' ye to be travelling alone at yer age," he said.
"Ah've goat a wee boy about yer age. You about twelve? He really likes
tae ride up front and play wi' ma CB radio."

He was only eleven, but he liked the comfort of the bigger number,
so Shuggie didn't answer. It was funny the way you could see only the
driver's eyes or his mouth in the mirror, never both at the same time.

"Dae ye want tae ride up front wi' me?" said the man's mouth in the
mirror. It split into a wide smile.

The taxi slowed to a stop, not at a junction or at a light but in the
middle of the wide empty road. Shuggie looked to the half-built houses
on the left and the flattened fields on the right. If he was to bring her

back safely, then Shuggie supposed he had no choice but to do as he was told.

The man told Shuggie to get out. The front door on the left opened; there was no passenger seat on the left side of the black hackneys, just a carpeted floor. He stood in the carpeted enclosure amidst the evening newspapers, an old coat, and a half-eaten packet of sandwiches. Shuggie tried not to stare at the food. The bread was thick with crust, but he was so hungry he didn't care, he would have eaten it crust and all.

"There ye go, that's better, eh?" The driver cleared his stuff off the floor and made some room for the boy. He held the sandwich in his hand. "Would ye like some?" he said. "It's just butter and bit of tinned ham."

"No, thank you," Shuggie said politely, but his eyes were burning into the half-eaten piece.

"Here, take it," said the man, thrusting it towards him. "I can hear yer belly frae here." Shuggie took the sandwich. The bread was damp from the butter, and he tried to eat it slowly, but the lager sat sour in his stomach, and he found himself pushing in large hunks of salted ham. It was so thick and rich it stuck to the roof of his mouth.

Even kneeling, Shuggie was still not shoulder-height to the seated figure. Glancing over the thick sandwich, he thought how the driver looked not at all like his father. The man's face was kinder, the edges of his eyes were creased from smiling. There was a crucifix on a silver chain around his neck, and the sight of it calmed Shuggie in an unexpected way.

"That there is the CB," said the driver, pointing to a handset that looked like an electric shaver. The driver switched a knob on the dial. "There ye go, ye can gabber all ye like, if ye want. It'll only be the long-haul drivers and the lonely hearts that follow them who'll hear ye on this channel." The man smiled at him with straight teeth, and Shuggie thought he would like Agnes to meet him, this man who gave him sandwiches.

With a snap of the handbrake the taxi took off again down the dark road. Shuggie fell back against the glass partition. "Whoa, there, wee man, haud on to something!" With his left arm he encircled the boy's waist, holding him tight and upright in the luggage space.

They drove on farther down the unlit road. Shuggie tried not to eat the sandwich too quickly. The ham was thick and so deeply salty it tickled his gums. The man said suddenly, "It happens mair than ye might think. Weans being left alone that is." He turned to Shuggie and smiled. "I see it aw the time, mammies and daddies that desperate to go down the pub that weans are fending for themselves. Poor wee things." Shuggie finished the sandwich. He tried not to lick the butter from his fingers.

"Was that good?"

Shuggie nodded and answered politely. "Yes. Thank you very much." The man's arm was still around his waist for support.

The man laughed kindly. "*Ooh, thank you very much,*" he repeated, like an amused parrot. "You're a polite wee fella, aren't ye?"

Shuggie tried not to look embarrassed. He fixed his eyes on the rear-view mirror and wished Leek was here. The empty country road seemed to go on forever; he was trying to remember the things they passed. He made a list of things he saw, like in a game of Granny Went to Spain, but after ten or fifteen trees and only one traffic light, all the things looked the same, and he gave up reluctantly.

Slowly the driver's arm went lower down the boy's side. With a slow hand, he pulled the back of Shuggie's shirt from his tweed trousers and insidiously pushed his fat warm fingers down the back of Shuggie's underpants. Without looking, Shuggie could tell the man was still smiling at him.

"Aye, you're a funny wee fella, aren't ye?" the man repeated. With a hard push, his hand reached further down inside the underpants, and he started searching the boy with his fingers. The waistband of the tweed trousers was cutting into Shuggie in the front. The strain felt like he was halving him in two, and he could have cried out for that pain alone. Still, Shuggie said nothing.

The cab was rolling slower. The driver made a funny sound like he was eating hot soup through his front teeth. Headlights tore in the opposite direction. Shuggie winced at the man now; his fat fingers were pressing down into him in a strange way. The custard made a skin on top of the sour lager, and the bread swelled and expanded in his gut so that he thought he might be sick. The fingers pressed and pressed. The driver's mouth was pulled tight in a grimace. Shuggie wished for the light of some houses.

"You know, my father is a taxi driver."

The driver stopped his grimace.

Shuggie kept on, trying to keep his voice casual and ignore the fingers that were searching his dirty place. ". . . And my Mammy's boyfriend, he's called Eugene." He took a shallow breath. "He might know you?" The question shot up at the end.

Slowly the driver slipped his hand out from the back of the tweed trousers. Shuggie slid his back down the partition and sat his dirty place safely on the floor of the cab. He put his fingers against his waist and in the dark he could feel the pink marks on his belly where the stitching cut into him. It felt like taking off school socks that were too tight, but worse.

Voices crackled over the CB. Some man in a Teuchter accent was talking about floods on the Perth Road. The driver wiped his hand discreetly on his work trousers. "So, did ye have a nice Christmas?" he asked casually, after a moment.

"Yes. Thank you," Shuggie lied.

"Was Santa guid to you?"

Christmas came from the Freemans catalogue and was slowly paid off. "Yes."

The black hackney finally reached the lights of a grey, worn-down housing scheme, and the driver asked, "Son. What did you say your daddy's name was again?"

Shuggie thought about lying, "Hugh Bain."

Something like relief swept over the driver, and he relaxed back into his chair. When he dropped Shuggie in Germiston it had already gone the bells. The boy offered the driver the bag of stolen fifty pences. The man looked at it closely, perhaps with pity or guilt, and said the ride was free because Shuggie had been such a good boy. The boy wished he had taken the coins; he didn't want the man to think he had liked the way his fingers had hurt him.

Shuggie could feel the man watch his back as he climbed all the stone stairs to the front door on Stronsay Street. Only when he turned around and smiled a brave smile did the driver pull away. When the taxi turned the corner, Shuggie tucked the black shirt back into the tweed trousers. He rubbed at the sourness in his gut. Each of the buildings were identical; the tenements crowded in on the narrow road and made a canyon of bricks and glass. Looking up, he noticed music and bright lights coming from a flat on the third floor, so he pressed the metal buzzer for 3R. Without anyone asking who was there, the door buzzed automatically open.

The tenement close was poorly lit. Somewhere above Shuggie loud music and happy voices bounced off the walls. Shuggie stepped inside. Any Glasgow wean could easily tell this was one of the poorer tenements. The six feet or so of decorative tiles that lined the entryway were cracked and missing. There was thickly applied council brown paint with a dirty cream stripe about adult eye level that pointed the way into the belly of the close. Every flat surface was covered in graffitied declarations of love and gang pride. From the sworn allegiance to the IRA, Shuggie could see that Germiston was certainly Catholic.

As he climbed up from the mouth of the close he could hear the party on the third floor. It sounded happy, like the night still hadn't turned sour. The boy took the steep stairs slowly, one at a time. They were hard granite that had been worn into a dip in the middle, and there was no curving banister; instead the stairway was built around a solid wall of poured concrete. As he climbed he couldn't see what lay around the corner.

He inched quietly upwards. As he turned the second bend, he came upon a woman and man sitting on the cold steps. They lay there rumpled like two piles of dirty laundry. They were doing things to each other that the boy had seen before. The old woman seemed barely conscious, and the man had his hand up her skirt, touching her in her dirty place.

Shuggie folded his arms over his chest and politely stepped back, away from what lay at eye level. He quietly stepped down some stairs and was almost back around the corner when the woman opened a rolling eye and noticed him. The man continued to rub at her like he was polishing a shoe.

"Whit ye looking at?" she asked, gummy-lipped.

"Are you OK?" he asked quietly. "Is he hurting you?"

Somewhere above them a door opened, and the noise of a grand party filled the close. People were leaving.

"Wid you stop that a minute, John." She pushed the hands away. The woman pulled her top closed and tried to bring more dignity to the scene. She lowered her eyes to the stone stairs. The drunken man continued chewing her neck regardless.

Shuggie took out one of the fifty pences and put it on the woman's bare knee. Then he darted past them, climbing up towards the noise at the top of the stairs. Men and women were pouring down in their winter coats. It took quick feet and effort not to be swept back down by their clumsy legs and long jackets. He reached the third floor, and finding the door still wide open, he went in. No one stopped him as he pushed through the legs into the small hallway. No one paid any heed as he went into the main room.

The room was a smaller version of the living room at home. It was covered in burgundy brocade wallpaper, and against one wall was a small electric fire with fake plastic coals throwing an orange glow into the sweaty room. In the middle of the room was a three-piece suite still covered in plastic. Around the corners were some borrowed kitchen chairs, and on these were sat men and women in their forties and fifties, faces Shuggie had never seen before. The men sat in heavy grey suits and wide ties, and the women were done up in pretty blouses. They looked stiff, as though they had come from chapel, but wet-eyed, like they had taken too much Communion wine.

The record player in the corner was spinning an especially melancholy version of "Danny Boy." A few older jakeys sat by it with their cans of warm beer and murdered the words in a howl, while an old woman sat teary-eyed nearby. The whole room was already sliding down the peak of the evening. He circled the room, searching from face to face for a sign of his mother. Agnes wasn't there.

In the corner near the window, sitting at a small folding table, was a young boy much the same age as Shuggie. He had been watching Shuggie the entire time as he did his searching circle of the room. He was dressed in his good clothes, and his hair was still neat from when his own mother must have parted it earlier. As they looked at one another, Shuggie wondered whether he was lost or searching too. The boy raised his hand in a small wave, and Shuggie made to cross the room and speak to the stranger. Halfway there he saw that on his little table sat a heaped plate of shortbread and some fizzy juice that still rolled with bubbles. Somebody here loved this other little boy. Shuggie turned away and went back to looking for Agnes.

Back out in the hallway he passed the tangle of legs once again. In the small narrow kitchenette was a woman with jet-black hair. His heart leapt and fell as he realized it was not his mother. Shuggie thought to ask her where Agnes was, but he was so embarrassed by the little shortbread boy that he said nothing. Pride clamped his mouth shut, and the black-haired woman sailed past him like he was invisible. There were three bedrooms in the tenement flat. Each was empty except for the odd lost partygoer having a quiet smoke or a quiet cry. He searched them all, but none of the drunks were his. The last room was the biggest bedroom, the one for mammies and daddies. The door was closed tight, and he had to pull down on the metal handle and push hard to get the sticky door open. There were no lights on in the room, but as the glow followed him in from the hallway he could see the large double bed was heaped high in winter coats.

Shuggie stood there and put his hand on the bag of coins in his pocket. It would be just enough to get him home. Perhaps he would find her there, frantic, sobered with worry, and waiting with hot tea and toast.

In the smoke and the dark, tears began to sting his eyes, and he sat on the coat-covered bed for just a minute. He was being a baby and he knew it. He had been a big baby all night, wanting his mammy, and he wished he was more like Leek, who never seemed to need anyone. Shuggie dug the nails of his left hand into the soft part of his right arm, and he willed the poor me's to stop.

Something stirred under the coats. Shuggie stood up in fright. Out from some old jackets came a small white hand. It hovered for a moment before it pulled a coat away from its face, and there, with a wet face and spoilt mascara, was his mother.

Agnes's hair was flat and matted on the right side. In the dim light the boy could see by the smallness in her eyes that she was no longer drunk. As she looked at him her lip trembled as if she would cry. This scared him into stopping his own sobbing, and he tried to stand up straight like a big boy. One by one he pulled the winter coats to the floor and uncovered her. Slowly she emerged, half-naked and crumpled, from the heap. In the half dark she held his eyes and she didn't say a word. Slowly he kept pulling the layers from the bed. From beneath the heavy coats emerged her white legs and small feet. Shuggie stopped and looked at her there, and in the tangle and the hallway light he saw that her black Pretty Pollys had been ripped from toe to waist.

Twenty-Four

The boy opened his eyes, and she was there, sat quietly on the end of his bed. She was the terrible half-a-person that always came in the mornings now. He watched her shiver for a while, trembling with the dampness that the drink had left in her. She held a piece of toilet paper to her mouth as she coughed up wet phlegm and then tried to hold in the rattling boak that followed.

Agnes cocked her head and looked at him with pleading, sleepless eyes. "Morning, sunshine."

"M-morning." Shuggie stretched his toes to the end of the bed.

Her hand was shaking as she gently pulled the layers of bedcovers away. The damp March air rushed in, and Shuggie whined and curled up in a tight ball. Agnes reached out her cold hand and put it on his clammy foot. He had taken another stretch: the old pyjamas cropped above his calves now, the hair on his legs starting to thicken and grow darker. "Another year and you'll be a man, and then what am I going to do?"

"Do you think I will be taller than Leek?" he asked. His brother's bed was already empty.

"Most definitely." She pushed his inky hair away from his eyes and tried to sound cheery. "How'd you like to stay off the school the day? Keep me company?"

Shuggie's eyes flew open at the offer. "I dunno. Father Barry says I've missed too much already."

"Och, you never mind him. You went nearly every day last week. I'll write you a note saying your granny died."

Shuggie groaned and stretched his toes into the cold. "He's not daft. You've done that three times already."

He knew what she wanted. As soon as the clock turned a quarter to nine he was put out on the frozen street with the Tuesday Book in his hand. He wore his thin cagoule and good trousers, and over one arm he carried a large, gingham nylon shopper bag. The shopper was a decoy; there would be no groceries to put into it, but it played the part and made the whole thing look more respectable. Like a greedy bookie, Shuggie flicked the pages of the Tuesday child-support book and watched the princely sum of eight pounds fifty appear on all the dated coupons. He found the one she had signed for this week, checked to see whether she had filled it out correctly in her desperate hunger, and then he dropped it into the decoy bag.

He knew she was watching from behind the net curtains, so he walked quickly and with a purpose. When he turned the corner out of sight, he slowed and spent a time squashing the white berries into a paste.

Shuggie had tried it all ways, rushing like the clappers up the street and back or going missing for hours in the peat marshes. Once he had even cashed the books and spent the child support on actual messages, provisions and meat from the butcher. It always ended up the same; she returned the messages that she could and bought what she really needed first, drink. So now when he cashed the benefit books, he just put his head down and got on with it with a sense of resignation.

She hadn't been the same since New Year's Eve. Whoever had left her half-naked under the pile of strangers' coats had taken the yearning for a good party out of her. Now when Shuggie watched her drink he could see she had lost the taste for a good time. She was drinking to forget herself, because she didn't know how else to keep out the pain and the loneliness.

The petrol station had turned her away. She had missed too many shifts, and with no one to cover, the station had gone dark too many times. At first Agnes had taken the rejection on the nose, like everything else, it was not meant to work out for her. When the catalogue bills started to pile up, and there was no money for drink by a Thursday, she started to talk about her sacking like it was a conspiracy. She had been too popular, too beautiful, she said, and the station owners hadn't liked how the place had turned into a social club for lonely taxi drivers. Leek had sat and listened to her, quietly spooning hot cereal into his mouth, and then he had asked, calmly, "How long are you going to keep lying to yourself?"

The queue took forever. It was silent but for rattling coughs, the swish of nylon anoraks, and the *stamp, stamp, stamp* of the agitated woman behind the counter. The way they fidgeted, he could tell that the people had waited a long weekend for their benefit books to be cashed. Some people would have been hungry, some running out of cigarettes by Sunday teatime, and others, like his own mother, were dying of a deep thirst. Shuggie pulled up to the counter and pushed the book into the little drawer that sat at eye level. With a slice it was pulled away from him. With a slice it came back.

"You've not signed it," said the postmistress.

Shuggie took the chained-down pen and wrote his name in the designee space in the way she had made him practice. He dropped it back in the drawer and smiled up at the lady. The woman took it up and looked at it closely on both sides. She wore rose-framed glasses and looked down at him like a teacher on a high stool. "Can Missus Bain not come and collect her child support herself?" she asked, a fraction too loudly.

Shuggie felt the queue behind him shift impatiently from one foot to the other. "No."

The woman leaned backwards as if stretching her tired back. "Young man. Should you not be at school?" He heard the queue clear its throat in agreement.

"My mother is not well," he whispered discreetly into the drawer.

The woman leaned into the safety glass, her face looming large above his. "Yes, but it comes to my mind that I see you every single Monday and Tuesday morning." She sniffed and held up the book, putting her finger under Agnes's signature. "It says here," she sniffed again, "that authorizing a designee is only for temporary purposes, and if the person cannot claim their own benefit then the book should be returned to the DSS."

Shuggie felt the threat of shit in his underpants. All he could manage was a quiet, "*Please, Missus.*"

"Shall I take this book from you, young man?" She adjusted her glasses with an ink-stained finger. "Should I send it back to the DSS?"

The boy shook his head and felt the leak start to worsen. "No. Please, Missus," he begged.

The woman seemed not to hear or not to care. She folded the book and put it closed on the counter. Solemnly, she folded her hands over the top of it as though in prayer. The back of Shuggie's eyeballs began to sweat. He could hear the hungry crowd start to moan. The child benefit was more than a quarter of all the money Agnes would get to feed them for a week.

With a trembling lip, Shuggie tried again. "Please, Missus."

The impatient crowd tutted and sighed behind him. "That boy's mammy is not well!" said a high voice from the very back of the post office. The postmistress looked up from the ashen face to the long queue. "Gie him his money, or he'll have nothing to eat!" it said again.

An old woman at the front joined in. She was tired of the wait and was shaking her pension book. "Oh, for the love. Gie the boy his money, ya heartless jobsworth."

The lady behind the counter looked at the queue and down at the fearful boy. She opened the book reluctantly. *Stamp! Stamp!* She marked it and ripped out the coupon for that week. Into the drawer she slipped the Tuesday Book, a fiver, three pound notes and a new fifty-pence piece. She held on to the drawer and leaned her face up to the little holes in the glass. Quieter now she said, "*You are a smart boy. Don't you let me catch you here again next week. Get yourself back in school. Study. Stick in at it and don't spend your whole life in a benefits queue."* There was a pity in her eyes, and with that she sent the drawer through. The boy nodded obediently and, licking the running wetness on his top lip, emptied the drawer of the money. He couldn't worry about next week. He'd have to worry about the rest of this week first.

Shuggie had hurried towards Pithead as quickly as he could. When he passed the school, he climbed the broken fences and ran down the dirt siding into the marshlands. When he was far enough from the road, he took off his trousers and his underpants, and hunkering down, he finished what the postmistress had started. Then he turned his white underpants inside out and tried to scrape them clean on some dried reed grass.

By the time he got home, it was still not half past ten in the morning, and the street was just starting to open its curtains. He opened the front door and ran right into her, standing in the middle of the hallway. She was dressed in her best mohair coat and had lined her eyes and put a deep lavender colour on her top lids. Her hair was set and curled, and the hairspray still hung wet and sparkling on its tips like dew. Under her left arm she had her best bag, and the other hand was out, palm side up, like a patient saint. It was itchy and red-looking.

"Where the hell have you been?" she asked, wanting no reply.

The boy opened the message bag and took the notes and single coin out from amongst his dirty underpants. Agnes clipped it securely into her purse. "Right, I need you to walk me up the road. If we meet anybody, I want you to talk to me."

"What about?"

"Anything. Bloody anything. Just talk to me and don't bloody stop, OK?"

Agnes spun him around and pushed him back out the door. As they reached the corner, he could tell she was relieved they hadn't passed a soul yet. At the bottom of the hill, leaning over a garden fence, was Colleen McAvennie talking to one of her and Eugene's cousins. They were smoking cigarettes, and Colleen had two big black bin bags full

of washing or sheets or the last of Big Jamesy's clothes. They looked up
as they heard the rap of heels on the concrete. Agnes made an unsteady
swerve, as though she were going to cross the road, but instead she
pulled her head up high and kept her path. She strutted out a confident
rhythmic clip and turned her head and said to the boy, "What would
you like for your dinner tonight?"

Shuggie looked up at his mother and did as he had been taught.
"Roast chicken, please. I'm a bit tired of sirloin every other night."

They passed the women, who stopped their own conversation, and
Agnes said with a light laugh, "*Oh, you!* You will have steak again and be
thankful!" She turned her regal profile and held her raw hand behind
herself. "Oh, hello Colleen, hello Molly. This one is growing like a
weed." The women said nothing as she passed, but she felt them draw
their eyes over the coat, over the shoes and hair. When she was safely
past them, her face froze in a rictus and she muttered, "*Aye, same to you
cunts*," and then crossed the street.

Dolan's general shop sat at the end of a row of three boarded-up
shopfronts perched at the top of the hill that overlooked all of Pithead.
When the colliery was still open it would have been a busy place, meeting the families' needs with fresh vegetables, the best meat, and a place
to pass bits of talk. Now Mr Dolan didn't even turn on the lights. If the
other nearest shop hadn't been over two miles away, then Dolan's might
have closed altogether. As though admitting this half defeat, the shop
sat with its metal shutters closed and the lights always off, only daylight
pouring through the bill-postered front door.

Mr Dolan himself was a kind and gentle man, although the sight
of him scared Shuggie. When the shopkeeper was a boy, and the mine
was still open, he fell out of a yew tree and crushed his right arm so
badly they had to amputate it. Now every time a wean climbed a fence,
mammies hung out windows and screamed, "*Get doon aff o' that or ye'll
end up like poor Mister Dolan.*"

As the shop bell rang, Mr Dolan looked both happy and sad to see
Agnes. The racks of lager cans and whisky bottles behind him said he
well understood the new economy of the scheme. Yet, when the beautiful

woman came up to the counter, the one-armed man couldn't help but sigh at the waste.

Agnes, trying to ignore the pity in his face, asked the shopkeeper how he was today. Mr Dolan just shrugged and nodded towards the boy. "Why are you no in school?"

"He's got a wee bug, Mister Dolan," Agnes interjected. "It's been going around."

The old man sucked his teeth but didn't linger on the lie. Agnes took out a piece of paper on which she had written a short message list. She ordered some innocent provisions: tinned custard, tinned peas, some mince, and a handful of potatoes. She asked for a little sliced ham and fidgeted nervously as Mr Dolan moved the meat skillfully in the slicer using his half stump. The butt end of cured pig and the pink-puckered edge of his stump looked to be one and the same.

"How much is that to be?" she asked, as he put the slices of gammon into her message bag.

"Five poun' two pence," said the man.

Agnes fumbled for a moment. "C-can I also have the day's paper, please?"

"Five poun' twenty seven."

"A wee bar of that Cadbury's for the boy."

"Five poun' fifty."

"Let's see," said Agnes, in a fake forgetful tone, "Oh, aye. I nearly forgot." Shuggie looked at his feet in shame. "Can I have twelve Special Brew, please?"

When the man turned to reach these from the shelf, Agnes licked all the lipstick off her bottom lip.

"Thirteen poun' even," the man said.

Agnes opened her purse and looked down at the notes and the single silver coin. "Oh, Mr Dolan, seems I'm a wee bit short the day."

The one-armed man reached under the counter and pulled out a big red ledger. He thumbed through the pages to *B* and found Agnes's name. "Hen, you already owe me twenty-four poun'," he said with gravity. "I cannae gie ye any more tick till that's all paid."

With a pained smile, Agnes looked through the message bag and placed the gammon, the tinned peas, and two potatoes back on the counter.

Whatever Mr Dolan thought, he never said. As terrifying as his loose sleeve was to the boy, Shuggie knew that he was a deeply sympathetic man. All the mothers in the scheme called him "the one-armed bandit," on account of his high prices, but Shuggie had never seen him be anything but kind. As Agnes stood shaking before him on a Tuesday morning, she looked as though she were shopping in the West End at the big brand-name shops. Mr Dolan never called out her little charade. Sometimes, when she was pulling food back out of the bag, he would wink at the polished boy with his hair washed and parted and would slide him a piece of ripe fruit. But not today. Today he took back nearly all the groceries and rang up the lager for Agnes.

Agnes clipped through the scheme with the message bag by her side. She glided faster now, and Shuggie struggled to keep up as she flew down the hill. When she got home she went into the kitchen without taking off her coat. Shuggie sat in the living room and let her gather herself. He waited for the hiss and splash of the cans and then the sound of the drink being hidden. He waited until he heard the tap running at the big metal sink.

"You feeling better?" he asked from the doorway.

She turned from the tea mug. The nervousness from her face was gone, but the worry was still there. "Much better, thanks. You were a good wee helper the day."

He went and wrapped himself around her waist. "I'd do anything for you."

All the way across the peat marsh he kept stopping and turning back to wave, until the house dropped out of sight and he couldn't see her at the window any more. As he cracked his way across the frozen burns he consoled himself, knowing exactly what her day looked like. There was comfort in the fact that whether sober or not, it largely followed the same trapped routine.

Shuggie flicked the brittle heads of the bulrush reeds and wondered whether the sadness would get her today. The frozen reeds were bone dry, and when he tapped the heads their seeds took to the air like little parachutists. They floated up and back to the scheme like a parade of little ghosts. He made a game of telling the ghosts that he loved her, and with a flick he sent them her way.

The trampled grass circle, where he practiced being a normal boy, was exactly as he had left it. On days when she had kept him home from school he had collected old bits of abandoned furniture for his flattened island. When she had a particularly bad bender; he spent a whole school-less week taking an old chair over, some carpet scraps from the bins, and odd pieces of cutlery and broken china. With ends of old rope he pulled things out of the rusty burns. He pulled out a broken telly and sat it facing the centre of the island. Even though it had no screen, just having it there made it feel more like a home. When he had all the furniture he wanted, he spent any dry days arranging and then rearranging the stuff into a shabby front room. He found an old-fashioned baby carriage and pushed it around, struggling through the long reeds, collecting the prettiest flowers for his new home. When he found a little black rabbit, dead and frozen one winter afternoon, he washed it in the burn and buried it in the dirt. Then he had buried the plastic ponies next to the rabbit, the shameful scented horses that he had stolen but that were not meant for boys. The following spring he searched the slag bings and took to laying sprigs of purple helleborine on the graves. With no friends to speak of, these little rituals occupied him well, allowing him to spend the day feeling house-proud, to attend to the shameful hummocks as dutifully as any mourning widow.

All that short day he walked around his trampled island washing the dirt off things. He took the fork, the spoon, and the cracked plates down to the burn and rinsed them in the water. He lifted the bits of carpet and tried to shake the stour from them. Then he hung the rain-soaked blanket over a chair to warm and crack in the low sun.

The sun was already leaving the sky after a short day's housework. As he climbed through the back fence he hoped to take a deep bath and practice his red book, but the front door was hanging wide open. Shuggie stood frozen on the bottom step for a long while, wondering what the omen was, tilting his head and listening like a guard dog. Creeping up the long hallway he could hear a commotion from inside the living room. He walked cautiously to the door and pushed it open a crack. Inside, prostrate on the floor, was Agnes. Sat on her chest, like a school bully, was Leek.

The crimson swirls on the red carpet were wrong. The pattern looked broken and disjointed. As Shuggie stepped closer, he could see that there was blood on his mother and that there was blood on Leek's face too. If he could have focused, he would have seen that there was also blood on the TV and the brown table and the fringe of the settee.

Leek was pushing down on to the heap of her. Around them were bloody piles of fabric that had once been clean tea towels. Agnes was writhing and cursing under Leek's weight. She called him names that Shuggie had never heard before, and his brother was crying strange tears and struggling to hold her down.

There was a broken razor blade on the carpet; to Shuggie it was small and thin and innocent-looking, like a tiny guillotine for a cartoon mouse. He only noticed it because it was funny that it should be in the living room, lying in the middle of his mother's good carpet. Leek was screaming something at him, but Shuggie couldn't understand. He wanted to know why there was blood on her tea mug. He watched his brother twist his face towards him as he held blackening tea towels over Agnes's wrists. When he had one of her arms secure under his knee, he reached out and grabbed Shuggie by the shirt front. Agnes's other arm flew free, and there was a low spurt of blood. Shuggie wanted to tell Leek, *Look! Look! That is where the blood is coming from!* but Leek had him by the collar and was shaking him so hard he thought his neck might snap.

"Shuggie. Listen to me." Leek's eyes were very wide, and there was white foam in the corners of his mouth. His face was coated in the thick white dust of a plasterer, and there was blood on the white of his teeth. "You need to call a fucking ambulance."

"You're a selfish cunt," she wailed. "Just let me go."

Her body was racked with deep sobs. Leek's tears were falling on to her face and mixing with her own.

"I'm too tired." Still she pushed and she heaved, and then her eyes rolled backwards as though they were looking for the relief of sleep.

"*You don't love me.*"

"*You don't love me*," she repeated, again and again.

The boy pulled the door quietly closed behind him. He sat down and composed himself before he called 999 and asked for an ambulance. Leek was screaming something at him, but he didn't understand. He didn't understand any of it.

When Agnes awoke in the psychiatric hospital she had no memory of getting there. The ambulance had taken her the many miles to the Royal Infirmary in the shadow of Sighthill. One of the emergency doctors skillfully stitched her wounds and stopped her blood loss. Then they put her on a drip and sedated her to keep her from clawing at herself again. As she rolled into a fitful sleep, they had admitted her to Gartnavel to begin the deeper healing. When she woke she was in a ward with thirteen other women: Grown women dribbling on themselves. Poor women crying at dollies to get dressed for school. Sedated women who didn't ever sleep a wink.

As Agnes, tiny and stitched up, slept through her sedation, Leek and Eugene drew the curtain against the unfortunates and stood sentinel on either side of her bed. It was the most time they had ever spent together. Each man was glad, in some way, to have this dormant body between them to focus on. It was a relief in the same way old people enjoyed having a child in the room, because it gave them something to fuss over when they had nothing left to say to each other.

Leek had not spoken to Eugene since the man had goaded Agnes into breaking her sobriety. Now they spent most of that first afternoon warily engaging with each other, avoiding eye contact, and talking about Agnes as though the other man had never met her. They agreed on only one thing. They looked down at the wrung-out woman and agreed how lucky she was to have survived. From the long, deep cuts on her wrists it was clear, she hadn't wanted to leave anything to chance.

"So it was the foreman, then?" asked Eugene, unable to meet Leek's clear gaze.

"Uh-huh."

"Lucky that."

"S'pose. I don't know how many times she had phoned that day. She's been calling my work a lot lately."

"Aye. My taxi rank as well."

Leek hunched his shoulders, like he sat heavy under the memory of it all. "It was a brass neck, but the gaffer was usually pretty good about it. Except this one time he came over and told me personally that I had better get home fast, there was some sort of emergency."

"He telt you that?"

Leek nodded. "He had my jacket in his hands, and at first I thought I was getting the sack. Then he told me to hurry. He even gave me money for a taxi." Leek brushed the hair back over his eyes. "That's how I knew something bad must have happened."

When Agnes finally woke up, it took a while for the realization of what she had done to sink in. First she smiled at them as if they had brought her morning tea. Clouds of memory passed over her, and then she looked down and saw her bandaged wrists. She had come closer this time than ever in the past. Leek's construction site was on the South Side. She hadn't meant for him to make it. She hadn't known the gaffer was a good-hearted man.

"Where's the wean?" she asked, her voice cracked with dryness.

Leek looked at her, and then, for the first time, he looked at Eugene. "He's OK," said Leek.

Agnes's eyes swivelled without her moving her head. "I asked where. Not *how*."

The blackness in her dilated pupils pinned him to the wall. Leek looked away and tried to busy himself with something to soothe her thirst. He poured her a phosphorescent glass of diluting juice, but she held her hand out in refusal. He looked at his shoes. "Well. He's with Big Shug," Leek said finally, wishing in that instant that he had lied.

Agnes did not say anything. She thought he was lying. The way her top lip curdled and stuck to her teeth warned Leek to stop taking the piss.

"Before you cut yourself, you must have phoned him and told him to come get Shuggie. It all happened that fast. I couldn't help you *and* help Shuggie." Leek exhaled upwards, and his fringe rippled like a curtain in an open window. "It's too much, Mammy. I can't be the one to save everybody all the time."

Twenty-Five

By the time Agnes awoke in Gartnavel Hospital her boy had been living at his father's almost a week. Before she cut herself she had called
the taxi rank to declare that Shug had finally gotten his wish, she was
leaving them all for good, and that he should come collect his winnings,
the boy. She said that she had bought a new suit for Shuggie from the
catalogue, and that Shuggie was to wear black dress socks to her funeral,
that Shug would need to be vigilant about that.

Leek never knew how that message got to Shug. Did the hackney
dispatcher broadcast it over the CB radio for all to hear? Did all the black
hackneys pull to the kerb and idle their engines as Joanie Micklewhite
relayed the last wishes of the woman she had helped kill?

Shug had not bothered to rush. When he finally came to Pithead he
was impressed that Agnes had actually gone through with it. He found
the boy eating tinned peaches, sitting stunned on the bloody settee,
consoling a wet-faced Shona Donnelly from upstairs.

Shuggie had never been to his father's new house before. As the
taxi chugged heavily through echoing streets, the boy counted on his
fingers and realized he had spent less than three hours with his father
since Joanie Micklewhite had stolen him away. He sat in the back of

the black hackney as good as a stranger. He couldn't really remember meeting Joanie Micklewhite either, but he could remember the yellow roller boots with a traitor's cramp that hurt his heart. Joanie had become like a villain in his mind; her reality and her legend were mixed deep inside him. Agnes's hate for her was as ingrained in him as knots in wood.

So Shuggie sat in stilted silence as the taxi rounded the corners of a brutal-looking council scheme. Each street was a scarred field of burnt-out off-licences, dirty canals, and cars on bricks. To the boy, this place looked a little like Sighthill; five or six tall high-rises pinned the heavy winter sky in place. Yet, unlike in Sighthill, the high-rises were ringed at the bottom with low, boxy concrete houses instead of flat empty forecourts. These low houses looked like ants gathered around trees, or scraps made of the council breeze blocks left over from the high-rises. What was once built to be new and healthful now looked sick with a poverty of hope. There was no grass and no greenery; every flat surface was concreted over or covered in large, smooth round boulders.

Big Shug stopped the engine at a vandalized telephone box. Shuggie could tell from the back of the taxi that it was a difficult conversation. It looked difficult, because after Shug hung up he stood in the phone box for a long time smoothing his moustache.

The boy opened the suitcase Shug had made him pack. Into it he had put all the possessions that meant most to him and very few clean clothes. He took out a faded Polaroid. It showed a shirtless Shug holding him as a newborn in one proud outstretched hand and smoking an ashy doubt in the other. He checked it now against the man in the phone box.

On dreich days Shuggie would take Agnes's wedding album and hide at the foot of her bed poring over the photos of his father. Shug didn't look like the person he remembered from the three Polaroids taken at the wedding reception. He looked smaller than the smiling man who had sat on the banquette with his arms flung open around drunken bridesmaids. Now, the years of sedentary taxi driving had taken what was already average and also made it round. The short Caesar cut of the photos was replaced by a wispy comb-over. The once cheeky eyes were set deeper into his pink flesh. Shuggie couldn't imagine any woman wanting to slow dance with this man now.

Shug hadn't really looked at the boy until he was in the back of the taxi and they were already on the North Side. He climbed back into the driver's seat and turned and looked at the mud and dirt and blood on the boy's school uniform. He asked Shuggie whether he had any cleaner clothes to change into. The boy said he had no clean clothes, but he did have pyjamas. It was a shameful feeling, taking off your clothes in front of a strange man, in a strange taxi.

Shuggie was in his clean pyjamas as they crossed Joanie Micklewhite's threshold. Her house was the middle in a strip of semi-detached houses that circled the fattest of the grey high-rises. She had a concrete front yard and an asphalt backyard, and therefore they paid a higher rent rate to the council. As the boy crossed the front door he noticed with awe that they had stairs in their house, two separate floors; that alone would kill Agnes.

Joanie Micklewhite was stood at the end of the short hallway with her fingers laced patiently in front of her round belly. She didn't say hello to the boy or to Shug; she just nodded and turned back into the kitchen. It was late supper time when they arrived, and Shug led the boy into what he called the "dining room," and Shuggie made a note to never tell his mother that they had stairs or a dining room.

The boy sat in the middle of the folding table, and Joanie scowled at one end, and his father glared at the other. Sat at the table already were six of Joanie's weans. They looked ill-humoured and hungry, like they had been made to wait for something not that special. The youngest of Shug's stepchildren was a boy aged about seventeen. Only one was a girl, called Stephanie, and it was the only name Shuggie could remember from his father's introduction. He remembered partly because it was the most Protestant name he had ever heard but also because, when Shug had first left, Catherine had threatened to kick the life out of Stephanie Mickle-Shite in an attempt to cheer up Agnes. Now, sat across from her, Shuggie could see Catherine would have lost. Stephanie had thick hairy forearms. Out of all of them, she hid her dislike for their new visitor the least.

Shuggie sat quietly while the Micklewhite-Bains recounted their days to his father. They had a lot to tell him. They had office jobs, they had cars, they were sticking in at school or were waiting to hear from a *university*. One was a training to be a teacher, and Stephanie worked in a place where everyone had something called a personal computer. They all called him *Dad*, which confused the boy, and they all wanted him to listen to them over the others, like he was an honoured guest. Shuggie was staring, he couldn't help it; Stephanie lowered her head almost on to the table, met his eyes with a cold glare, and asked if he would like to take a picture.

After that Shuggie tried to keep his eyes moving. He tried to surreptitiously soak in all the details of his father. He knew almost nothing about him, and while the others ate, he stole sideways glances at the man and wondered why he tolerated these other children but had left him.

The strange man lifted his glass and drank his milk, and all the while his eyes scoured the others like a searchlight. He would lower the milk glass and with his other hand smooth the lines of his glossy moustache in satisfaction. Shuggie was nervously rubbing his own top lip when his father finally looked at him, and they regarded each other in silence.

After dinner, Joanie led the boy to where he would be sleeping. Despite the dining room, the Micklewhite house seemed very small. The eldest boy slept on a single bed in a narrow cupboard under the glorious stairs. He was a professor of chemistry or something, and his cupboard was decorated with Star Trek memorabilia all suspended from the ceiling by invisible fishing gut. If their brightest and eldest was in the cupboard, the boy couldn't think where they were leading him.

Joanie took Shuggie upstairs and passed three or four small bedrooms. There was another Micklewhite, a seventh, a boy also called Hugh, who was away in the Army cadets. Joanie switched on the bare bulb and said that he, the new Hugh, could sleep here, "temporarily, mind you." The room was messy and felt stuck in a limbo between a child's and a man's bedroom. There were little green soldiers glued along the windowsill next to posters of a naked Samantha Fox. Hugh Micklewhite had kept his clothes, clean and dirty alike, in a heaped pile next to his bed. Shuggie cleared a space on the sheets and sat on the dented mattress. His head was swimming.

He counted on his fingers. If you included Leek and Catherine, then Shug had fourteen children. There were four of his own from his first marriage, then Shuggie, and he'd added Catherine and Leek and then collected the seven half-grown Micklewhites. His father had three sons named after himself: one Hugh per woman. After he had done the sums, Shuggie felt lucky to have had those three hours of his father's time.

Big Shug took to hiding in his taxi: double shifts, back shifts, night shifts, early shifts. For his part, Shuggie skulked around the shadows of the high-rises and hid from them all. In the mornings Joanie turned the boy out of the house. She told him that his father needed peace to sleep, "that was what the night shift did to taxi men." At the front door she pushed a jam piece and a peeled carrot into his hand and told him to go and play and not to come back till it was dark. She pointed out into the distance and waved her hand wide across the scheme, meaning he could go anywhere he pleased for all she cared.

While every other wean was in school, Shuggie spent the time wandering the high-rises. Each floor of the high-rise had a shared laundry room between the flats. These were cavernous concrete rooms that had a wall of breeze blocks and so were open to the elements on one side. Housewives would hang their clean washing there and wait while the Glasgow wind battered it dry and froze it solid. Shuggie rode the lift, floor to floor, till eventually he would find a laundry room that was unlocked and open. The higher was always better, and he would sit with his legs and arms through the breeze blocks and look out over the sandstone city all the way to Sighthill. The north wind would scald his face as he dropped little green soldiers to the ground below. He strained to see the black line on the horizon and tried to imagine her there. Was she missing him? Was she even alive?

The boy had been dropping the green men to their deaths for nearly three weeks by the time Agnes came. Eventually she had discharged herself. She telephoned, and Shuggie watched with a dark curiosity as Joanie Micklewhite spat hate as good as she got. He felt like a traitor, to be inside the hoormaster's house, to have Joanie hang up on his mother, and then to watch them laugh and degrade her and pick her apart like old chicken. The boy was heartbroken to watch them take joy in her misery. He died for the fear she might think he was now one of them, laughing down the phone at her. He thought about her wrists and the blood on the tea towels, and like a big baby he cried from frustration right there in front of them.

In a way Joanie changed her tune then. The boy didn't understand why she suddenly became sweet as sugar towards him. Shuggie had gone from being an imposition to being a useful pawn. To her he was now a wonderful, magical, hurtful way to show Agnes Bain once and for all who was the winner.

Agnes grew sick of all her threatening and all her tearful begging. She sat at her dressing table and set her hair into a hard crown of black roses with layer after layer of her expensive hairspray. She pulled on her tight black skirt and a fresh white blouse, and over this she wore her good purple mohair coat, making sure it was long enough to cover her tender, bandaged wrists. She sank three cans in quick succession, and then she burst the gas meter open and called a taxi.

Agnes had threatened to do it, and they hadn't believed her. Like bullies they had felt safest in a crowd, and they had laughed down the phone in big *HA-HA-HA*s. Now, as she stepped out of the black hackney, she asked the driver to kindly wait.

"I won't be a minute," she said. "I'm only away to have the last laugh."

With a proud clip, Agnes walked down the street counting up the odd numbers. Opening the metal gate she stood in the small front yard and rubbed at her heart when she saw the double-glazed windows. She looked at the new windows and then at the two storeys, and her mouth pulled wide in a sickened grimace. She checked the address on the torn piece of paper and then pulled down on the cuffs of her purple coat one last time.

Agnes hammered on the door, but no one answered. There was a scurrying of feet by the peephole, and then there were voices giggling. Agnes hammered again, and then she stepped backwards.

"*SHUG!*" she shouted. "*SHUG BAIN! SHOW YOUR FACE, YOU WIFE-BEATING HOORMASTER.*"

She waited. There was no answer from inside the two-storey house, but people on the street stopped dead in their tracks. They milled about behind postboxes and parked cars; children laid their BMX bikes down in the dirt and scurried to get a better look. She could feel them all watching, and it emboldened her.

"*SHUG BAIN! YOU BALD-HEADED FUCKFACE. STOP PLAY-ING WITH YOUR TINY COCK AND SHOW YOUR FUCKING SELF!*"

Her voice bounced off the low buildings and carried clear across the high-rise flats. Agnes straightened her back and drew up her chest to scream again, and then something caught her eye. There was nothing in the paved front yard; its concrete was perfectly flat and grey. There was nothing except for a few straggling weeds and, in the corner, two large silver rubbish bins.

Agnes picked up the first bin; it was not yet full, not yet too heavy. In one clumsy motion she twisted her body, her thin heels wobbling under her, and then slinging back around let go of the bucket. Still weak from the hospital, she almost fell backwards, gracelessly, through the gate. The metal bin flew through the air, and for a moment she thought it would bounce off the thick windows and do her a damage. She held her breath in fear it might miss.

Agnes didn't miss.

The bin found the centre of the window and crashed with an almighty clatter into the room. The glass broke into small, ice-cubed pieces, and the proud net curtains were pulled down from their rod. The old women who had stopped in the street screamed for mercy. The children on BMX bikes whooped with excitement.

The Micklewhites had been sitting, Walton-style, at the dining room in the back of the house when Agnes had started hammering. Everyone but Shug jumped when they heard the noise from the front room. Joanie, who had been laughing at Agnes over a serving dish of golden potatoes, was up and through first. When she saw the glass and the garbage, she screamed as if she had been knifed.

By the time Shuggie had pushed through the tangle of Micklewhite legs, Joanie was standing amidst the debris and rotten rubbish with her mouth open and hands flaccid by her side. Stephanie put her arm around her mother, lest she should keel over. The big colour television lay smashed on its face. Shuggie noticed it didn't have a coin meter; *wait till I tell her that*, he thought.

There in the front yard, smiling, stunning, and mostly sober was Agnes Bain. The boy wanted to scream, *Goooooooooaaaaal*. He wanted to run a victory lap around the scheme with her.

Shug made it to the front door first. With his arms pinned on either side of the door frame he stopped the rest of the Micklewhites from spilling out into the street. Their arms clawed at her around the bulk of him; it looked like the zombie horror films Leek let him watch. Agnes calmly put her hand into her bag and pulled out a long cigarette. Lighting it slowly, she took a long elegant draw. "You bastard," she said, quite calmly. "Get my boy out here now."

Joanie, who was still amidst the glass, found her sharp tongue at last. She let out a shriek, the kind that starts at your toes and tightens all the muscles in the body till it erupts out of your mouth. "You auld drunk hoor! You're gonnae pay for that window, so help me God!"

Agnes picked at a fresh chip in her nail. She looked disappointed as she held her hand up to Joanie. "Now look what you made me do. *T'chut*." She mugged and made her painted nails dance in a wave. She turned her cold eyes back to Shug and hissed through gritted dentures, "Get my boy out here now."

Joanie pushed her way into the hall, past the boy and the other roaring bodies that Shug was using his girth to hold back. His face had flushed between scarlet and puce. "You auld drunk, I'm going to fucking kill ye," Joanie spat, her talons wildly scraping the air.

"Shug Bain, I am warning you!" Agnes took another draw on the cigarette and looked down the street as more neighbours emerged from their homes. She moved closer to the second silver bin. "If you don't get my son out here now, I'll put in every window in this fucking street."

Joanie kept clawing at the air around Shug and started spitting watery gobfuls into the street. Agnes only looked at her distastefully and went back to picking at the chipped nail. Joanie kept screaming like a banshee. "Ye're fuckin' mental. They should never have let ye oot o' the maddie house."

In a fluid motion Agnes dropped her cigarette on the ground and had her black high heels off and clutched in her hands. Agnes, who couldn't throw a ball straight, was feeling brave after the bin had found its mark. The first sharp stiletto sailed through the air and clattered against the door frame and fell to the ground. Agnes shifted forward in her stocking feet and like an experienced shot-putter let fly the second heel; it found its mark on the side of Joanie's face. Joanie staggered back into the hallway with a bloody yelp.

The boys on bikes howled with wicked delight. They fell to the ground and furiously started gathering chuckie stones, holding them out to this warrior woman and chanting for more blood. "*Here! Here! Missus. Again! Again!*"

There was blood, a small amount only, but enough for Joanie to wipe on her hand and rile up her brood. At the sight of the blood the Micklewhite boys started to push harder to get out and lynch Agnes. Shug looked like his heart might burst from the strain.

Shuggie could hardly see his mother standing in the front yard. The hallway was so full of bodies pushing against his father, and if he couldn't see through the mess of angry limbs, then he would never be able to reach her. He turned and retreated slowly up the hall and sleekitly slid into the room on the left. He crossed the glass-strewn living room and stood on the large upended TV, using it as a step to climb up on to the window ledge. In one leap he jumped up and over the jagged edge of the broken window and dropped down on the hard concrete outside.

Shuggie moved cautiously towards his mother. She was gaunt and pinched-looking, and underneath her paint she was a grey anaemic colour he had never seen before, but she was alive. Shug watched his son tread delicately across the broken glass. "Shuggie, come here, *now*," he barked. The claque of Micklewhite voices behind him started to protest. They were braying for blood; they were telling Shug to let the boy go. He ignored them. "She's no gonnae get any better, son. Come away from there."

Shuggie paused for a second, he looked over his narrow shoulder bone and shrugged. "But she might."

Agnes was glaring up at Shug, her hand outstretched to her boy. "You can't see green shite but you want it."

"I know what's good for the boy." His lip curdled under the bristles of his moustache. "You cannae look after yersel, never mind him. Fuck's sakes, look how twisted you've made him."

In her stocking feet Agnes bent over and folded the boy in a deep embrace. The buttons of her good coat scratched at his face, but he didn't care. He choked her middle and tried to bury himself back into her flesh. His bottom lip started to tremble; it protruded and rose like a heat blister. Agnes put her thumb gently on it and kissed the pale skin above his left ear. Her words were as warm and easy as the Fair Fortnight sun. "Shhh, we've been greetin' in front of them long enough. Not here, don't give them the satisfaction."

She drew herself to her full height again, somewhat diminished without the black heels. She looked up at Shug and the grotesque chorus that longed to do her a damage. "Sometimes you don't even want a thing. You just can't bear anyone else to have it."

Without another word Agnes took Shuggie's hand and led him out of the gate. The BMX boys were still screaming for blood. Agnes raised a hand to quiet them, but they took it as a salute, and then the whole street broke into a cheer: "*Gaun, yersel, Missus!*"

By the time they got into the back of the taxi, her boy was mute and staring up at her like she was an apparition. She cupped Shuggie's face with her painted fingers and turned his gaze out to the low house. "Get a good look. God help me, you'll never see that fat bastard again."

As they drove away she held his chin. Shuggie watched his father struggle to push the Micklewhites back inside the hallway, as if he was stuffing an unpegged tent back into a bag. Now there was a deflated roundness in his shoulders; all the gallus swagger of the past few weeks was gone.

As they left the scheme, the BMX bikes circled the hackney, soaring and diving like little starlings. Agnes pulled the boy into her side, and he clung to her like a limpet. She held him tight for a long time and tried to ignore the scent of another woman's soap on his hair. He let her cry, he let her talk, and he didn't contradict her when she made him fine promises he knew she would be unable to keep.

Twenty-Six

Eugene parked the hackney just beyond the house. He waited for the morning sun to come over the scheme and watched Leek come out the gate and lumber towards the bus stop. The young man dug his hands into his overall pockets, the weight of the tool bag digging into his right shoulder. From where Eugene watched him, he looked like a half-shut penknife, a thing that should be sharp and useful, that was instead closed and waiting and rusting.

When Leek was gone, Eugene used the key she had given him. When he went into the house, she was snoring in that thick way he had come to despise. Her knew her head was backwards off the edge of the bed, and that her larynx was struggling to cope under the clogged bile of last night's drink. He stood outside the door and knew he wouldn't stay today. Some mornings he had found that if he timed it correctly, he could find her after the drink of the previous day had left her and before she had soaked herself in fresh sadness. Then she would be small and a little pitiful, but she would be present, charming even, a thing he could look after like a spindly plant he wanted to coax towards the sunlight.

As he passed along the hallway, there were small sounds from the other bedroom, neat footsteps, the sound of Shuggie's fingers searching through his tidy pencil case. Eugene went into the kitchen and placed his bags on the counter. He filled the fridge with fresh liver and butter, and at the back of the small pantry he stacked four tins of tomato soup and four tins of sweet custard, like he had been doing every morning. It sat before him now, a wall of overflowing rations, the shelf groaning under the weight, and it made him feel better somehow.

He made tea and toast for himself and for Shuggie. He left Shuggie's on the carpet outside his bedroom door and then sat at the kitchen table alone. There was yesterday's newspaper, but it had been a slow night, and he had read it forwards and backwards already. He had even read the agony column, which he enjoyed reading and found truly insightful, but would never admit to anyone. Agnes's paper was split open to the classifieds: jobs wanted, caravans for sale, and lonely hearts. She had been circling ads in her fat bingo marker, and as he drank the tea he glanced at them.

The pages of house exchanges were soaked with ink. She had circled anything that sounded far away from here, and Eugene was surprised not to feel saddened by it. Since Gartnavel Hospital, he had watched how she paced around like a caged animal, and when she wasn't picking at her arms, she'd pick at the window paint, the bed frame, the loose threads on the settee. He had come up behind her one morning and had needed to hold her tight, almost crush her between his arms, until the picking anxiety left her. Now, from the bleeding ink, he could see she was picking a different scab. She had told him how she longed for a house in a more central, less-insular scheme. He had been rubbing her back one morning as she told him she wanted to live somewhere she could have her anonymity back, a place her pride could be restored. Then she added timidly, somewhere Eugene could live with her like he was her man. He had said nothing then, he just continued to rub her back until she grew restless and picky and moved away.

Eugene knew that if you asked the council to find you another house in another neighbourhood, they would place you on a long waiting list. Even the truly desperate had to wait for years for a council house, and if you already lived in one, you became very low priority. The wait to be rehoused was interminable. So, if you already occupied a council house, the better approach was to try to execute a straight swap of houses, off the books, on the fly. The council didn't mind this; it cleared the backlog, and anything that kept the complaining masses from filing through the chamber doors was welcomed. In their view, exchanging one house for another only moved the problem around, but at least it kept it from their desk.

Eugene stretched and tried to straighten his hunched spine. There was an old gas-bill envelope next to the newspaper. She had been writing an advertisement and then scratching it out, again and again, till the wording was perfect. He could see Agnes had spent a long time thinking of the phrasing of her request, and that she had gotten slowly drunker as the evening wore on. When she was closer to sober it read almost pitiful and pleading, and later as she slid towards spitefulness it sounded more demanding. She had eventually taken all the versions and cut them into one. In thirty words or less she had made Pithead sound lovely, a pastoral and friendly place, neighbourly and thriving. In the ad she stated she was willing to consider any offers. Eugene thought, had it been a lonely hearts ad, she would have been both desperate and a liar.

He drained the dregs of his tea and stood up to leave. If he left now, she might never know he had been, and he could sleep peacefully in his own bed. He turned to go, but the boy was in the doorway. Shuggie was neatly dressed, his school bag lashed tight across his body. He saluted Eugene, as had become their way. "Night shift clocking off, sir."

Eugene put down his money belt again. He tried not to sound too deflated as he returned the limp salute. "Aye, day shift reporting for duty."

"I don't like ye when ye've got a drink in ye," was how he told her they were finally done.

Eugene had come by, as he had taken to doing, at the end of his night shift, knowing it was the best chance to find her sober. Some nights, without undressing, he would lie with her in the warm bed, and they would talk about the funny punters he had seen or the shiny things she wanted for the house. If she was not too hungover, he would unzip his trousers and roll on top of her then. Agnes would try to push the sleep from her limbs and ignore the painful rubbing of his sheriff's belt on her belly. He would shove away at her, and before long they would both want it to stop. With a grunt he would roll off her and kiss her on the cheek. He would say he was too jumpy to cuddle, and already dressed he would go sit in the dark kitchen and wait for her with the lights off. Agnes would get up and cook him something hot in the black frying pan and make him two mugs of strong black tea. She would set both mugs in front of him at the same time, side by side, and watch as he drank them in the one go, scalding hot, like they were glasses of water. They would talk a little longer, about nothing really, and he would slip her some money, just a few notes, enough for a loaf and perhaps some hairspray. Then he would kiss her, their first proper kiss of the visit, and he would go home to his own house and his own grown daughter and get into his own bed.

Agnes waited until he had rolled on top of her one night, and as he shoved his way into her, she asked softly, "Genie. When I get a house exchange, will you move in with us?"

Eugene stopped his thrusting, and she felt him slip out of her. His thick face was flushed round the edges. The look of boyish concentration dissolved as his features hardened themselves, preparing her for disappointment. "No," he said simply, sliding out from between the warm sheets.

Agnes felt so embarrassed that she couldn't sit up. For a long time she just lay there in the dent they had made. She listened as he went to the kitchen, and she heard him pull out his chair and wait for the service. It took all the strength she had to raise herself. She poured herself on to the floor as though she were boneless. When she got into the kitchen he spoke first.

"I don't like ye when ye've got a drink in ye."

She knew what he meant. He had said it not as if they were lovers coming apart but as if he had thought about it and was resigning from a job he hated.

She wanted to tell him she didn't much like him when she didn't have a drink in her, but she didn't. She didn't have the strength to lie. There was no face left to save. Instead, she pushed two link sausages around in the pan until they burst. Then she made him two identical cups of dark tea, with the tea bag left in. He drank them, and then he left.

Shuggie never saw Eugene again.

Agnes's boys could tell something was different. It was like how you can tell when a bonfire has petrol in it instead of just wood. In a fury, she drank herself into a sadness with lager, and when she was done with being sad she changed to vodka and made herself angry again.

For weeks the door swung back and forth, with Jinty and Bridie and Lamby and all the others who brought bags full of drink. For two weeks Shuggie stayed away from the school and tried to keep her contained in the house. He locked the doors and ran all the outside messages. When she fell asleep sitting up in her chair, Shuggie took out his schoolbooks and tried not to fall so far behind.

"I'm getting out of here," spat Agnes one afternoon. "Phone me a taxi."

"But where?" Shuggie asked, looking over the top of his textbook.

"Don't ask me where!" she screamed. "Anywhere, anywhere away from here. Away from you."

He tried not to flinch. "But what will I tell the taxi man?"

"Tell him I want the lights, the action." She smacked her lips. "Tell him to take me to the bingo, for fuck's sake."

Shuggie picked up the phone and pretended to dial the number. He pressed 111-1111. He waited a moment and then blethered cheerfully into the empty receiver. "Taxi? Yes, please, Bain, that's right. The big bingo. OK, thanks." He gently placed the receiver back on the cradle. Clearing his throat, he said, "The taxi man said it will be at least half an hour."

Agnes was already by the front door, her hand tugging on the handle. She danced from foot to foot like she needed the bathroom. "Fuck!" she squealed like a spoilt child. "Does nobody want me to have a life?"

"Mammy," soothed Shuggie, "your hair is sticking out on the one side. You can't go out like that. Come away in, and we'll fix it."

"No!" she spat, running her fingers through the tangles.

"Come on, you can have another wee drink."

At that Agnes let the leather bag slide from her shoulder on to the floor. She stumbled along the hallway. When he got her back into her chair, her head was already bobbing sleepily on her shoulders, as if she were on a very bumpy bus. On his knees at her side he poured her a tall mugful. He used more vodka than Irn-Bru. He handed it to her. She drank it like water. Her eyes sprang open.

"Are you going to fix my hair, then?"

Sitting on the arm of the chair he began to run the brush through her black hair. Agnes held the mug against her chin and slurped the sugary liquid into her mouth. "Has it been half an hour yet?" she asked.

"No, Mammy," he sighed.

"I was going to go out and get you a new daddy."

He ran the thick brush around the side of her hair, and the hairspray cracked and dusted the air like sweet pollen. He liked the way the hair started to soften and feather. "That's OK. I don't need a daddy."

She shook her head mournfully, like she strongly disagreed. "Has it been half an hour yet?"

"No, Mammy."

"Has it been half an hour yet?"

"No, Mammy."

"I wish you would phone them again."

She fell asleep on the chair, her head dipped forward on to her chest, her breath throaty and irregular. As Agnes snored, Shuggie let his shoulders soften. He took the mug from her loose fingers. He knelt in front of her and gently unbuckled the strappy heels, sliding them off slowly, taking care that the buckle shouldn't rip her new tights. With steady hands he unclipped the mismatched earrings. All these things he returned to her room in the hope that when she woke up she would forget she had been trying to go out.

Shuggie picked up the schoolbook again and, like a loyal dog, sat at Agnes's feet and listened to her heavy breathing. Through the front window he watched the children start to trickle back from the day's school, shirt tails out, ties around their foreheads. They were sat together like that for only an hour, when Leek came in from work and slammed the front door shut. Shuggie looked nervously to his mother, then down the hallway to his brother, spook-faced with white plaster dust. Agnes made a sound like a generator starting, and Shuggie laid his head on his knees.

"I want my dig money," were the first words out of her mouth.

Leek didn't answer his mother; he glared straight at Shuggie as if to say what a terrible job he had done keeping her from the drink. He mouthed a silent, *nice one*, and turned, with a slam, into his bedroom. Through the wall came the crashing guitars of Meatloaf, and Shuggie tilted his head back like a baying dog and shouted into the air, "I did my bloody best."

"Give us peace! Who are you to scream like that?" She jabbed her thumb sharply into her own chest. "I am the man of this house! *Me!*" Agnes tottered along the hallway and rapped her rings on the thin bedroom door. The volume went up. Shuggie watched her sink back on her heel and stick her jaw out. He could see the short hour's sleep had only given her back her fire but not taken any of the poison from her. Agnes rapped the big rings on the door one more time.

There was the sound of a little snib sliding back in its bed. Leek stepped out into the hall. He had changed out of his work clothes and into his best denims, the ones he saved for the gambling machines in the city centre.

"I raised you to answer me when I am talking to you."

Shuggie could see Leek was trying to be civil, to placate her. He bit the tip of his tongue before he answered her. "Yes, Mammy. What is it?"

"What is it? What is *iiit*?" Agnes spun around the hall, looking at the ceiling in dramatic disbelief. "You expect me to cook and clean for you all week, and when I try and have a civil conversation with you, all I get is, '*Yes, Mammy. What is it?*'" Too late Leek opened his mouth to apologize, but Agnes battered on. "I'll tell you what it fucking is. I'm sat home all day rotting away with baw-jaws there"—she thrust her thumb towards Shuggie—"and you come home and can't even say two kind words to me."

"I'm sorry."

"Sorry? Not half as sorry as I am." She drew her eyes up and down him, and they stuck on his blue jeans. "Are they new denims?"

"No."

"I've not seen them before. They must have cost you a bob or two. Are you going down the pub in them?"

"Maybe."

"What do you mean, *maybe*? You think I'm that daft?"

"Aye. I *am* then."

"Well, I only wanted to know. Would you like some hot dinner before you go?"

Leek blinked; Shuggie winced. "Yes, please." Leek fell for it.

"*Aye, I bet you fucking would.* Well, you don't pay me enough to keep hot food on this table."

Leek turned his back to her to lift his nylon bomber from the bed. The sight of his sharp shoulder made her furious, and Agnes jabbed her ring finger hard into the middle of his back. It caught him funny; Shuggie saw him twist from the pain. "Don't you turn your back on me when I am talking to you. Who do you think you are, pal?" She laced her fingers under her chin like a delicate fan. "All dressed up in your fancy-boy denims. Off up the pub with all your wee woofter mates. You're nothing but a big old jessie. A big old ponce, aren't you?"

Something in the words made Leek look to Shuggie, who had turned the colour of grey ash. Those were the same words Shuggie heard every day on the streets of the mining town. The words he heard in the playground and at the back of the class. Something in that look told Shuggie that Leek knew he was not right.

She was still roaring with the drink, but neither boy heard what she had been saying. The finger came out again and caught Leek in the middle of his bony chest. Something instinctual in him brought his hand up, and there was a loud crack as he swatted her knuckles away. Shuggie could see by the way she curled her sore fingers that it had hurt. Worse than that, it had hurt her pride.

Agnes and Leek were both shaking in anger. "You think you are the man of my house? No way!" There were tears of fury on her face. She uncurled the finger into his chest again. "Get. Your. Stuff. And get the fuck out of here. You're papped."

"Mammy." Leek sounded like a little boy again.

"*PAPPED.*"

There was a tremble in Leek's jaw. Shuggie saw it. It shook a moment, then it stiffened. A kind of locking started in his knees and travelled up his whole body, vertebra by vertebra, till he was standing solid as a stone pillar. Leek's shoulders straightened, and he held himself tall, taller than Shuggie had ever seen.

Shuggie waited until his mother was hammering a number into the telephone before moving. He slunk along the hallway and slid into the bedroom. Around the walls were the cabinets and shelves Leek had made by hand from old pieces of YTS wood. Beautiful, functional things, rich with inlaid doors and sliding drawers for hidden stashes. Under the bedroom window was a massive plywood unit that housed Leek's turntables, his speakers, and his records. Into the face of it he had made dozens of little compartments to neatly hold exactly ten albums apiece. The precise and careful hand was gone now as he stuffed his life frantically into black bin bags.

"Shut that fuckin' door," he barked, as Shuggie came in.

Shuggie did as he was told, closing their door gently, easing the ball lock into the socket. Leek was leafing through albums, deciding what to bring and what to discard. Shuggie crossed the room and put his index finger into a belt loop at Leek's waist. He twisted and twisted until all the blood was cut off from his fingertip. "She's only saying this to you a'cos Eugene's done it to her. Just wait. It'll pass."

Leek turned, he twisted his brother's hand free from his waist. "Jesus, Shuggie! I want to say something to you, and I want you to *heed* me, not just *hear* me, OK?"

The boy nodded slowly.

"Look. You are the man of the house now. So you are going to have to grow up and do some things. You are going to have to look after her money for her. When she cashes the Monday and Tuesday Books, you are going to have to keep a bit back to get you food through the end of the week. Do you think you could do that?"

Shuggie wanted to say he already did that. That he had done that since he was seven.

"You are going to have to keep her in and keep the rest of those alky bastards out. Unplug the phone when she is not looking; if they come to the door, try and turn them away. Tell them she's out. That goes double for men, alright?" Leek was still filling bin bags with the contents of his life; unwanted things no longer of use to him, he threw into the corner. Even in his hurry he made it look easy, as if he had thought about it a hundred times before. "Men will only want to hurt her, take advantage." He paused. "Do you know what I *mean* by that?"

"Yes." He knew all about it, more than Leek could ever imagine.

"Are you going to stick in at the school?"

"I'll try."

"Well, try harder. Don't make the same mistake as me, Shuggie. Make something of yourself." Leek took a handful of Shuggie's hair in a tight fist and gently shook his head. "If you are worried about leaving her, then hide all the pills from the bathroom. While you are at it, hide the razors and steak knives as well. Wrap it all up in a tea towel, take it outside, and hide it in the bushes, alright?"

Leek studied his brother for a moment. "What are you, like, *thirteen*?" Leek exhaled upwards into his own fringe. "Shit. Your balls will be dropping soon. Look, it won't be for that long. Just a wee while longer, till you can go too."

Shuggie's head pulled back on his neck in disgust. "Then who will look after her?"

"Well. She'll have to look after herself."

"Then how will she ever get better?"

Leek stopped his packing. He lowered himself on to one knee, so that he was looking up at Shuggie. His lips were moving silently, almost like he didn't know quite where to start. "Don't make the same mistake as me. She's never going to get better. When the time is right you have to leave. The only thing you can save is yourself."

Whatever weak power Leek had held over the house faded away as he left with the last of his black bin bags. The lowest of the demons came out of the off-licences and bookies, and they filled her with the drink. They drank and they smoked together, and then they fell asleep, sat upright in her armchairs, only to wake and start drinking again. Shuggie tried to keep them away; he tried to hold on to a little money and get himself to school. He only wanted to do his best for Leek, to prove that she could get better, and maybe that would bring him home again. But it was hard.

Twenty-Seven

It was the first day in three weeks she hadn't woken up to a living room full of clammy, sodden bodies. It was a funny kind of lonely. Agnes sat and whimpered poor me's to herself for a while. She sat in the chair, which was surrounded by overflowing ashtrays, and put her head between her knees and tucked her hands up in her armpits to stop the shakes.

She was unsure how long he had been sitting there clutching the red mop bucket, but when she called his name he looked as surprised to see her there as she had been to see him.

"Can I have a cuddle?" she asked pitifully.

He crossed the room obediently and sat on the arm of her chair. He was taking a growing stretch again, and his arms easily encircled her shoulders. Each time he held her he was less like a child. He was becoming something else, not yet a man, something like a stretched child, waiting to be inflated into adulthood. She clung to him while she could. He smelled fresh, like the fields outside.

All he said was, "I don't want to live here any more."

"No. Me neither."

Agnes ran herself a hot deep bath. To sweat felt good, and she felt some of the sourness leave her. She sloughed herself with a rough towel and got dressed in her best, taking care to match her jumper to her coat and shoes. With mutinous hands she put on her face and combed her black hair carefully over the start of white roots. Finding the last of the Tuesday Book money, she put it carefully into her pocket and left the house. The day was hot and close, two weeks of sunshine trying to soak up a year of rain. Still, she buttoned up her coat. They were watching as she came out the gate, standing in clusters with bean sauce down their jumpers and weans wrapped around their stretchy leggings. Agnes could hear what they were saying, and she knew that was the point. She pitied them for not even having the pride to run a brush through their hair. *Please, God. Not long now*, she thought, as she waved and held her head high.

Grey men stood around the mouth of the Miners Club, drinking their lager in the weak sun. Even though the weather was muggy and close, they all wore the thick black donkey jackets they had worn under the ground. As she passed, they turned in to one another like shy penguins, talking in hushed tones. She heard her name whispered, heard her legends discussed. The bolder of the men watched her with hungry eyes over their pints of amber. She knew they only wanted to degrade her, bring her to a new low. She knew a handful of them who had taken her comforts in exchange for a bag of carry-out. When they were done, they all went home again to their scrawny wives and their mismatched bedding. It was all too small, too pitiful to care about any more.

After a long walk she reached the string of shuttered shops on the side of the thoroughfare. As the cars screamed by, she realized now that this was the only time she got out of the Pit town, the only time she was guaranteed to cross the marshes, to be around people who didn't believe they knew every sordid thing about her. She was walking in the sunshine, allowing herself this rare daydream of freedom, when she saw her. Like a cat being cornered by a dog, the woman jumped and looked about herself nervously. For a minute Agnes thought the woman might dart out, climb the low barrier, and try to run across the four lanes of screaming traffic. In a way, Agnes hoped that she would.

"Hello, Colleen."

The woman tried to circle around her on the narrow pavement. Agnes might have let her go but not today. She stepped into her stride and said louder, "I said, *good morning*, Colleen."

The withered woman was stuck, blocked from escaping by the screaming traffic. "What are ye saying that for?" she asked.

"Why should I not say hello to you in the street?"

The woman lifted her eyes to Agnes's face for the first time and tried a vinegary smile. She pursed her lips in a grimace, which Agnes thought was a shame. The only thing that was plump and feminine on her face was her lips. "I dunno."

"So, how is your brother keeping?"

The woman batted her light eyes. "Aye, grand, thanks."

Agnes hoped she was lying, but it hurt anyway. "Well, do you think now that we are finished you could stop phoning me?"

Colleen placed her hand over her silver crucifix. "I don't know what ye are on about."

"I see. So you must take me for daft. *T'chut*." Agnes clacked her lips in the same way Lizzie had done when she was having none of it. It surprised her, then she laughed. "Colleen, you breathe like an old cocker spaniel. In the future when you phone someone to harass them, maybe you should try to shut your mouth and breathe through your nose."

The look of innocence slowly slid off Colleen's face like an ice lolly melting in the sun. The smug smile returned. "Well, youse stay away from ma brother, and we'll see."

Agnes reached into her pocket and took out the old gas-bill envelope. It listed the "House Wanted for Exchange" notice, the same one she had placed in the paper; she now planned to advertise in the newsagent's window. She handed it to Colleen, and as her eyes peered over it, Agnes noticed that the woman was a slow reader, her lips moving with each syllable. Agnes was glad she had taken the time to do it in her best cursive. "See. I'm trying to get away."

The woman snorted. "Too good for us, eh?"

Agnes rocked back on her heels. She folded her arms. "You put me in mind of my second husband. You know that? You don't want me here. You don't want me away from here."

"Yer jokin', right?" Colleen dropped her jaw in mock shock. "Ye come here to our wee scheme thinking yer some kind of big *I Am*. Walking around thinking yeese are better than the rest of us, with yer hairspray and yer handbag there." She thrust her finger at Agnes. "Ye and that funny wee boy try and rub oor noses in it, and the whole time yeese are lying in yer own piss and fucking other wummin's men. Lord. I've never seen such a hypocrite."

"Here's hoping you never fall on hard times."

"Aw, shove it! Ah nearly died when ma Eugene came home and telt me that he's taking up with the hoor in the purple coat! My mammy was being tortured in heaven just watching the two of ye carry on."

Agnes shook her head. "Those would be some bloody binoculars."

"I suppose it's all a big joke to the likes of ye?"

"Well, it's all finished. You win. Your mother can rest her net curtains now."

Colleen's face had worked up to such a shade of red that the woman looked as if she might burst. "It's much too late for that, lady. Do ye think his poor wife is going to want him now when he joins her? There's nothing he can do to make it up after bein' with ye."

Agnes sank back on her heel, she twisted the back of her earring. "Well, I can say I've heard it all now."

There was a look of pure hate in Colleen's eyes. "Ye've heard nothing. He only came to ye in the night because he was that embarrassed by ye. Creeping around like a thief! That's why only taxi drivers will have ye, int'it? So they don't have to be caught by yer side in the daylight."

"Is that so?"

The thin woman smiled, triumphant. She looked unburdened, happy to have said her piece. "Aye."

"We'll never get on, will we?"

"Never! How does that grab yeese?"

"Fine," said Agnes. She turned and headed towards the bombed-out shops. "Oh, and Colleen—" She motioned to the woman's neck, then she ran a painted finger across her own pale collar bone. "You've got a ring of dirt there around your neck. You maybe want to take a cloth to that afore you step over the door in the morning. It fair spoils the lovely glint of your crucifix."

The woman sneered. "That the best ye've goat?"

Agnes closed her coat against her neck and smiled goodbye. "Oh, and I fucked your man. It was lousy." She sniffed distastefully at the memory of it. "He had a line of skidmarks on his underwear that was a pure embarrassment."

The door went all afternoon. At first the McAvennie girls tried to lure him outside. Told him they had sweeties that they wanted to share, but he knew the McAvennie girls, and he knew their brothers would be hiding amongst the council bushes. They kept coming to the door, and when he stopped answering they took to spitting through the letter box, big long gobbets of sugary phlegm that stuck on the metal flap and slid slowly down the inside of the wood. Shuggie hid in the corner, watched them gob their mess, and tried to wipe it with a rag before it slid on to her good carpet.

Whatever Agnes had done now, Shuggie couldn't say, but they had filthy words for her. New names that sounded dank and foustie; woman's words that put spittle on their lips and made sucking sounds like a boot in the coal slag. The imaginary moat Eugene had laid around the Bain house was gone now; he rolled it up as easily as a carpet when he left. Now the McAvennie weans hammered their feet against the locked door. They shouted all the familiar poncey names at him. They made slurping kissing noises, then they made sing-songs of kissing noises, and then started the dirty names again.

When the girls grew tired of tormenting him, Francis McAvennie finally came to the door. Shuggie was ready to open it. He was so tired that he wanted to end it, take whatever was due to him, and close the door again.

Francis was nearly two years older than Shuggie. He was at the big school now, separated from his brother Gerbil, and there was thick hair on his top lip. He had started fingering a Protestant lassie. His little sisters told the scheme all about it with an odd mixture of disgust and pride. When Francis's eyes appeared at the letter box, Shuggie thought he would spit through it like his siblings had. He folded the soaking rag and readied himself to catch the dribble. Instead, Francis's big pink lips just started to talk softly through the slot. "*Shuggie. Shuggie! I know you are in there. Open the door. Go on. I want to talk to ye.*"

He had never spoken so sweetly to Shuggie before. The words poured out slowly, like the trickle from a hot tap. "Will ye no open the door, Shuggie?"

"No."

Their eyes met through the slot, and Shuggie noticed that the sallow-skinned boy had thick eyelashes like the bristles on a scrubbing brush. Francis said, "I heard youse were flittin'. I came to tell ye I was sorry for being a wee prick." Shuggie heard him ferret around in his pocket. He came back to the slot and pushed the body of a gold robot through the letter box. C-3PO's severed head was bound on with clumsy Christmas Sellotape. An old, childish toy, long ruined, a measly peace offering.

"If ye put a wee dab of glue on it, it'll be good as new." The older boy moved his eyes away and lifted his mouth to the slot to show he was smiling. His teeth were as big and smooth as white beach pebbles. "Jist open the door."

"No."

"Why do youse hate us?" asked Francis quietly.

"I don't. You hate me."

"Naw!" He sounded offended. "It's only banter like." Shuggie could tell Francis was thinking hard about what to say next. "I want to make it up to youse. For always noisin' ye up." His brows knotted. "Dae ye want to kiss us?"

"*What?*"

Francis put his lips to the slot again. There was the faint blemish of an old scar on the top bow. His father, Big Jamesy, had been fast with the back of his hand. "I mean, I will let ye, if ye don't tell anybodies. I'll let ye kiss us. That's what ye were always after, eh?" He sniffed. "Jist open the door."

Shuggie waited, he didn't trust the feeling that was writhing in his belly now. "Why would I want to kiss you?"

"Come on. Ye know what ye're like."

Shuggie peeled away the clear Sellotape, the head fell off the gold robot and rolled across the carpet. "Francis. Are we friends now, really?"

"Aye. Surely."

"OK. Then put your mouth up to the letter box."

"Naw, jist open the door." The boy sounded almost pleading.

"Just do it, alright." Shuggie could hear the McAvennie boy hesitate. He was certain that at any moment Francis would balk, that he would call his bluff. It was silent for a painful moment. Then he heard the scrape of shirt buttons on the door as Francis pressed himself against the outside.

"One kiss, then ye'll open the door?" The voice was so clear it sounded like it was inside the room.

Shuggie closed his eyes and got on his knees. He put his face to the letter box. Francis's breath smelled sweet and sugary, like supermarket jam. Shuggie could feel his sticky breath flood over his lips, and for a moment he wanted only to put his fingers through the hole, to touch Francis gently.

But the moment passed.

Shuggie brought his hand to the opening and, as quickly as he could, he pushed the wet rag through, the one soaked in the spit of his tormentors. It was folded so the greenest, phlegmiest part was to the outside. He felt it touch the other boy's face, felt the resistance, then he felt Francis pull away from the door as the tea towel slid out. Shuggie leaned against the door. He could hear Francis hacking the sour spit out of his mouth.

Francis brought his teeth back to the letter box. They were snarling now, nipping and biting to tear at Shuggie. "Aye, ye better no open the door. I'm gonnae fuckin' stab ye, ya poncey little prick."

There was a *thump-thump* against the door, like a hard fist against the wood. Shuggie recoiled as Colleen's kitchen knife shot through the slot and jabbed wildly in the air. Shuggie pressed himself against the inner draught door and watched as the silver blade darted in and out of the letter box. It searched blindly for his flesh, its edge so keen and sharp it screeched as it sawed back and forth against the metal flap.

Davey Parlando, the rag-and-bone man, came to the door three times with his wagon. He took anything Agnes offered and paid her with a roll of grubby pound notes bound by an old Elastoplast. He couldn't believe his luck at the beautiful woman's generosity—or blind stupidity. When he talked he was jumpy and nervous, like he was constantly improvising, because he couldn't tell which it was: Was she daft or was she good? It was hard to tell because her eyes were glazed with a kind of apathy.

When Davey offloaded the remnants of Lizzie's wedding china, he made a last trip to the wagon. He usually gave weans a whistle or plastic toy, but he handed Shuggie a whole boxful of grubby balloons, enough to last him the entire rag season, all misprinted seconds emblazoned with the smeared offset of proud corporate sponsors. Davey did a trick where he blew up a balloon through clamped lips by slipping the rubber neck between the teeth he was missing in the front. He handed the damp balloon to the neat boy, and read it slowly, as if Shuggie could not read for himself. "See, it seys, *Glasgow's Miles Better*."

"Than what?" asked Shuggie pointedly.

The ease with which Agnes was now willing to part with things was unnerving Shuggie. Whatever furniture the rag-and-bone man did not cart away at a steal, Agnes returned to the rental centre. She sent back all the furniture that was on hire purchase that she could. Then she took out a hobbling Provident loan to buy new and better when they made it to the city.

He could sense the fever that had fallen on her, the dream of being a new person surrounded by new things. It made her clammy as any flu. She gathered up all the years of Kensitas cigarette coupons and counted them obsessively. All bound together, they made dense little bricks, little ingots that still smelled of sweet golden tobacco. Shuggie lay on the carpet and built walls and forts from them as Agnes went through the Kensitas catalogue, tabbing the corner to mark lamps and tea trays she only half-liked, and kept a worried-looking total on a gas-bill envelope.

Shuggie watched her and said under his breath, "Why can't I be enough?"

But she wasn't listening.

Agnes had packed up the house quickly, starting as soon as the exchange was agreed upon. She looked at most of their belongings as though they had hurt her in some way. The packing was mostly done in an afternoon, both of them keen to be gone and preferring to live the last weeks in a packed-up house full of unsullied dreams and anticipation. Shuggie helped her wrap the precious ornaments, taking care to fold them all into old newspaper and then tuck them in a box amongst her underwear. When her back was turned he took things of Leek's from the pile of discarded items—some old records, half-filled sketchbooks, and an old stuffed leprechaun of Catherine's—and then hid them safely amongst his mother's moving boxes. The last of his siblings' belongings she gave to Davey Parlando for a roll of dirty notes.

The night before they moved she burst the television meter one last time and bought handfuls of chocolate at the ice cream van. She laid all her old clothes out for Shuggie, and they sat with their knees touching, deciding what versions of her to bring and what to leave behind.

"People don't really wear stuff like that any more," Shuggie said. She had slipped on a fuzzy black jumper, the yarn like a trillion droopy eyelashes.

She nibbled a corner of mint chocolate. "But what if I belt it?" She pressed her hands against her cinched waist.

Shuggie reached inside her jumper, unbuttoned the two white shoulder pads, and removed them. Suddenly she seemed less severe; she was softer and younger-looking. He squinted. "If you'd wear denims, then maybe that's better." He put the pads inside his own school jumper, and his shoulders raised to his jawbone.

Her face puckered. "Uck. I'm too old for denims. They make everything look common now."

Shuggie leaned forward and took up a wool A-line skirt the colour of dead heather. It was tight but not too tight. He had never seen her wear it. "I like this one."

Agnes considered it. She flicked the zipper as if checking to see whether it still worked and then tossed it aside. "No. I don't want to be *her*. She wears men's house slippers and keeps her pinny on all day."

"You would be comfortable."

His mother lay back on the carpet with a huff. She turned and ran her eyes the length of him. "So, who do you want to be when we move?"

He shrugged. "I dunno. I've been too busy worrying about you."

"God, it's Mother Theresa herself." Agnes looked crabbit then. She propped herself up on one elbow and took a drink from her lager mug. She scowled into the cirrus patterns that were forming on the top of her ale. "Look, when we get to the tenement, I'll give up the drink, I promise."

"I know." He tried a smile.

"I'll get a wee job like other mammies."

"I would like that."

Agnes picked at a hangnail. "Your bastard of a father never liked me to work. A woman's place and all that guff." It was true: Shug had never suffered her to work, nor had Brendan McGowan. For the Catholic it had been a matter of pride; he worked his hardest so the neighbours knew he could provide for his entire family. For Shug it had been that he was not to be trusted, and therefore he was unable to place his trust in anyone else, least of all his own wife. He preferred her at home, to know where she was all day. Her men never liked her to work, so she never really developed the taste for it.

"You're too good to work. You're too lovely." He knew what to say; they had talked like this a hundred times before. It came out too flat, but still Agnes seemed assuaged. Then he said something unexpected that froze the smile on her face. "But, like, *if* you did work, it would be OK. Like, if you get a night shift, you don't have to be in for me at nights any more. I can watch myself."

Agnes sat up and downed the last of the lager. She seemed like she wanted to change the subject. Shuggie watched her as she pulled together two effigies from their unwanted clothes. She arranged a pink angora jumper of hers and a too-small gangster outfit of his into a pair of hollowed-out Guy Fawkes dummies. Shuggie followed her into the kitchen, where she hung them on the clothes pulley. She pulled on the rope, and the pulley ascended to the ceiling again. They twisted there, full of life, two versions of their old selves hanging in wait for the new family.

"The woman's named Susan," said Agnes. "She's nice. She has four weans and a carpet-fitter for a man. Never claimed the dole in his life. Wait till they get a load of him round here."

"Are we tricking her?" asked Shuggie, full of concern for the new tenants.

Agnes rubbed her cheek like she was trying to soothe herself, like her dentures were pinching at the back. She poured herself a fresh mug of lager. "No. She has a motor *and* a man. They didn't seem that bothered to be so far out."

She put her finger down the neck of Shuggie's jumper, pulled it out, and rubbed his skin, like she was checking whether a lazy maid had hoovered under a carpet. There was fine hair starting to bud on the plain of his small chest. She worried it with her nail, but said nothing about it. "You're awful pale. When was the last time you were outside?"

He didn't want to tell her about Francis McAvennie and the kitchen knife. He didn't want to admit he had been too scared to linger outside since that day he had threatened to stab him. In the end he didn't have to say anything. Agnes's mind was a jumping slide projector. She said, "You'll not remember the city. You were too wee. But there's dancing, all kinds of dancing, and big shops. You can be outside all the time, because there's that much to do." He thought he saw her inflate with false hope, like she was trying to puff herself up with a delicate excitement. It seemed as fragile as thistledown. "You'll not remember. But you'll see."

"I can't wait." It was a lie, but only half of one. He couldn't admit it to her, but the city scared him slightly, the vast uncontrollable nature of it: all the alcoholics he could lose her to, the dark pubs, the men who might take advantage, all the unknown streets she could slip down and he could lose her on. At least the Pit had been a known element. It had held them stuck like flies on paper, bounding them in on four sides by nothing. She could harm herself here, but he could not lose her.

Shuggie tried not to dwell. "When we flit, will you really try to stop the drinking?"

"I said so, didn't I?"

There was a faint look of disbelief in his eye; he couldn't help it. He turned to the sink to wash the last of the dishes, to hide his face.

It got her goat. "Are you calling me a bloody liar?"

She had been drinking all day. Her mood was a low-level haar, foggy, dark and heavy, but holding steady without rain. Shuggie did not want to burst this cloudiness and force the bad weather. "No. Sorry."

Agnes stubbed her cigarette out on the edge of the sink. She lifted her lager mug and tossed the contents down the drain. It all happened so forcefully, so fast, that Shuggie got sprayed with the dregs and stepped back, soaked and blinking.

Agnes opened the planking place under the sink and took out her last two Carlsberg. She handed one to him, and tore open the other herself. She held it over the sink, and the lager poured down the drain in a choking, sputtering torrent. When it was empty, and the last of the white yeasty foam had fallen into the sink like damp snow, she threw the can at the bin and missed, the tin rattling on the linoleum floor. All Shuggie could do was step back wide-eyed and hold on to the worktop for balance. Agnes, possessed by something now, ran around the house; he could hear her clawing underneath furniture and scrabbling behind the wardrobe. She came back with a half dozen bottles, all the forgotten dregs of vodka, all the last slugs she had passed out before finishing. She emptied them down the sink with a dramatic flourish.

Shuggie had never seen her do that before. He had never seen her waste good drink.

On the rare occasions she promised to get sober, she would still drink it all first, every single drop, before she started with the fierce withdrawals and the boaking and the shaking. There were other times she fell sober because she had no choice. On the weeks when all the benefit money was gone, and no man would bring her a carry-out, then a type of grudging sobriety would start. If that happened on a Thursday, then her sobriety had a four-day running start. Shuggie always rooted for it. But the drink rarely lost. It was like a bully who gave Agnes that running start in the grinning confidence he would catch her easily, and she'd be battered again when the benefit book was cashed again the following Monday. Still, Shuggie always fell for it.

He opened the last bronze can. He watched her out of the side of his eye as he poured it down the sink, in a gentle, tentative trickle, ready to stop at any moment.

Agnes watched him do it, her held tilted back like she was a fine lady. "Do you believe me now?"

Shuggie pushed his thumb knuckle into his eye socket to steady himself, to stop the hopeful tears. "Thank you."

Agnes stiffened, but she smiled, a faint tremulous thing. "No more drinking for me. I'm not saying it'll be easy, but that's the best thing about the city. No one will know us from Adam." She picked some oose from their hanging effigies. They spun in the quiet kitchen. "And you. You can be like the other boys. We can be brand new."

1989
The East End

Twenty-Eight

After the isolation of the slag hills, the tenements felt like a thriving hub of life. The main road was lined with thick sandstone buildings, and set into the base of them were hundreds of little shops, a post office every mile, a chip shop nearly every block, and all sorts of dress and shoe shops where Agnes could shop on tick. Shiny cars waited at lights and then inched along in patient lines; there were double-decker buses, two at a time, stopping every block or so. There was a cinema, a dance hall, a big green park, and as many chapels and churches as he had ever seen. The pavements were full of people going about their messages, and nobody paid any mind to the others. They moved independently, in oblivious, anonymous, take-it-for-granted freedom. The people didn't even nod hello to each other, and Shuggie could bet there was not a single cousin amongst them.

The moving lorry made some sharp turns on to tighter side streets. The sky felt far away now, and the only break in the wall of tenements was at the corners, where streets of even more tenements branched outwards. Shuggie looked up, it felt like they were dug into the very earth, deep inside a sandstone valley. They came to a stop, blocking the street completely, and with a loud rattle the men from the AA dropped the tailgate. Agnes looked at the piece of paper and stood looking up at the tenement. It was a greyish-blond building sat in the middle of a long wall of the same. The door had buzzers for eight flats, and Agnes found the ones for the third floor.

"This is us now," she said, pointing to one for the boy to see.

He was too old for it, but he let her hold his hand, if only to keep her moving forward and not send her itching for drink. Shuggie hooked her hand in his, it felt small to him all of a sudden. She was wearing every ring she still owned, but despite the chilled metal he could feel the nerves and the clammy want in her palm.

"Let's promise to be brand new. Let's just promise to be normal," he prayed, as they held hands like newlyweds.

The close mouth was clean and cold. The walls, the floor, and the stairs had the look of being carved from a single piece of beautiful stone, and it all smelled like it had been recently wiped out with bleach. They climbed the stone stairs slowly, stepping to the side to let the men get up and down with the boxes. On each landing two heavy doors faced each other, each floor neatly and evenly divided. As they passed each landing, floorboards squeaked behind some of the doors. Agnes held her head high and carried on up the stairs.

The door of the flat was on the right-hand side of the third stone landing. As they stepped inside, Agnes made a quick inventory of the dirt that remained, the carpets that needed to go, pointing at finger marks here and there like she was a tour guide. "Aye, she wasn't very clean," she said coldly. "She'll likely do fine out in the Pits."

The new flat was small. It had a stubby L-shaped hallway, and he found himself wondering where she would put her telephone table. At the front of the tenement, looking out on to the street, was a big bay-windowed living room, and next door to that was a very small master bedroom. At the back of the tenement was the narrow kitchenette and a tiny box bedroom. Shuggie paced the small bedroom, measuring it heel to toe in both directions, hoping it would fit two beds, but it never could. It suddenly felt final, and it made him miss Leek.

Agnes stood by the big bay window and looked out over the street. Shuggie encircled her with his arms, and these brand-new people allowed themselves a minute of quiet, peaceful daydreaming. Agnes scratched the back of her calf with the other foot. Shuggie knew it was in her nature to be contrary.

The moving men had finished before long, and as they took the last of the cardboard with them, Agnes gathered her mohair coat and promised Shuggie hot tea and apple pastries for their lunch. Shuggie closed the door behind her and ignored where her shoe buckle had snagged the back of her tights. He stood alone a long time at the kitchenette window and stared into the enclosed back green. Completely walled in by the tenements, the space was divided by five-foot walls, so that every building had an equal square of scabrous grass, dominated by a concrete bin shed.

Every square of green was teeming with weans, like petri dishes hoaching with life. The air was filled with echoing screams and laughter, amplified by the sandstone enclosure. Every so often a wean would shriek up at the back of a building, and shortly thereafter a window would swing open and a bag of crisps or a set of keys would be tossed down four storeys to the ground.

Shuggie sat and watched the scene—a coliseum of sorts—for most of the afternoon, wondering what it must feel like to play, to be so carefree. He watched the weans climb the walls and invade other back greens. He saw heads get cracked and toddlers get shoved off of bin-shed roofs. A window would open, and an officious finger would single out the offending gladiator, and then that child, wailing in fear and contrition, would not be seen for the rest of the day.

Shuggie eventually grew bored with the brutality.

As he waited for her to return with the tea things, he fell on the little red football book and for the hundredth time started at page one. He was reading the results for Arbroath when he heard the key in the new lock. From the seat at the window in the kitchenette he could already tell.

"Hello, son." She stood in the open doorway, her eyes loose in her head, and there was a wide, too-toothy smile on her face.

"Ha-have you been drinking?" he asked, already knowing the answer.

"*No-ooo.*"

"Come here. Let me smell you." Shuggie crossed the empty kitchenette.

"*Smell me?*" she said. "Who do you think you are?"

He was getting taller every day. He took hold of her sleeve and pulled her towards him with all the command of a grown man. She wobbled on her feet and tried to wrench her sleeve free. He sniffed at her. "You have! You have been drinking."

"Look at you. You love to spoil my fun." Agnes tried again to pry him from her sleeve. "I just had a wee hauf with my new pal Marie."

"Marie? You promised we would be brand new."

"We are! We are!" She was becoming irritated by her gaoler.

"You lied. You didn't even try. We are not new. We are just the fucking same." Shuggie pulled her sleeve so hard the jumper stretched and the neck slid off her shoulder. There, on the soft white skin, was a single black bra strap. He reached out to grab it.

"Get off of me!" Agnes looked frightened now. She tugged on her jumper and twisted away so abruptly that the boy took to the air. He landed with a crack against the wall and slid to the floor in the corner of the hallway.

Agnes was mumbling to herself. "Who do you think you are to speak to me like that?" A thought crossed her mind and she turned on him again. "Your father? Do you think you are your bastarding father?" Her head sat back on her neck in ugly defiance, and she spat down on him. "That'll be the fucking day, sunshine."

He watched her put the stretched jumper back on her shoulder and go back out the front door without shutting it behind her. In the echoing close he heard her go from door to door. She chapped each door, and when someone answered she introduced herself with a slurring politeness.

"Hello. I am *SO* sorry to bother you. My name is Agnes. I am your *NEW* neighbour."

Shuggie heard the good people of the tenement pause and then return awkward greetings. He could almost hear their eyes running up and down the length of her, taking her in, making up their minds. This woman, with her bottle-dyed, jet-black hair, in the shiny black tights and the black high heels, was already drunk by lunchtime.

The secondary school was bigger than any he had seen. He had waited and cautiously followed a boy that lived on the landing downstairs. The boy was tanned the colour of summer holidays. At the street corners he turned around and with big brown eyes he looked suspiciously at the pale boy who was following him like a stray.

Shuggie had set up the ironing board and ironed his own clothes for the first day. His trousers were a grey school wool and were topped with a smart red jumper that Agnes had bought for him with cigarette coupons. He ironed them till they were perfectly flat and two-dimensional. Then he ironed the underwear and the socks.

Following behind the boy, Shuggie rounded a corner, and there it was. It sprawled forever and looked like a city of its own: big concrete cubes and rectangles that intersected at different angles and were surrounded by lower buildings that looked like Portakabins but more permanent. There were no windows to the outside, just this giant concrete mess of shapes in the middle of a flat expanse of asphalt and stone and brown mud.

He followed the boy in through a main gate. The schoolyard was big, and it was full. Inside it was a moving mass of Protestant blue, and white and some red. Nearly every boy had a Glasgow Rangers shirt on, a training jacket, or at least a sports bag. Everywhere he looked, *McEwan's Lager* was spelt out in big white letters. Shuggie put his hand in his pocket and felt better feeling the dog-eared red book there.

The bell rang, and he followed the boy in through some glass doors. For want of a better idea he followed the boy to his class. The children took familiar seats and set about talking at the top of their voices. Shuggie put his bag on a desk at the back and tried to hide behind it. A short middle-aged man with a white beard came into the classroom. He looked like an angry terrier, and he spoke with a very loud Glaswegian accent. "Right, shut yer faces, youse lot. Let's go fur the record and then youse kin all get back to talking aboot earrings and perms an' that." He paused. "An' that's jist the boys."

The room made a bored huff. The man took the register and when he got to the end the room fell about shouting again. The teacher folded his arms and closed his eyes and leaned back against the edge of the desk, trying to steal five minutes more sleep.

Shuggie put his hand in the air and then took it down and then raised it again. "Sir," he said, too quietly. "Sir!"

The teacher opened his eyes and looked at the new boy. "Aye?" he asked, still not familiar with the new year's faces.

"I'm new," said Shuggie, too quiet to cut through the rabble.

"Everybody is new, son," said the man.

"I know. But I think I am a late enrolment." He used the term Agnes had told him to use.

The room fell quiet. Thirty heads turned as one to look at him, boys with top lips dirty with hair and girls already with women's bodies and faces broken out in little white spots. "Ye're whit?" asked the terrier-faced teacher.

"I'm. I'm a late enrolment, sir. From another school." The room was now silent.

"Oh," said the teacher. "Whit's yer name?"

Before he could answer, it started. It sounded like a murmur, and then someone said it out loud, and the whisper became outright laughter. "Is eht Gaylord?" said a rat-faced boy at the front. The room erupted.

"*Big Bobby Bender?*" said another.

Shuggie tried to talk over them. His face burned red. "It's Shuggie, sir. Hugh Bain. I'm transferred here from Saint Luke's."

"Listen tae that voice!" said another boy, with tight curly hair. He opened his eyes wide like he had hit the bullying jackpot. "Ere, posh boy. Whaur did ye get that fuckin' accent? Are ye a wee ballet dancer, or whit?"

This went down the best of all. It was a divine inspiration to the others. "Gies a wee dance!" they squealed with laughter. "Twirl for us, ye wee bender!"

Shuggie sat there listening to them amuse themselves. He took the red football book and dropped it into the dark drawer of this strange school desk. He was glad, at least, to be done with that. It was clear now: nobody would get to be made brand new.

Twenty-Nine

The brown-eyed boy who lived downstairs in the tenement knocked on the door as though they were old friends. In the months since they had moved in, he had done his best to ignore Shuggie. Now, when Shuggie answered the door, the brown-eyed boy tilted his head in greeting, told him to get his coat and follow him.

"What for?" asked Shuggie, rather ungratefully.

"Cos ah need your help." The boy was already halfway back down the close.

Keir Weir was a palette of warm tones all chosen because of how well they went together. He was more tan than anyone Shuggie had ever known, and his brown hair shone with memories of a sun it had rarely seen. His eyes were richly grained, like walnut wood, and his lips were shaped and arched in a way that made Shuggie stare. He would have looked like a teen pinup if it wasn't for the dripping tip of his nose and the continual cold sore that bothered his top lip.

Shuggie pulled on his jerkin and followed like an obedient footman. When they got to the mouth of the close, Keir spun on his heels and stopped him in his stride. "Look, you're no going out wi' me looking like that."

Shuggie looked down at himself. He was wearing what he wore every day: old wool school trousers, old black shoes, and a blue anorak from the catalogue that looked like one of Agnes's old coats that she would be embarrassed to run the messages in.

"You'll gie me a brass neck. Does your maw still dress ye?" Keir pushed his hands into Shuggie's anorak. He reached around into the small of Shuggie's back and with a tug pulled on the adjustable cords there. The jacket cinched in at the waist till it almost cut him in two and fluted at the hem like an Edwardian doublet. The brown-eyed boy took the neatly ironed collar and flipped it up, then he roughly pulled the plastic zip all the way to the top till Shuggie felt like he was peering out from inside a ship's funnel.

Shuggie tilted his head back and talked over the top. "Where are we going?"

"Ah'm gonnae introduce ye tae some lassies. But ah cannae have ye looking like a fanny." Keir drew a cheap black comb from his back pocket; one end was chewed to uselessness. He spat a foamy white gobful on to it and scraped a line down the dead centre of Shuggie's head. Shuggie recoiled in horror, but Keir put his long fingers around the nape of Shuggie's neck and braced him in place. It was how men pulled women towards them in all the pictures Agnes liked on telly. It meant nothing to Keir, but Shuggie felt like the back of his eyeballs were sweating.

The drag of the buckled comb made his skull feel like it had been cleanly and evenly split. The boy roughly rearranged Agnes's neat side-swipe and parted the black hair sharply into heavy curtains. "There!" he rubbed the back of Shuggie's head, fair pleased with his work. "You look mair hardcore now." He turned and went out on the street. "Just dae what ah dae and there'll be nae problems, right?"

"OK," agreed Shuggie, lurching after him, imagining ways he could make Keir grab at him again.

Keir Weir swaggered bandy-legged up the street. The bottom of his face was obscured by his anorak collar, and his hands were tucked deep into the pockets of his jacket. Shuggie walked a little behind and tried to use a wide gait like Leek had once shown him. "We're gonnae meet a couple of lassies. One's ma bird. The other is her wee pal. She's a right wee ride," he said. "Have ye already goat a bird?"

"Yes," lied Shuggie.

"Who?" asked Keir. Only his frown and his eyes were visible over the high neck of his anorak.

"A girl from where I used to live."

"Oh, aye? Whit's her name then?"

Shuggie couldn't tell if Keir was sneering now. It was hard to talk when you couldn't see the person's lips. "Eh," he stuttered. "Um. *Madonna*." As soon as the word escaped he was grateful for the collar. His face flushed a liar's pink.

Keir looked at him with narrowing eyes. A shadow passed his face that said he was beginning to regret having asked him out. "Aye, is that right?" His eyebrow arched high above his collar. "Have ye even finger-er-ed her yet?"

Shuggie's mouth went slack behind the facade. He nodded slowly.

Shuggie heard the bored air escape Keir, watched his hair curtains bounce from the draught. "Well, ma bird's pal is right dirty. She'll gie you a ride if you ask." He sneered again. "That's if Madonna doesnae mind." He lowered a cigarette doubt into his collar, like a bucket into a well. "Anyway, ah just want ye to stop her botherin' us. Goat it?"

They walked through the blond-tenemented streets, not stopping to watch women pour buckets of bleach water out on the pavement. Keir cut through the estate with a man's stride, clipping corners, jumping benches and small stone walls. He made a direct and efficient line to her. Shuggie half-jogged behind. Keir slowed his stride only when they got to a block of modern-looking flats. He stubbed out his wrinkled cigarette doubt and reached around in his pocket and took out a piece of chewing gum. He put it in his mouth and chewed it quickly. Shuggie could smell the sweet peppermint casing break between his big white teeth. He chomped it like a hungry dog and then drew it out of his mouth. "Here," he said, offering the wet gum to Shuggie. "You're gonnae want tae be fresh for the ladies."

Shuggie blinked at the grey gum between the boy's wet fingers. He was glad again of the upturned collar, as his mouth turned down in a distasteful frown.

"Don't be a fucking poof. *Here!*" Keir thrust the gum at him. Reluctantly, Shuggie took the wad and put it in his mouth. It was slimy and warm, and it tasted of mint and beans and cigarettes. He found he didn't mind; he rolled it slowly around his mouth and savoured it. He used his tongue to push the last of Keir's spit up into the dry pocket above his teeth, behind his lips, like it might last longest there.

They climbed the stairs to the top-floor flats. Every landing had a big open balcony, and Shuggie was happy to stop at each and admire the view, like a contented pensioner. When they reached the top, Keir turned to him and said, "Try not to sound like such a posh boy, alright. I don't want them tae laugh at us."

Keir pushed the bell at the side of a mottled-glass door. Inside, a door opened and tinny pop music filled the hallway. They watched a cloud of blond hair get closer and closer through the bubbled glass. There in the doorway was a short plain girl, pale-skinned, with big green eyes obscured behind thick pink glasses. Her gelled hair was scraped back from her face and erupted in a large, permed ponytail. On the side of her head, arranged in neat rows, were pink-coloured hair clips that looked like a rack of ribs from a pig.

She was a little younger than the boys. The messy paint on her fingernails made Shuggie think of the McAvennie girls, when they would slide around clumsily in Colleen's low heels. "Hi-yaa," said the girl through the crack in the door.

"Hi-ya, doll." Keir wore a sideways smile. He put his palm possessively on the door.

The girl giggled and then eyed Shuggie suspiciously. "What do you two want?" She closed the door slightly.

"Is your maw home?" asked Keir.

"You know fine well she's out workin'."

"Can we come in for a wee while then?"

"Naw." She squirmed and closed the door more.

"How no?"

"Cos I said so. My maw said she would batter me if I let you in when she was at work again."

"Aw, come on." He stepped out of his shoes.

"Naw," she squawked childishly. "You ruined it last time! You peed all over the toilet seat and the skirting board. My maw went spare when she saw it. I got leathered." She closed the door till only her face fit in the crack.

They stood this way for a moment. Inside there was the sound of a pop cassette tape being turned over. Keir spoke first. "Well, I brought ye this." In his hand was a bar of soap wrapped in clear pearlescent cellophane; it looked like the cheap soaps that were piled high at the Barras market, the ones Agnes turned her nose up at. It said clearly on the side, *Not to be Sold Individually*.

Her small white hand came out from behind the door and cautiously took the soap. The cellophane made a crisp, crinkling noise. The young girl gasped in delight, then added, "That changes nothing."

"Are ye still wantin' to be ma bird?"

She looked at the bar of soap and back at the tall boy. "Aye. Mibbe."

"Dae ye want tae come out then? Ye know and kick around for a wee while?"

"Na-aw. I cannae," she pouted.

"How no?" Keir Weir was batting his brown eyes as hard as he could.

"Cos Leanne is here, that's how no."

Keir nodded and presented his prepared plan. "Well, this is Shuggie. He fancies Leanne." Shuggie stepped from the shadows of the close. "So she can come an' all."

The girl's eyes went wide. She let out a squeak, and her little head popped back into the hallway as the glass door slammed shut. Shuggie watched the distorted puff of blond hair race down the hall.

Was this to be the moment that would make him normal? All the practicing at walking, all the chasing of a bladder ball and learning outdated football scores: it was all for this.

The door opened, and two small faces peered out. Then the door slammed shut again. There was a riot of laughter from inside the hallway. Keir shifted nervously. "Try and look less like a big poof, would ye?" he hissed without turning.

Shuggie inhaled a deep breath and tried to stand up broad and straight and then like an unhappy turtle he lowered his face into the anorak with a scowl. The door opened again, wider this time. The two girls stood there, fidgeting with delight. Leanne Kelly was a good foot taller than the other girl, and peered out at them over the bush of blond perm. Her jaw was set firm, and she wore no make-up or trinkets in her hair. From the way she stepped forward and squared herself to the boys, it was clear that she had been raised with a colony of brothers. When she spoke, her mouth was pinched like it was guarding her teeth. Shuggie thought her eyes were like little watchful raisins.

"How can you fancy me? I've never even seen ye," she asked bluntly.

Shuggie went blank, and Keir kicked him hard in the soft of his ankle tendon. "Well, it's . . . it's just that I heard so many nice things about you."

The girl wrinkled her nose in disbelief. "Whit, now?"

"I heard that you were very attractive."

"Why do you speak so funny?" she said without smiling, the wrinkle still on her nose. "Whit school do ye go tae?"

The girl stepped further out into the daylight of the close, and Shuggie realized her face wasn't actually dirty but covered in a thousand beautiful freckles. Her raisin eyes still shot about, taking him in suspiciously. "Um, I go to the school up the road," he said.

"That Proddy dump?"

"Yes."

The girl sighed, and the wrinkle fell off her nose. "Too bad. Ah go tae Saint Mungo. It's for Cath-licks."

"That's OK. My mother is a Catholic. So I'm a halfer, I suppose."

A thin smile spread across her lips. "Doesnae matter round here. Ma brothers would skin me if they knew I was going around with a dirty Orange dog."

Shuggie tried to hide his relief. It flooded over him, and he wanted to exhale long and low. He could tell her he was mostly Catholic, that he had taken Communion, but instead: "Oh. Well. OK, then. It was nice to meet you." He turned away with a gentlemanly wave goodbye. He wanted to run.

"Don't play so hard to get," Leanne exhaled loudly. "At least let me get ma fuckin' jumper then."

It was smirring lightly by the time they went back out on to the grey streets. They walked in neat sets of two. Up and down, up and down, between the identical tenements. At first Shuggie could feel the girl steal sideways glances at him; then she was openly gawping in the puzzled way that he himself stared at starving African babies on the telly. Her mouth hung open and her eyes wanted to look away but couldn't, because they were confused by what they saw. All the while she played absent-mindedly with the end of her long brown ponytail.

"Ye look funny," she declared finally, her assessment complete.

"Sorry?" He wondered how long it would be until he could go home.

"You don't have a da, do ye?"

Shuggie turned his head in the funnel neck. "Why do you say that?"

"I can just tell," she huffed, like a bored clairvoyant. "I'm just guid at guessing things like that."

"My dad is dead," he said, and then he wondered if he would even ever know if it were true.

"*Really?* Mine too!" She was brightening. Then she added, as though she had forgotten, "I mean, sorry. That's dead sad."

Shuggie shook his curtained hair. "No. I think it's great."

Leanne giggled. "That's a terrible thing to say. God's going to get you."

"It's OK, my dad was a bad man."

They walked on a little further before she spoke again. "Do ye even like lassies?"

"I don't know." It fell out of him unexpectedly, almost like a loose fart, and he regretted it instantly. His face flushed, and his eyes darted to her. She was his best chance at being a normal boy, and already he had ruined it.

But the girl simply sighed. "Aye, me either. Like boys that is." She chewed on it for a moment and then added, almost defeatedly, "So, do you want to be my boyfriend anyhows? Ye know. Just for the now."

"OK," said Shuggie. "Just for the now."

She slid her hand into his; her hand was longer than his own, but he liked the way it felt, safe and warm. They came to a ragged bit of muddy grass with blue-legged weans playing football. At the far side Keir and the blond girl pushed through a split in a chain-link fence.

Leanne stopped stubbornly and folded her arms across her bony chest. He was half-stunned by how her teeth ground together in the tight mouth. "Dirty perverts!" she spat. "That's all they want to do. Go in there and suck the scabby faces off one another. It makes me sick the way they paw at each other. She's been a right nympho since she turned thirteen."

The pair watched Keir and his date receding into the waste ground. Shuggie spoke first. "They'll just think we are funny if we don't go in."

The girl thought about it for a minute. She dug at the dirt with her toe. "So," she pouted, "ah'll get my brothers to murder them."

Keir turned around, waist-high in the weeds, and with a flick of his wrist commanded Shuggie to *hurry the fuck up*. Shuggie held the wire back, and with a sigh Leanne warily went through the hole, bending her height almost in half.

On the other side of the fence the grass crested in a gentle unkempt hill. On the down slope of the hill ran the motorway to Edinburgh. Traffic screamed by at terrifying speeds less than twenty feet away. They walked along the grassy knoll beside the hard shoulder until they reached a pedestrian footbridge. One by one the children crawled under the bridge and shuffled along the concrete embankment that slid down and on to the motorway. It smelled of piss and car fumes, but it was dry, and if they sat directly behind one of the broad structural columns, it was almost private.

They sat there, the two couples, in a fidgety silence, watching the Saturday-morning day trippers rush by. They rolled chuckie stones down the side of the embankment and cheered when the stones raced to the bottom, got caught in the wheels of the speeding cars, and flew dangerously backwards down the motorway.

"You goat any fags?" asked the blond girl. She was flattening an unruly hair into a piggy hair clip.

"Naw," answered Keir.

"Honest to God! I don't know why I am your bird," she moaned. "Stookie telt me he'd gie us a packet of fags a week if I went wi' him. Didn't he, Leanne?"

"Aye," said the tall girl, absent-mindedly.

Keir shrugged; he would call her bluff. "Away ye go wi' Stookie then. See if I care."

It was freezing under the bridge, away from the weak sunshine, and Leanne started to rattle with the cold. Shuggie slipped off his anorak. He watched her put it on with a glad smile, and laughed when her long arms stuck out the bottom of the too-short sleeves. She put her long arm around him. They sat quietly like this for a long time, watching the traffic rush by. When Shuggie looked around, he saw that Keir was lying on top of the blond girl. He was opening and closing his mouth on to hers in a way that looked like he was trying to be sick.

Shuggie watched a long thin hand slide up inside the girl's sweatshirt. Keir pushed himself against her leg, the muscles in his arse tightening with concentration, and Shuggie watched him move his head up and down on her mouth like he was chewing her. He was moaning and grinding as the girl squirmed clumsily underneath him. Shuggie savoured the sight of the ropes in the boy's arms, the tide of his back, the pulse of his arse. Keir opened his eyes and met Shuggie's hungry gaze. The outline of his mouth was wet and red and chapped raw. He narrowed his brown eyes. "Were ye lookin' at my fuckin' arse?"

"No . . ." Shuggie turned back around. The cars had thinned out.

The blond girl's glasses were moist and crooked on her face. She looked like she had been assaulted. "Leanne, hen. You alright, doll?" Her tiny voice echoed off the concrete bridge above.

Leanne, cold and bored, simply shrugged without looking back. The pair of them sat in silence, listening to the young lovers behind them. Keir spoke first, in a voice that was deliberately too loud. "See!" he said to the crushed girl. "Everybody but you thinks I'm pure shaggable."

"Ye're a stirring bastard," moaned the girl, but she was squirming beneath him again.

Keir hauched a chewy phlegm wad out on to the concrete. Shuggie could feel Keir's eyes burning into his neck. The boy turned back to the crushed girl. "Can I finger ye for a wee while?" he asked bluntly.

"Naw. It's too cold."

"Aw, please," he pleaded. "I'll blow on them first to warm them up. Ye don't even have to take yer pants off."

"Naw."

"But I telt you I love ye. And I bought ye soap."

"*You stole that soap*," the blond girl said, before she sighed and added, "Alright then. But just for a wee minute and ye need to warm up yer fingers first."

Shuggie's face had turned scarlet. He could feel the heat radiate off of it. He took Keir's chewed comb out of his pocket and slowly slipped the end into his mouth. It smelled like cigarettes and boy's hair gel. It smelled like Keir.

"If ye want, I'll let ye touch my tits," said Leanne next to him. "That's if ye want?"

He shook his head without looking at her. "No, thanks." He let a handful of small grey stones roll down the embankment and on to the motorway.

The girl dug at a line of green moss. "Well, I'm no sitting here to catch my death."

Shuggie drew the chewed comb from his mouth and wiped the wet end of it on his trousers. It left a wet, dark patch on his leg. "Maybe I could comb your hair?"

The girl didn't answer, and he felt the red flush back into his face. Then she sighed and slowly drew the furry elastic band from her hair, and the thin, straight ponytail fell around her ears. The tightness in her face softened. Her eyebrows lowered and her freckled skin looked less taut and transparent. She looked kinder now and much younger. Shuggie took the comb and ran it the length of her hair. The brown was more than just brown. It was a million shades of glossy reds and a melange of dark chestnuts. The hair slid through his fingers like silk, each strand light as gossamer.

They sat like this for a long while, listening to the clumsy moaning behind them and watching the buses come and go to Edinburgh. Shuggie drew the comb gently through the girl's hair, and soon she closed her eyes and relaxed her head against his chest. "Does your maw take a drink?" she asked abruptly.

"Sometimes. Just a little," admitted Shuggie. "How can you tell?"

"You are too worried-looking." She raised a hand and found the bridge of his nose. She rubbed it gently. "Don't worry, though. Mine does an' all," she said. "I mean. Well, sometimes. Just a little."

Shuggie fixated on the comb gliding through the hair. He watched how each strand separated like burn water. "I think she is going to drink herself to death."

"Would you be sad?" asked the girl.

He stopped combing her hair. "I would be gutted. Wouldn't you?"

She shrugged. "I dunno. I think it's what all alkies want anyways." She shivered. "To die, I mean. Some are just taking the slow road to it."

Something shook loose inside him, as if the old glue that was gumming his joints together had failed. His arms felt unexpectedly heavy, like the knotted muscles that stopped his shoulders from spreading were suddenly unravelling. He felt the words start to pour out of him. It felt good to tell her things. He hadn't known how much lighter it would feel. "It's hard to not know what you are coming in to at nights."

"Aye, but it's never a hot dinner, is it?"

"No," admitted Shuggie. His stomach turned over with fresh worry. "Do you have many uncles?"

"Aye, of course," she said. "Ye know, I'm a Cath-lick."

"No! I mean, you know, *un-cles*."

"Them. Oh, aye. They don't stay that long, the scavengin' bastards. They always end up battering her, and then my brothers always end up battering them." She yawned like it was too ordinary to explain. "My job is to dip their pockets for money."

"Really?" He was surprised at her barefaced pride.

"Aye. I clean them out. Every single penny." She shrugged nonchalantly. "I need to. Ma maw spends that much of the message money on drink."

Shuggie picked long broken hairs from the old comb and wound them thoughtfully round his finger. "I wonder if my mother knows yours?"

"Doubt it."

"I mean through the meetings. Through the AA," he said.

"Naw. Auld Moira is well past that shite." She shook her head. "Has she ever tried to send you to Alateen?"

"No. What's that?"

"It's like AA but for families. Moira said it was a support group. She said it would help me to cope with her illness."

"Did you go?"

The girl sat up and took her hair in her hand. "Once. But after that, no fuckin' way! Why should I go when she hardly makes the meetings herself. Eh?" She pulled the short sleeves down over her blue hands. "Anyway, you should have seen some of the posh wee bastards that were there. All moaning that their mammy drank all the Christmas sherry and fell asleep afore present-opening time." A cruel smile crossed her lips. "So I telt a story of how ma maw opened all the presents and drank ma brother's Christmas aftershave by mixing it wi' a bottle of fizzy ginger. You should have seen their faces." Leanne grinned like the devil and put on a fancy Edinburgh accent. "I'll have an Obsession and Diet Coke, please."

"*Diet* Coke?"

"Aye, she's worried about her weight."

Shuggie laughed, then felt bad for laughing. "Did she really drink that perfume?"

"Oh, aye. Well, she tried it. Drank the whole thing. It near kil't her. She was vomiting for days." Leanne rubbed at her chilled legs. "Her sick smelt nice though."

Leanne's face fell again; the end of her nose was purple with cold. "The next Christmas she wised up. Auld Moira Kelly got the itch and took some of the presents up the far end of Duke Street on Christmas Eve. She stood in the knee-deep snow and sold them at the side of the road for some drink money. She sold a cassette player for five pounds and a wee colour portable for twenty."

"I'm sorry."

"The worst part is that I'm still paying the catalogue for them."

The words were on his lips before he realized he had spoken them out loud. "My mother tried to kill herself last night."

Leanne turned to face him. "Did she take some pills?"

"No."

"Slash her wrists?"

"Well, no," he paused. "Not this time anyway."

"Put her head in the oven?"

"No. She has afore. But I think the one in the new flat is electric."

"Ugh, that'll not stop them." Leanne took a strand of hair between her fingers and inspected its frayed ends. "Ma maw did it once when I was away on a school trip. I'd had a lovely time at the Edinburgh Zoo looking at the penguins, but when I got home my brothers were all stood around her laughing. She looked like she had been on the sunbeds. She'd tried to do hersel in and baked her face instead. Half her hair had grill lines on it from the oven rack." She plucked violently at a broken hair. "It was mental. She permanently crimped half her head and set the other side in a semi-wave."

Shuggie couldn't help but laugh. The girl giggled lightly and then sighed sadly almost as quickly. "Well, what did yours dae, then?"

"She tried to throw herself out of the window." He lowered his eyes. "With no clothes on."

"Jeezo," the girl whistled. "Auld Moira has never tried that. Thank fuck I live on the ground floor."

Shuggie rubbed at his arm; he felt the fresh welts from her struggle scream from under his jumper. Agnes had sure enough taken to the window ledge. It was a new tactic, and it had terrorized him. She had been casting up on the telephone, and then she went quiet. When he found her, she was at the kitchenette with one leg in and one out the window, her bare cunt on the stone sill. She was naked and screaming, and he had to use his whole strength to drag her back inside. There were slivers of her skin still stuck under his fingernails. A tired, damp feeling ebbed over him now. "I think the drink will kill her, and I feel like it's my fault."

"Aye. It probably will kill her," she said, much as if she were only discussing the weather. "But like I said, it's a slow road, and there's nothing you can do to help her."

The desperate slurping sounds behind them stopped. Leanne sat forward, her hair so shiny it was almost wet-looking, her face calmer and kinder now. The cold motorway air rushed between them. Shuggie let a little ball of her loose hair roll down the embankment, and suddenly he felt lonely, like he wanted to sit on Agnes's knee again as he had when he was little.

Leanne turned and regarded him over the curve of her shoulder. In the bright headlights he saw how pretty her eyes really were, not only brown but gold and green and a sad flat grey. He knew now that he couldn't keep his promise. He had lied to Agnes as she had lied to him about stopping the drink. She would never be able to get sober, and he, sat in the cold with a lovely girl, knew he would never feel quite like a normal boy.

Thirty

The first thing he said to her as he came in the door from school was, "I'm hungry."

Nobody ever cared how she felt or if she was hungry. They just told her what they wanted and what they were going to take from her. She sat in the armchair and lit another cigarette while listening to the cupboard doors in the kitchenette open and shut. "Mammy, there's nothing to eat!" he shouted from the kitchen. His voice had broken, and although it was not deep it had the entitled timbre of a grown man's. He didn't even bother to come through and see if she was there. He knew she would be. Agnes took a mouthful from the mug and asked no one in particular. "Why do you all have to take me for granted?"

She could hear him drag his school bag along the carpet. "Ma-mmy, I'm hungry. Ma-a-ammy, I'm hungry," he whined. It was almost a song to him by now. The living room door opened, and he dragged himself through. He was changing, getting taller, taking a stretch. He was always hungry.

Agnes looked at him there, his hair parted differently, the clothes hanging off his skinny shoulders, and decided she didn't like this change. "Are you not going to ask me how my day was?" she drawled.

Shuggie ignored her and swept around the room efficiently, like a hotel maid. He drew the curtains and put on the lamps. He turned on the electric fire, the one that he used when he tried to make her fall asleep.

"Turn that off," she barked. He looked at her, and then looked straight through her and left the fire on. "*I'm-fine-thank-you-and-how-are-you?*" she said with a snide sneer.

"I told you I was hungry, and there is nothing in the house to eat." He turned to face her, and although he drew himself to his full height, he looked tired. "What are you going to do about it?"

Standing there now he looked like his granny. She could see Lizzie with her hand on her hip, shaking her head in disappointment, lamenting that only hell would mend her. It caught her off guard, then it got her goat. "Don't you look at me like that."

Shuggie had had enough. He sat across from her and rubbed at the side of his temples as if his head hurt. "I said I was hungry." He was deliberately pushing her. "What are *you* going to feed me?"

"Oh, you are all the same, eh? Take! Take! Take! Well, let me tell you, I have no more to give."

"Drink! Drink! Drink!" he mimicked. "Well, let me tell YOU, I'm bloody starving."

"You cheeky streak of piss." Her false teeth ground together in her tight face. Only her eyes were loose and half-detached, rolling under the waves of the day's drink.

Shuggie rose again and stood in front of the fire. "It must be so easy for you staying here all day, but I've got to go out there and mix with *those* people." He let out a long sigh like a punctured bike tyre. His shoulders lost all of their bones. "Most of them can barely speak English. I can't even understand what the teachers are teaching."

"Easy for me?" She was slipping out of time. "They feed you a hot fucking lunch up at that school, don't they! Three hot courses, I bet. That's more than I get sat here on my own."

Shuggie put his tongue between his teeth and bit down on it hard. Only when he had mastered his breathing did he speak again. "Look. Just give me some of the social. I will go back out and get us some dinner."

"You'd like that, wouldn't you? Well, there isn't any money."

"How?" The life returned to his shoulders. "So. Monday Books, Tuesday Books. Where has all the week's money gone?"

"*Pfft*," she said, with a flourish of her hand; it looked like a fluttering bird that wore its only colour on the very tips of its wings. "It's gone away. *Vanished.* Just like all the bad bastards I've ever known."

Shuggie leaned over her now and looked down the secret side of her chair. There were only the six cans of cheap lager. It wasn't enough to waste the entire benefit. "Gone where?"

"Oh. Up the bingo. It was the snowball the day," she said. "Well, that and I bought a wee filled roll. Excuse me."

"Agnes," he said, "we'll starve."

Agnes cleared her throat. Then she shrugged her shoulders. "Aye. Probably."

Shuggie sat down in the middle of the settee and looked into the hot bars of the fire. Agnes took another can and with a painted nail slipped the ring pull off with a delicious hiss. The fight started to seep out of her. "Look, you better eat all the lunches. That'll be one hot meal, I suppose."

He spoke very quietly. "They've been taking the tickets off of me. I've not been getting the free lunch." He looked at her face; she had sucked her head back over her neck in affronted confusion. "These boys in fourth year. They don't like how I speak. They said I was too posh. They took the tickets. They've been eating my lunch."

Something cleared in her eyes. The fire made its pinging song, the coiled bars bursting with orange heat, but now she felt only cold. "We'll starve," she said quietly.

"I know."

They sat in the beaming heat of the electric fire for a long while before Shuggie stood up again. The fire was making him sleepy, and the lager smell was making him sick. He had to get out. He thought he might go up to the main road to try what Keir had taught him and steal some crisps from the newsagents for their supper. Four or five packets, he thought, and then neither of them would be hungry any more.

Agnes watched him stand and silently shuffle to the door, his feet flattening the carpet as he went. The stretch he had taken meant he was almost as tall as his brother. He was nearly fifteen and the growing pains had made him irritable. He looked to her like a piece of pale sugar toffee, pulled too long, ready to break in the middle. She could see her sons had the same old man's stoop, Alexander and Hugh, the same burdened shoulders. Watching him, she felt a longing for her other boy. She tried to cover it up. "Oh, so are you leaving me now as well?"

"What?"

"Taken all you could get, and now you are done."

"What?" He couldn't take in what she was saying.

"You've never gone hungry before. Never once in all these years."

"I know," he lied. There was no use in fighting her now.

With difficulty Agnes got herself up and out of the chair. She shoved the boy, who was hovering aimlessly between here and there. "Well, here, let me bloody help you." She stoated out the door into the hallway; her shoulder connected with the door frame and rattled with a crack.

He listened to her nails click on the buttons of the telephone. He heard her complain to herself under her breath and then, "Hello! Yes. Taxi, please. For Bain. That's right. Off the Parade."

She came back into the room looking victorious. "Well, I never thought you would leave me."

"Come on," he pleaded, his hands open and stretched out towards her. Nothing inside him wanted to harm her. "*I'm not leaving.*"

She slid back into her drinking chair. "Aye, you are. They all leave. Every last one."

"Where would I even go? I don't have anywhere to go."

Agnes had started to turn inwards. She started talking to herself. "I've raised nothing but a shower of ungrateful swine. I've seen you looking at that door, watching that clock. Well, to hell with you."

Out on the street the horn of a hackney pumped three times. The thrum of the diesel engine echoed up the canyon of tenements. "Go on!" she spat. "Go! Away to your fucking brother's. See if he'll feed you. See if I care."

"No, I don't want to go. I am meant to stay here with you. Just you and me. Like we promised each other." His lip started to tremble. He crossed the room to her and tried to hold her, tried to lace his fingers behind her neck.

Sounding impatient, the taxi pumped its horn again. She took his arms and pressed her nails into the soft flesh by his wrists. "You and your fucking promises. I've never met a man who kept one yet. You can all sit around and stuff yourselves till you are full, and then you can laugh, *Agnes Bain*. Ha fucking HA!"

"No!" He struggled to grip her hair, her jumper, her neck. Anything.

"Look!" she reasoned as she unpicked him from herself. For a moment her eyes cleared of the fog, and his mother seemed like she might actually be in there. "Don't you ask me to phone you a taxi and then stand there and make a liar out of me. Get your bag. You're papped!"

The telephone rang. She shoved him away, and a great shower of beads ripped from the neck of her jumper. The telephone kept ringing. The ringing bells were hammering his skull. Shuggie answered it in a daze, and a gruff-sounding man asked, "Taxi for Bain, pal?"

"Uh-huh." He wiped his face on his sleeve.

"Well, your driver's downstairs. He's no got all bloody day."

Shuggie put the phone back on the cradle and stood in the hallway, waiting for her to say something, anything. Agnes could have said anything then, and he would have taken it and he would have forgiven her. He would have sat back at her side and wrapped his arms around her legs. He could starve, as long as they starved together.

No. Agnes wouldn't look at him. She didn't say a single word. So Shuggie picked up the school bag and went out the door, down the winding stairs, and out of the tiled close. The driver folded his newspaper as the boy got into the black hackney.

Agnes went to the bay window and looked down into the narrow street. She watched her baby come out of the close mouth and search the sky for her. She nodded smugly that she had been right, that she had always known he would leave her, like they all did. She watched him climb into the waiting taxi, and she knew then that she had lost him.

* * *

The driver asked Shuggie where he was going. The boy just sat there and had to think for a long time, unsure of where to go now, stalling for any sign of hope. His eyes flitted nervously to the mouth of the close. He wiped his eyes on the sleeve of his school jumper, hoping each time he pulled his hand away, that she would be there.

The driver watched him in the mirror and then turned round with a concerned look. "You alright, wee man?" he asked with thin patience.

No one came to the close mouth. "South Side, please."

The taxi took the boy through the busy heart of Glasgow, in a rambling line from the East End to the South Side. They passed the Victorian train station, and he saw lost-looking boys his own age standing in bubble-shaped anoraks and tight denims, loitering around the arcades and amusements that clustered nearby. The taxi went down one of the streets lined with office buildings, and people were leaving their work and queueing at the bus stops on the corners. The lights came on in the pound stores, and he watched women with shopping bags full of Christmas presents. Several times he cleared his throat to ask the taxi to turn around, but he never did. They flew across the wide grey Clyde, with its disused blue cranes and shipbuilders' yards. "Where to exactly, pal?" asked the man.

Shuggie didn't know the exact address. He knew it was on the Kilmarnock Road, and he was pretty sure it was above the savings bank, so he told the man as much. The driver sighed and lowered his head, driving slowly along the congested main road and looking for a bank with a blue sign on a corner.

Here the Victorian tenements still had a grandeur to them. They were cut from expensive red sandstone, and not the porous blond of the East End that sucked up all the dirt and black damp of the city and held on to it for decades. This road was alive with the transient energy of students, immigrants, and young professionals. The taxi passed wine bars and delicatessens. There were small bookstores, pubs with tables out on the street, and shops that sold the latest clothes from down south.

Shuggie was watching a young woman with flowers in the basket of her bike and almost missed the bank. It was there, on the left, old and draughty-looking, with a big blue sign, just as he had remembered it.

The taxi did a neat pirouette. "Twelve poun'," said the man, punching the meter.

Shuggie felt the panic rise. "Wait a minute, please," he said, reaching for the door handle.

"Naw, pal." The old driver locked the door remotely. "Twelve poun', please."

Shuggie tried the locked handle; it wouldn't budge. "Please. My brother will pay, and he lives in that building there."

"Son, you must think I was born yesterday. If I open this door, you'll be off up that street like a dirty Mick wi' a hot potato."

Shuggie slid back in the seat. "Mister, I don't have any money."

The driver barely winced at what he had seen coming. "Then we are going to the polis." He took the handbrake off, and Shuggie felt the taxi shudder and roll. Its front wheels pulled out into the evening traffic.

"Mister!" spat Shuggie in panic. "Ah. I'll let you touch my willy."

The driver looked at the boy in the mirror for a while. His eyes sat deep and small in his pink face. They were hard to read. His lips barely moved beneath his moustache. "Son, how old are you?"

"Fourteen."

The man didn't take his eyes from the boy's face. His head seemed to roll back on to his thick neck, and his moustache danced unhappily. Shuggie tried to smile, but his lips had gone dry, and they wouldn't pull away from his teeth. "I mean it. I do. You can touch my willy or you can play with my bum," he said earnestly. "If you like."

With no warning the red lights above the locks went out. There was a pity in the man's eyes, but Shuggie was too scared to let it rip at his pride. "Son, I only take cash."

Shuggie tried the door and almost fell out on to the street. Tired women with thick bags of messages criss-crossed hurriedly on the wide pavement. Clumsy with nerves, Shuggie stumbled through the lines of busy shoppers and stood in the sanctuary of the tenement mouth. He found the name Bain on the big panel of buzzers. He pressed the button and waited, but no one answered. His legs started twitching in a jittery panic, threatening to run. He pressed the buzzer again and looked up and down the street for a thickness in the crowd, or an open close to lose himself in. Behind him, the taxi driver sighed. "Right, son, get back in the taxi."

Just then a voice crackled over the buzzer. "Hallo?"

When Leek came downstairs, he was still in his work clothes. The thick stour of white plaster chalk made him look like a baker's ghost. He crossed to the taxi and paid the man his twelve pounds. Shuggie watched him count out the last of his change in ten and five pences. When he was done, he turned his white face to his little brother. His shoulders unknotted. "Christ!" he spat. "She's started early wi' you."

Leek led his brother all the way up the tenement stairs. They got to the door of the flat and entered a windowless hallway. Off the hallway came five or six doors; behind each door lay a single bedsit room. Leek slipped his key into a thin Yale lock and opened his door.

Shuggie had been here only once before, a time that Leek had come for him unexpectedly. Agnes had been drinking, and a steelworker from the tenement next door had been gladly refilling her mug. By lunchtime, they had made him feel like he was in the way, and somewhere, deep inside, Shuggie had lost the energy to watch over her.

So he had gone looking for Keir along the Parade in the drenching rain, ducking in and out of newsagents and pub doorways. Something cold ran down the back of his neck, and he had turned and seen his brother watching him from a dry tenement doorway, just watching. Shuggie couldn't tell how long Leek had been there. He hadn't seen his brother in nearly eighteen months. Shuggie raised his hand in a shy wave and crossed the road cautiously. He was scared, for he knew Leek didn't like to be cornered, and he was afraid that his brother might use his long legs to run. But Leek hadn't ran. He had only nodded and then clouted Shuggie on his shoulder.

On that rainy Saturday, Leek had taken him across the city for a few hours of peace and quiet. He had filled him with a bowl of sugary cereal, and then they had sat on the settee and watched *Dr Who* together. Shuggie had pretended to fall asleep and slid slowly into Leek's narrow side. Leek didn't move him, and Shuggie had been unable to tell him just how much he had missed him.

Leek never said more. He never mentioned how often he had gone to watch over Shuggie. Shuggie never knew if it had been his first time or his hundredth. He was just glad he had been there.

So Shuggie had seen this room once before. The room itself was large and proud, and what once would have been a smart living room was now stuffed with borrowed furniture. The ceiling was higher than the room was wide, and at the front were large bay windows that let the evening light and the traffic noise spill in from the main road. Shuggie looked around; there was something different about it this time, but he couldn't tell exactly what.

Leek took his seat again in front of the blaring telly and started spooning in mouthfuls of hot noodles. Leek caught him staring. "The kettle's just boiled."

Shuggie burst the foil on the top of some noodles and poured in the galloping water from the steaming kettle. He knew he had to let it stew for five minutes, but the tub burnt his hand, and the smell of the cheap noodles stoked the hunger in his belly. His lips must have been wet with hunger, and when he lifted his eyes, Leek was holding out his only fork towards him. He cleared clothes from the end of the narrow bed. "Sit down, you're giving me the heebs."

Shuggie sat where he was told, and the two of them huddled around the colour television in silence. The boy tried not to eat the food too fast, tried not to make a pig of himself, to be a good guest, like she had always taught him to be. "Thank you very much for my dinner," he said, as though it were a fine Sunday roast.

After a while Leek asked, "So how come she finally papped the golden boy, then?"

"I dunno," said Shuggie.

"How long has she been on the drink this time?"

Shuggie shook his head. "I stopped counting. She stopped drinking for a short while near Halloween, but I don't know why, and it never caught on."

Leek let out a disappointed sigh, as if to say that was all he needed to know. "I thought you knew better by now. She's never going to get off the drink."

Shuggie was staring into the swampy broth. "She might. I just have to try harder to help her. Be good to her. Keep myself tidy. I can make her better." Then he added, "Anyway, you could help some."

Leek rubbed at a pocket of wind trapped in his chest. "Ah! I see. You were papped for being a nagging moan."

Shuggie ignored the taunt. He looked around at all the things Leek had gathered to make a little home: one cup, one bowl, a single set of towels. There were found things, cobbled together, a kerosene camping lamp on a bedside table, a kitchen chair used as a clothes horse. The room looked disjointed and tatty, like a spare room in an old house where people put the things they didn't want any more. Still, amongst the shabby cramped furniture, were expensive electronic toys: a telescope, a Japanese camera on a tripod, a remote-controlled Lamborghini. It looked like a boy's den, the lair of someone who was spending money on all the wrong things. Then Shuggie realized what was different this time: it was organized. It was tidy, because Leek had been packing his life into a set of brown moving boxes. They sat ominously in the far corner. He was going away.

As Leek watched the television, Shuggie felt lonelier now than he ever had. He looked around the rented room and now saw what it was. It didn't look dingy any more. It looked wonderful. It wasn't a hidey-hole from her, or a secret den. It was a last raft. Leek was leaving.

He studied the side of Leek's face. His older brother still had the stoop, the knotted shoulders, the tight mouth, yet now his eyes looked green instead of grey, and his hair was pushed confidently away from his face. Shuggie regarded him as he watched the television and envied this new peace in his faraway eyes. "What do you think will happen to her?"

"She'll sober up. She'll beg you to come back. Then she'll do it all over again," said Leek bluntly. "But she'll have a taste for papping you now."

"I meant in the long run."

"Oh. The drink will put her out on the street," said Leek, very quickly and too casually.

"On the street? No way! She won't even leave the house without colouring in the scratches on her shoes."

"Shuggie, she's getting too old for this. It's only a matter of time before it all catches up with her." He picked the inside of his nose. "What's she gonnae do when you leave? What's she gonnae do when the men stop wanting her?"

"Then I won't leave," said Shuggie with certainty.

Leek sniggered. "So are you gonnae be one of those middle-aged saddos that still lives with his mammy? Still lets his mammy buy his clothes for him and stoats up and down to the post office wi' a pensioners' trolley." He rolled up the mucus and flicked it into the corner. "'Asides, if she was gonnae get better she would have got better by now." Leek scratched his chin, but his eyes went back to the little television. "The drink will put her out on the street. You will come to your senses. Sooner or later."

Shuggie felt sure now that they had been playing "you touched it last" and no one had bothered to explain the rules to him. He hadn't known he was going to ask this, but as soon as he had, he knew he had wanted to ask it for a very long time: "Why did you never come back for me?"

Leek took his eyes from the television and met Shuggie's stare. He hooked his hand around the back of his brother's neck. "That's not fair, Shuggie. How am I meant to raise you? What have I got? 'Asides, you're still lying to yourself. Look at you! No one can help you but you, Shuggie. I mean, think about it. Think how long it took for me, and in all that time Caff never once came back for me."

There was a loud buzzer sound from the carpeted hallway.

"Shuggie. You. *You didn't*." He was staring at his brother with a wide-eyed fear. The shrill buzzer went again, more insistent and angrier. Leek scuttled out into the hallway, and Shuggie heard him scream into the handset, straining to be heard over the noise of the busy road.

"*I didn't mean to.*" Shuggie was talking to himself, apologizing to no one in particular. "I only told her it was the Kilmarnock Road." He was only making it worse. "Oh. I might've said it was above the bank."

"You little grassing bastard." Leek lifted a jam jar full of coppers and dumped its contents on the single bed. A dirty metallic smell filled the air. With quick fingers he pored through the coins and counted out around ten pounds. He slipped the coins into his dusty coveralls and clattered out the door and down the wide close mouth. Shuggie listened to him jangle into the distance.

When Leek came back, his face was flustered and angry, red from the stairs and knotted with outrage. Shuggie felt the warm noodles in his belly turn to worms. Leek stood at the door with a plastic bag in his hands. The bag was full of tins of Bird's yellow custard. Leek pushed his damp fringe back from his face. His forehead was pink and dust-free now. "That custard," he said, catching his breath, "has just spent the last of my wages on a sightseeing tour of Glasgow."

A bubble of sick, nervous laughter rose inside Shuggie. He tried to put his sleeve over his mouth but the sound escaped regardless.

"It's not fucking funny," spat Leek, but he was smiling, then he was laughing. "Bad news always follows you, Shuggie. It always has." A telly turned up the volume on the evening news in another bedsit; Leek made the two-finger salute at the adjoining wall and shut his thin door. "Turns out Mammy phoned the taxi company and tells them to come and get her. When she comes down out of the close she puts the bag of custard in the back and tells the driver to bring it over here. He telt her, 'no way,' but she says her boy will pay the fare at the other end. That I would even give the driver a two-pound tip!" Leek stopped laughing. He slumped against his moving boxes. "I don't even think I have enough left for my work's bus fare."

"Why did she send the custard, though?" asked Shuggie. He wondered what terrible thing she might have done to get the money for the food.

Leek had started to step out of his work shoes when the buzzer howled again. The two of them looked at each other in disbelief. Leek went out to the intercom in the hall. He came back in looking crushed and worried; his smile was gone. From his pocket he took a small pen-knife, and on his knees he burst open the lock on the gas meter till a handful of shiny silver coins fell out. Without speaking he gathered them up and went down the stairs.

Leek was gone an age this time. Shuggie stood rooted to the floor. He whispered to himself, over and over, "I shouldn't have left you, I'm sorry, I shouldn't have left you, I'm sorry," in incessant prayer.

The door opened and Leek stepped through the darkness and back into the bedsit. Under the whiteness of the dust was an even whiter face. Leek cradled something in his arms, and when he spoke it was the quiet shy voice that he used to use. He definitely wasn't smiling any more.

"Shuggie," he whispered. "The taxi driver is waiting downstairs. I gave him a handful of coins, and he said he would take you home again. He needed to go back east anyway. Gather your stuff and take yourself home."

Shuggie nodded, slowly and obediently. He *had* touched it last. He could never be free. "What's in the bag?"

Leek looked down at the white plastic shopping bag in his arms and undid the knotted mouth. Shuggie watched his shoulders rise behind his ears. Whatever it was, it had turned Leek's anger into concern; it had scared him almost. Leek put his hand inside and slowly drew out the tan-coloured plastic with its looping spiral tail. "I don't think this is a good sign."

It was the telephone from his mother's house.

It was an end to all contact, a sign she would hurt herself and this time she would not call for help—not to Leek's gaffer nor to Shug nor to Shuggie. The tinned custard wasn't a fuck-you to ungrateful sons. She was making sure her baby was fed, and now she was saying goodbye.

Thirty-One

It was March and it was her birthday. Shuggie stole her two handfuls of dying daffodils from the Paki shop. Since the afternoon at Leek's, he had hidden the benefit books and made sure they had enough to eat before she bought her weekly drink.

Since Christmas he had held a little of the meter money back, out of her sight, to give her a few pounds to play at the bingo on her special day. She had taken the envelope half-full of coins and held it to her chest like it was the crown jewels. She had been so happy.

When the police brought her home the next morning, the air in the flat was already thick and sickly with the pollen of the decaying daffodils. They had found her wandering by the River Clyde. She had lost her shoes and her good purple coat. She hadn't even made it to the bingo.

Agnes couldn't look at Shuggie for shame, and he wouldn't look at her for a deep sense of his own stupidity. The chill of spending a March night outside was rattling sore in her damp lungs, so Shuggie poured a deep bath and sprinkled it liberally with cooking salt. He ironed and laid out clean clothes. He made her some milky tea, which he set outside the bathroom door, and then he left without either of them having said a word.

Dressed for school, he ran across the main road with the other children and was surprised to hear two fifty pences from the gas meter jangling around in his anorak pocket. It stopped him cold. He turned them over in his hand. He climbed aboard the first bus going anywhere and asked the driver how far the money would take him.

The view from the sixteenth floor of the Sighthill tower made him feel tiny. The city was alive below him, and he had never even seen a half of it. Shuggie pushed his legs through the breeze-block wall of the laundry room and looked out over the endless sprawl. For hours he watched as orange buses snaked through the grey sandstone. He watched as leaded nimbus darkened the Gothic spires of the infirmary, while elsewhere, obstinate sunlight brought the glass and steel of the university to life.

His arms and legs felt heavy hanging out over the city, but he found the envelope in his jacket pocket and took it out to consider it for the hundredth time. It had no return address on it, only a postmark that said Barrow-in-Furness. He didn't know where Barrow-in-Furness was, but it didn't sound like Scotland.

It was a Christmas card that had arrived two months too late. Leek had found work someplace else. They were building new houses, and they needed young men who could turn to any trade: tiling, plastering, roofing. He said the money was decent, and he didn't know when he would be back. There had been no art school yet, maybe next year, he had said, or the one after. Instead there was a nice girl, and she worked in a tea room, and they liked to go walking together on something called a moor. The card had a twenty-pound note taped inside, a new note, crisp and never folded. Shuggie had wondered about that money for a long time. He allowed himself a brief daydream of Leek waiting for him at some distant bus station. Then he spent it on fresh meat and surprised Agnes with a heaping bowl of stovies.

There had been something else inside the Christmas card; a page from a lined school jotter covered with a pencil drawing of a small boy. He was sat cross-legged at the foot of an unmade bed, his back to the artist so you could see the base of his bare spine where the top and bottom of his pyjamas didn't quite meet. Whatever was holding the boy's attention was nestled discreetly in the curved crook of his body. The boy was engrossed, his face in shadow, and he looked like he was playing with small toy horses that could have easily been wooden toys, military or Trojan. Shuggie knew what they really were, that they were the scented dolls, bright and cheerful and for little girls. They were the pretty ponies, and Leek had known. Leek had always known.

The cold north wind roared around the concrete laundry room and pinched Shuggie's nose red. When he couldn't suffer it any longer, he put the card inside his coat and went home again.

All the lights were on when he returned. The stolen daffodils still wilted on every surface, and he could smell the yeast and the rot of her confinement. Shuggie listened to the whine of the operator's warning as he replaced the abandoned telephone on its cradle. She had been busy; the red pen was out on the phone book, and there were fresh scratchings through old names.

Agnes was asleep in her chair. She looked like a melted candle, her legs lifeless and her head lolling to one side. Shuggie walked around the far side of her and shook the hidden Tennent's cans to see how much she had drunk. He held the vodka bottle up to the light and measured its remaining dregs. It was all but gone.

In the silence he listened to her cough through the stupor, then she wretched and a trickle of thick bile appeared on her lips. Shuggie reached inside her jumper sleeve and took out her toilet paper, carefully enough not to wake her. With a practiced finger he reached inside her mouth and hooked out the bronchial fluid and bile. He wiped her mouth clean and lowered her head safely back on to her left shoulder.

There was an emptiness in his belly. It was below his stomach; it went deeper than hunger. He sat at her feet and quietly started to talk to her. "I love you, Mammy. I'm sorry I couldn't help you last night."

Shuggie gently lifted her foot, first unbuckling the tiny ankle clasp and slipping off each high heel and then carefully pulling the hard seam of her black tights out from between her toes. He rubbed the balls of her cold feet tenderly, and then he set each foot gently back on the floor. He talked to her quietly as he did.

"I went up to Sighthill today," he whispered. "I looked out over the whole city."

He set her high heels to the side of her chair and stood up over her again. With skill he searched under the soft sag of her breasts until he found the centre of her chest, and through her thin jumper he undid the butterfly hook of her bra. He watched as her heavy breasts poured free.

"You must have loved living there. There was so much to see," he whispered. "It made me feel dizzy to think of it all."

Hooking his fingers he found each bra strap. He moved them on her shoulder line and freed her burdened flesh from the digging pressure of the nylon. Agnes stirred but did not wake. She coughed again, a deep damp cough that was miners' houses and mould, warm lager and now a cold night by the river. Shuggie rubbed her breastbone and wondered if the police cells were very cold. Her head rolled backwards on to the soft back of the chair, and quickly, from instinct, he placed his fingers on her temples and gently rolled it safely forward again.

"I'm going to leave school as soon as I can. It's no good arguing. I need to get a job and get us out of here," he said. "I was thinking maybe one day I'd take you to Edinburgh. We could see Fife, Aberdeen even. I could even save enough for a caravan maybe. Do you think maybe then you could get better?" Shuggie smiled down at her unconscious face. "What do you think?"

He listened to her breathing for a while, and then he reached to her side and undid the zipper on her skirt. It slid down easily, and her soft stomach rose gratefully, almost like bread dough escaping the pan.

"No? I suppose not," he whispered.

Shuggie reached into her snoring mouth, and with a damp sucking sound, he pulled out each set of her dentures. He wrapped them in toilet paper and placed them neatly on the arm of her chair. With soft fingers he massaged her head and made waves through her black hair. He rubbed at her scalp just how she liked. Her roots were obscenely white.

Agnes coughed again, a dry tickle in her throat that rumbled into her belly and became all at once heavy and thick. The bile was on her lips again. Shuggie stopped running his fingers through her hair and reached for the toilet paper, but something made him stop. He watched her cough. "Suppose maybe Leek was right."

She gurgled again, and her head fell backwards till it rested on the soft back of the chair. Agnes wretched, and he watched the bile bubble over her naked gums and painted lips. Shuggie stood there and listened to her breathing. It grew heavier at first, thick and clogged. Her eyebrows knotted slightly, as if she had heard some news that was unpleasant to her. Then her body shook, not hard, but like she was in the back of a taxi and they were bumping down the uneven Pit road again. He almost did something then, almost used his fingers to help, but then her breath hissed away slowly; it just faded, like it was walking away and leaving her. Her face changed then, the worry fell away, and at last she looked at peace, softly carried away, deep in the drink.

It was too late to do something now.

Still he shook her hard, but she wouldn't wake up.

He shook her again, and then he cried over his mother for a long while, long after Agnes had stopped breathing. It did no good.

It was late now.

Shuggie arranged her hair as best as he could. He tried to cover the brazen whiteness of the roots, to arrange it just the way she liked to wear it. He unwrapped her dentures again and gently placed them back inside her mouth. Then, taking the toilet paper, he wiped the sick from her chin and pulled fresh paint across her lips, taking care to push the colour into the corners and stay neatly within the lines. He stood back and dried his eyes. She looked like she was only sleeping. Then he bent over and kissed her one last time.

1992
The South Side

Thirty-Two

There was no real stour to be wiped away, but Shuggie wasted the morning by wiping Agnes's porcelain ornaments. In the move into Mrs Bakhsh's bedsit the tiny fawn had chipped an ear, and the beautiful girl who sold rosy apples had lost a whole arm, still clutching her McIntosh red. For weeks it had made him feel terrible just to look at them. Now he took real care to wipe them all gently and set them back exactly in the right place.

That morning he picked up the long-limbed fawn and turned it carefully in his hand. He had expected the chip on the fawn's left ear, but as he looked closer he saw how the paint was fading away from her lashed eyes and the white markings were rubbing off her flank. It angered him. He had always been so careful. He had always tried his best.

Shuggie squeezed the ornament until his knuckles blanched white. The fawn kept beaming its same serene smile. He pressed against the dainty front leg, lightly at first, then he pressed harder and harder until the porcelain gave. It made an awful grating, *snicking* sound as it broke. He stood without breathing for a long while. Under the shiny porcelain veneer the ceramic was rough and chalky. He ran his finger along the sharp broken edge. Then, without thinking, he pulled again and again until he had snapped all the legs off the ornament. When it lay in pieces in his hand, he found he could not bear to look at it again. He dropped the broken fawn into the space between his headboard and the wall. Then he quickly gathered his coat and the bag holding the tinned fish he had bought from Kilfeathers, and locking the bedsit door, he went out into the bracing rain.

Shuggie floated in a daze towards the main road. Despite the rain, Pakistani men were still busy putting boxes of brown vegetables out in front of their shops. Screeching music blared out of the Bollywood video store; its windows were jarring with bright posters of swarthy-looking men holding doe-eyed women in swooning embraces. He stopped for a moment to study them, then he walked on, passing by unnoticed.

He boarded an orange corporation bus, and with a noisy clunk the driver issued a long white ticket, half-price for children. He climbed the stairs and sat on one of the last dry seats on the top deck. The bus crawled through the slow traffic, but Shuggie didn't mind. He wiped a peephole in the condensation and watched the city fall away. The bus shuddered and turned into an abandoned scheme on the right. The gable ends of half-demolished tenements lay exposed in the rain. Brightly painted front rooms and wallpapered hallways stood bare and embarrassed-looking above piles of rubble. In one backcourt there was still a line of clean washing strung proudly between two makeshift poles. In another, happy weans kicked a bladder where whole blocks had been torn down around them.

The bus rumbled over the Clyde. The river water reflected the grey hulk of the Finnieston Crane as it loomed lonely and idle over the water. Shuggie wiped again at the damp windows and thought of Catherine. His mind always went to her when he saw the rusting cranes. She had not come home for Agnes's funeral. She had told Leek, who had told Shuggie, she would rather remember her mother in the good times. It would do her no good to see how the drink had whittled her. Now, looking at the cranes, Shuggie realized he couldn't picture Catherine's face clearly any more. He wondered exactly what Catherine could still see when she thought of their mammy. Maybe she could see only lovely things.

They had burnt Agnes on a bright cold morning.

Shuggie had sat with her body for the best part of two days. At night he tucked a blanket around her, and the next morning he took it off again. He turned on the fire when she grew cold, but it was no good, her skin could retain no heat. He called Leek at the boarding house down south to tell him their mother was dead. Leek waited a long while for him to stop crying, and then he told Shuggie what to do, step by step, and then very patiently, he repeated it slowly, as Shuggie wrote it all down in Agnes's phone book. That was good of him, Shuggie thought later, not to lose his temper.

Leek came north on the overnight coach. He travelled all those miles and then stopped ten feet away from Agnes's body. He never seemed to be able to come any closer. He let Shuggie fuss with their mother, and later he simply watched as his brother bent over on the undertaker's carpet and smashed and glued cheap stones together till he made her a pair of earrings that almost looked like they could match.

Leek organized the cremation. Shuggie followed Leek the entire week, too tired to cry, too stunned to be of further help. From the procurator fiscal to the undertaker, then on to the chapel, Shuggie followed behind him, pallid, useless, mute. Several times Leek stopped in the middle of whatever he was doing and turned to his brother. He said nothing; he left empty space for Shuggie to confess whatever was heavy on his mind. Shuggie tried, he wanted to tell Leek what had happened, but the words wouldn't come, he couldn't admit it. All he would say was that he had been tired, that he wished he had tried harder.

The DSS would pay to have her cremated but would not stretch to the cost of burial, because there was no space left in Wullie and Lizzie's plot. Leek kept her death from the paper; there was no announcement in the *Evening Times*. Still, a woman in the next close had been intermittently in the AA with Agnes, soon the word spread through the fellowship, and there were strangers at the door. Then word of her death leached out to Pithead, and all the old ghouls came out to Daldowie Crematorium.

Big Shug had not come to Agnes's cremation. The only black hackney that came to Daldowie was Eugene's, and although Big Shug must have heard the news through Catherine or Rascal, he never showed face. Shuggie had packed a backpack full of clean clothes, just in case, then felt stupid for having done so. Throughout the service he searched the faces for his father, but Shug never came.

Leek frowned at Shuggie, like he was angry at his hope, disappointed that Shuggie was stupid enough to still believe. Leek said Big Shug was a selfish shitebag. It made Shuggie sad then, not only because it was true but also because Leek had looked so much like their mother when he had said it.

Inside the crematorium the mourners sat along the outside edges and towards the back. Only Shuggie and Leek sat in the front. Eugene sat near the door, flanked by Colleen and Bridie. Jinty, half-cut already, hung off young Lamby. When Shuggie turned around he thought how nobody looked truly sad. After they rolled Agnes into the ritual chamber, he heard a woman's voice behind him tut, "Cremation? They'll never get the bloody flame out with that old soak."

Until then, Shuggie had not thought properly about her being cremated. When they put her coffin on the guide rollers, his mind was filled with supermarket conveyor belts. Then it dawned on him. He found himself straining, peering wide-eyed and wild, to see where she was going next. As he looked across at his brother, Leek only nodded calmly and said, "Aye, that's her away."

It was what Leek used to say as they watched Agnes get into a hackney. "That's her away," he would say, as he emerged from behind the good net curtains, grinning down at his younger brother, and then set about tormenting him in front of the evening news.

That's her away. It was what you said when you disposed of something.

Outside the crematorium there were white buds on the bare trees, and the smell of thawing greenery hung across the memorial garden. Some of the mourners crossed the grass to offer their condolences to the boys. The bravest came themselves; others, like Colleen, sent a delegate, in the form of Bridie. Jinty had a difficult time crossing the damp ground. She looked perplexed when Leek said there would be no reception, no drink to celebrate.

"What, no a single drop?" she asked.

"Are you fuckin' kidding me?" he spat, the front of his false teeth locked tight.

Eugene took Jinty by the arm then, to steer her away. He turned to Agnes's boys to say something kind. But Leek simply turned away.

Shuggie rested his head against the bus window and tried not to think about the funeral any more. His fingers separated some coins from the others. He thought to call Leek later, from the payphone outside Mrs Bakhsh's bedsit. He knew now how it should go: Shuggie would ask how the new baby was, but he would not ask about art school. Then when Leek asked him how he was, Shuggie would say he was doing fine, because he had learned that was what his brother wanted to hear. They would both pretend to be fine, and then they would talk awhile about a train ticket and a visit south, something small and distant to look forward to. Then Leek would go quiet. He knew Leek didn't ever like to talk much. In one way that was good; to call south on the greedy phone box was expensive, and Mrs Bakhsh refused to install a phone of the boarders' own.

The bus rumbled on. The Clyde shipbuilding yards were dead now. The wide river was quiet and empty, except for a lonely boatman in a small boat. The reflective strips on his raincoat shone bright as diamonds through the steady smirr. Everyone knew of this man; he was always on the front page of the free *Glaswegian* newspaper. Like his father before him, the man patrolled the Clyde without rest. He rescued those old men who, with a skinful, had fallen in over by Glasgow Green. Other times he pulled out the bodies of the men and women who hadn't wanted to be rescued, those who slipped silently, deliberately, from the side of stone bridges into the brackish water.

Shuggie got off the bus at the back of Central Station. Even thick with grime and dabbled with pigeon shit, the riveted glass arches of the train station were still proud and magnificent. The mass of the glass station ran above some of Argyle Street and made a dark tunnel of the wide street below. The overhang was filled with fish and chip shops, bright places that sold half-priced denims, and a windowless pub that opened as early as it could in the morning and was already thick with smoke by lunchtime. Shuggie stopped outside a bakery. The ovens of the shop made it glow bright and warm, and the air was sweet with cheap icing sugar and white bread.

Sometimes he would just stand here and pass an empty hour, pretending to wait for a bus but only warming himself in the sugary dream of the air vent. He had found himself squinting at the taxi rank opposite on one such visit. He had been bending down slightly, buckling his knees and searching the faces of the drivers, before he realized what he was hoping for. Ashamed, he straightened up quickly and hurried away.

Shuggie went inside the bakery. There was a long queue of damp office girls dripping over the hot pastry cabinet. Shuggie waited patiently, his eyelids drooping in the sweet heat. A rosy-cheeked shop assistant scratched the back of her hairnet, and he asked her for two strawberry tarts. As she started to slide the tarts into a paper bag the glossy red jam began to spoil and stick to the paper. "Excuse me, Missus. Could I please have them in a box?"

"It's fower cakes to a box, son," she said, with a hot, bored chew.

Shuggie folded the five-pound note around his fingers. He would not be paid again until next week but said, "OK, then. I'll take four, please. They are a present."

The woman huffed, but she was not unkind. "Ye should have said so, Casanova. Ah didn't know ah was serving the last of the big spenders."

"It's not like that," Shuggie mumbled, his chin to his chest.

With two quick turns of her wrist the woman snapped a cardboard box together. The red tarts looked like four ruby hearts. He paid the woman, pulled up his hood, and went back into the dreich. The money did the thing it always did: now that the fiver was broken, he found himself in a small shop, spending some shrapnel on a large bottle of fizzy ginger. With the tinned fish in his bag and the ruby hearts he walked the length of the long street. He wandered through the old part of Merchant City until he had covered the Trongate and the Saltmarket and found himself back at the wide river. He walked along the empty riverbank until he came to the mouth of Shipbank Lane. Under the overhang of the old Saint Enoch railway, groups of men huddled in T-shirt sleeves and thin suit jackets. They shivered and jangled as they hawked pirated videocassettes off flattened cardboard boxes. Women ignored them as they came down the narrow alley carrying bags filled with second-hand clothes they had bought from the market at the top.

She was there, exactly where she said she would be.

The girl was opposite the market mouth, sat on the low boundary fence as though she were rusted on to the very metal. In the soft rain her long hair was poker straight and the large hoops of her earrings made her seem more childlike than she was. It hurt Shuggie to see her looking so drawn and pinched. When he had first met her, with Keir Weir in the year before Agnes died, there had been a defiant bravery to her. She had been wise, and she had been gallus, and he knew now it had all been a childish front, a mouthy bravado that covered the hurt inside her. Now her pretty, freckled features were set in that closed, self-protecting way she had developed. Her lips were almost always pursed, and her raisin-coloured eyes were constantly scanning the busy crowd for trouble. There was a calcified hardness to her now that she wore like armour and too often forgot to take off.

"You took yer time. I'm soaked to ma skin," said Leanne Kelly. There was a small pile of shopping bags tucked defensively between her legs.

"I'm sorry," said Shuggie. He climbed the fence next to his friend and sat just as she did. He checked his stance against hers and then altered it, till they were the same. He was as tall as her now, taller even, and he reached out and rubbed her wrist where her anorak never seemed to cover her skin. "So what do you want to do? Walk about a bit?"

Leanne smirked. "Good thing we're no winching." She flicked her grey chewing gum into the puddle. "Ye're pure predictable."

"Sorry."

She ran her hand over the side of his face and then shoved him roughly. "I'm jist kidding. Course we'll walk around, what else is there?" She fidgeted with the bags at her feet. "Jist let me do this one thing first, OK?"

He knew what she meant to do. If Agnes were alive, if he still had the chance, he would want the same thing for his mother. Still, as he watched Leanne pick at her lips in worry, he could not help himself: "Leanne. Come on. If I was at this nonsense you would batter me for it. It's useless. I'm sorry, but it is."

She cut him off. "Don't start. Ah fuckin' know." Leanne scowled up at the rain like it was a nuisance she could tell to just go away. "'Asides, I'm no even sure ah'll see her."

Even in the soft rain Paddy's Market was busy. The alley snaked the length of the disused train lines and into each of the abandoned railway arches were stalls full of children's clothes, bright floral sunloungers, and bedside lamps in gaudy football colours. The market used every available space: clothes hung from the sooty ceilings, and folding tables were covered with odd ornaments and old watches. Vendors spilt out messily into the tight alley, their second-hand furniture already water-logged and ruined in the spit.

Shuggie watched a blond girl with black hair roots. She crouched over what looked like all of her belongings, which she had laid out thoughtfully on a muddy piece of ground. He thought how Agnes would have both loved and hated it here.

Leanne handed him a polystyrene cup full of tea, and when he took the lid off he saw that it was already cold and filmy. He looked at the milky cataract and felt bad that she had been waiting for him a long time.

"Agnes would have been fifty-two the day," he said, then he added quickly, "although she would have denied it blue in the face."

Shuggie tilted the fizzy ginger towards Leanne like an arrogant sommelier he had seen on the television. "I thought we could have a wee birthday party. Cheer us up." He was grinning as he passed her the sweet strawberry tarts. She opened the box with a soft coo, and he was suddenly disappointed at the mess of blood-red jam squished against the lid. "Bugger! I carried them as carefully as I could."

Leanne shoved her shoulder into his. "Don't worry. They're gorgeous."

The tarts that were so lovely an hour ago now sat between them looking spoilt and damp. Shuggie reached out and snatched one. He wanted them gone. With a hand like a shovel he forced a whole tart into his mouth. The sweet sticky jam and the warm cream filled his throat to choking. He sucked the cake down and felt better for the weight of it in his gut. He reached into the box for a second, and this time Leanne turned her body away from him and squealed, "Get aff! They're mine, ye greedy beggar."

Shuggie laughed; he liked to see her look less worried. He mashed the last of the jam between his lips till it coated his mouth like a messy lipstick and made great gurning faces at her. Leanne shoved him away. She ate two tarts, slowly and delicately, taking care to separate the jam from the cream and then handing the unloved shortbread pastry to Shuggie to finish. She closed the lid on the last.

They sat together in that huddled way, as the rain stopped and started, and stopped and started, just drinking the cold tea and sweet ginger and talking and waiting for something that might not even happen. Leanne spoke first. "So, our Calum's got a lassie from Springburn pregnant."

He took a handful of her fine hair and ran his fingers through it. He squeezed it between his forefinger and thumb, like an old clothes mangle, and it released the dampness with a squeak. "Is he the one just above you?"

"Naw, he's two above me, between our Stevie and our Malky. He's fair enough looking, but he's no very bright, and that's how ye've got to keep yer eye on him. He'll try to dip his wick in jist about anything."

"Charmer."

"Aye. Last Easter he must've met this lassie up the dancin' on a Saturday, and by all accounts she must have been pregnant afore they opened the chapel doors on the Sunday." Leanne shook her head at her brother's stupidity. "Her father just came to our door last night. He'd found us in the phone book. Our Malky leathered Calum when he found out. Not for getting the lassie pregnant but for being stupit enough to tell this wee lassie his real family name." Leanne took up a separate strand of her own hair and started checking it for split ends. "Our Calum couldnae even remember this lassie's first name, never mind what she looked like. Ye should've seen his face when he saw her. He would have passed her on the street. Now he's a daddy. Stupit eejit."

Shuggie heard the woman before Leanne saw her. It was a girlish laughter, too young for a woman so old, and it rang hollow and forced, as if she were performing for someone. Shuggie thought about ignoring her; he considered pointing Leanne's gaze down the river, away from the laughing woman. When he turned to his friend, she was gnawing the skin around her thumb and worrying the contents of her plastic bags. When he pulled her hand away from her mouth, there was hardly any skin left around any of her fingers. He could not bring himself to lie to her then, so he sighed and pointed to the woman. Then Leanne sighed for herself.

The woman had not seen them yet. Her pale hand snaked through the arm of one of the short-sleeved men from the alley, his young mouth a closed knuckle of toothlessness. Clear across the busy market, from the other side of the lane, Shuggie could hear her cajoling the young jakey for a little company. With wet lips he told her *naw*, flatly, and Shuggie watched as the man used sharp pinching fingers to free himself from her grasp. The jakey jangled off and left her standing alone.

The pair watched the woman for a while; she looked trapped in the centre of the alley, not sure where to go next. She was more of a ruin than the last time Shuggie had seen her. Her mouse-brown curls were becoming a peppery mat of tangled locks, and her skin was overrun red and royal blue with broken veins. There was a little cornflower eye-shadow on her face and around her lips a trace of a happy pink lipstick. It comforted Shuggie to see her still wearing tan tights, even though there was a ladder in one leg, and she stood demurely with her knees and her ankles somewhat together.

Leanne rolled her eyes. He could see that it took all her strength to force herself forward. She slid from the fence and picked up the shopping bags at her feet. One of the plastic bags was heavy with folded laundry and clean underthings that were long past white. The other held sweet soft foods, like toddler's yogurt and jars of mashed apple sauce. Shuggie remembered his own contribution then and pulled from his pocket the bag with the dented tins of fish. "You said these were her favourite."

Leanne opened his bag and peered inside at the tins.

"Ta very much, Shuggie." She turned the salmon in her hand. "But she's out on the street. Where's she gonnae get a tin opener for that?" Leanne shook her head at her own question. "Sorry. That was dead ungrateful." She exhaled slowly, and she swung the small bag in a wide arc like a clubbing weapon. "Listen, auld Moira will find a way. She always fuckin' does."

Leanne crossed the mouth of the market towards her mother. Shuggie saw the woman clock the approaching girl and roll her brown eyes. He couldn't help but smile at the family resemblance.

They greeted each other without affection. The smirr had stopped for a moment, and Mrs Kelly followed Leanne out of Paddy's Market and over to the Clyde side. Shuggie flattened an old cardboard box and laid it over the wet railing. He let the two of them sit close together, and they watched the boatman thanklessly skim the water.

"Ah knew some of the poor lassies he fished out o' there," said Moira Kelly. "He didnae even knock a single thing. Every damp cigarette was still in their pocket, every Claddagh ring. He took not a penny. Now isn't that a thing?"

Leanne opened the box of tarts and offered the last one to her mother. Shuggie tried not to look as the woman fingered a gobbet of the sticky red jam and popped it in her puckered mouth. There were deep, drawn cavities around her eyes, as if she hadn't been eating again. The strawberry sugar glistened in the corners of her mouth like gloss, and it looked obscene.

"Are we just gonnae sit here aw day?" she asked, not uttering a word of thanks.

"Why don't we just sit a little while?" Leanne slid the cake box on to her mother's lap, trying to pin her under the sugar, as you might draw a dog closer with a tin of meat. The woman was bobbing with the drink, but she lifted the last cake and stuck her tongue deep into the exposed cream. He could see there were new teeth missing on the side, teeth that had been there in the autumn. There was cream on her knuckles, and she licked the length of her finger in a suggestive way. Leanne looked pleased to see her try to eat, but it was too vulgar for Shuggie. As he looked at Mrs Kelly's ripped tights, with the gooseflesh of her legs poking through, suddenly all he wanted was to see his mother again.

They sat together for a while, and Shuggie watched the Clyde as Leanne told her mother about the soap opera her five brothers created on the daily. Several times Mrs Kelly just laughed at the Kelly boys' nonsense and said, "Thank feck ah'm no there to clean that shite up."

When she said things like that, Shuggie found he had to keep his face turned to the river. Leanne then told her mother she was to be a grandmother. Shuggie felt the fence wobble as the woman shrugged.

When Leanne had run out of things to tell her, she asked her mother to stand up. She made Shuggie hold Mrs Kelly's old overcoat out wide; and as the woman hopped from one leg to the other, Leanne drew off her tights and then her dirty underpants from underneath her skirt. The woman didn't enjoy being fussed with. She grumbled to herself but turned her eyes to Shuggie. Shuggie kept his own eyes firmly on the wet pavement.

"Ah don't understand ye, son. You should be oot fingerin' lassies and getting drunk. No houndin' auld Moira for some company."

"I'm not here for you, Mrs Kelly," he mumbled. He lifted the coat higher, trying in a way to turn her damp gaze from him.

The woman was unperturbed. "Well, ah should be oot there havin' a guid laugh. No dancin' the fanny fandango for a funny wee fella lit you."

Leanne was still on her knees. She buckled her mother's shoes again. "Shuggie brought you salmon. Don't be so bloody cheeky."

"Well, hurry up then. It's giro day. The men will have it spent afore ah can even get a drink oot o' them," Mrs Kelly hissed and bounced like an impatient child.

Shuggie had nothing to say to Mrs Kelly, but for Leanne's sake he wanted to hold the woman there with them, just a little longer. "So? How have you been keeping since I last saw you?"

Mrs Kelly mocked him: "Oh, it has been a sihm-ply marvel-louse spring. Hasn't it just?" Then she pursed her mouth, impatient with the bother of it all. "Nosy wee bugger, 'int ye?" For a moment, that seemed to be all she was going to say. Then her mouth pulled downwards in a sour sneer. She did have something to tell, and she was suddenly glad of the audience to tell it to. "Here! Ah got back the gether wi' wee Tommy for a minute." She rubbed instinctively at her jaw, where the teeth were missing, in remembrance of this unknown man. "He wisnae aw bad. He had a good grift gaun up the back of the Caley railworks. Used tae spoil me rotten. Used tae stoat frae pub tae pub and pretend he was blind. He was that blind he had tae feel along the bar for his drink." Mrs Kelly was bubbling with laughter now. "He necked his fair share of other folks' whisky afore they found oot his eyes worked just fuckin' fine."

She was roaring to herself. Shuggie could see it made Leanne happy to see her laugh. It was clear in the way she looked up at her mother and in how the tightness around her mouth softened a little. But too soon it passed. Leanne seemed to remember herself and tried to recover her defences. It was like she had been scolding a badly behaved child, but the child had won her over with its charm, and she had caved against her better judgement.

Mrs Kelly had noticed. "See, ah'm good company. Ye like seeing auld Moira, din't ye?" Mrs Kelly was rubbing her daughter's shoulder. "Aye, ah could always cheer ye up."

Leanne said nothing to encourage her. Shuggie lowered the coat and went back to watching the boatman. Mrs Kelly prodded at her sore jaw again and finally asked, "So, any chance ye've got money for a wee bottle of fortified?"

"No." Shuggie shook his head.

She sucked at her missing teeth. "Aye, well. Ye don't ask, ye don't get. Eh?"

He held the last of the fizzy ginger out to her. She glared at the sweet drink like it offended her, then she took it from him anyway. They had been enjoying it slowly, but now Mrs Kelly swallowed it like she was parched. Shuggie looked at the gummy line her lipstick left on the neck of the bottle. He tried to bite his lip, but he could not help himself. "Why do you have to get in such a state?"

Leanne stopped pushing the dirty clothes into plastic bags and sat back on her haunches. She looked up at her mother again, as if this were something she would very much not like to miss.

"Who says ah don't *like* tae take a drink?" Mrs Kelly pouted and ripped the coat from Shuggie's arms. "Yer aw just jealous. Ah have a rare time! Helps the day tae dance along a wee bit. Cuts oot the flat parts." She took a tube of lipstick out of her pocket. It was worn down to the canister, and as she pushed too hard the colour missed the line of her lips. Shuggie tried to ignore the particular shade of pink.

"She loves you," he said.

"*Shuggie!*" Leanne pleaded.

"Oh, tweet-tweet, kiss-kiss," Mrs Kelly snorted, and she thumped her chest to release some sugary gas. "Well, ye know what ah think? Ah think the more ye love someone the more they take the piss out of that. They will do less and less of what ye want and more and more of just as they fuckin' please." She thumped her chest again and belched this time.

Leanne roughly gathered the dirty laundry and stood up again with a tired huff. She put herself between the boy and her mother. Shuggie could see her cheeks were scalding red and her eyes were liquid as she started chewing her lips again. He turned away and went back to watching the boatman.

"Pubs will be filling soon," said Mrs Kelly, closing her coat. "Ye've had your money's worth."

"Oh, bloody charming!" Leanne stood back from her mother and checked her work. She talked to Mrs Kelly as though the woman were only a child who was anxious to go back out and play before the scheme lights came on. She knew she could hold her no longer. "Right, Moira, away ye go then. Try to look after yersel, alright. I'll look for ye again."

"If ye must."

Shuggie found he had balled his fists. He stepped forward then and forced his hands inside Mrs Kelly's coat. He wrapped his arms around her waist and searched her softness till he found the familiar slippery wetness of the rayon warp knit. He roughly pulled at the underskirt till it sat properly and correctly back inside her clothes.

Mrs Kelly's mouth hung open in shock, but she let herself be handled, as if she didn't mind the warmth of his arms around her middle. Then she licked her bottom lip with a fat tongue and flashed a wicked grin to Leanne. "Oh, ye want to watch yersel wi' this one, hen."

The boy let go of her waist. He put his hands on her upper arms and gave her a sharp shake. Mrs Kelly blinked like a tossed doll. Her eyes took some time to focus on his face again. "Here you!" She pulled herself from his grip and walked around him without breaking her scowl. "Whit a funny wee bastard ye are."

With that Mrs Kelly turned towards the market, towards the dark pubs that lay under the railway line. They watched her go, stumbling along the alley, with her arms full of shopping bags. She stopped at the corner and, with a low swing, launched the bag of tinned salmon at the girl with the blond hair and black roots. Mrs Kelly raised her arms as though she had scored a goal, and then she stumbled onwards and was gone.

"Jist don't start!" Leanne warned. She closed the zipper on her anorak till it covered the lower part of her face.

"I won't." He kept his eyes on the damp pavement and tried to calm himself. "Do you feel any better?"

Leanne scoffed and then she shrugged. She pulled her wet hair away from her face, and caught it in the elastic band she kept around her wrist. He was sad to see her pretty face grow so taut and hard again.

Shuggie wiped the mud from his shoe on to the back of his trouser leg. He reached out and pulled a loose thread from Leanne's sleeve, her wrist was cold to his touch. "My mammy had a good year once. It was lovely."

Leanne said nothing. She put her chewed thumbnail back in her mouth and sat alone with her thoughts. Shuggie let her be. It had stopped raining, and he watched the boatman tether his dinghy to the riverbank and straighten his bent back.

They still had the rest of the day together, and even in the damp the thought warmed him. "So!" Shuggie tried his hardest to sound brighter. "What do you want to do now?"

Leanne wiped her eyes. She turned out the empty pockets on her denims and held them out like flapping flags. "Hows about we jist walk around for a wee while, eh?"

"Jeezo. Who's predictable now?"

"*Me?*" She laughed for what felt like the first time in a long while. "No way. We both know ye just want to go gawp at the big handsomes up the Virginia arcade!"

He felt the flare of shame. He shook his head as if to deny it, but something in her eyes stopped him then. He drew a sharp breath between his front teeth.

Leanne reached out and jabbed him sharply in the ribs. "Pack it in. 'Asides, I think the one ginger lad with the pierced ears might have been making eyes at youse."

"Really?"

She grinned. "Mibbe. Mind you, he does have that one gammy eye, so who the fuck knows."

Leanne swung the bag with her mother's dirty underclothes and pretended to launch it deep into the Clyde. Then she slipped her free arm into his and tried to shake him loose of his worry. He nudged into her shoulder like a tugboat, until they both were turned away from the river.

Shuggie dropped their rubbish into a council bin. "You know, hearing about your Calum did make me wish we could go up the dancin' one time?"

Leanne was still swinging the dirty bag, and now she howled with laughter. It was so loud, so vibrant, it made the videocassette jakeys jump with fright. "Ha! *You?* Get to fuck wi' those poncey school shoes," she squealed. "There is no way Shuggie Bain can dance!"

Shuggie tutted. He wrenched himself from her side and ran a few paces ahead. He nodded, all gallus, and spun, just the once, on his polished heels.

Acknowledgments

Above all, I owe everything to the memories of my mother and her struggle, and to my brother who gave me everything he could. I am indebted to my sister for encouraging me to set this into words and share it with you.

This novel would not be in your hands without the belief and passion of Anna Stein, a slow reader but a courageous agent. Thanks also to Lucy Luck, Claire Nozieres, Morgan Oppenheimer, and all at ICM Partners and Curtis Brown. Thanks especially to my editor, Peter Blackstock, for his patience, his bravery, and for being firm but gentle with Shuggie. Morgan Entrekin and Judy Hottensen were enthusiastic supporters, and my gratitude to Elisabeth Schmitz, Deb Seager, John Mark Boling, Emily Burns, and all at Grove Atlantic. Thanks to my friends in the north, Daniel Sandström and Cathrine Bakke Bolin, and to Ravi Mirchandani and all at Picador UK for bringing this novel home. My sincere gratitude to Tina Pohlman, for first steps and her incredible generosity. Debts are also owed to my early readers: Patricia McNulty, Valentina Castellani, Helen Weston, and Rachel Skinner-O'Neil for all your insight and encouragement.

The last words of this book belong to Michael Cary, he read it first, and nurtured the heart of it, like he always does.